# WERGEN:
# THE ALIEN LOVE WAR

# WERGEN:
# THE ALIEN LOVE WAR

Mercurio D. Rivera

NEWCON
PRESS

NewCon Press
England

First edition, published in the UK November 2021
by NewCon Press

NCP263 (hardback)
NCP264 (paperback)

10 9 8 7 6 5 4 3 2 1

ISBN: 978-1-914953-00-2 (hardback)
978-1-914953-01-9 (paperback)

Cover art by Jim Burns
Cover design by Ian Whates

Editorial interference by Ian Whates and Kim Lakin
Text layout by Ian Whates

# CHAPTERS

For my brother, Jesse, who fueled my imagination with *Fantastic Four* and *Spider-man* comic books before I could even read.

*"Of all the pain, the greatest pain*
*It is to love, but in vain."*
—Abraham Cowley, *Anacreontics*

# CHAPTER ONE
## Longing For Langalana

### Langalana – Years 2500 – 2600

Transmission to Earth/Human Colonists in the Sol System
1/12/2622
Duncan McGuire of corpship *Rapprochement*

Historians will start at the beginning, perhaps with a description of the reactions to the alien transmissions received by the Sagan-Xi Yu station orbiting Neptune. More likely they'll focus on the content of the messages, three simple words repeated in over six thousand Earth languages: "Can we help?" Those words, after all, would go on to alter the course of human history.

I'm no historian. This particular tale, I believe, like most stories about life and death, love and loss, is told best by skipping straight to the ending.

If you're old enough, you remember the awe, the optimism, the hope, those first years following first contact. We accepted the aliens' gifts without ever thinking through the consequences.

Only in hindsight is it obvious: our relationship with the Wergens never stood a chance. For all our attempts to learn about our respective cultures, we never really understood each other. But the following transmissions might help you do so.

So let me tell you the ending. Or an ending.

At unimaginable distances from the Sol System, human and Wergen settlers began colonisation of Langalana, a planet twice the size of Earth orbiting a blue star in the outer spiral arm of our galaxy. This is the life story of Shimera, the legendary Wergen ambassador. This is the story of the human-Wergen partnership.

I wince at the intensity of the Earth Emissary's beauty and take a step backward. Despite my decades of exposure to his people, the mere sight of this uniformed young man, this stranger, still causes powerful feelings to bubble to the surface. As he strides into the room, his emerald-green eyes glittering, the resemblance to Phinny is uncanny. He nods a greeting and sits down at the conference room table. His smooth-skinned brilliance makes me squint, and I have to turn my back to him to combat the giddiness. Facing the thick-plated window, I observe the dull, grey moonscape, the dead dust dunes stretching off into the horizon, softly lit by the indigo glow of Langalana overhead.

I struggle against the urge to stare at his hazy reflection in the glass.

"An Emissary, eh?" I say, leaning heavily on my red-furred walking stick. "Your father would be proud." Peeking over my shoulder, I point to the wicker bowl on the glass table, my finger trembling ever so slightly. "Please, help yourself to some *chapra*. But chew the leaf slowly. Its nectar is very sweet. Your father used to love it when he was a boy, you know."

I slowly rub the scales on my chin and gesture toward the massive reddish planet that fills half the black sky. "Magnificent, eh?" Mauve clouds encircle its equator and dark purplish seas stand out starkly between three large landmasses.

"To think, our peoples travelled so far, endured so much. But in the end, Langalana spurned us," I say. "And so, we've been left to pine from afar, to dream about what could have been."

I turn around and dare to look directly at him again.

The young man sucks gingerly on the tip of the red-leafed *chapra*. Like his father, a majestic swath of thick yellow hair sheathes his closed cranium, falling to his shoulders. Emotion makes me shudder; I shake my head and avert my gaze again.

"I know why you're here," I say.

From my sleeping quarters I spied the silver landbuzzer – a glinting pinprick in the distance – speeding toward us. As if riding choppy waves, it skimmed atop the undulating, scarlet-furred grasslands that stretched in every direction. The buzzer clattered up to the reed fence surrounding our hurth and two humans – an older female and a young boy not much taller than me – clambered out of its sidecars.

I froze, open-mouthed, for I had never seen an actual alien before. In the weeks since landfall – when our Wergen brethren left us and continued onward to the Northern Continent – these were the first pilgrims we had encountered. I'd been told they came in magnificent shades of pink and brown and yellow, like the Visian demigods of our mythology, but to actually see them with my own eyes… Rather than a single breathing canal, they bore two tiny holes in the centre of their faces beneath a protruding skin-covered bone. Coloured fibers covered the tops of their rounded heads. But most striking of all, a rainbow-coloured aura I can only describe as a coating of pure beauty shimmered about them.

I bent down and peeped at them over the windowsill as they approached our front yard. The older female conversed casually with Father and Elkah, both of whom worked the fields with the bots. Although I longed to see the aliens up close, I felt paralysed by a sudden overwhelming shyness.

"Shimera!" Father called out. His voice, though loud, sounded shaky.

I hesitated before bolting through the central fireroom to the hurth's front archway. Father and Elkah stood side by side, both clutching their bunched-up tether – for when they stood so close together there was a chance one of them might stumble over it or become entangled.

"Shimera, these are our new neighbours, Dr. Zooey Crest and her nephew, Phineas." As he spoke to me, Father kept his eyes fixed on the humans.

When I tried to return the aliens' greeting, I found myself breathless. I could only nod.

"I was hoping, young lady," Dr. Crest said, "that you might be able to tutor my nephew in the Wergen tongue." She said this in perfect, unaccented Wergenese. "I'm inundated with lab work, and Phinny could really benefit from some personal instruction. He knows just a few words and phrases."

As Dr. Crest spoke, the boy, Phinny, stood behind her, gawking at the tether connecting Father and Elkah's craniums.

"Say hello to our neighbours, Phinny," Dr. Crest instructed the boy, switching to Earthen. "In Wergenese."

The boy stayed hidden behind his aunt's pleated black skirt and shouted out a badly accented "hello." While the adults continued speaking, he shifted his gaze to me and stuck out his dark pink tongue. I smiled, marvelling at this strange and wonderful human greeting.

"Shimera would be honoured to tutor the boy," Elkah said.

When Phinny looked at me again, I bashfully stuck out my own colourless tongue, which couldn't extend nearly as far as the human's.

The boy laughed delightedly and Dr. Crest glanced at me, raising an eyebrow. "Yes, well… Phinny will come by around midday tomorrow."

"You really must visit for dinner," Father said.

"Yes, please, we insist," Elkah added.

Dr. Crest shot us a strange look, one I had difficulty reading, and shook her head slowly. "That's very kind of you, but I'm afraid we're going to have to pass. Some urgent gengineering experiments require my attention."

"Can we come by and help clear your fields?" Father asked.

"Perhaps assist you with your lab work?" Elkah said. "Really, there must be some way we can help."

Several lines appeared across Dr. Crest's forehead. "That's quite all right. The Wergen bots are managing the fieldwork just fine, thank you. And I work best alone."

"Are you sure –?"

Her glare cut Father off mid-sentence. "Good day." She grabbed the boy's hand, turned, and marched off.

Father and Elkah bowed their heads.

As the landbuzzer receded into the distance, Phinny looked over his shoulder, and I thought I saw his long pink tongue stick out once again, greeting me in his special way.

"We were planetary pioneers, the 'heroic trailblazers' of Langalana," I say, my voice tinged with bitterness. "My father and Elkah performed the traditional Wergen function: maintenance of the fieldbots used by the pilgrims to clear large patches of the grasslands in preparation for the settlement's expansion. Dr. Crest studied soil samples and, months later, headed up a team of human gengineers responsible for crop production. This was years before the construction of the Science Institute, Emissary, years before the devastation had begun, before the landfall of hundreds of human exobiologists, anthropologists, and entomologists."

I pace slowly, shifting my weight to my walking stick, and rub the scales on my chin.

The young man stares at me silent, impassive.

"But what did Phinny and I care about the logistics of settlement? We were just children, children exploring a vast new playground." I can't help it; my voice becomes wistful now. "Every morning Phinny came to my hurth for his lesson in Wergenese. Our conversations in those first few days – in Earthen, of course – were formal and very brief for, you see, I was still painfully shy around him.

"And as the days passed we became more comfortable in our surroundings, more comfortable around each other. Oh, the afternoons Phinny and I spent in those breathtaking grasslands! How many games we played! How many secrets we shared! One day, he told me he'd discovered a natural trail through the grasslands, a trail twisting out towards the Purple Sea."

Elkah oversaw the skittering bots that cleared the growing grass in front of our hurth while Father prepared the meals inside. At that time, their cranial cord extended for almost a full ten metres and still sported the great elasticity typical of the recently tethered.

When we strolled past Elkah, her head jerked upward and her charcoal eyes zoomed in on Phinny. "Where are you going, Phineas?" she asked.

"To the overlook," he replied in slightly accented Wergenese. "For my lesson."

"*Very* well spoken," Elkah gushed. She patted his head and her fingers lingered in his yellow tresses. "You're an excellent student." At that very instant Father must have moved toward the rear of the hurth because Elkah's tether pulled slightly, causing her to take two steps backwards. "Olbodoh!" she shouted over her shoulder. "Phineas is here!"

Before Father could join us, Phinny grabbed my hand – which pulsed with pleasure at his touch – and pulled me along to the recently discovered path that curved in a southwesterly direction. Because the blue sun hovered directly over us, we cast no shadows as we wandered through the trail. The grasslands resembled nothing on Earth apparently, judging from Phinny's wide-eyed reaction every time we moved through them. A deep crimson fur lined each blade of grass, and the fields literally swayed – not from the warm wind, but of their own volition – left, then right, in perfect rhythm.

From the twisting dirt path, the fields fell away and we emerged onto a jutting rocky overlook. Shielding our eyes, we stood at the lip and marvelled at the glorious, placid Purple Sea, kilometres below, lapping against the crystalline cliffside. A steady breeze blew, warm and silky and impossibly salty.

We set down our blankets and I began Phinny's lesson, instructing him on the nasal twangs punctuating Wergenese verbs. I found Phinny had an impressive facility for languages, so much so that his skills approached Wergen levels. He always picked up the nuances quickly, biting his lip and concentrating intensely. Before long, however, a dam seemed to burst in his head. He'd hurl stones into the sea, or recite the Wergenese alphabet while standing on his head, or break off a reed and challenge me to a duel, or lay on his stomach and spew a dewy substance from his mouth over the edge of the overlook – signalling the end of the lesson.

As we began our long hike back, I could sense he had something on his mind he wanted to ask me. His reluctance surprised me since Phinny had questions and opinions about everything. In the weeks I'd been tutoring him, he'd never once hesitated to voice them:

"Do you have any brothers or sisters?"

"I had two sisters who died at birth."

"Why do fieldbots look like giant spiders? The Wergens should make them look, I don't know... friendlier," he said.

"The bots are modelled after Scythians – our pets on Ocura."

His barrage continued: "I wish I had those white Wergen scales. You shouldn't say you're 'colourless' – you're white, like chalk;" "The math and science holoprograms are boring, don't you think?" "I'm glad Aunt Zooey got assigned to Argenta rather than Inlandia;" "We're the luckiest kids ever, to be the first pilgrims on this continent;" "They say you can fit two Earths into Langalana, but I don't believe it!" And so on.

I always answered in Wergenese and we spent hours on that overlook, the afternoons vanishing into the sun's blue blaze as we chatted and played.

As was our practice, I accompanied him back to his habitation. Sometimes I wandered inside to catch a glimpse of Dr. Crest in her spacious laboratory, the rectangular gene-splicers humming in the background. But today she waited at the entranceway in her lab coat and waved for us to enter when she saw us approach.

She stood in front of a table with a microscope. A blue syringe and oddly shaped metallic devices scurried about the table on their own. "Did you have a good lesson, Phineas?"

"Yes, Aunt Zooey," Phinny said in Wergenese. "Learned a lot."

"The watermelon is ready."

Phinny jumped up and down and let out a whoop. Dr. Crest had been trying for some time to gengineer Earthen fruits and vegetables to grow in the garden behind their habitation.

"Can we have some right now?" Phinny said.

She hesitated. "Come here, Shimera."

Despite her wrinkled dermis, Dr. Crest radiated waves of beauty – like all humans – that made me feel tingly and happy to be alive. She gently grabbed my hand – an electric tickle buzzed through me – and placed it on the table, palm up. Her five fingers, so pink and dainty and dexterous, brushed my three digits with a sandpapery substance. "Let me do a quick run of your cell samples to make sure it's safe for you to eat these fruits," she said. "Phinny, run outside and cut up a melon."

Phinny scrambled out the door.

"Shimera, I've received Elkah and Olbodoh's daily dinner invitations, their notes and messages." Dr. Crest removed a bundle of red slips of paper from her lab coat jacket and dangled them in front of me. "Please tell them to stop." She crumpled the invitations in her five-fingered, white-knuckled fist and tossed them into the waste bin. "You Wergens can be so goddamned overbearing."

The scanner beeped. Dr. Crest stared into a monitor and made a peculiar gesture, raising her opposable digit in the air. "All clear. Enjoy the watermelon."

I face the Emissary, but make a conscious effort not to look him in the eye. He has finished the *chapra* and fingers the edges of the empty wicker bowl.

"From that brief exchange with Dr. Crest, I learned how important it was to suppress our feelings around humans, how our emotions make them uncomfortable, and can potentially drive them away. At that moment, I promised myself I would never make Phinny feel awkward around me. I would bottle up my feelings for him deep inside rather than ever risk losing him," I say, my voice trembling.

"Keeping that promise proved more difficult than I could ever have imagined. Your father's kindnesses, his generosity, his humour, all touched me deeply. I tried my best to contain myself around him, mind you, not always with success."

I limp over to the window and press both my hands against it.

15

Following Phinny's lessons, he and I would sit in Dr. Crest's garden in what he called the "watermelon patch." He'd split the melons with a long blade and we'd lifted out the pink centres, eating them heartily, juice dribbling down our chins. We also occasionally sampled the succulent *chapra* that grew on the reeds of grass. I preferred the taste and texture of the watermelons while Phinny loved the *chapra*.

One day, intoxicated with sugary *chapra*, Phinny finally blurted out the questions I sensed had been weighing on his mind.

"Shim, why do Wergens love humans?"

His directness made it difficult to respond.

"What makes *us* so special?" he asked.

"Well… I mean, you're all so… beautiful." I blushed.

"You think so? Aunt Zooey thinks it might be biological. Maybe the way we smell or something."

I didn't know what to say.

"Your father? And Elkah? Why are they, you know, tied together that way?" he asked. From the look in his eyes, I could sense this subject, the tethering of Father and Elkah, was what interested him most of all. But I was painfully shy about the subject.

"They're tethered," I said, embarrassed.

After a few seconds, when he realised I would volunteer no more information, he asked, "Are your scales soft?"

I shrugged.

Phinny shyly reached out to me. "Is it okay if I…?"

I nodded, and he gently brushed his hand along my cheekbone.

I know it's silly, but, sometimes, all of these decades later, I can still feel the warmth of his fingers tracing the crevices between my scales.

"They feel… rubbery, nice," he said. "On Earth only reptiles have scales." His gaze shifted to the *coronatis*, the leafy headdress covering my cranium. "And what about your head…"

"That's personal," I said quickly, and he withdrew his hand sheepishly.

"Why do Wergens wear those things? Those leaf hats?"

"To cover our… areas." I looked away from him again. "That's where our cords emerge. When it's time."

He digested this information. "Shim, do you think a Wergen could ever tether with a human?"

My hearts skipped. I shrugged.

"Do all of you get tethered?" he asked.

"After the tests are done, yes, for the most part."

"Tests?"

"Our medics always test our genes to make sure we're... compatible. Some persons have diseases that don't let them tether. And some people just choose not to," I said, looking downward. "That's not a good thing."

"Oh." And just like that, Phinny jumped to his feet and sprinted in the direction of my hurth. "Race you!"

I leapt to my feet and chased after him, laughing. "Wait! Wait!"

Perhaps because I stood slightly taller than Phinny, or because he constantly took instruction from me on Wergenese, he resented whenever I told him what to do outside of our lessons. Looking back, I suppose I did sometimes take a superior tone with him, but this only sprang from my desire to protect him from the dangers that existed alongside Langalana's natural wonders.

All of that changed on one cool day, a day just like any other with magenta clouds looming overhead in the pink-tinted sky and the smell of snow in the air, the day Dr. Crest sent Phinny to my hurth to obtain an extension blade. One of the fieldbots had damaged a claw and she needed to replace it. I decided to accompany Phinny on his walk back home. The truth is, I not only wanted to be with him, I also wanted to experience soaring over the grasslands in his landbuzzer, which his aunt had let him borrow.

As we accelerated away, Elkah and Father waved goodbye to Phinny from a window. "Goodbye, Father!" I shouted, smiling broadly, one hand on the handgrip and the other holding my headdress in place. "Goodbye, Elkah!"

"Why don't you call Elkah 'Mother'?" Phinny asked.

"Elkah isn't my mother, silly," I said, laughing. "Elkah is Father's second mate. My mother, Hexa, was his first."

"So your parents are divorced?"

"Divorced?"

"Yeah, divorced. Like mine. They separated when they realised they couldn't get along any more."

"Separated mates?" I shuddered. I had never heard anything more horrible, more... alien.

17

"Mom decided it would be best for me to stay with Dad," he said. "She's a really important person on EarthCouncil and doesn't have time for kids. But then Dad enrolled in the Delta Expedition. So he left me with Aunt Zooey." Phinny had a sad, faraway look in his eyes.

I didn't know what to say, so I simply stared ahead.

The buzzer skimmed the apex of the red blades, and we both held on to the handlegrips as we surfed the waves of grass.

"So. Where *is* your mom?" he said. "On the Northern Continent?"

"Hah! She's encorporated!"

"What do you mean?"

"Don't you know what encorporation is?"

Phinny straightened up. "Well, I've heard of it…"

"Oh, look! A manticola!" I shrieked. "Stop for a second."

I jumped off the sidecar and pushed my way through the feathery grass to the bright yellow-and-white petals of the budding manticola. When I stooped down to take in its scent, I heard Phinny scream.

He shoved me hard from behind, sending me sprawling to the ground.

As I tumbled, I saw it there on a patch of grassless sand, emerging from a shadowy burrow. With a clicking sound, the thing twitched and unfolded its carapace segment by segment until it stood eye level with Phinny. It was as thick as my leg, with a lightning-bolt shaped torso. Thorns covered its muscular chitinous sections, and it bore the same deep-red colour as the surrounding grasslands. As I tried to figure out whether it was plant or insect, the creature screeched. It seemed poised to sink its sharp teeth into Phinny when he pulled the extension-blade from his pocket and lunged. He drove it right between the thing's four black, bulbous eyes, pounding the creature again and again, even after it had slumped to the ground.

I watched from ground level as Phinny flattened the creature's head with his blows until it lay in a red pool of viscous fluid. Only then did he stop.

I walked behind him and placed my hand on his back. "Did it bite you?" I asked.

In response, Phinny made a bizarre choking sound and disgorged chunks of semi-digested food onto the ground.

"Are you ill?"

18

He wiped his mouth. "Why did you run into the grass blades?" he shouted. "There's no path here! You *know* it's dangerous." He stomped off toward the landbuzzer.

I ran after him. "I can't wait to tell everyone, Phinny. You saved me. What *was* that thing? Weren't you even a little afraid? The way you struck it down…? Why, I've never seen such courage!"

He ignored me. But as we rode back and I chattered on and on about his bravery, Phinny's mood seemed to brighten. He stood straighter, with his chest puffed.

Following the incident, we were both so excited and flustered we got turned around without even realising it and wound up back at my hurth. As we approached, I saw Elkah tending the fields and I leapt off the landbuzzer as it slowed − this time carefully staying on the sandy walking path − shouting what had happened as I ran toward her.

"That sounds like a grubber! There've only been a few of them spotted on the Northern Continent − uncommon, but dangerous creatures − but I didn't know we had them here. How'd you know its weak spot, boy? Right between the eyes! I certainly wouldn't want to be fighting off one of those things with nothing but a blade." She patted Phinny on the back and shoulders. "Shimera, you have to be more careful. The boy could have been hurt."

From that day, the dynamic changed between us. It's hard to explain, but I no longer felt the same need to protect Phinny. I knew he could take care of himself. Not only that, I knew he could protect me too.

I circle the table slowly. The young Emissary looks at me curiously, as if staring at an experiment gone awry.

"Despite the increase in the number of incoming human pilgrims over the years, Argenta's population grew only slightly. Most arrivals settled in Inlandia or in provinces in the Northern and Western Continents.

"As for my people, you have to understand, Emissary, the Joint Venture Compact only permitted five percent of the population to be Wergen, and the locations where we lived were the subject of extensive negotiation. Given Langalana's sheer size, we were spread thin to put it mildly. At the time, our arriving pilgrims lived primarily on the large continent in the north − an inconceivable distance from Argenta. As a result, I went almost a decade without seeing another of my kind – except for Father and Elkah, of course. A decade! Nevertheless, surrounded by beautiful humans – most importantly, in the company of Phinny – I consider these days on Langalana, these idyllic days of my childhood, the happiest moments of my life."

The Earth Emissary nods.

I saw Phinny less frequently as he began to spend much of his time assisting other pilgrims with the construction of the farmhouses and plantations. Often I would visit him at the worksite where he helped Aunt Zooey's team with the irrigation system. We would eat together at midday and discuss the latest developments on Langalana.

He stopped by my hurth one morning to share the news that a starship carrying over ten thousand humans was expected to arrive early that next year. The plans to expand Inlandia to accommodate them needed to be expedited.

"I'm going to be working twelve-hour days, Shim, programming the bots to process grassland reeds, working with the engineers to diagram the city layout."

"Phineas!" Father shouted, lumbering closely ahead of Elkah. With the cord fully extended, they could now walk only a metre apart. "My, but you've sprouted. What broad shoulders! You've been working the crop fields, eh?"

And, indeed, Phinny's transformation had been dramatic. He'd grown much taller and his yellow hair paled by the sun to an almost golden white. His skin had browned and his body had become lean and taut.

After I guided him away – his beauty mesmerised Elkah and Father and prompted them to earwig him far beyond the point of rudeness – he turned to me and whispered, "I never noticed before, but their tether... It seems to have shrunk."

I blushed. Of course their tether had constricted. Father and Elkah had been mated for quite some time now. "I-I..."

"It's okay, Shim. I know you don't feel comfortable talking about it." He turned to me. "It's going to happen. I'm moving to Inlandia."

"Really?"

"Aunt Zooey's getting older. She needs to continue her research in a less challenging environment. With the grubber swarms and the constant evacuations, it's getting to be too much for her."

I heard the words, but had trouble registering their meaning. "I think it's admirable you're so loyal to Dr. Crest."

"It's the least I can do after everything she's done for me."

My spirit sank. Although he'd been talking about this for some time, I never thought the day would actually come. "When?"

"Next week. The bots need major reprogramming to assist with the construction of the highways and office buildings and sewage systems. And we need to clear several more kilometres of Inlandia's grasslands."

As we walked our familiar path to the overlook, the field's colour shifted from red to purple.

"What about you, Shim? There's plenty of opportunity in Inlandia, you know. The grubber infestation here has only gotten worse. And with your language skills –"

"I can't leave my hurth, Phinny. Not until my Passage."

"Your 'Passage'?" He raised an eyebrow. "Isn't it time you finally told me what this is all about?"

I hesitated, for our rituals are sacred, intimate. But then again, this was Phinny. "When a Wergen reaches the age of maturity, there's a Passage ceremony," I explained. "A male stands with the female through the rites. But in my case... the nearest Wergens are restricted to the other side of the planet. What am I to do, Phinny, swim across the ocean under the cover of night?"

"Let me speak to Aunt Zooey. She has connections at EarthCouncil. She might be able to arrange for the restrictions to be lifted to allow more Wergens to live in Inlandia."

"It doesn't matter. I couldn't perform the rites with a stranger."

"I'll stand with you," Phinny said, just like that, his green eyes aglitter.

I felt as if flut-fluts flew circles in my stomachs. "You *would?*"

"I'd do anything for you, Shim. You know that." He reached out and caressed my cheek with the back of his hand, tracing the lines of my scales.

I couldn't speak.

When we reached the overlook, he bent down to pick up a stone, which he shucked sidearm into the coruscating waters below. How many times had he done this over the years? Something about the familiarity of this act made my hearts swell.

And so on a chilly day, with the rising sun peeking from behind an amethyst cloudbank, we stood atop Pine Peak, the highest point nearest Argenta, and performed the rites. For as far as I could see, the grasslands shone like a vast coverlet of scarlet, shimmering in the indigo sunlight. Father, Elkah and Dr. Crest stood by me at the Passage ceremony. According to our customs, my companion should have been a potential tethering mate; here, my sweet Phinny accompanied me, wearing the traditional *coronatis* and ivy-laced ceremonial raiment.

Father and Elkah – thrilled at Phinny's participation – presided over the ceremony. They moved awkwardly, their tether now not more than six inches long and so taut Elkah's head leaned slightly to the left and Father's slightly to the right. By this time Father had attained dominance; Elkah rarely spoke. As Father sang the Old Words, I removed my headdress, exposing my cranial cavity, and sang the song of adulthood.

I caught Phinny peeking for a second before averting his eyes.

My cheeks flushed and I felt my cranium moisten.

Father raised his arms and spoke the final words. And then chaos erupted.

Father drew his sidearm and a laser pulse fired. Phinny yanked on my arm as he stumbled, pulling me away from the sudden movement behind us. When I turned, grubber carcasses lay strewn on the ground, steaming. Another one sprung at us, and Father fired again. At the same time, a purple-thorned grubber loomed over Dr. Crest, who held her hand over her face. Everything was happening in a heartbeat, and the shock rendered Dr. Crest – indeed, all of us – silent. Unable to move quickly, Father and Elkah stumbled over each other and fell to the ground, the sidearm dropping out of Father's hand. Without thinking, I hurled myself at the creature before it could strike at Dr. Crest. As I collided with it, the grubber turned, a blurry streak, and clamped onto my upper leg with its mandibles. While I rolled on the ground, the creature on top of me, a shot rang out and I found myself staring at the grubber's headless carapace.

"Are you all right?" Phinny asked, clutching Father's smoking firearm. But I could barely hear him over the scream – my own scream,

22

I came to realise – as I spotted the thorns embedded in my thigh and the clear blood streaming from my shredded leg.

I lift my walking stick in the air and waggle it, shifting all my weight to my healthy leg trunk. "A memento."

The Emissary scratches his chin.

"Phinny and Dr. Crest delayed their relocation to Inlandia for several weeks during my slow and painful recovery while Father and Elkah programmed the medbots to tend to me. But the venom proved beyond the bots' ability to treat. At first Father thought the bots might find it necessary to amputate my leg, but Dr. Crest developed what we then thought would be an all-purpose anti-venom. You must realise, Emissary, this was before we understood the true nature of the grubbers."

He stares blankly at me.

"Eventually the infection waned and my fever subsided. Although my body ached during this period, my spirits were high. Your father sat with me every night, held my hand, read to me. I dreaded my recovery, for I knew when my condition improved, Phinny would leave."

I fell into a deep depression after Phinny's relocation to Inlandia. I couldn't get out of bed to attend the scheduled tutorial sessions in Wergenese – or even to help Father and Elkah with the clearing of the grasslands. Phinny must have sensed the impact his departure had on me, because he made an effort to call and visit regularly. Over time though, the bi-weekly visits became monthly trips, then just random stop-bys several times a year. But we would still speak almost every day. During our holo-chats he would confide his problems, his adjustment to life Inland: how the grasslands had been cleared away and glass towers erected, how he'd obtained a position as an intern on the new Settlement Council. He told me in great detail about debates with his new friends and co-workers, ranging from political discourse about settlement policy to petty squabbles about who got the offices with the best views. Some of the councilmen had supported the strong political push on Earth to pursue more profitable alliances with another alien species at the expense of current human-Wergen joint ventures. Phinny told me that even though it wasn't his place to do so, he'd passionately defended the Wergen alliance, invoking loyalty, the deep friendship between our species, the vast amount of knowledge and philosophy humanity still had to learn from the Wergens.

During these years that Phinny lived in Inlandia, I spent my days waiting for his projection on my holo-monitor. I longed to hear his gentle voice, to laugh at his self-deprecating humour. These chats became more difficult to schedule, however, as the grubber infestations increased. It seemed the evacuation sirens blared every few days and full-blown laserfire blasted on the outskirts of Argenta.

At the time, a personal matter also concerned me. My body ached to tether, but being isolated from my own kind made this impossible. By then – although I had not discussed it with Father or Elkah – I had already made my decision. I would not tether. More than anything, I wanted to commit myself to the person I cared for more than anyone else in the universe. I wanted to spend my life – in the way humans share their lives – with Phinny.

Phinny knew about my dilemma; I had confided in him about my need to tether, but not about the decision I had made. During one of his unexpected visits, we took our familiar jaunt together. A bioelectrical field – quite effective at the time – kept the trail and the overlook clear of grubbers. During this hike, I confessed my intentions.

"I don't plan to tether," I said to him.

"You're just saying that because of your circumstances. I'm sure if there were others of your kind among us you'd feel differently."

"Maybe I'll just get 'married,'" I said playfully. "I've practically lived my life like a human anyway. After reading up on it, I must say, Phinny, there's something quite intriguing about the human marriage ritual."

"When do I get to read the book on Wergen mating customs?"

"Phinny, you *know* we wouldn't write about such things…" But when I saw his warm smile I realised he'd just been teasing.

"I know, I know," he said, holding his hands up as if surrendering. "Shim, I have something in mind." And at that moment – I don't know what gave it away, really – it finally dawned on me: Phinny had been planning to 'propose' to me. I tried then – as I had on so many prior occasions – to imagine our lives together once we formally committed to each other. Human marriage was such a pale shadow of tethering. But if it was with Phinny, with my sweet Phinny, it would suffice.

"Why Phineas Crest, I can't imagine what it might be," I said, mimicking his teasing tone. Then I spoke seriously. "Thank you,

Phinny. Thank you for always being there for me." I kissed him on the cheek.

He hugged me, and I felt a buzz surge through my body.

"Phinny!" a familiar voice shouted. Father and Elkah lumbered toward us.

Phinny took a step backward, a look of horror etched across his face. In hindsight, I suppose I should have realised he would react this way, never having seen this stage of encorporation before.

Father plodded on four legs, his and Elkah's. Elkah's left arm protruded from Father's midsection. Their two torsos were pressed so tightly together Elkah's left side melded into Father's right side. Elkah's head had disappeared within Father's – another sign of his dominance – save for her right ear, which still remained visible. In several months, all traces of her body would vanish.

"Don't be afraid, Phinny," Father said, skittering towards us, a magnificent tumbleweed of extremities. "It's still us."

Phinny stood silently, his mouth agape, his eyes bulging.

Father chattered away for a long time while Phinny gawked. Finally, I grabbed Phinny's arm and gently led him away.

"B-but, Elkah. What about Elkah?"

"She'll be encorporated completely within Father. Like my mother. Some of Elkah's skills and random memories will survive. And when encorporation is complete, Father – the new Father – will be impregnated with a brood."

"That's how your people…?"

"Phinny, I can't believe you didn't know. You've been seeing this with your own eyes for years." I placed my hand on his shoulder. He flinched.

"I've never heard of anything more horrific. Wergen females die when they mate?"

"The dominant partner – male or female – encorporates the weaker one and then propagates. Father's genetic dominance was determined when he and Elkah first tethered. My genotype is such that I would surely be dominant if I ever tethered."

"I see," he said. Deep lines formed across his forehead. He folded his arms across his chest and walked a few strides ahead of me. "Poor Elkah."

"It's part of who we are. Trust me, Elkah looked forward to the day when she could pass on her best qualities to Father, when she could provide the raw materials necessary for the birthing of a healthy brood."

He said nothing for a long while. During this interminable silence I cursed Father's unbelievably poor timing. His appearance had upset Phinny just at the moment when he was about to 'propose' to me, I was sure of it.

"Phinny, what were you going to ask me?" I finally said, breaking the silence.

He shook his head slowly. "Encorporation. I'm surprised Aunt Zooey didn't tell me about it, or that it hasn't appeared in the xenobiology literature."

"You know it's something we don't talk about. It's very... personal to us. So much so it's an express provision of the Joint Venture Compact that humans not write about it or discuss it."

He smiled now, that wide angelic smile which could light up all of Langalana. "Nature is marvellous, wondrous, isn't it?"

I exhaled loudly and returned his smile. Phinny was so gentle, so broad-minded. Of course he understood. Of course he accepted our ways.

"Tomorrow," he said, "I want you to wait for me at our special place."

"Oh?" I felt weightless. "Whatever it is, can't you tell me now?"

"No, no." He shook his head and smiled bashfully.

"Please, Phinny?"

"Don't make me ruin it!"

He squeezed my hands and kissed them. "My dear loyal, Shim. I have so much I've wanted to tell you. *Tomorrow.*"

"Tomorrow, then," I said.

I arrived at the overlook almost an hour early, dressed in the shimmering golden robes Phinny had purchased for me in Inlandia. I brought blankets and sat down in the same spot where I had first begun Phinny's lessons in Wergenese. In my mind's eye, a ghostly version of that rambunctious boy from long ago sat on the blanket next to me, concentrating intensely then jumping to his feet to toss a rock into the ocean.

From the position of the sun, I could see Phinny had scheduled this moment to coincide perfectly with the sunset.

Where would we live? Phinny had mentioned the spaciousness of his Inlandian apartment. But we had not spoken about children. Although biological procreation could never happen, Phinny had often mentioned the numerous orphaned children left behind by pilgrims killed during the grubber swarms.

I heard the rustling blades of grass and turned around. Phinny stood there. His face glowed with joy to see me; his long yellow hair ruffled in the ocean breeze. I rose to my feet and he came to me, held my outstretched hands in his. My entire body tingled; I felt incandescent.

"This is my gift to you, Shim," he said, his voice hoarse with emotion.

How many times had I dreamt of this moment?

And how many times in the hundred years since have I relived that moment, a moment forever preserved in my synaptic amber?

He released my hands and swept his arm backwards as if clearing a messy table, as if avoiding a charging grubber.

I followed the direction of his hand, which pointed to the grasslands behind him, to the squat silhouette of a male figure. A figure unmistakably Wergen. He stepped toward us, emerging into the light of dusk.

"Remember when we were children, when Aunt Zooey took your cell samples?" Phinny said. "I transmitted your samples to the Northern Continent. They ran the normal genetic tests and found a perfect match. When the last human starship arrived, I arranged... Well, it doesn't matter. Shim, this is Korte. Korte, Shim."

Confusion overwhelmed me. Phinny's words initially registered as gibberish. But as their meaning sank in, I staggered backwards.

The Wergen knelt and bowed his head. "A profound honor, Lady Shimera."

I turned and bolted into the grasslands as quickly as my legs would carry me, dashing through the chest-high blades into denser brush that rose higher and higher over my head.

"Shim! What's wrong?" Phinny called out behind me.

Running blindly through the fields, I heard Phinny's voice become fainter and fainter. "Shim! Shim!"

I lost all sense of time racing through the grasslands, the blades' gentle fur brushing against my skin. Had seconds passed? Hours? I dropped to my knees and heaved suffocating sobs. My breathing canal begged for oxygen but my body shuddered with each spastic sob. I rolled to the ground and hugged my knees. What had happened? I couldn't understand. Rocking myself, I wept uncontrollably.

When I finally opened my eyes, the twilight had faded and the stars blinked on. Occasionally I heard a buzzer whiz over my head and voices calling my name. But I only wanted the grubbers to appear and end my agony, to seize me in their mandibles and mercifully rip me to shreds.

A knock on the door of my room woke me the next morning. Sitting up, I looked around and found myself in my hurth. A dream. Yes, it had all been a horrific dream.

Phinny entered. And all at once I knew yesterday had really happened. His dishevelled appearance and the creased semi-circles under his eyes suggested he had been part of the search party.

"Shim. What happened? Why did you run away like that?" He sat beside me on the edge of my bed. "Don't you know the grubbers are everywhere now? It's a miracle we found you in one piece."

I glared at him.

"I thought you'd be happy. Korte is a perfect genetic match; he'll make an exceptional tethering mate."

My eyes brimmed with angry tears.

"What is it?"

"Oh, Phinny, you idiot. Don't you realise I'm in love with you?" I said, the words finally pouring out of me. "That I've been in love with you from the first day we met? That you mean everything to me? That I can't imagine a life without you?" The tears stung my eyes. "I couldn't care less about tethering."

He seemed stunned. "Shim... I understand," he said. "You're Wergen. Of course you love me."

"No, you don't understand. You don't understand at all. This goes beyond that. I don't love you because you're human. I love you... because you're you!"

He shook his head. "How can you say that? You know every Wergen feels that way about every human." His face filled with unmistakable pity.

"I don't feel this way about any other human!"

"That's because you've spent more time with me than you have with anyone else. It's only natural you would have a stronger attraction toward me."

"Your kindness, your humour, your generosity, those are the things I love… not your beauty."

"Shim…"

"How can I convince you?" I clutched his hands. "How can I make you understand that what I feel for you… It's real. *I swear it.*"

"On a rational level, you have to know this just isn't true. You're too intelligent not to realise that the biological impulse driving your species to be attracted to mine… It's affecting you."

"Fine." I let go of his hands and crossed my arms. "So you've known how I felt about you all these years? It must have provided you with such amusement."

"Shim." He shook his head. "I need you to understand." He gently ran his hand across my cheek.

I slapped his hand away. "Don't touch me!"

"You're my dear, dear friend…" he said, his voice cracking.

"Leave!" I jumped out of bed and shoved him.

"Shim…" He hung his head and stepped toward the door.

"Don't you care that the very sight of you tortures me? That your touch is agony to me? You're a monster!"

"You have to understand…" He turned and grabbed my shoulders.

"Get out! Get out!" I slapped him hard. He took a few steps back, his hand over his red cheek, and I slammed the door in his face. "Leave me alone! I don't ever want to see you again. Do you hear me? Let me live my life in peace." But even as I said the words, I longed for him to break down the door, to take me in his arms and beg my forgiveness, to kiss me and hold me tight, and tether with me in the fleeting, short-lived way of his people, were it possible. My back to the door, I slid to the floor and stifled the sobs with my hands. After several interminable seconds, I heard him retreat, his footsteps daggers in my hearts.

"Don't look at me that way, Emissary," I say. The look of pity – even after all these years – still stings. "It wasn't easy, but I eventually got over your father."

The Emissary nods his head slowly.

"I redirected my energies towards… more productive endeavors. I taught classes in Wergenese to thousands of arriving humans. And years later, I turned my attention to politics. I travelled to Inlandia every month and sat on the Settlement Council as Argenta's elected representative. And eventually the World Council was established. Remarkably – even though I remained untethered – my people selected me to serve as Langalana's Wergen Ambassador.

"My feelings for your father have been dead and buried long, long ago. The way we'd left things, I never thought I'd see him again."

Against the advice of my military advisers, the remains of Father and my half-siblings, Valik, Lyrra and Olsinore were set ablaze on the summit of Pine Peak. An entire platoon of armed soldiers surrounded the procession, on the lookout for grubbers. Blue-tinted snow fell around us in sheets, forming a covering that made the grasslands appear tired and aged. The pyre still smoked – the final words having been spoken – and, out of respect, the humans and Wergens congregated around me to sing a brooding threnody.

That's when I saw him, standing off in the distance, his face covered by a scarf, his yellow tresses blowing in the wind. Ten years later and I recognised him instantly. It seemed like only yesterday since we'd spoken.

When Phinny realised I'd spotted him, he approached, accompanied by an obese female human wearing a fur-lined hooded coat.

"Shimera," he said, hugging me. "I'm so sorry about your family."

"Phinny? It's really you! I'd heard you relocated to Earth."

"Yes, I was near the Langalanan system when I got word of Olbodoh's passing."

"The grubbers are everywhere, Phinny. *Everywhere*. The swarms now overwhelm our strongest forcefields. When I found Father and the children… it was too late…"

Phinny embraced me again and this time I fell into his arms. After a few seconds, he pulled away and gestured to the pot-bellied female. "Shimera, this is my wife, Lois."

"Your wife?" I shook her hand in the way humans greet one another, and my hand tingled. How I hated myself in that instant; how I hated that this woman's touch brought me pleasure. "I'm honoured," I said.

After we exchanged pleasantries, Phinny whispered something into his wife's ear and she nodded. A Wergen patrolman took Lois's arm to help her with the slippery footing.

Phinny hooked his arm with mine, and I handed my walking stick to the patrolman. We strode several steps ahead of them, our footsteps crunching in the snow. "Wergen Ambassador?" he said. "My, my, my. What happened to the farm girl and teacher I knew?"

"Without distractions, she found she could expand her horizons."

Phinny looked away from me uncomfortably.

I didn't intend to sound so bitter. I changed the subject. "How's Dr. Crest?"

"Aunt Zooey died a few years ago. She stayed in Inlandia, convinced to the very end the solution to the grubber problem lay in gengineering. Then the locust storm hit."

"We lost so many good people that day. I didn't realise she was one of them."

"Shimera, isn't it time for you to abandon this world? It isn't safe here."

"I can't give up on Langalana, Phinny. I just can't," I said. "Remember how easy we all thought this was going to be? Simply power up my people's fieldbots and welcome the arriving starships, right?" I shook my head and smiled. "Well, just because things have gotten difficult is no reason to quit. I have responsibilities here."

The snow had intensified as we walked toward the settlement, but I could still make out the Wergen security forces in our perimeter, following with their weapons drawn.

"Shim, about the way we left things all those years ago… I'm sorry. It was wrong not to stay in touch."

I stopped. "Does she love you, Phinny?" I whispered.

He nodded.

"Let me ask you something," I said under my breath with a ferocity that surprised even me. "How do you know?"

"Excuse me?"

"How do you know? How do you know that she isn't just physically attracted to you, that she isn't just driven by a biological compulsion to propagate your species, to combine her DNA with yours?"

"Shim…"

"How do you know it's true love?"

Flakes of blue snow hung on his hair, and he looked as if he carried a great weight on his shoulders. "I suppose I don't. But I know this much: she doesn't *have* to love me."

His words deflated me. We took a few more steps in silence before I responded. "I've read medical journals about your species' state of 'love': the increased dopamine levels, the heightened neural activity in the ventral tegmental area of your mammalian brains. It's all chemical, you know. All driven by the evolutionary urge to breed. You look down on us, but I don't think your kind is *capable* of true love."

"I don't look down on you," he said. But even as he said the words, he stared at me with an unmistakable pity.

Lois and the patrolman had caught up to us so we started to walk again. I coughed and cleared my throat. "As I was saying, Phinny, we're not giving up on the grasslands. We'll figure out some way to drive back the grubbers. I have absolute faith in that. Tell me, can you and Lois stay a few days?"

Phinny glanced back at his wife who gave a small, near-imperceptible shake of her head. "No, I'm afraid not. We're on our way to visit Lois's parents in the Scornian system. Plus, Lois is pregnant and it's not really safe for us to stay here too long."

"Oh?" I stared at her midsection and tried to recollect my lessons in human procreation.

We stopped in front of the neighbourhood's row of hurths.

"Well, things have certainly changed here," he observed.

"Yes, a lot more Wergens, eh? Development of the suppressor has allowed us to renegotiate our population quotas." Many Wergens now wore transparent masks – whiffers – that allowed them to manage their emotions around humans. But after a lifetime of suppression, I needed no drug to help me hide my feelings. "Can you and Lois come in for a few minutes? Perhaps share a bowl of *chapra*? Or maybe some preserved watermelon? For old time's sake."

He looked at Lois again and this time she rolled her eyes and tilted her head back slightly. I could have sworn this caused Phinny to take a step backward, as if an invisible tether pulled at him. "No, no, we really have to be going." He placed his hands in mine. "I promise, I'll keep in touch this time."

"That's good," I said. But as I gauged Lois's expression I knew this would be the last time I would ever see Phinny.

I circle the table again slowly.

"Langalana rejected all of our efforts to tame her, Emissary. We had to evacuate the settlements three sun-cycles ago and relocate here. The grubbers kept multiplying exponentially. We've concluded they're a form of biospheric antibody, keyed in to our alien DNA. They burrowed through our forcefields, rendering the grasslands uninhabitable. Then Inlandia fell. The Northern and Western Continents fared no better. Eventually we tried relocating to the frigid peaks of Langalana's highest mountains – but the grubbers followed, scaling the vertical walls unimaginable heights to pursue us. We even tried constructing new settlements on remote islands, but in time the grubbers honed in, swimming across the vast oceans to find us. For a few years we thought we'd found a solution when the gengineers developed chemical signatures that camouflaged our alien DNA. The grubbers actually stopped attacking and multiplying, then disappeared altogether. One day, however, they suddenly saw past the chemical mask and the swarming recommenced. Hundreds of thousands of pilgrims have since been killed.

"We have no choice. It's time for us to move on, Emissary. For all of our dreams of settling Langalana – so many seedships travelling such vast distances – we're not welcome here. So I've given the order," I say. "The Wergen contingent will be moving out of this system, joining humanity on some other new world. That's why you're here, isn't it? To coordinate our relocation to the next human colony?"

The Emissary stands up and clears his throat. "Thank you for telling me so much about my father's childhood. The truth is, we had a falling out a long time ago and we were never as close as I would have liked… Before he died, my father heard I had business on Langalana.

He asked to see me and requested I seek you out to give you a message."

"A message?"

He reaches into the inside pocket of his blue uniform jacket and pulls out an envelope. I stare at the extended hand and, shivering slightly, take it from him.

"My father believed in this quaint form of ancient written communication. He was an eccentric man." The Emissary pauses. "As for the business I have here…"

"Eh?"

"Yes, we'd heard about the decision to move your people." He rubs his hand over his mouth. "I realise with your displacement to this satellite you may be unaware of recent developments." He hesitates. "I'm here to inform you humanity has decided to pursue a different path."

"Excuse me?"

"EarthCouncil believes our most profitable joint ventures with the Wergens are behind us. We've learned a lot from your people, Ambassador, for which we're deeply grateful. But we're now able to produce our own bots on par with the best the Wergens can produce… And the new alien species we've encountered, the Eremites, have offered us new technologies and new opportunities."

"I… I understand. Well… at least there will be ongoing cultural exchanges between our peoples. We still have much to learn from one another."

"I'm afraid I haven't made myself clear. Our disassociation must be total. You have to understand, Ambassador. My people have difficulty coping with the Wergens'… deep, unconditional adoration. I'm afraid it's brought out the worst in a certain segment of our population. There have been some… abuses… on other colonies. Then there was that ugly matter of the Wergen renegades. No, I'm afraid it's not in anyone's interests for our worlds to interact any further." He stands at the window and stares at Langalana. "So many precious resources. What a shame." He turns. "In any event, Ambassador, thank you for your time. I have other pressing matters to attend to."

I clench my fists. "What about the agreements in place between our people? The Joint Venture Compacts that have been signed?"

The Emissary strides to the door and pauses at the threshold. "I'm sorry. If you wish to file a grievance, I'm sure some financial settlement can be reached."

After a long pause, I answer. "I'm sorry too, Emissary."

"Yes, well... Good luck to you," he replies awkwardly, and nods goodbye.

As he turns the corner and his footsteps fade down the hall, I hold up the yellowed envelope in my hand. I don't need to open it; I know what it says. Phinny loved me. He came to realise over the years that he'd made a terrible mistake not asking me to marry him, that the love we shared was pure, genuine. But once he'd realised his terrible mistake, circumstances had conspired against him. By then he had responsibilities to Lois and to his son.

Ah, Phinny, I've been over you for so long now. It doesn't matter any more.

I fold the envelope, unopened.

Leaning against the window, I focus intensely on the cold beauty of Langalana. The planet hangs there, so close, so close I can almost snatch it out of the sky and cradle it in my bosom. I reach for it, but find the glass thick and impenetrable, and the proximity only an illusion.

I sigh and slowly run my hand along my cheek, tracing the crevices between my scales.

# CHAPTER TWO
## In the Harsh Glow of Its Incandescent Beauty

### Triton – Year 2498

So there you have it, an ending. With Ocura, the Wergen homeworld, now receding on my viewscreen, I'm tempted to tell you of our covert mission to rewrite that ending. But if you're to understand how we got here, if you're truly to be free, I need to tell you of the first human-Wergen settlement, the Axelis Colony on Triton. This was long before colonists ever set foot on Langalana, at a time when the 'Love Panel', as it came to be known, a clandestine organisation dedicated to learning the secrets of Wergen physiology, had first formed. I don't think anyone understood the dark path we were pursuing and where those efforts would ultimately take us.

Our seedship landed at the Lassel Airstrip near Axelis Colony where I was sure my wife, Miranda, had arrived a month ago with Rossi. Joriander and Hexa, my Wergen minders, hauled my bags down our seedship's ramp while I hugged my hooded fur coat tight. Neptune hovered high in the pale viridian sky. Even with the Wergen forcefield doming this airstrip, Triton's tenuous atmosphere still managed a bitter breeze that stung my face like razors.

The three of us trudged across the empty tarmac toward the terminal entranceway. To our left, the towering, cathedral-like glaciers of Triton's North Pole glittered blue-green, capturing Neptune's luminescence.

"Here, Maxwell," Hexa said, removing a leathery scarf and exposing her scaled face to the elements. She threw it around my shoulders and pressed close to me – too close, I thought – for a few seconds longer than necessary.

Joriander followed suit, removing his temp-mitts and offering them to me.

I resisted the urge to slap the gloves to the ground. "Knock it off. I'm fine."

The Wergens stooped their shoulders at my curtness, and I felt a pang of guilt. They continued their steady gait at my side. The ground rumbled and a geyser exploded on the horizon, spewing ice-lava kilometres into the sky.

*Oh, the distances you've travelled, Miranda. He's taken you so far from home. But don't worry; I'm here now.*

After a few paces, Hexa placed her four-fingered hand on my shoulder, letting it linger there. "I wish my people could have produced a more effective field over this area, one that could generate more comfortable temperatures for humans. I apologise."

"No need," I said, shrugging off her hand. "After all, where would we be without you?" Digging caves on equatorial Mars, I thought. Wergen fieldtech had opened up every planetesimal in the Solar System to human colonisation, the limitations of temperature, radiation, gravity and atmosphere all conquered in one fell swoop. Without their help I would never have obtained transport to Triton to track down Miranda and bring her home.

Joriander removed a jewel-encrusted sphere from his inside robe pocket and tapped several of the gemstones. In response, the terminal's circular doorway irised open and we entered a cavernous holding area. As soon as the door rumbled shut, a dozen mantis-like bots, big as terriers, skittered towards us. They herded us into an enormous decontamination pen where they scanned our retinas, removed and sterilised our clothes, and ran us through a battery of tests to screen for contagious diseases.

I caught the Wergens staring at me with rapt attention, their large mooning eyes probing my body. I cupped my hands over my crotch. Despite the Wergens' notorious reticence to discuss their sexual practices, they showed no bashfulness at their own nakedness. They were squat, husky, with reptilian scales speckling their bleached-white skin, and no visible genitalia. Hexa, the female, matched my height, while Joriander, the male, stood half a metre shorter. Rumour had it their sexual organs lay hidden within their flat-topped craniums, which they kept covered, even now, with a leafy headdress. I shuddered. For all of the Wergens' courtesies, I still felt an instinctive aversion toward them. But they offered us so much. And I had to do whatever necessary to save Miranda.

One of the bots injected a tracker into my earlobe. Local officials carefully monitored all new arrivals, a practice I was counting on to find Miranda among the hundreds of thousands of Axelis's inhabitants. The bots then sprayed our naked bodies with a microfilament that produced an electrical field evident only by the faintest of blue tinges.

"This will maintain your body temperature at a more comfortable level," Joriander said. "We won't need the heavier protective clothing any more."

I turned away and donned the standard two-piece blue uniform provided to us, feeling the Wergens' eyes on my back. The bots proceeded to guide us to a raised monorail where the three of us boarded a private railcar headed to Axelis.

We sped above smooth, dark-green ice plains formed over millions of years by a slurry of water and ammonia. As the minutes turned to hours, the topography below us shifted to a landscape of what I'd heard described as "cantaloupe skin," an endless expanse of circular depressions separated by deep rounded ridges. Ahead of us, Neptune crept across the skyline, growing smaller as it moved to the west but still filling a quarter of the sky. The massive storm system of the Great Dark Spot stained its southern hemisphere behind half-formed rings.

"A spectacular sight, isn't it?" Hexa said, leaning toward me.

*What did you think, Miranda, when you saw these alien vistas? Were you in Rossi's arms, then? How much had the neuromone warped your thinking?*

The railcar wound around a bend between two icy mountain peaks, then, all at once, Axelis came into view. The settlement sat in the thousand-mile Great Gulch, a valley of low, neon-lit hills beneath a silver web of monorail tracks. The blue wisp of the Wergen forcefield stretched from one peak to another. Below us, more than five hundred thousand colonists from Earth, Luna and Mars populated Axelis.

Joriander locked eyes with me in that intense Wergen manner. "Did you leave it on the ship?" he asked.

I reached down and unzipped the side pocket of my bag, revealing the airpulser. "No, I'll be needing this."

Joriander averted his eyes.

The administrator sported a platinum-blonde crew cut and hunched over a comm terminal. Her height – well over two metres – pegged her as Mars-born. "Yes, they do reside in Axelis."

"Do you have an address?" I said.

It turned out Miranda and Rossi had temporarily settled in the Pretori District in southern Axelis. They were on the long waiting list for the human/Wergen expedition to Langalana, an unexplored but potentially habitable planet hundreds of light years away.

"Thank you for your help," I said.

"My pleasure to serve, sir." She bowed. "Welcome to Triton."

Joriander, Hexa and I retreated to the rotunda of the Visitors' Centre. From within this hollowed-out hill, the space resembled the lobby of any office building on Earth or Mars, except for the Wergen companions accompanying each human who walked by.

We boarded the jam-packed public monorail to Pretori. Among the Terrans and Martians, a small contingent of Wergens wedged into the crowd, their pasty faces frozen in ecstasy. While Joriander and Hexa stood dazed by the human crowd, I felt relief at the brief respite from their constant attentions.

The complex where Miranda and Rossi resided, like all the habitations in Axelis, consisted of a green, rocky knoll riddled with scores of catacombs and caverns. I disembarked from the tram and hiked a paved path that snaked up the rocky terrain. Hexa and Joriander, eager to please as always, lugged my bags up the side of the hill.

Row upon row of windows pocked the entire hillside, standing out like grids on an emerald anthill. Faces stared from behind them, surveying our arrival. I searched for Miranda among them.

As we made our way through crisscrossing catacombs, I asked for directions from passersby until I reached the shelter where Miranda lived. I pounded on the door. When no one answered, I lowered my shoulder into it, but the door held firm.

"Can I help you, sir?" A Martian neighbour poked his long neck out into the corridor at the sound of the commotion.

"I'm searching for the man and woman who live here."

"Who are you?"

"Miranda's husband."

"Her husb – Oh. I see." The man tilted his head and scrunched his nose in an expression I couldn't read.

"Do you know where they are?" I said.

"They left last week to attend basic training for the Langalanan expedition. They're due back any day."

On my adrenaline high, I had to resist the urge to break down the door anyway. Joriander thanked the man for the information and gently pressed his hand against the middle of my back, moving me away. Hexa mentioned that the ships to Langalana departed from the Cipango Planum Plateau in the western hemisphere of Triton, which is where training would take place. Our Joint Venture Compact with the Wergens required humans to work side by side with them on Triton or Europa or one of the other spaceports for at least six months to qualify for these colonisation missions. The Wergens provided their tech to humanity – wormhole-generating seedships for intergalactic travel, forcefield devices, and low-level AI bots that performed the physical labour. In return, we gave them our art, our ingenuity, and – what they desired most of all – our companionship.

A trip to distant Cipango Planum risked delaying my reunion with Miranda for weeks if she were already on her way back. So despite my frustration, we settled into the closest available shelter to wait. The Wergens shared the single sleeping room while I camped out on the sofa in the living area, staring out a window overlooking the pathway approaching the complex. The cavern smelled musky with a trace of burnt rubber – a sure sign of recently lasered rock. Stoked on stims, I spent two days observing every approaching individual, hoping to see Miranda's sweet face, a familiar streak of red hair, her pale soft skin. Water geysers exploded sporadically on the horizon.

The Wergens prepared meals for me and supplied the stims. When they weren't engaging me in annoying small talk, they would sit in two chairs and study me silently, a half-smile on their flat faces. They gave off a vinegary stink that made me gag.

"You're very diligent," Hexa said. "Very devoted to your mission. That's an admirable trait, Maxwell."

I twitched from the stims.

"Why did Miranda leave you?" Joriander asked.

I had already explained this back when I negotiated their price for using the seedship – eight months of my companionship – but they still couldn't grasp the situation. I had left out many details, of course. I told them nothing about how Rossi and I had served on the Wergen Study Group – the so-called 'Love Panel.' We were selected to work with a committee of fellow scientists to understand the nature of the Wergens' obsessive infatuation with humanity. Rossi and I were specifically tasked with examining the aliens' brain chemistry, a near impossible assignment given the Wergens' taboo against revealing anything to us about their physiology. But military operatives had surreptitiously obtained Wergen skin cells and body scans, which proved invaluable to our research.

We discovered that the introduction of a strand of the aliens' triple-helix DNA into the cells of the medial temporal lobe of a human test-clone caused a new neurotransmitter to be generated in the amygdala, one that stimulated the firing of very specific postsynaptic neurons – the ones responsible for feelings of love. After synthesising the neuromone, while we were in the process of presenting our findings, Rossi disappeared with the sample. And with Miranda. It never crossed my mind he would think to *use* the neuromone, on my wife no less. I thought of the three years I'd worked side by side with him, the weekend swivelball games, the times I'd tried to cheer him up over watered-down beers at Helen's Pub during his rancorous divorce. How many times had Miranda and I hosted him for dinner?

"She's been drugged, brainwashed," I said to the Wergens, fingering the airpulser in the inside pocket of my jacket.

Joriander and Hexa seemed perplexed. "She doesn't understand what she's doing?" Hexa said.

"Her feelings have been... warped." When they remained bewildered, I added: "I miss her. I need to be with her."

This they understood. They bobbed their heads in empathy.

"She's my *wife*."

Joriander and Hexa looked confused again. During our uncomfortable trek from Mars, I had tried my best to explain the concept of marriage to them, with no success. The Wergens had trouble understanding how mere vows could connect two people. I had finally thrown my hands up and escaped to the ship's sleeping quarters for some rest. I'd wake up, however, to the unnerving sight of their flat smiling faces. How many times had they stood there staring at me? My skin crawled.

"It's difficult for us to understand 'leaving' after you've been joined together in what you term marriage," Hexa said.

"It's complicated," I said.

When I stopped talking, Hexa changed subjects and asked: "Why are these black hairs sprouting on your face?" She reached out to touch my cheek.

I flinched. "I haven't had a chance to shave."

They continued to gawk at me.

"Do you have to stare all the time?" I asked.

"You're just so…" Joriander struggled for the words. "Luminous. Incandescent. It's difficult not to admire your beauty."

Joriander's response didn't make me feel any more comfortable. The Wergens' unconditional love for us transcended gender or species. As always, I did my best to ignore them and focused my attention on Triton's horizon.

On the third night, I spotted her. She walked hand in hand with Rossi before he stopped to kiss her. A Wergen companion followed close behind them. Miranda waved goodbye to Rossi and he proceeded onward past the gates with the Wergen while she entered the residential catacombs alone.

"You're looking stressed, Maxwell," Hexa said.

"Are you well?" Joriander said.

I shoved past the Wergens and bolted out the front door, down the curving corridor. When I arrived at the entranceway, I found her by the elevators, her back to me.

"Miranda!" I grabbed her arm and spun her around. Her face blanched, her eyes widening. A long strand of red-orange hair draped across her left eye. She looked exactly as if she'd seen the ghost of the husband she'd cheated on.

"Max! How did you…?"

I kissed her cheeks, her lips, her forehead. "It's okay. I'm here, I'm here."

She pushed me away. "What are you doing?"

"I came to bring you home."

She stepped backward.

"You've been drugged! It's a chemical, a neuromone we discovered." The words came in a flood. I explained it all to her, how the single vial of the substance had disappeared the night before she left, how Rossi must have slipped the neuromone into some food or beverage she'd consumed.

"Oh, Max," she said. "I told you to stay away."

"None of this is your fault, Miranda. There would've been no way for you to resist. You would've fallen instantly in love with the first person you saw."

"Max, I need for you to listen to me." She put her hands on my forearms as if both to steady me and keep me at a distance. "I *know* I'm drugged." She paused for a beat as if to let the message sink in. "Rossi confessed everything to me."

"What are you saying?" I felt as if the floor shifted under me. "I'll work on a treatment, Miranda —"

"No, you don't understand —"

"I'll find a way to counter the effects —"

"I want to stay here with Rossi."

Her words stunned me.

"I know I should be furious, I should feel victimised. But after discussing it with Rossi, that's not how I feel anymore. I'm an adult, I'm lucid, rational and... I'm in love with him. Deeply, totally, unconditionally in love. I'm the happiest I've ever been in my life."

"You're not thinking straight."

She shook her head vigorously. "Look, the chemical simulates the processes in the brain when a person is in love, correct? In other words, if you compared my brain chemistry with that of a normal, happy newlywed there'd be no difference between the two, isn't that right?"

"Well, yes. But in your case it's been triggered by a foreign substance, a drug!"

"So what?"

"Miranda...!"

"*So what?* What difference does it make what the origin of these feelings are? The point is that they're real to me. I'm in love with Rossi."

I couldn't believe what I was hearing. "And what about me?"

A long pause followed. "I've behaved unforgivably. You have every reason to despise me for what I've done —"

"It's not your fault."

"No, I should've settled things with you before leaving, Max," she said. "But I was too much of a coward. Maybe someday you'll find it in your heart to forgive me for what I've done, but right now you need to forget about me and get on with your life."

"I can't do that." Not while she remained under the neuromone's spell.

"Please, don't make me hurt you any more than I already have." She turned to leave. "Rossi will be here soon. You should go."

I hoped it wouldn't come to this, but I had no choice. I lunged and grabbed her from behind. Peeling off the synth-skin covering my thumb, I pressed the dermaplast-soaked digit against the back of her ear. She struggled for just an instant before letting out a sigh and falling back into my arms.

I cradled her as Joriander and Hexa approached.

"Maxwell! What did you do?" Joriander said.

Hexa grabbed Miranda's wrist. "Is she dead?"

"She's fine. Help me take her back to the ship. We're putting her into spacesleep for the trip back to Earth."

Joriander crossed his arms and wiggled his stubby fingers, a gesture I'd never seen before, but which I later came to associate with Wergen anxiety. Hexa mimicked him.

We walked half a block to the monorail line, passersby gaping at Miranda's limp body in my arms, and boarded a private railcar back to the Lassel Airstrip.


Joriander stood watch over Miranda's body in the ship's medroom while Hexa prepared the ship for departure. I stared out of the plexi and saw the terminal's metal door whir open, two silhouettes emerging from the bright interior, one human, the other Wergen. Their appearance was inevitable, I supposed, given our implanted trackers.

I strode down the ramp onto the tarmac.

"What do you think you're doing, Max?" Rossi flashed an angry smile when he spoke. He looked thinner than I remembered, younger. Somehow he'd managed to find the time to maintain his tan on Triton. As he approached, he pulled an airpulser from his bomber jacket and pointed it at me.

"Don't do this!" the Wergen accompanying him pleaded. The alien regarded me with lovesick eyes.

"Don't worry, Olbodoh," Rossi said to the Wergen. "I won't hurt him... unless he forces me to." He moved closer, his Wergen companion shuffling right behind him. "Board that ship and retrieve Miranda."

"But are you sure you'll be –"

"Do it!"

The Wergen crossed his arms and wiggled his fingers while striding up the ramp, disappearing into the vessel.

"I trusted you, you son of a bitch," I said.

I thought I saw regret flash in his eyes for a microsecond. "Don't play the victim here, Max. It doesn't suit you. Miranda's happy now."

"I'll make sure you're charged with assault and kidnapping. You'll be digging pits on Mars the rest of your miserable life."

"I don't think Miranda will be pressing charges, Max," he said. "Not against me, anyway."

I moved closer to him and he jerked the gun upward, pointing it at my head.

"Do you think I'm so stupid I wouldn't have expected you to have a gun?" I said.

"Keep your distance." He pointed the airpulser at my feet and attempted a warning shot. Nothing happened.

I laughed. "My Wergen companions set up a dampening field."

He lunged forward and knocked me hard across the mouth with the barrel of the pulser, dropping me to my knees. The force of the blow made my bodyfield blink off and on, then disappear.

Subzero temperatures assaulted me. I reached inside my jacket for the gun – the one immune to the dampening field – and fired. The shot went wide.

At that moment the ground rumbled and a geyser exploded in the distance.

I stumbled and dropped the gun.

It slid forward and Rossi dove for it ahead of me. I realised I had no chance of wresting the gun from him before he could fire it.

Scrambling backwards, I raced along the tarmac away from the ship, in the direction of Triton's towering glaciers.

I sprinted through narrow, zigzagging pathways inside the pine-green glacier. I made out Rossi's black bomber jacket far behind me, appearing and disappearing with each bend. The air-pulses struck the sides of the walls, sending chunks of ice flying.

I dropped, hugged the frozen ground, and waited.

An air-pulse whooshed past me and the ground to my left exploded. Another shot rang out and I darted into a crevice in the green ice wall.

My teeth chattered. I was headed in a dangerous direction, away from Lassel, where the Wergen forcefield would become more and more tenuous. After a few seconds, I stopped running. Eventually nothing would protect me from the moon's deadly natural environment. There was no trace of Rossi. The sensible thing for him to do would be to forget about me. But I suppose he was no more sensible than I was when it came to Miranda.

At that moment, he came around a bend, firing.

My chest ached as I sucked air.

After several hundred metres, the trail before me opened into a wide, bowl-shaped arroyo. The peaks of the glacier circled high above. Ahead, the ground broke into layered ridges that sloped downwards. I twirled around, looking in all directions for any sign of Rossi.

Then I glimpsed movement. Like a charmed snake, an arm rose from below an ice step and Rossi fired the airpulser. It struck a glacier wall, scattering icy splinters that rained down on me. I rolled to my left and hugged the frozen soil above his line of sight, trying to control my ragged breathing.

The ground shook again and an explosion boomed. Above us, a plume of slush shot into the air.

When I caught sight of him again, Rossi's distant form darted into another crevice in the far ice wall.

I leapt down the levels, my spikes crunching in the snow. I could barely feel my feet. Mucus had frozen above my lip.

As I clambered down the final step, inhaling needles, I slipped and fell. My entire body slid sideways to the left and stopped just short of a crevasse two metres across that opened up into a black, bottomless pit. I crawled away from the edge and found my feet before bolting into another steep sided passageway. Like the prior trail, sharp corners lay ahead, only this time the path forked into multiple arteries, forming a maze. I slowed down at each corner, expecting Rossi to be lying in wait. I hit dead end after dead end, turning and veering back, looking upwards to see if I could climb out, but spotting only glassy scarps that stretched into infinity. When I made my way around a long curved bend, I saw him.

Rossi was up to his waist in an icy slush. He'd taken a misstep and found himself in a quicksand-like slurry, no doubt precipitated by the gushing geysers that surrounded us and filled up crevasses.

I strode towards him, careful to stay on solid footing.

"This isn't about you, Max. It's about me and Miranda." He clutched my ankle; I kicked his wrist with my other foot until he let go. I kicked his arm, his shoulder, the side of his head, until the blue aura around him faded and his bodyfield collapsed. He let out a gasp that turned into a howl as the subzero temperatures assaulted him and he sank further into the ice slurry.

This was it. The moment I had waited for, ever since I came home to an empty house and a note in Miranda's familiar scrawl that simply said, "It's over, Max. Please don't follow us." *Us*. And she had expected me not to do anything?

I picked up the airpulser, which lay on the ground several metres beyond his reach. My arms shivered uncontrollably so I grasped it with both hands, pointing it at Rossi.

"I love her, Max." He barely got the words out through chattering teeth.

I fingered the trigger.

"That's enough, Maxwell."

Joriander, Hexa and Olbodoh stood behind me. Scores of metal bots swarmed from behind them over the ridges of ice. One darted over my legs and crawled onto my chest. Another crawled over Rossi. The blue veneer of my bodyfield blinked back on, as did Rossi's.

"What are you doing?" I screamed. "This isn't your concern!"

"We've deactivated your weapon," Joriander said. "We can't just stand by and allow you to kill each other. It would be blasphemous."

"Stay out of this!"

"Maxwell, we do what you ask, what your people ask, because we love you." His every word oozed compassion. "All of you. You're all precious. You're all beautiful. It would be immoral to stand by and let you hurt yourselves this way. We want to protect you, to nurture you."

"He needs to pay for what he's done!" I trembled, but not from the cold, and my voice broke.

"You're both suffering from frostbite. You need to be tended to."

The carapace of one of the bots opened like a blooming flower and a syringe emerged, penetrating my thigh.

I woke to the muted glow of the ceiling lights in the ship's medroom. Joriander sat by my bed, stroking my hair. I pulled away from him. On the other side of the room, Miranda and Hexa stood next to a bare-chested Rossi, who was buttoning his shirt.

I lurched off the table, but lost my footing as the room tilted. Joriander grabbed hold of me before I collapsed.

"You need to lie back down, Maxwell. The sedative the bots gave you won't lose its effect for another thirty minutes." He helped me back onto the table.

"You alien bastard," I muttered. Joriander turned away as if I'd slapped him.

Hexa and the other Wergen, Olbodoh, accompanied Miranda and Rossi to the door of the medroom.

Miranda stopped at the threshold and looked back at me. "Can I have a moment alone with him?" she asked the Wergens.

As they exited the room, Rossi placed his hand on her back and she gave him a nod, as if assuring him it would be all right. He smirked at me – a smile of triumph – and followed the Wergens.

Miranda sat on the chair next to my table, her red hair draping the side of her freckled face. "Are you okay?"

I didn't answer.

She took a deep breath. "Remember when we first met, Max? We were on that climbing tour of Olympus Mons and you offered to help me secure my rocklock. Remember? When I met you I felt the same… giddiness, the same butterflies-in-my-stomach feelings I feel now for Rossi."

And, oh, how I'd reciprocated those feelings! Beautiful women like Miranda had always been out of my reach, and when she confessed her feelings for me it was if I'd been shunted into an alternate magical reality.

"I found it so endearing when you'd wake up with your hair uncombed and sit on the balcony reading your retinal messages until you were late for work every morning." She smiled sadly. "But things change, people change. My brain chemistry adjusted over time and those feelings faded."

"I can't accept that," I said. "What we shared was… *deeper* than dopamine coursing through our brains."

"So says the man of science." She laughed softly. "The man who studies the biology of love for a living."

"You've got it all wrong, Miranda. It's love that causes the chemical reactions in our bodies, not the other way around. I have to believe that."

She covered her mouth and shook her head.

"Don't go with him, Miranda."

"I'm talking about *us* now, Max." She pushed her hair out of her eyes. "What happened to us? To our passion for each other?"

"Every relationship settles into a... comfortable dynamic. You can't maintain that 'giddiness' forever," I said. And as I spoke these words, I couldn't help but think of it in biochemical terms, the dopamine replaced slowly over the course of time with oxytocin and vasopressin, intense passion replaced with feelings of companionship and bonding. I pushed the thought away.

Miranda's expression turned deadly serious. "There's something I need to tell you. Something I think you deserve to know." Her eyes met mine and I could see a trace of fear in them. "Rossi and I became involved about a year ago."

As the meaning of her words sank in, I felt as if I'd been sucker-punched.

"Yes, that was long before you two developed the neuromone." She paused as if to make sure I fully grasped the ramifications of what she'd said. "Rossi would visit me whenever he knew you'd be working late at the lab. For him, you have to understand, it was all about the thrill of lying in his friend's bed and screwing his wife. The 'wrongness' of it excited him. I knew that; I'm not stupid. But for me, over time, it became something more. I started to feel like a lovesick schoolgirl. Rossi would actually talk to me. He'd tell me about your work, about your concerns. The truth is, I couldn't wait for you to message me that you'd be working late, so I could be with him."

I flinched. A stranger was talking to me.

"I'm sorry. I'm not saying these things to hurt you. Honestly. And I realise it was wrong of me to leave the way I did without explaining this to you. I see that now." She took a deep breath and continued. "After a few months, Rossi began to lose interest and moved on to his next conquest. I felt foolish, furious. By then he'd told me all about the neuromone you two had synthesised. I went to the lab one morning to visit and…" She looked up at the ceiling. "Max, Rossi didn't drug me. I drugged *him.*"

I heard the words but I couldn't believe them. She had to be lying. "You have the drug in your system," I said. "I checked for it when you were unconscious."

She sighed, as if that bit of information now required her to reveal more than she intended. "You have to understand, Rossi loves me now, wildly, passionately. It's everything I'd dreamed of. But on the trip here from Mars, I started to have… doubts. My own feelings had started to wane, and by then I had already left you, I'd quit my job, I'd travelled across the Solar System to Triton. There was no turning back, so I took the last dose of the neuromone myself. So I could reciprocate his feelings."

I opened my mouth, but no words came out.

She stood up to leave. "When you surprised me at the catacombs, I thought it would be kinder to let you think I was the victim. That my feelings for you hadn't died on their own, that they'd been erased by a drug. But that's not the truth, Max."

"So I did all this for nothing."

She bent down and gave me a light peck on the forehead, squeezed my hand. "Be honest. You didn't come here for me. Not really. Your friend stole something of yours and you wanted to get revenge. That's what this has all been about."

"That's not true," I said. But even as I denied it, I knew she was right, if only in part.

"I confessed everything to Rossi and he forgave me."

Of course he would. "What about me, Miranda? What about what you've done to me?"

She remained silent for a long time. When she finally spoke, she said, "After everything I've done, you could never love me again."

"And yet I do."

A familiar tenderness flashed across her eyes, but only for a second. "It's over, Max. It's been over for a long time now. You just didn't know it."

"Miranda —"

"You know the truth now. All of it. Please leave us alone. Don't come after me again."

With that, she turned and left the room, left my life.

If what she said was true, if what we shared had died a long time ago, why did her words cut so deep?

I staggered over to the porthole plexi and looked outside. Rossi waited at the end of the ramp. Miranda ran to him and he lifted her off her feet in a tight hug.

The door behind me slid open and Joriander entered. "You shouldn't be standing up, Maxwell," he said, exuding concern as always.

"Where's Hexa?" I said. "I want to leave as quickly as possible."

"Hexa has decided to stay behind with Olbodoh, Miranda and Rossi. She and Olbodoh are much more compatible for mating than she and I would have been."

"Oh?" This was the first time I'd ever heard a Wergen talk about mating. I didn't know what to say. "I'm... sorry."

"Why?" Joriander seemed perplexed. "They make a perfect genetic match. In fact, they've already tethered."

"Tethered?" I said.

Joriander stared at the ground and didn't respond.

But then I peered out the plexi and I caught sight of Hexa and Olbodoh. They no longer wore their leafy headdresses. Instead, a single rubbery cord extended out of Olbodoh's flat cranium into Hexa's skull, binding them together. Olbodoh carried much of the long, bunched-up tether in his hands to avoid tripping over it.

"So *this* is how members of your species commit to one another?"

The Wergen seemed embarrassed by my question.

Neptune had retreated all the way west and was now just a distant blue-green marble. A dark emerald hue filled the night sky.

"I'll never get used to the way that planet sets in the sky," I said.

"Millennia ago," Joriander finally said, breaking his silence, "this world was an asteroid floating freely in what your people call the Kuiper Belt. Then it came too close to this beautiful planet, Great Neptune, too close to its harsh glow – its incandescent beauty – and got captured in its orbit. That's why it rotates in the opposite direction of the other moons."

Joriander recited more facts about Neptune and Triton, but I tuned him out. I was focused on Miranda, almost a speck now, walking hand in hand with Rossi toward the terminal, the two Wergens trailing close behind.

# CHAPTER THREE
## For Love's Delirium Haunts the Fractured Mind

### Mars – Years 2530-2535

While the Wergens remained in contact with human enclaves in the outer Solar System, they refused EarthCouncil's invitations to visit Earth itself. Perhaps they feared the consequences of being in the presence of nine billion irresistibly beautiful beings. But they did creep ever closer in Earth's general direction. Fifty years after the establishment of the Axelis Colony – while the settlement of Langalana had begun half a galaxy away – we'd established the joint equatorial colony on Mars.

By this time, the dynamics of our relationship had shifted dramatically. For we'd finally grasped the depths of the Wergens' fascination with us, and used it to our advantage in negotiating the terms of the Joint Venture Compacts.

In the highlands overlooking Valles Marineris, human performers had erected a massive red-and-white-striped tent supported by poles planted in the orange dirt. As I steered our buzzer closer, Master Alex pointed excitedly, his light brown hair flapping in the wind, a huge smile stretched across his angelic face. He leapt out of the side of the buzzer as soon as it slowed down and bolted into a bustling crowd of humans. I took a deep breath to maintain my composure at the sight of so much concentrated beauty.

When I caught up with Master Alex inside the arena, the dazzling humans sitting on wooden benches applauded and whistled as I accompanied him down the aisle, assuming me part of the performance. I made it a point not to make eye contact with any of them. I had sworn to Lady Madeline that I'd be able to remain sufficiently clearheaded to tend to Master Alex.

A redheaded little human darted in front of me. "You're disgusting," she said, scrunching her nose.

I couldn't help but smile at her squeaky voice and adorable manner.

"Can it juggle?" she asked Master Alex.

"No, stupid," Master Alex answered. "He's no clown. He's *my* Wergen."

I suppressed a laugh. Master Alex was cuter than a Bendellian bug. How it pleased me to hear those two words. "My Wergen." I had wanted for so long to be his Wergen, Lady Madeline's Wergen. It meant they finally considered me part of their family. For five years I had toiled in Lady Madeline's vineyards in Medusan Vallis, monitoring the fieldbots and tending to the grapes before I finally ascended to the position of household domestic and caretaker. At last I could be close to her. For the remaining year of my service, I could bask in her fluttering laughter and honey voice and revel in her devastating beauty. I could prepare Master Alex's meals and play with him. And in the course of performing my duties, I'd enjoy their clever conversations and sweet attentions and learn everything I could about their culture to report back to the Explorata.

We settled into our seats and a moment later the lights dimmed. Even in the dark I had to take deep breaths and avoided staring overtly at the throng around us. Individually, their beauty tickled me and made me feel warm and happy. Collectively, it was a force of nature, a blast of hot wind that swept through me and made my head spin. I shut my eyes for a second, but couldn't resist opening them. A male with slicked-back yellow hair sat to my left. A female to my right, just in front of us, wore a bright blue dress that exposed the smooth flesh of her back. Another female, much older, flashed a warm smile that made me ache for Lady Madeline. It reminded me of her expression whenever she spoke to Master Alex. And all around us precious wide-eyed children perched forward in anticipation.

"I'm really happy you brought me, Joriander," Master Alex said. His innocent joy made me feel euphoric. When Lady Madeline learned she had meetings scheduled today with buyers, I had volunteered to bring Master Alex. She had objected, expressing concern about how functional I might be among the human crowd, but Master Alex had pleaded for her permission and I had reassured her I could still perform my duties.

Master Alex punched my arm. His touch brought a familiar thrill. "I'm sick of waiting!"

I wondered why he often behaved this way, but then I remembered that, like most humans, he was a single-birth. I had grown up with a brother and two sisters in my brood so I could understand the boy's loneliness might lead to bad manners. Still, Master Alex loved me. He would call for me whenever he needed anything. And he would actually seek me out to play with him.

"Look, Joriander!"

Up-tempo music played and the parade of performers took to the stage. First came a long-limbed Mars native, a towering human in pinstriped attire and a tall hat that hid his head – unusual since humans ordinarily flaunted their craniums. He introduced other performers, either Earthborn humans like Lady Madeline and Master Alex or the taller Martian variety like himself.

One pair of Mars-born humans entered the arena riding atop an enormous four-legged creature with two protruding teeth, floppy ears and a prehensile limb that jutted from the centre of its head. The woolly behemoth blared its disapproval of the whiplashes, but picked up various blocks and rings with its face-limb at the direction of its handlers. I marvelled at its girth and power – clever humans had resurrected this animal on Mars without our help – and I noted from Master Alex's wide eyes and huge grin that, like me, he had never before seen anything like it. Other unimaginable acts followed: an Earthborn human wrestled a monstrous feline that resembled Lady Madeline's housecat, only fifty times as large and with sharp fangs; lanky Mars-born Earthers painted their faces white and hid their noses behind a red ball; and it seemed as if adjustments had been made to the gravity field on stage that allowed other performers to fly through the air and swing from ropes dangling high above us.

Although I had grown somewhat accustomed to human company after my six years living in Northern Mars and from my prior excursion to Triton, moments like this reminded me of their alienness. I had no doubt reporting today's events to the Explorata would prove to be challenging.

The audience remained enraptured by the performances while my attention wandered to the faces around me, to the incandescent smiles and awestruck expressions.

A performer blew a whistle that startled me. That's when I saw them.

Two Wergens. Mated, tethered, their cords coiled from one open cranium into another. Their handler shoved them forward until they scuttled into the centre of the stage.

The audience murmured and clapped and hooted. Several of the humans sitting near us gawked at me, pointing at the leafy *coronatis* I wore atop my head.

The whistle blew and the Wergens grabbed hold of their cord and flung it around and around, slapping it against the ground while the human skipped over it and performed feats of agility. I was both mortified and amazed. Although I didn't know the pair, if stationed here they could only be cultural ambassadors like me. Their treatment plainly violated the treaty between our peoples. But as I gazed into their eyes, I saw their love for the man with the whistle. I could imagine them objecting at first but then relenting before the persuasiveness of his striking beauty. After a few moments he blew the whistle again and the Wergens positioned themselves farther away from one another, stretching their tether two to three metres apart. The humans took turns taking a flying leap over the taut tether and landing with a flourish. One of them climbed atop a bouncing stick that sprung over the cord. The audience erupted in applause.

I rubbed my shoulders and wiggled my fingers nervously. Breaking the tether would mean instant death to the pair.

"What's that thing coming out of their heads?" Master Alex asked.

I was too embarrassed to discuss Wergen tethering with any human, let alone with an innocent child.

At that moment, a cloaked figure rose from the crowd and took centre stage. Several performers stopped in their tracks and the music came to an abrupt halt. She had the unmistakable size and shape of a Wergen, wide and thickset with ivory scales visible on her bare legs. Perhaps she felt ill because she raised a blue inhaler to her breathing canal and took a deep whiff.

"Freedom!" she shouted, raising her arms skyward. "Freedom from love!"

She dropped her robes, revealing the glow of a blue bodyfield that grew blindingly brighter.

I hurled myself at Master Alex and pinned him to the floor as the deafening explosion rocked the arena and shook the ground and the world around us went dark.

I sat up and gasped.

Lady Madeline gently pushed me back down onto the bed. "It's okay, Joriander. You're fine." Her touch immediately soothed me and slowed the beating of my racing hearts.

"Master Alex...!"

"He's unhurt. Your body shielded him from the blast."

I felt sore and confused, but none of it mattered with Lady Madeline sitting at the edge of my bed. Two medbots skittered across my leg, injecting and slicing at my right foot, which was sheathed in a bloody bandage. Having this additional Wergen tech inside the house violated the terms of her contract, but Lady Madeline had obviously made an exception for my injury.

Master Alex stood in the corner of the room wearing a worried expression.

"Are you okay, Joriander? Can you play with me?"

"Alex, please go outside," Lady Madeline said. "I need to talk to Joriander alone."

The boy peered over his shoulder at me as he reluctantly exited the room.

Lady Madeline turned to me. "Others in attendance were not as fortunate as you and Alex. They're still pulling bodies from the rubble."

I rubbed my shoulders. I'd read reports of similar incidents in colonies on Titan and Earth, but I couldn't believe it had happened here and that a Wergen could be capable of such an act. "I should go help..." I shooed away the medbots and tried to sit up without success.

"Spare me any further heroics, okay?" Lady Madeline said. "You'd only cause a commotion if you showed up down there. No, you Wergens have done more than enough." She glared at me. "The medics on the scene didn't have the means – or the inclination – to treat you, so I had you transported here, where your bots could tend to you."

I couldn't bear it when she glowered at me this way. It was as if I'd scarred her beautiful face with displeasure. It hurt even more than my throbbing foot.

"It's just a small group of disturbed fanatics committing these acts," I said.

"I'm sure that's a comfort to the victims." Her lips trembled.

"I'm sorry," I said. "Whoever's responsible will be captured and executed by the Explorata. Violence against your people – even the mere thought of it – is anathema to us. You know that." I dared to reach out and touch her arm, but she pulled away and stood up. "I can't pretend to understand what drives these extremists to turn their back on love."

To this, she said nothing. She walked to the bay windows and pulled open the curtains. Phobos hovered partially behind Olympus Mons. The forcefield my people had erected over the Amazonis Quadrangle tinted the orange sky blue – a shade we knew comforted the humans – and made Northeastern Mars fully habitable, just like Europa and Triton and so many other locations our fieldtech had transformed into suitable spots for joint human/Wergen colonisation. We'd given the humans the galaxy. All we asked for in return was the pleasure of their company.

"I've brought in the Wergen assigned to the vineyards to tend to the house while you recuperate," Lady Madeline said. "You can move to the guesthouse in the meantime."

"Trax? There's no need. I'm already feeling better." The thought of Trax stepping foot inside the main house made me want to scrub my scales. He had worked in the vineyards for only twenty months while I had put in more than four years there – hoping every day for even a fleeting glance of the humans. That Trax might benefit from my injury and prematurely receive the loving attention of Master Alex and Lady Madeline seemed utterly unfair. He could wait his turn as I did.

I lumbered to my feet, the medbots scuttling around my ankles. "See?" I suppressed a wince. "I'm fine."

Lady Madeline turned and regarded me with a mixture of pity and contempt. "Why are you this . . . way, Joriander?" she said.

I didn't know how to respond.

She sighed. "Fine. If it makes you happy, go prepare dinner. The kitchen is a sty."

She marched past my bed, avoiding my eyes as always. When she got to the doorway, she paused, her back still to me. "Thank you, Joriander. Thank you for protecting Alex."

She continued down the hall without looking back.

Lady Madeline had thanked me! If my foot could have tolerated it, I would have jumped for joy.

When I limped down the stairs and into the kitchen, I found Trax there, scrubbing the floors on hands and knees.

"Joriander," he said, startled at my appearance. "You're not well. You should be resting."

"You can return to the guesthouse," I said. "I'll be in touch tomorrow about the status of the fieldbots."

Trax swallowed hard before responding. "I can't tell you how pleased I am to see you've recovered so quickly." But he spoke these words in our native tongue, which made his true feelings quite evident. "Has Lady Madeline approved my reassignment?"

"Don't question me, Trax. Your day will come," I said. "In the meantime, you can serve your term in the fields like I did."

"Why can't we *both* —"

"You know why." Lady Madeline had specifically negotiated the terms of our assignment here, forbidding more than a single Wergen at a time from staying inside the house.

"What if she decides to move off-world? What if I never get what's coming to me after all my sacrifices?" His jaw dislocated and clicked left and right. "How can you expect me to simply walk away from such beauty?"

"I'm sorry, Trax."

He whirled about and stormed out of the kitchen onto the veranda.

I surveyed the counters littered with dirty dishes and spoiled food Trax had failed to refrigerate. He knew nothing about the humans' exotic diet, the proteins they consumed from the flesh of other creatures. It would take me several hours to clean and reorganise. Of course bots could have accomplished the same task in a few minutes, but my people had attached some conditions to the technology they provided Lady Madeline. She was required to interact with me regularly. That meant allowing me in her home and not using bots to replace the labour I provided. Given how often she retreated to her room whenever I worked inside the house, I didn't think Lady Madeline had exactly lived up to the spirit of the bargain.

After I finished in the kitchen, I escaped to the veranda overlooking the vineyards and sat on a stone bench to rest my foot, munching on some sweet *chapra*. A rustling in the grapevines startled me.

I rose and leaned over the edge. It was difficult to see in Phobos's dim moonlight, but something scuttled in the dusty path between the vines below me.

Since the fieldbots didn't operate at night I could only assume Trax had deigned to intrude once again upon the sanctity of the main house. The clunk of heavy footsteps grew louder and a figure emerged, shorter and wider than Trax, but unmistakably Wergen.

"Who are you?" I said. "What do you want?"

"Joriander?"

I didn't respond.

"Are the humans asleep?"

The voice sounded familiar but I couldn't place it.

"How do you know my name? You don't belong here."

He stepped out of the darkness, the porchlights illuminating his face. "Joriander, it's me."

Korte. My brother. The Explorata had assigned him to the colonisation of Langalana, a planet hundreds of light years away. When last I heard from him, he had been matched with a mate. I never imagined I would see him again.

"You weren't tethered?" I said, stating the obvious.

"My mate spurned me," he said. He gazed towards the heavens as if it were Langalana orbiting Mars and not Phobos and Deimos. "A lovely mate with a lovely name – Shimera, my perfect genetic match – and yet when she first saw me she fled into that world's scarlet grasslands. She claimed to be hopelessly in love – with a human. So deeply in love she refused to tether with me."

I unlocked my jaw in shock. Yes, we loved the humans, but no Wergen would ever spurn his or her genetic match. We all bore a responsibility to tether and to propagate.

"It was a sobering experience." He continued speaking as he climbed the stone steps up to the veranda. "I left Langalana at the first opportunity. And in colonies across the Milky Way, I've met others of our kind who have suffered the same type of humiliation."

"I can't believe this."

Korte laid his hands on my shoulders in greeting. "Do you remember studying bot-tech together? Before our encounter with humans? If only we could go back to those days when we could proudly call ourselves Wergen." He reached down and plucked a *chapra* leaf from the bowl. "What about you, brother? How did you wind up here?"

"I spent some time on Triton, a satellite in the outer Solar System," I said, "assisting a human in his search for his missing mate. Can you imagine?" Nothing drove home how truly alien the humans were more than the notion of untethered mates. But then I remembered Korte's situation, how his mate had refused to tether with him, and thought it best to change the subject. "When I returned to the inner system, the Explorata assigned me to work with Lady Madeline and to continue our study of human culture. Why are you here, Korte?"

After a long pause, he said, "I came for a very specific purpose, brother. I'm here to free you."

"Free me?" I laughed. "From what? Do you know how many Wergens envy me for this position?"

"Don't you see what's happened to you?"

"I don't understand."

"You've been enslaved and don't even realise it. What you feel around humans, that exhilaration, that false happiness, is purely the result of biochemical processes we don't understand."

"As are all emotions." I glanced back to see if any lights had turned on inside the house. "Korte, you need to leave. If someone were to see you…"

He reached into his robes and removed a metal inhaler and displayed it to me. "This is a suppressor."

I took a step back at the sight of the blue device, the same type of inhaler the murderer at the circus had used. "No."

"A deep, single breath will allow you to view the humans through unfiltered eyes for several days. It affects the cell swaths of the upper mandible. We don't fully understand how human seduction works on us, but this compound blocks the neural receptors and allows us to temporarily resist their charms."

"You're one of them?" I said. "A member of my brood. My own brother."

"This can set you free."

I shook my head. "We shouldn't be trying to free ourselves from love, we should be celebrating it. What I feel for Lady Madeline and Master Alex brings me great joy, Korte."

Korte's face contorted in disgust. "Listen to yourself! 'Master Alex,' 'Lady Madeline.' They are not your masters, and you were not born to be subservient to them." When he saw my downcast eyes, he said, "I know their presence makes you feel blissful, but is it truly love if it's physiological? If it's irresistible?"

"You can say the same about a father's love for his offspring, about –"

"What you feel is unnatural!" he said. "We're on the verge of being conquered, Joriander. By a false love."

His words made no sense. "*We're* the ones who offered them our bots and fieldtech and ships in exchange for their companionship," I pointed out. "The humans didn't demand this."

"We're at war. You just don't know it." He had the desperate air of a wounded soldier. "We're losing the desire to breed and propagate. It's the end of our species. And what a miserable end it is! Taking our last breath as fatuous, fawning –"

"Lower your voice!"

"– pathetic slaves. And we don't even realise it!"

"Don't you think the Explorata considered all of this when negotiating the Joint Venture Compact? This is why we only have a small number of Wergens stationed on any particular colony –"

"The members of the Explorata who negotiated those agreements are no more immune to the humans' charms than you are! It was the humans who demanded caps on the numbers of Wergens permitted on any colony."

"The humans were being cautious. They feared invasion and conquest."

"It wasn't fear of conquest that drove their demands." He smiled angrily. "All this time living with them and you still don't understand, do you? *They loathe us.* The mere sight of us sickens them."

I couldn't accept this. Yes, we sometimes made the humans uncomfortable, but Lady Madeline and Master Alex had great affection for me. "You're wrong."

"Is *this* love?" he said. His eyes darkened and swirled and I realised he wore recording lenses. He projected a holographic image of the tethered Wergens performing at the circus, the female Wergen stepping out of the audience, the blinding flash that preceded the explosion. "Now others can learn of the indignities, and of the noble sacrifices that have been made. Others of our kind, not yet exposed to these humans, can see the dangers. And they can understand there's reason to hope. We can still conquer love, Joriander."

"What about the innocent –"

"There's nothing innocent about them. And I'm not asking you to kill them, though they deserve it." His lenses flickered and the projections shut off. "I'm here only because you're my brother and you deserve to be free." He placed the inhaler in the palm of my hand and closed my fingers over it. "Take this and use it. And then spend a few minutes with your beloved slavemasters. If you still feel that same undying devotion towards them, so be it. But the suppressor will allow you to break the spell that binds you to them, Joriander. At last you'll be able to hate."

"That's what I'm supposed to aspire to? Hatred?"

"Not hate for hate's sake. But hate for what it represents. Freedom. The freedom, the dignity, of being true to ourselves."

"My feelings *are* true."

"Then you have nothing to fear." He pressed his hand against my chest as if to feel the beating of my upper heart. "There's a revolution coming. I hope you'll be part of it." He leaned in and whispered, "Freedom. Freedom from love!"

With those words he turned and made his way into the vineyards. And as his silhouette disappeared into the cool night, I knew only fear. Fear of what he might do next.

The next morning, I sat in my room and stared at the metal inhaler in my hand. Korte's ravings had kept me awake all night. His suggestion we were somehow at war with the humans was madness. Our technological superiority was beyond question. With a simple command our bots could destroy Earth and every human in the joint colonies in one fell swoop. Yes, the humans elicited profound feelings in us – no one could resist their beauty and cleverness – but why was this wrong? We felt what we felt.

No, best to dispose of this drug and to forget Korte's troubled words. Could all of this be the result of what happened with his mate in Langalana? Could she truly have refused to tether with him? Then I thought about the tethered Wergens at the show yesterday. The love and devotion on their faces as they debased themselves in front of the human audience.

My hands shaking, I slid my fingers along the side of the inhaler and viewed myself in the mirror. Humans constantly reminded themselves of their beauty by studying their reflections in this manner. But I saw only the ugliness of self-doubt in my visage. How could I go about my daily chores wondering whether my feelings for Lady Madeline and Master Alex were real? And what did it say about me that I even entertained such thoughts? I loved them. Of that I had no doubt. Surely my love could withstand whatever temporary numbing effect this chemical provided.

I placed the inhaler over my nasal canal and took a deep whiff.

"Joriander!" Master Alex screeched from the hallway.

I shoved the inhaler beneath my sleeping mat just as he flung open the door.

"It's playtime!" he shouted.

I followed him downstairs to the living room where Lady Madeline waited for me. I felt off balance, as if the floor had a slight tilt to it I'd never noticed before.

"How can I serve you, Lady Madeline?"

She cringed as I approached. "Keep Alex busy for the next couple of hours. I have calls to make to buyers in the Amazonis Quadrangle."

She seemed unfamiliar somehow. Normally she had an aura about her – warm, soft lighting that shimmered along the edges of her body. But now I just saw sallow flesh and a pronounced sneer on an alien face.

"About yesterday," she said. "I'm sorry if I was a bit short with you, but you have to understand, I was in shock. I still am." She paused. "It might be best if you don't go into town today to run any errands for me. It might be dangerous given what happened."

Normally I would have been touched by her concern for my wellbeing, but today it all seemed... different. I had a better sense of her real apprehension. She simply wanted to protect her Wergen servant, her property.

"Why are you just standing there, Joriander?" she said.

I would usually exult in her attention, the fact she'd addressed me directly by name, but today I recognised she simply wanted me out of the way and tending to Master Alex as quickly as possible.

63

"I asked you a question," she said.

"I'm fine."

"Then get to it. Alex is waiting outside."

I made my way out through the kitchen doorway to the veranda, then down the stairs to the dirt path that led through the vineyards. The sunlight and fresh air would help clear my head. Alex had a head-start and raced ahead of me, swerving in and out from behind the plants. He'd switched into one of his costumes and activated a VR bracelet that sent miniature spaceships buzzing around his head while he swatted at them with a holo-sword. Whatever effect Korte's drug had on me, I still found Alex adorable, I still found his imagination amusing.

"Joriander!" he said. He raced around me, wielding his sword and pretending to stab me with it. "Get down on your knees, alien."

Normally I would've complied in an instant, but today I found his request distasteful.

"I said bow down!" His fleshy lips sneered; his sickeningly smooth-skinned face took on a grotesque expression.

"I'm still not feeling well, Alex —"

"Shut up!" he screamed. "Bend down!"

"Run ahead and chase some VR ships."

His alien face turned a red shade. "Why. Won't. You. Play with me!" He stabbed at my bandaged foot with his sword and I recoiled from the pain. Without thinking, I shoved him backwards and he landed hard against the ground, his head snapping back and hitting a rock. He bawled like a wounded desert-trog and blood trickled down the side of his temple. His howls startled me out of my stupor.

What had I done?

I picked him up and staggered toward the house, signalling to the medbots that awaited us on the porch alongside Madeline, who had no doubt heard Alex's screams. He struggled in my arms.

"What happened? Did you fall?" she said, snatching him from me.

"Joriander! He – he" he said. He gulped in heaps of air.

Madeline held him still while the medbots swarmed over him, stitching the wound and spraying it with disinfectant.

"Jor-Jor —"

"Joriander's right here," Madeline said. "Now hush."

Water trickled from his eyes down his smooth face.

After a few minutes of soft crying, the words finally came. "He pushed me! Joriander pushed me!"

Madeline paused and looked at me apologetically. Then she turned back to the boy. "Alex!" She leaned down so her face was only inches away from his. "Stop it! You know I don't like it when you fib."

Her scolding tone shocked the boy out of his crying jag.

"Joriander loves us. He risked his life to save you!" she said. "Why, he couldn't hurt us if he wanted to. Isn't that right, Joriander?"

I nodded, but instead of feeling happiness at Madeline's faith in me, I felt only a deep shame.

When I went to bed that evening I resolved never again to use the inhaler. What I had done to Alex was monstrous, unforgivable. Korte's drug, I realised, didn't 'free' me from anything. It distorted the real world; it transformed beauty into hideousness and suppressed my true feelings. No, it was Korte and the misguided rebels who needed to be 'freed' – from the effects of this drug.

I slept late – perhaps another side-effect of the inhalant – so I was surprised Alex hadn't come bursting through my door the next morning, barking orders at me to play with him. Because the drug's effects could last several days, I decided to avoid Alex and Madeline and devote the day to scrubbing the floors and supervising Trax's work in the fields. It wouldn't be too difficult to limit my interactions with them until I felt more like myself.

I strode past Madeline's room and poked my head in. She'd made her bed today. I heard voices downstairs, Alex shrieking a command at someone. This was unusual since he never spoke in such a manner to his mother. I descended the winding staircase to the living room.

I found Madeline sitting on the couch, two Wergens wearing the blue-leafed *coronatis* of the Explorata on each side of her. The officers' eyes flitted in my direction then returned to staring at her adoringly.

"Here he is," she said, pointing at me.

One of them made a gesture with his fingers without taking his eyes off Madeline and several dozen security-bots skittered past my feet and up the staircase. Five remained behind and surrounded me.

"Joriander," one of the officers said. "Lady Madeline summoned us because of a serious charge that has been levelled against you. You were seen consorting two nights ago with someone. An individual believed to be connected to the rebels."

I froze. Someone had seen me with Korte?

Madeline stood up and approached me. "Tell me it's not true."

"I'm devoted to you, Madeline. Completely, with every fiber of my being."

"Did you meet with one of them *on my property*?"

"I condemn them. I reject what they stand for. You know that!"

"Answer my question!"

At that moment, the bots scuttled down the stairs and into the living room carrying the metal inhaler I had hidden under my bed-matting. One of the officers plucked the inhaler from the bot's pincers and held it at a distance, as if it were a poisonous perpuffer.

Madeline's brow furrowed and she placed a hand over her mouth. "I gave you what you wanted. I let you into my house. I left my son in your care!" Spittle spewed out of her mouth and her contorted face accentuated her alien features: her savage brow and round hairy cranium, the skin-covered bone jutting out of the centre of her flat scale-less face. "And this is how you repay my kindness?"

*Kindness?* I had trouble at that moment recollecting a single instance of kindness or compassion in my time with her. How could I ever have seen things so differently?

"I've done nothing but serve you faithfully," I said. I had to avert my eyes; not because of her beauty but because I couldn't bear her hideousness.

"He's one of them," she announced and turned her back to me. "Get him as far away from my son as possible."

"Madeline!" I said. One of the officers shoved me forward as I continued to shout her name.

As they led me out of the front door, one of the officers said to the other, "To be surrounded by such striking beauty... and to throw it all away."

I spotted Alex on the veranda as we exited the house. He was dueling with Trax, barking out orders to him in a sharp unpleasant tone that was difficult to tolerate even from this distance. Trax, smiling ecstatically, looked in my direction. His smile faded.

I knew at that instant he had been the one who spotted me talking with Korte. He had been the one who reported me to Madeline.

"We're blinded by love," I said.

The officer set down two bowls filled with salt pellets and Bendellian bhar-roots. I lifted up the deep dishes from the table and poured their contents down my gullet, storing the food in my phagial pouch so I could continue speaking while I ate.

"*Now* you decide to talk?" he said. The officer was young, a fresh recruit with barely hardened scales. "A bit late for that, don't you think?"

"Perhaps." I'd refused to answer their questions because I knew they had no interest in hearing the truth. The truth of our subjugation to the humans. Teams of doctors and diplomats had tried to persuade me to reveal what I knew about the rebels, but I'd refused to tell them anything about my brother, about the coming revolution. Instead, I urged them to try out the suppressor, to see the humans as they truly were, but this only produced shaking heads and whistles of disapproval and further medical evaluations. The drug, they insisted, had damaged my neural swaths. It had skewed my perception of the humans' true beauty.

They even tried to seduce information out of me through human interrogation, but the lingering effects of the inhalant protected me. My questioners were unaware of the temporary nature of my immunity. *How much longer could I resist?* Korte had said the drug's effect would only last several days.

"Let me ask you something," I said. "What good is love if it's unreciprocated? What purpose does it serve other than to debase us?"

"You're speaking nonsense," he said. "And treason." But I could tell by the way he rubbed his shoulders that my question had shaken him.

"When I look back at how misguided I was, the years I wasted…" I said.

"This is not a productive use of your time. I suggest you clear your mind and savour your meal."

The fluorescent light flickered and the door irised open. A dozen bots scuttled into the room.

The young officer accompanied me down a long white-walled corridor and we entered a vacant room with a chair at its centre. He guided me to the seat and a forcefield strip activated around the armrests and legs, holding my wrists and feet in place. One of the walls was made of glass and behind it sat an audience of several dozen humans, most of them, I had been told, relatives of the victims of the circus blast.

The Explorata officer froze at the sight of the mostly human crowd and I, too, felt a wave of titillation wash over my cranium. The suppressor's residual effects were waning.

Then I saw them.

Madeline and Alex occupied the front row with Trax, who sat to their left. Trax gazed ecstatically at Madeline. He never seemed happier—or more pathetic. Meanwhile, she stared at me impassively. I was her Wergen. It made sense she'd feel obliged to attend.

At that moment I spotted a familiar face on the other side of the glass, standing guard in the rear behind the seated humans and dressed in an Explorata uniform.

Korte.

He'd come to Mars for another reason besides freeing his brother. He'd apparently infiltrated the Explorata's ranks long ago. So maybe we did still stand a chance. Maybe someday we would be free from love. He gazed at me with an intense concentration that indicated his recording lenses were activated.

A black bot scooted up my leg and torso and rested on my left shoulder.

Alex jumped to his feet and pointed excitedly in my direction. I felt the old, familiar rush in my hearts and in my head at the prospect he might ask me to play with him. Then I realised he was pointing at the bot on my shoulder. His mother pulled him back, scolding him. Just seeing Alex made me made me want to smile and laugh.

*No! Stop it!* I took deep breaths and tried to draw on specific memories from when I had seen them after using the suppressor. Madeline's scowl. Her contempt for me. Mast – Alex's screeching orders and disrespect. A spark of hate came back. And I tried to make it glow brighter inside my head.

Madeline sat there with Trax at her side. I thought I saw something in her moist eyes. A trace of regret? Sorrow? But then she blinked and it was gone.

The bot on my shoulder released a long syringe from its carapace and plunged it between the scales on my jaw.

I winced and the humans leaned forward in anticipation. It reminded me of the audience at the circus.

A warm tingle coursed through my body, though I couldn't say whether it was the result of the injection or the pleasure I felt at bringing joy to these humans at this moment.

*Fight it!* The audience became blurry. That was good. Maybe if I couldn't see them clearly, I'd be able to hold on to my blessed hatred. Maybe I could nurture it and make it grow and take my final breaths with dignity, as a free Wergen.

I searched for Korte in the fuzzy crowd, but I couldn't find him.

I saw only Trax and his silly grin as he now played on the floor at Lady Madeline's feet with Master Alex.

*Hold on to it!*

I struggled to embrace the sweet hate, but the only one I truly loathed was Trax. And I hated him profoundly, with all my heart. I hated him because he got to be with Master Alex and the beautiful Lady Madeline.

I hated him because he'd taken my place.

# CHAPTER FOUR
## Tethered

### Titan – Years 2540 – 2555

The secret experiments conducted by the Love Panel – experiments that resulted in the discovery of the 'love' neuromone – had been kept under wraps for years. But development and modification of that chemical compound had surreptitiously continued. More problematically, the wealthiest one tenth of one percent of the population purchased access to the neuromone for their own purposes – purposes that quickly became evident as the Charismatic Class rose to power. Using their chemically induced charms, the Charismatics convinced the enamored masses to vote against their own interests, to place the yokes around their own necks.

EarthCouncil came to be dominated by Charismatic representatives. Faced with growing poverty, many Earthers fled to the joint colonies in search of a fresh start, and those settlements thrived and expanded with the massive influx of immigrants.

Meanwhile, efforts to better understand Wergen physiology continued. And Wergen renegades, confronted with what they perceived as a threat to their civilisation, continued the modification of their own chemical cocktail, a suppressor that rendered them temporarily immune to human charms.

On the shore of Ontario Lacus on Southern Titan, Cara molded castles from the windblown sediment that served as sand. Her parents stood at the threshold of their shelter in the distance, chatting with their sponsor, the Wergen responsible for transporting her family from Earth. Cara lay on her stomach while the methane waves lapped against the shore, tickling her bare feet.

She held up her hand against the smoggy orange sky and studied the barely visible blue tint that covered her skin. Her mother had described it as a special "coat" that protected them from the cold weather. The Wergen forcefield over Ontario Lacus shielded them from radiation and modulated the gravity, but they still needed the 'coat' to protect them from the temperatures. It certainly didn't feel cold, Cara thought. It didn't even look chilly, although Cara's mother had told her Titan was colder than the coldest place on Earth.

A young Wergen, their sponsor's daughter, tentatively stooped down next to her. "Soy Beatrix,"the alien girl introduced herself. She was squat and scaled and spoke with a slight accent so she must have just learned Spanish. It took Wergens about a day or so to speak a language fluently. "My brother and I were wondering... What are you doing?"

A fat, grey-scaled Wergen boy with round eyes peeked at them from behind a red boulder.

"Why is he hiding?"

"He doesn't like the way humans make him feel."

"Really? I've never heard that before."

"You make him feel *too* good."

Cara shrugged. Of course the boy felt good around humans. He was Wergen.

She was amused to see Beatrix wore a red, skintight swimming cap over her flat head. Every Wergen she had ever seen before wore green, leafy wreath hats.

"I'm building a sandcastle," she said.

"What's a castle?" Beatrix asked.

Cara giggled. "A house where a king lives."

The Wergen stared at her. Cara wondered whether the alien girl knew what a king was.

"Can I help?" Beatrix said.

Every Wergen Cara had ever met asked her parents that same question; her mother and father were sick of it. But it was the first time a Wergen had asked *her* and it made her feel grown up and important. Normally, her parents sternly said "no" and the aliens would slink away with their heads down and their shoulders slumped. But Cara didn't want to make the alien girl unhappy.

"Yes, you can help." She showed Beatrix how to pack the sediment and mold it into towers for the castle she was building. After a while, bored with this activity, Cara said, "I know something even more fun. Let's go for a swim and catch perpuffers!"

"What are those?"

Cara displayed her left forearm, which was covered with furry bracelets. "They're pretty, aren't they? I have all the colours except purple. Purple perpuffers are the hardest to find." She shuffled to the edge of the lake.

Beatrix stood up and looked out at the thick pink waters sloshing back and forth in slow motion. "I... don't. I mean..." She stared silently.

"Follow me," Cara said.

Six bots scampered around Beatrix's feet. They were as large as cats, but Cara thought they looked more like praying mantises as they crouched on their spindly rear legs. Three of them stood in front of the Wergen girl, blocking her path. Red lights glowed at the end of their six appendages. Beatrix clapped her hands and the bots scattered to one side, allowing her to walk past them.

As they waded into the lake, Beatrix pulled off her robes and tossed them to the bots. Cara didn't know what she expected to see beneath the alien's clothes but the Wergen girl simply stood there naked, unashamed. Beatrix had smooth white skin speckled with silver scales that sparkled when they caught the light at certain angles. Cara considered taking off her own bathing suit but then remembered the Wergen boy spying on them from behind the rock.

They dove into the water together, their blue bodyfields bright in the red murk of the lake. They were less buoyant in this liquid than in water and its ruddy colour made it hard to see. Cara forced herself to go deeper, reaching out blindly and hoping to latch onto one of the furry perpuffers that filled the lake.

Cara heard a muffled scream.

She barely made out the Wergen girl's blue bodyfield far below. Beatrix waved her arms over her head, sinking deeper. Cara dove closer, hooked her arm around the Wergen's waist and kicked hard until they broke the surface.

"Don't struggle!" Cara gasped. "Don't struggle!"

She shouted for help but there was no one nearby to hear her. "You're okay, I've got you."

After a few panicked seconds, Beatrix relaxed in her arms and they floundered back to shore.

Cara's screams had alerted the medbots, which immediately scoured over Beatrix's face and chest. Cara's parents and their Wergen patron came running and stood watch until the medbots eventually blinked yellow, signalling that Beatrix was unhurt.

The adult Wergen, who Cara believed to be Beatrix's father, said, "You need to be more careful," before turning his attention back to

Cara's parents. "Are you sure I can't help you with anything?" he said to them. "Perhaps I can assist with the interior decoration of your shelter?"

Her parents turned away without answering and the Wergen followed close behind them.

Once the adults had left, Cara sat silently beside Beatrix for several minutes. Cara burrowed her toes beneath the pasty sediment. There was no longer any sign of the Wergen boy. He hadn't approached, even when the medbots had examined his sister.

Cara finally broke the silence. "We can't drown, you know," she said, pointing to the blue tint that coated their bodies.

Beatrix paused, staring out at the pink waters. "Then why didn't you just leave me?"

"I wasn't going to swim back to shore while you were out there, all alone and afraid."

At this, the Wergen girl turned to face Cara. She tilted her head to the left and nodded, smiling warmly.

"Don't you know how to swim?" Cara said.

Beatrix shook her head.

"Then why did you go in with me?"

"You said it was fun," Beatrix said. "And... I wanted to make you happy."

"Oh."

The steady wind blew and neither of them spoke for a long time.

"Can I see your hand?" Cara said. She removed a red perpuffer from her left arm and placed it around the Wergen girl's wrist. "Here. This is for you. A gift."

The Wergen girl's eyes brightened. "That tickles," she said.

"Sometimes the perpuffers expand and contract a little bit when they're fresh out of the lake."

"No," she said. "I meant your hand. When you touched me."

Later that evening when Cara lay in bed, she couldn't get the words of the Wergen girl out of her head, the Wergen girl who so wanted to be her friend that she would risk her own life to make her happy.

[Encrypted] *Medical Journal Entry No. 223* by Dr. Juan Carlos Barbarón:

The Wergen headtail, or 'tether' as it is referred to in common parlance, originates at the base of the secondary spine. As the subject matures, the headtail extends, lining both the secondary and tertiary spines, and, ultimately, coiling into the hollow cavity of the cranium. (Note: Wergen physiology has no analog to the human brain. All neural activity is centred in a swath of cells that surround their upper and lower jawbones. (See *Med. Journal Entry No. 124.*))

Every day after VR school, Cara met Beatrix at the lake. They waded up to their waists and jumped up and down in sync with the slow, swooshing waves. The winds never stopped on Titan. After what happened at the lake, Beatrix's father programmed bots to swim alongside them at all times and ensure their safety. Like all Wergens, Beatrix only had one parent, but to Cara he seemed awfully distant, spending most of his time with humans instead of with Beatrix or her brother.

Over time, Beatrix became less afraid of the water and Cara taught her to swim and to hunt for perpuffers. It didn't take Beatrix long to get the hang of it. In fact, she became so skilled at perpuffer hunting that she and Cara would often leave the lake with their arms and legs draped with the furry creatures. When they weren't swimming together, they would spend hours sculpting intricate castles and spacecraft in the pasty orange sands. Or Beatrix would try to teach Cara how to sing like a Wergen, which Cara found challenging given the chirping and rumbling noises Beatrix's throat made.

During the rainy season when the waves were too choppy to swim, she and Beatrix would play outdoor VR games. As the settlement by Ontario Lacus expanded, more human children took to the lakeshore and joined them.

Cara pointed out the human boys she found cutest and what she liked most about them – their swaggering walk or broad shoulders or dimpled smiles. Beatrix found this fascinating, as she did everything about humans. She mentioned how beautiful she thought the other adolescents were – girls and boys alike – and became animated whenever they huddled together and shared their secrets. As they spent more and more time together, Cara found herself forgetting Beatrix was a Wergen – except for those occasions when Beatrix stared at Cara intensely and mentioned the bright, rainbow-like auras she saw around all humans, how her upper heart fluttered at the mere sight of them, and how she spent every waking hour thinking about what she could do to make them happy. Cara didn't like to hear this. It made her feel less special.

"What about *Wergen* boys?" Cara asked Beatrix one day while they were treading water far from shore. "Which ones do you like?"

There were few Wergens present on Titan because of a treaty between their peoples that restricted their numbers. But Wergen children occasionally gathered at the shore to watch the humans.

"It's different for us, Cara," she said. "We don't think about things that way."

"Well, how *do* you think about them?"

The waves washed over them as they bobbed in the lake.

"I can't explain…"

"Try."

"I don't like them in the same way you like human boys. At least not right now. But when I reach a certain age my body will change…"

"Change?" Cara said.

Beatrix hesitated as if struggling to find the right words.

"Is it like having your period?" Cara said. She had explained menstruation and making babies and every aspect of human reproduction in excruciating detail to Beatrix, who, of course, had found it utterly captivating. *Was there anything about humans that didn't enthrall her?*

"No. My cranial opening will expand. And my cord will release. It will connect with the cord of a perfect genetic match. And then I'll be tethered."

Cara stared at the red swimmer's cap on Beatrix's flat head.

"After years of tethering, the cord retracts and the mated couple…" Beatrix looked around to make sure only bots swam near them. "We become one," she whispered. Our bodies… merge."

"You mean you have sex?"

"Not like your people, Cara. *Real* sex. The merge is… permanent."

"What do you mean 'permanent'? How can that be?"

"The passive partner is absorbed. The dominant partner then becomes pregnant with a brood of children."

Cara stared at her in horror. "So… if you have a baby, you die?"

"It depends on whether my genes are passive or dominant. But I don't think about it in terms of dying. It's the best part of being alive, Cara. I can't wait to be tethered."

"Okay," Cara said, trying not to think about it. She decided to change the subject. "What's your home world like, Bea?"

"I've never been there, but I hear the orange skies and the green-sand deserts are so beautiful the mere sight of them can make a grown Wergen cry."

"I wish I could see it," Cara said. "I wish I could travel to all the amazing planets in our galaxy. I want to be an explorer." She wanted more than anything to be like her parents, working with the Wergens to colonise the universe. So many other worlds had been opened up to them thanks to Wergen fieldtech. Colonisation efforts were already underway on Triton and Enceladus as well as incredible alien worlds hundreds of lights years away, such as Langalana and Verdantium.

A wave splashed over them.

"What do you want to be when you grow up, Bea?"

Beatrix looked up into the orange sky. "I hadn't thought about it before, but being an explorer sounds wonderful, Cara." She tilted her head to the left in that familiar manner and nodded, smiling. "Especially if I can explore the cosmos with you."

"Beatrix!" A voice shouted from the shore. Her brother, Ambus, called for her to return to her hurth as he always did when dusk approached. Cara knew that by the time they made it back to shore he would be gone. She had yet to see Beatrix's brother up close.

"Let's race!" Cara said. She stroked furiously, leaving Beatrix behind in her wake.

A moment later, Beatrix jetted past her, propelled by the bots, a huge grin plastered on her face.

[Encrypted] *Medical Journal Entry No. 224* by Dr. Juan Carlos Barbarón:

A contractile sheath gives the tether a pronounced elasticity as it emerges through the cranial canal. The tail end is laced with thousands of microscopic nerve fibres and pore receptors. Muscle spindles allow the tether to unfurl and undulate toward the Wergen mate. When two tethers come into contact, the fibres bore into the receptors of the Wergen with the passive genotype. This signals the commencement of macrofusion.

One day Cara agreed to meet Beatrix by the lake, but a kilometre farther north where fewer ice boulders dotted the shore and three-metre orange dunes draped the surface. Perpuffers were said to be even more plentiful in this area.

As she approached, Cara heard someone shout her name from behind a red dune. She recognised the voice immediately. "Ambus?"

"Stay where you are, so I can't see you."

"What do you –?"

"And don't speak! Your voice is too… sweet. I don't want to give in to it like my sister. And my father. Just listen. If you respect my sister, you'll stay away from her."

Cara fought the urge to answer him.

"She doesn't have the will to resist you. How can she choose her own path with you around? How can she be her own person? If you really consider yourself her friend, just leave her alone!"

Cara couldn't stay quiet any more. "Bea can pick her own friends. Why should you decide for her?" She scaled the dune to confront Ambus, but when she reached the top he was no longer there. His footprints receded into the distance, behind the sand drifts in the horizon.

[Encrypted] Two items merit future study: First, the Wergen version of DNA consists of three strands, two of them analogous to human DNA though the nucleotides are most unusual and require additional examination. The purpose of the third strand with its dormant alleles remains a mystery. Second, the evolutionary purpose of Wergen gender is hard to fathom, as it appears to play no role in their procreative processes. One hypothesis is that a diverse gene pool created the Wergens' varying physical characteristics and that it is human perception that assigns gender markers to those attributes.

Cara rode the buzzer a metre off the ground, clutching the handlebars tightly. She had made arrangements to meet Beatrix in the Aaru region, at the viewing post at the foot of Tortola Facula, an active cryovolcano outside the colony's forcefield. Normally she might have visited Beatrix at her hurth, but she didn't want to run into Ambus. Even after all these years, he still made it a point to avoid contact with humans, believing they fogged his mind and skewed his perception of reality, Beatrix had explained. He'd even taken to wearing special earplugs and visors that he hoped might protect him.

When Cara arrived, she found Beatrix waiting for her on a bench at the overlook, staring raptly at some newly landed seedships. The colonists stood near the yellow hash marks that signaled the forcefield's perimeter, and viewed the volcano shooting spumes of hydrocarbon-rich materials kilometres into the atmosphere. It would later rain down onto the surface as liquid methane, feeding the thousands of lakes and tributaries in the region.

Beatrix approached when she stepped off the buzzer. "You let your hair down! You look more beautiful than ever, Cara."

"Come on, I bet you say that to all the humans." She paused. "No, *really.*"

They laughed and hugged.

"I'm so glad you suggested getting together," Beatrix said. "It's been too long."

While they spoke every few days, it had been several weeks since they'd seen each other. Ever since Cara graduated and her parents relocated to Axelis Colony on Titan, she'd been working with EarthCouncil's Colonisation Subcommittee – thanks to some strings her parents pulled before departing – helping to plan the next great human-Wergen expedition. The target world was a rogue planet that had escaped Cancrii 55's orbit and now roamed freely through space.

"What did you want to tell me, Cara?" Beatrix asked. "It sounded important."

"I think I'm in love, Bea."

Beatrix stopped in her tracks. "Oh?"

"His name is Juan Carlos. We've only gone out a few times, but we seem to have made that instant connection, do you know what I mean?"

"Yes, yes I do."

She hesitated to see if Beatrix was joking, then continued. "He's a doctor who works with Biotech at CE. He's got a reputation for being quite opinionated, uncompromising to a fault – except with me."

She described his thick eyebrows and slicked-back black hair, his lean muscular physique. She told Beatrix about everything they had in common, about their three dates together – including how they'd kissed in the empty office at CE until they were interrupted by guardbots.

Cara and Beatrix strolled arm-in-arm along the edge of a great gorge that overlooked a river. Southern Titan teemed with ridges and crevices and chasms, all filled with flowing ethane and methane.

Cara noticed that Beatrix had stayed quiet for a long time after she'd spoken about Juan Carlos. Sometimes she forgot Bea was a Wergen and that, like all Wergens, she couldn't help but love her, and perhaps be jealous of her new relationship. Maybe it had been a mistake to confide in her, but Bea was her oldest and dearest friend.

She decided to change the subject. "How's Ambus?"

Beatrix stopped. She released Cara's arm and rubbed her shoulders nervously.

"What is it?" Cara said.

Beatrix turned away and started walking again.

"Tell me. What's wrong?"

Beatrix stood at the lip of a precipice. "You know how Ambus has always felt about humans."

She nodded. "Yes, he wants to avoid humans – so, of course, he lives in a colony of humans on Titan."

"That's not fair, Cara. He was brought here as a child. He had no say in the matter. And now that he's on the verge of reaching maturity… I'm afraid for him. He's found others who believe as he does, that co-exploration with humans was a huge mistake."

"Really?" Cara had always found Ambus eccentric but basically harmless. "Well, it isn't as if Wergens would ever harm humans."

Beatrix looked away.

"Bea?"

"There's been a drug developed off world recently, Cara. A suppressor that distorts the way Wergens perceive human beings. It's horrible. It mutes our natural love for your people."

"And Ambus took it?"

"Its effects are only temporary – no longer than a few minutes. He views it as a way to 'free' his mind. You mustn't say anything, Cara. You have no idea of the consequences if anyone were to know. This is a serious crime."

"Does your father know about this?"

"My father left a few weeks ago to start work on a new project, the construction of another cityfield over Xanadu, on equatorial Titan," Beatrix said. "Maybe I'll go join him. Get away from all of this."

"That's really what you want?"

After a long pause, Beatrix said, "Now that you've met someone… I'm not sure there's anything left here for me."

"Bea, I don't want you to worry about Juan Carlos. That has nothing to do with our relationship. We've always been friends and we're going to stay friends forever. No man can change that."

Beatrix's face brightened and they continued their trek along the edge of the gorge, the ethane-filled tributaries churning far below.

[Encrypted] *Med. Journal Entry No. 225* by Dr. Juan Carlos Barbaron: Adsorption:

The first step in macrofertilisation is the penetration of the headtail fibres into the specific pseudo-protein receptors of the passive Wergen's tether. Enzymes quickly dissolve the base plate, and the tethers become one, triggering significant changes to the aliens' body chemistry. (See *Journal Entry No. 6*).

Cara lowered her head and trudged forward into the driving pink snow. Her boots sank into the slushy drifts as she made it over the hill and Beatrix's hurth came into view. The dwelling resembled the upper half of a metallic egg with two arched openings on opposite sides. The Wergens had a very rigid conception of exits and entrances.

Juan Carlos had wanted her to spend the day visiting with his parents, but she'd grown increasingly concerned that she hadn't heard a word from Beatrix in over a week. Usually the problem was keeping Beatrix from calling too often – something else Juan Carlos bitterly complained about. But Beatrix couldn't help herself, Cara had explained to him for what felt like a thousand times.

Juan Carlos didn't want to hear it.

Cara stepped through the archway, stomping the snow from her boots. Her blue-tinted bodyfield clicked off automatically. Welcoming bots skittered at her feet, unlaced her boots and laid out slippers for her on the scale-patterned floorboards.

This was the only time she could remember visiting the hurth when Beatrix hadn't been waiting for her at the entranceway. Could her friend be jealous? Is that why she'd stopped calling? When last they spoke, Cara had told her Juan Carlos had finally proposed and that she had accepted. After expressing some confusion over how an engagement differed from dating or from marriage, Beatrix had asked whether it still meant they would someday join a human-Wergen expedition and go colonise some strange new world together. Cara had reassured Beatrix that she and Juan Carlos had promising careers at CE and that they were both on track to join the colonisation efforts.

Beatrix emerged out of the fireroom in the centre of the dwelling and Cara staggered backward.

In all the years she'd known her, Cara had never seen Beatrix without some head covering. Usually she put on a *coronatis*, the leafy headdress that all Wergens wore. But today the flat top of her head was exposed and a rubbery cord extended out of her cranium, dragging along the floor to another room in the hurth.

"Cara!" Beatrix said, smiling. "I'm sorry I haven't returned your messages. It's just... these past few weeks have been a very private time for me."

Cara pointed to the tether. "You... you're..."

"Yes, it was my time." She looked at the floor, embarrassed.

"Why didn't you tell me, Bea?"

She rubbed her shoulders nervously and didn't answer.

Cara understood Wergens were notoriously private about their reproductive cycle, but this was her best friend. She felt wounded by the fact Beatrix hadn't confided in her. Then she remembered what Beatrix had told her all those years ago about the absorption of one Wergen into another based on their genetic makeup, about encorporation.

"Bea, tell me you're genetically dominant. Please!"

Beatrix continued rubbing her shoulders.

A moment later the Wergen at the other end of the tether entered the room. He was shorter than Beatrix, with grey-flecked scales he covered with a dark blue robe.

Ambus.

Cara gasped. "But..."

"A pleasure to finally see you up close," he said.

But there was no pleasure in his voice, no Wergen servility. Only an undercurrent of hostility.

Care turned to Beatriz, eyes wide. "Your brother?"

"Of course. There are very few of us on Titan. And we're genetically compatible. We can safely interbreed for another generation."

"You don't owe her any explanations, Beatrix," Ambus said.

"I apologise for his tone, Cara," Beatrix said. "When he saw you approaching our hurth he took a dose of the suppressor. He'll be more himself in a few minutes."

"What does it feel like to hold so much sway over another person's life?" Ambus said to Cara. "Do you realise how unfair you've been to her? That she's your loyal slave because she has no choice?"

"She's not my slave!" Cara said.

"Your people and ours are at war. A secret war. We're all soldiers in this great battle and don't even know it."

"Bea," Cara said, "I just wanted to make sure you were all right. I really have to get back to Juan Carlos."

"What, you're leaving before we can bow down to you and wash your feet?" Ambus said.

Cara stepped into her shoes and walked back through the archway to the hurth, which reactivated her bodyfield.

"Cara, I'm sorry," Beatrix said. "Don't leave!"

"Look, I can't… I can't deal with all this. I can't believe you're with him." The sight of the tether repulsed her.

"Cara!" Beatrix shouted from behind her. But Cara marched through the gusting snow without looking back.

[Encrypted] *Med. Journal Entry No. 226* by Dr. Juan Carlos Barbaron:

The rate of tether contraction varies, but can commence as early as six months [Terran] after adsorption and accelerates, bringing the passive and dominant mates ever closer together. This triggers the growth of nerve fibres on the dominant Wergen's dermal scales in anticipation of the final stages of corpus contraction, i.e. encorporation.

Cara floated through the thick liquid hydrocarbons with her eyes closed. It felt as if she had left the present behind, as if she had travelled back to when she was ten years old, hunting perpuffers for the very first time. She broke the surface of the waters and threw her head back.

Beatrix sat on the shore, hugging her knees and watching her. She had said it might still be possible to swim despite her tethered status, but that she preferred not to because Ambus didn't much enjoy the lake. He sat about eight metres to her left, clutching their bunched-up tether and examining a bot. They could move almost fifteen metres apart given their cord's length and elasticity. But Ambus couldn't be far enough away as far as Cara was concerned.

In all the years she'd known Beatrix, her friend had never seemed more alien than she did at that moment with the flesh-coloured cord dangling from her head, snaking across the shore toward Ambus. Poor Bea. How much time did she have left?

Cara descended again, peering through the muck of the methane. Something caught her attention. A circular shape pulsed by her feet. She reached down, pushed her hand through the ring and the creature instinctively contracted on her wrist.

Cara rose up out of the viscous methane and raised her fist in the air, flashing her find to Beatrix. A phosphorescent-purple perpuffer.

Beatrix clapped her hands and shouted, "Well done, Cara! Well done!"

How many times did they dive together for perpuffers, searching for the elusive purple one, the top prize? Cara couldn't imagine ever doing this without her best friend at her side.

She swam back to shore.

Ambus moved as far away as his tether would allow, sitting on the other side of a dune with his back to them.

"Cara, it's lovely," Beatrix said, fingering the perpuffer.

Cara sighed happily. "After all of these years, I was beginning to think the purples ones were just a myth."

"Are you going to dive for more?"

"No, I have to go meet Juan Carlos for lunch."

"Don't go." Disappointment washed across Beatrix's face. "Cara, don't take this wrong way, but… I don't like what you've told me about him."

Cara raised an eyebrow. It was unlike Beatrix to make a negative statement about a human – let alone express her disagreement so openly. Normally, if her opinion differed from Cara's, she would hesitate or turn her head away when responding. If something moved her, she would tilt her head to the left and nod. Cara had learned to read her subtle mannerisms.

"You don't know Juan Carlos," Cara said.

"Why doesn't he ever join us?"

"He's busy." Cara could never bring herself to tell Beatrix the truth. Despite Juan Carlos's many fine qualities – his drop-dead looks, his sharp wit and analytical mind, his love for her – he had a low threshold for socialising with Wergens. He made it a point to minimise the time he spent in their presence. "They're lapdogs, Cara," he had said to her that morning, trying to persuade her not to visit Beatrix. "Doesn't it offend you? That such intelligent beings can be so fatuous, so sycophantic... They're like lovesick schoolchildren."

Undeniable, really. But he had never met Beatrix, and their friendship transcended that species drive; Cara had to believe that. And certainly she had no biochemical reason for the fondness she felt for Beatrix.

"If it's so offensive," she had answered, "maybe we shouldn't be accepting their technology, hmm?" She made a face and kissed him on the cheek. "I know you don't want me to go, but I really need to visit Bea at the lake." Juan Carlos's objections had dissuaded her from seeing Beatrix over the past few weeks. "I don't like the way I left things with her the last time we met. I'll see you at lunch, okay?"

Now, as she towelled off, Cara spotted a shape Beatrix had sculpted in the sand. Instead of a spaceship, it was the familiar oval outline of a Wergen hurth. "Are you going to talk to your father about joining one of the next few expeditions?" Cara said. "Juan Carlos and I were thinking of Langalana..."

"No, I don't think that's a good idea," Beatrix said.

"What do you mean?"

"CE doesn't need any more Wergens. The Explorata is already swamped with qualified volunteers. Ambus thinks we might be better off staying here."

Cara didn't know how to respond. She stuffed her towel into her carrytube and said, "I'm sorry to hear that."

Beatrix stared in Ambus's direction. "I found where Ambus kept the suppressor, Cara. And I threw it away. That's why he's keeping his distance. He knows if he speaks to you, if he sees you up close, he'll feel the same way I feel about you."

"Bea, once you're... encorporated..."

"You'll see, you and Ambus will be good friends, I know it."

Cara's eyes filled, and she nodded. "Yes, of course we will." But she said this only for Beatrix's sake. She knew that Ambus wanted to resist falling under humanity's spell and she'd respect his wishes by keeping her distance. It wouldn't be fair to him if she didn't. Then again, how fair had she been to Beatrix all these years?

Beatrix's lips quivered and she reached out and clutched Cara's wrist. "Promise me we'll be friends forever."

"Bea…"

"Promise me?"

"Friends forever, Bea," Cara said. She hesitated. "Does it still feel… good to hold my hand?"

"More than you can know."

Maybe Cara had been fooling herself all these years. Maybe Beatrix's loyal unconditional love *was* just the product of a biochemical reaction. Maybe she'd been as unfair to Beatrix as Ambus claimed.

"I have to go," Cara said.

"Now?"

"I'm afraid so," she answered. "I don't want to have another fight with Juan Carlos." She took a few steps away from the Wergens, then turned and hurried back to Beatrix. Without saying a word, she slipped the purple perpuffer onto her best friend's wrist.

*[Encrypted] Med. Journal Entry No. 227 by Dr. Juan Carlos Barbaron:*

*Encorporation. As the headtail continues its relentless contraction, dermal contact follows, and nerve fibres penetrate the pore receptors on the scales across the passive Wergen's body. This quickly disintegrates cell walls as the mates merge, commencing macrofusion. Genetic materials, primarily nucleic acids, flow from the dominant to the passive Wergen and impregnation of the rear sac results. Scales along the dorsal spine grow into multiple nubs – fetuses that develop outside the Wergen's body, attached to its back. The semi-fused Wergens and their developing fetuses are at their most vulnerable at this stage. Perhaps for evolutionary reasons, encorporation accelerates at this point and the Wergen's natural instinct is to isolate itself. This period of vulnerability may be exploitable. (See Related Entry No. 195 on 'Multiple-Birth Wergen Broods and their Susceptibility to Dopamine Neuro-transmitters as a Counteragent to Suppressor Drugs').*

Cara and Juan Carlos stepped through the hurth's archway as the bots scooted into the back rooms to alert Beatrix and Ambus of their arrival.

"Five minutes," Juan Carlos said. "Not one second longer." He'd only permitted her to come on the condition that he accompany her to ensure she'd be out quickly. He said he feared they'd encounter more Wergens than necessary since they tended to mob around humans.

"It's not safe for you to be walking around these Wergen neighbourhoods. With the terrorist bombings at the Martian colony, how long will it be before they strike here on Titan? We may be forced to make some difficult decisions at Biotech, but we need to protect ourselves." He turned away and tapped his eyelids to open up a retinal connection to the newscasts. "Five minutes." He blinked and made a connection, his eyes glazing over.

Juan Carlos enjoyed being in control but Cara knew he had her best interests at heart. She thought about objecting – she had no doubt he was overreacting – but didn't want to provoke an argument. The media had blown out of proportion an incident involving a faction of so-called "Wergen rebels" – an oxymoron if ever she'd heard one – that had caused some unrest on Mars and other sister colonies.

A minute later, Beatrix and Ambus entered the room. They now stood no more than six inches apart. Their tether had lost its elasticity and Beatrix's head drooped to one side. Her left leg had disappeared inside of Ambus's right leg so they walked awkwardly, like a three-legged monstrosity lurching forward. In a matter of months, Beatrix, her friend, would be gone forever, absorbed into Ambus's form and broken down into the chemical components that would leave him impregnated.

Beatrix's face had a semi-glazed look, a blank stare. But when she caught sight of Cara, a brightness washed over her face.

"Cara?" she said. But then the spark of recognition faded.

Cara stood to hug her, but couldn't do so without also putting her arms around Ambus.

"Thank you for visiting," Ambus said.

Juan Carlos blinked off his retinal connection. He had a strange expression Cara couldn't quite identify – disgust? fascination? – as he greeted them.

"It's kind of you to come," Ambus said. "I know how much Bea wanted to see you." From the way he smiled and bowed his head, he clearly had no suppressor in his system.

"Oh, Beatrix," Cara said. "Bea…"

"No, it's fine, it's fine," Ambus said. "How have you been? How are your parents?"

She told them about her mother's death, about her father joining the expedition to Langalana. And as they conversed, Cara noticed that only Ambus spoke. She gazed directly into Beatrix's eyes and tried speaking only to her. "Do you remember the seasons we spent diving off the shore of Ontario Lacus? We practically covered ourselves head to toe with perpuffers."

A brief smile flashed across Beatrix's face. Then it went blank again.

"Yes, those are strong memories, Cara," Ambus said. "She'll remember them right up to the point of encorporation. After that, it's even possible I may still retain a stray experience, a random memory, but I can't guarantee any particular one will survive."

Cara placed her hands over her Beatrix's. "Hey, Bea. Are you in there?"

"She's in there," Ambus answered. "Fully cognisant of everything you say."

"Can't she answer me?"

"I speak for her now."

Cara paused.

"So will there be nothing left of her?"

"Of course there will!" Ambus said. "Her knowledge of nanotech, her facility with plants, a few random experiences. Her most useful skills will survive encorporation, creating a new, improved me."

"What about her ambitions, Ambus?" Cara's voice trembled. "What about her dreams of exploring the universe?"

He paused. "I've come to like it here on Titan, Cara. I can't say…"

Juan Carlos shot her a look and glanced dramatically at the time on his palmscreen.

"Bea, honey," Cara said, patting her hand. "I have to go, I'm sorry. Juan Carlos needs to be somewhere right now and I promised I'd accompany him."

"That's fine," Ambus answered. "But Cara, you have to promise you'll come visit again soon. Beatrix would love to see you once more before encorporation is complete."

Beatrix's eyes remained rolled back in her head and a bit of clear drool oozed out of the corner of her mouth. Cara couldn't bear to see her like this. But she would never abandon her friend in the final moments of her life.

"Of course I'll be back, Bea." She leaned in close and whispered in her ear. "We'll go to the lake again and you can sit on the shore and watch while I dive for perpuffers for us, okay?" She felt the tears well up and fought them back.

87

"Cara," Juan Carlos said softly. "We should get going."

She took a deep breath and waved goodbye to her friend, wondering how much of her would remain when next they met.

[Encrypted] *Med. Journal Entry No. 228* by Dr. Juan Carlos Barbaron:

Nano-indentation tests have revealed that a tether is comprised of a biopolymer – a sinewy substance not easily broken, but certainly breakable.

Cutting the tether of mated Wergens results in an instantaneous loss of identity, followed by a rapid and painful death.

The smog blanketing Titan was thinner than usual on this day. So much so that Cara could almost distinguish the outline of ringed Saturn filling half the sky. In all of her years living on Titan, this was the first time she'd ever seen the planet with her naked eye. Its proximity caused the tidal winds that drove down from the poles towards the equator.

She felt awkward visiting Beatrix's hurth. So much time had passed that her friend was certainly long gone by now. *Damn Juan Carlos!* She would never forgive herself for allowing him to keep her away all this time. She had made a promise and she would keep it. If nothing else, she owed it to Beatrix's memory.

As she followed the winding trail down a steep hill toward the familiar hurth, she slowed. *What if encorporation wasn't complete? What if pieces of Bea were still visible?* She imagined the segments of an arm jutting out of Ambus's chest, two half-heads merged together into a disfigured monstrosity. She wouldn't be able to bear the sight of it.

No, more than a year had passed. She began walking again.

When she got within five metres of the hurth, two Wergen children raced out through the archway in her direction. They ran in circles around her, saying, "Good morning" and "Can we help you?" over and over.

She stooped down. "Are you Beatrix's children?"

The stocky female said, "My name is Antillia."

"I'm Umar," said the boy. "Ambus is our father."

"Is he inside?"

The children nodded excitedly and followed close behind her.

When she entered the hurth's archway, Ambus stood there as if expecting her, even after all this time.

"I knew you would come," Ambus said. There was no longer any sign of the Ambus she remembered, the Wergen who spurned all contact with humanity. He threw his arms around her and she hugged him back. He looked different. Thinner. And his scales had familiar flicks of silver.

He guided her into the fireroom, where a transparent tube that ran from floor to ceiling blazed with flames. "Your children are beautiful, Ambus," she said.

The Wergen children tittered and whispered to each other.

"I need to speak alone with Cara for a moment," he said to them and they slowly, reluctantly, left the fireroom while staring over their shoulders, trying to sneak one final glance.

Housebots skittered at Cara's feet, removing and taking away her boots while others brought in a tray with cups of steaming spicy sap.

"How is Juan Carlos?" Ambus asked as they took their seats in front of the roaring fire column at the centre of the room.

"I broke off our engagement."

The Wergen gasped.

"He was so possessive. So secretive about his work at Biotech. I thought I could change him. But it didn't happen." She set down her cup of cider-sap. "He didn't like it when I visited with friends, when I did anything without him. And I went along with what he wanted. But then I started to feel... suffocated. I couldn't continue living that way, under someone else's thumb. I didn't like the person I was becoming."

Ambus stared incredulously. After a long pause, he said, "Sometimes I forget how truly alien you are."

She smiled. "Of course you wouldn't understand."

They drank their sap and, all the while, Ambus leaned forward on his elbows and fixated on her every word; he offered her food; he asked whether she wanted him to feed the flames so she could luxuriate in the warmth of the fire column.

"Are you sure I can't get you something else?" Ambus said.

The initial joy Cara felt at being back in Beatrix's hurth began to drain away as she listened to Ambus's steady stream of fatuous remarks. She had to face the bittersweet truth: her best friend was gone forever. It could never be the same with just any other Wergen. She couldn't imagine herself without Beatrix. Before she even realised it, she started to cry.

"Cara, what is it?"

"I was thinking about something you told me once. That it was unfair of me to have remained friends with Beatrix for so many years." She wiped away the tears and regained her composure. "I think you may have been right. I should have... freed of her biochemical shackles."

"Again, I wasn't myself at the time. I had taken the suppressor, which skewed my perception of reality. Please forget about what I said to you. It was unkind of me."

"Unkind, but true."

"Cara... did Beatrix explain what happened to my suppressors?"

Cara recalled their conversation on the lakeshore, when Beatrix had explained how she'd found where Ambus hid the drugs and destroyed them. "Yes, she kept them from you."

"On the day we met you at the shore..." Ambus paused as if considering the consequences of his words. "Beatrix had taken the suppressors herself."

"What?"

"She said she wanted to have... a better understanding of her relationship with you, Cara. Its effects were temporary – only a matter of minutes – but in those minutes she experienced a clear understanding of her true feelings."

Cara dreaded asking, but she did. "And how did she really feel about me in that moment of clarity?"

"She never told me. The memory didn't survive encorporation. I'm sorry, I don't know."

After an extended awkward silence, they talked about other subjects: politics, the acts of violence by Wergen renegades on the Martian settlement, the future of human-Wergen colonisation efforts. And when it came time for her to leave, Cara knew she would never return.

As she stood and the bots re-laced her boots, Ambus said, "Before you go, there's something I need to give you." A few seconds later, a bot entered the room, carrying a small metal box. "Beatrix wanted you to have this."

"It's a stasis box," Cara said. She carefully lifted the lid and looked inside.

A purple perpuffer sat at its centre.

"Beatrix preserved it for so many months," Ambus said. "I don't understand its significance."

Cara slipped it onto her wrist. Removing it from the stasis box meant the perpuffer wouldn't last for more than a day or two before decaying. But it didn't matter.

"Thank you, Ambus," she said softly.

Ambus tilted his head to the left in a familiar manner, and nodded.

As Cara made her way out the exit archway, she told herself she'd never see this hurth again. But after only a few seconds she couldn't resist looking back over her shoulder. She saw Ambus out front and the two Wergen children at his side, all staring raptly at her as she trudged through the methane snowdrifts.

# CHAPTER FIVE
## Tactics for Optimal Outcomes in Negotiations with Wergen Ambassadors

**Earth – Year 2565**

The trigger for the war between humanity and the Wergen renegades remains a mystery. Some believe it originated with a single leaked EarthCouncil memorandum.

**TOP SECRET – CLASSIFIED**
DRAFT #3  9/10/65 [BRACKETED COMMENTS BY JCB: DOES THIS DRAFT INCORPORATE FEEDBACK FROM EXOBIO?]

### R E T I N A L
### M E M O R A N D U M

To:    Members of the Outer Colony Committees on Human-
       Wergen Relations
       *(via entanglement encryption)*

From:  Tessa Kornbluth
       Senior Diplomat, Colonisation Planning
       EarthCouncil

Re:    Tactics for Optimal Outcomes in Negotiations with
       Wergen Ambassadors

Date: October ___, 2565 [LET'S ACCELERATE TARGET DATE FOR DISTRIBUTION. NEGOTIATIONS FOR A PLUTO COLONY ARE IN THE BEGINNING PHASES.]

As we continue our long and mutually beneficial partnership with our friends, the Wergens, this memorandum (1) sets forth 'lessons learned' from prior negotiations with the Wergen Explorata in establishing joint colonies on Mars and Triton, and (2) delineates specific strategies going forward to optimise the results of negotiations in connection with the establishment of human/Wergen outposts on Pluto, Enceladus and Ceres.

## I. Critical Metrics Regarding the Triton and Mars Colonies

### A. The Unsuccessful Triton Talks

Negotiations for establishment of the Axelis Colony provide a roadmap for 'What Not To Do' when interacting with Wergen representatives. Discussions were hampered from the onset by our ignorance of the Wergens' ~~primary weakness~~ agreeable nature. The talks were such a fiasco that each human colonist on Triton is currently required to be accompanied *at all times* by three Wergen shadows. This unfavourable Wergen to human (W2H) ratio has resulted in decreased productivity and high rates of depression ~~and suicide~~ for Axelis colonists exposed to the Wergens for such prolonged, uninterrupted periods of time. [TESSA, THE COMMITTEES ARE SENSITIVE TO COSTS. LET'S DRILL DOWN & QUANTIFY, AND INCLUDE THESE FIGURES AS AN ATTACHMENT.] Even more troubling, the Commitment Period for each colonist to partner with his or her alien shadows runs eight Earth years – an excessive length of time by any measure. These unfavourable metrics are directly attributable to the following factors:

- Information Control: Due to first contact with the Wergens being established by our manned space stations orbiting Neptune and Saturn, the aliens immediately understood our aspirations to settle the Solar System and mine the asteroid belt. Having discovered the numerous challenges we faced, they used this information to their advantage, offering us the assistance of their bots and forcefields *provided that* we agreed to partner with them in our colonisation efforts. This underscores the importance of ~~keeping our cards close to the vest~~not burdening the aliens with our private affairs. ~~The less the aliens know about our goals and needs, the better.~~

93

- **Location of Participants**: The terms of the joint colonisation project on Triton were discussed and agreed upon primarily via virtual conference at the request of the Wergens. Also of significance is the short duration of the negotiations, which commenced and concluded within a span of only one Earth day.

- **Role of Earth**: Because of the aliens' peculiar phobia about interacting directly with Earth, the heads of our Neptune and Saturn space stations served as intermediaries between EarthCouncil and the Wergens. Discussions between the Wergen ambassadors and their own leaders in the Explorata via video-con added yet another layer between both sides' ultimate decision-makers – which worked to the Wergens' advantage.

According to one account by a typical Axelis colonist:

<VIRTUALBLINK>: "I was overcome – we all were – by the miraculous nature of their tech." A woman with red curly hair and pale skin speaks rapidly, excitedly. "Wergen bots swarmed over ten square kilometres of Triton terrain, reshaping and transforming it into a suitable footprint for colony construction. And their forcefields…" She smiles and shakes her head incredulously. "Their forcefields shielded us from radiation and allowed us to regulate gravity and temperature."
A pause follows. The smile fades and her face goes blank.
"Then we realised what we had bargained away."
She hangs her head. The image pans back to reveal three Wergen colonists standing directly behind the woman, their chalk-white, scaled faces barely visible behind hooded robes, their black, owl-like eyes trained on her in a lovestruck expression.
*Testimony of Ariel Ambrose, taken on March 10, 2517 at 18:22 – 19:07.*
[EXCELLENT SELECTION OF WITNESS. SHE'S MUCH MORE ARTICULATE THAN THE WITNESS YOU USED IN PRIOR DRAFT.]

B.  The More Favourable Mars Negotiations

Martian colonists are the happiest and most well-adjusted settlers in the Solar System. [LAYING IT ON A BIT THICK HERE. DO WE HAVE PRODUCTIVITY METRICS WE CAN POINT TO?] Having only one Wergen shadowing four humans (a W2H ratio of 1:4) ensures every settler some measure of privacy. In addition, Wergens are required by the terms of the joint colonisation agreement to 'earn' their time with humans by sharing information about their bot tech and working the vineyards of Medusan Vallis for contractually negotiated periods. These favourable terms reflect a positive trajectory in our relationship with the Wergens and are attributable to the same three factors that worked to our disadvantage on Triton, namely:

- Information Control: The fact that we had already established a belowground outpost on Mars strengthened our bargaining position. Having undertaken colonisation efforts without assistance from the Wergens, we could credibly threaten to walk away from the partnership proposal unless they ~~gave us what we wanted~~ showed more flexibility. [TESSA, KEEP OUR AUDIENCE IN MIND. PHRASING HERE IS OFF-PUTTING. COMMITTEE MEMBERS LIKE TO TELL THEMSELVES WE'RE ACTING IN A FAIR AND REASONABLE MANNER.]

- Location of Participants. Wergen ambassadors appeared *in person* on Mars to discuss proposals for the construction of an aboveground colony and to demonstrate the effectiveness of their fieldtech. Those Wergens, however, ~~craftily~~ understandably required all proposed terms to be approved by their off-world superiors – still not the optimal situation for us.

- Role of Earth. EarthCouncil diplomats travelled to Mars and participated directly in negotiations with the Wergen ambassadors.

An average Martian colonist describes the living conditions on equatorial Mars as follows:

<VIRTUALBLINK> A heavy-set, middle-aged man wearing a straw hat and blue jeans sits at the edge of a porch in a rocking chair, the orange sky visible over his left shoulder.

"The Wergen bots do a bang-up job tending to the crops. We're growing corn, wheat, oats – and, I swear, Medusan Vallis wine is better than any I've ever tasted on Earth. Sure, I have to put up with my Wergen coming in to the house twice a week to sit around and stare at me. Makes my skin crawl. But it gets pretty happy when I play the guitar, so I'll sing the alien a few tunes – it doesn't seem to mind that I'm so off-key."

He laughs so heartily he has to reach up to steady the hat on his head.

*Testimony of Abe Sidowski, taken on February 10, 2523 at 15:32 – 16:17.* [CAN WE BRIGHTEN THE COLOURS TO PROVIDE MORE OF A CONTRAST WITH THE TRITON TESTIMONY?]

## II. Lessons Learned and Stratagems to Employ

A rigorous comparison of negotiations regarding the Triton and Mars colonies provides valuable insight on the best approach going forward. When negotiating with the Wergens, it is critical to never lose sight of our primary objectives. First and foremost, we ~~should~~ must strive for the most favourable W2H ratios and Commitment Periods possible for each outpost to improve the ~~productivity~~ quality of life of our hard-working colonists. Second, we ~~should~~ must [USE MANDATORY TERMS THROUGHOUT MEMO] attempt to obtain information about the location of the Wergen homeworld. Lastly, when possible, we ~~should~~ must continue to encourage the Wergens to make direct contact with Earth itself ~~so that they succumb to our demands~~ to strengthen our partnership. The prevailing theory is that the Wergens are being overly cautious about revealing the location of their homeworld because they fear ~~conquest~~ direct contact between us and their leaders – who may find our arguments too persuasive, our positions too compelling, our personal charm too irresistible – and accede to our reasonable demands. [WHO WROTE "CONQUEST"? IT'S

RIDICULOUS – AND DANGEROUS – TO STATE THIS SO OVERTLY.] Given their ~~biochemical compulsion to love us~~ fondness for humanity, one would have expected the Wergens to jump at the invitation. While they may yet bring their tech gifts directly to Earth, their reticence to set foot on our planet remains a mystery. [A BIT HEAVY-HANDED. OBVIOUS TO EVERYONE WHAT THEY'RE AVOIDING. CONSIDER RE-WORDING OR DELETING.] Whatever it is they're hiding,[1] we strongly believe we may be able to ~~exploit~~ leverage that information in future negotiations.

## III. Tactics for Ongoing Negotiations with Wergens: Action Items

A. In-person Negotiations

Prior talks highlight the importance of up-close, in-person contact with those members of the Wergen Explorata responsible for signing off on joint colonisation terms. In close proximity to humans, any Wergen ~~enslaved by their biochemical compulsion to love us~~ – overcome by their natural affection and fondness for us – will ~~inevitably cave~~ more likely agree to our demands. For this reason, we must avoid repeating the mistakes of Axelis where the Wergens cleverly utilised a layered communication chain. On Mars, the mere act of EarthCouncil diplomats sitting in the same room with their Wergen counterparts produced a more favourable outcome. Eliminating as many of these layers as possible provides us with a crucial tactical advantage. Accordingly, we ~~should~~ must refuse to participate in negotiations going forward unless the ultimate decision-makers for each side are present.

B. Spare Setting

---

[1] See *Memorandum on Efforts to Surreptitiously Debrief Wergen Colonists*, dated December 2, 2525, which notes that most Wergen colonists were born off-world and appear to have been purposely kept in the dark about the location of their home planet. However, certain ~~love-smitten~~ Wergens stayed silent when interrogated on this subject. This suggests they hold relevant information about their homeworld but may have been protected by some form of mental shield that prevents its disclosure.

The Triton negotiations between human and Wergen surrogates took place aboard the spacious, 1000 square metre viewing deck of the *Engagement* with its spectacular views of the storm clouds of Uranus. In contrast, the more successful Mars talks occurred in the Pavonis Mons Caverns, in a shadowy den measuring only three by six metres. Based on the foregoing, negotiations should take place in cramped quarters with no tables or other barriers between the attendees. Close physical proximity is likely to produce optimal results. The room must be spare, with no decorations, windows or other distractions for the Wergens.

C.  Extended Duration

During Martian negotiations, the lead Wergen representative interrupted the talks and took frequent breaks. As described by one of the attendees:

<VIRTUALBLINK> A bald man in a dark rumpled suit sits at a table. He speaks directly into the camera, slowly, with haunted eyes.

"Our interactions were polite at first, becoming more and more informal with each passing hour, before turning noticeably chummier. By the end of the day, the aliens had to take numerous breaks, staggering out of the conference room every few minutes, hugging their shoulders. On one occasion, while I don't recall their exact words, I overheard them whisper to each other." He imitates the Wergen, raising the pitch of his voice to a sickly sweet singsong: "'So, so, beautiful... Their delicate forms... their soft speech... the warm sparkle in their eyes.'" His voice returns to normal. "Their white scales turned from a light grey to an ivory white. They averted their eyes, pulling the hoods of their robes over their faces while they retreated to compose themselves."

*Testimony of Representative Marcus Decinces, taken on August 1, 2525*
*at 45:32 – 46:44.*

Accordingly, we must object to these numerous breaks and extend the duration of negotiations as long as possible. Most of our diplomats can tolerate being in close quarters with the Wergens for no more than a few days before experiencing extreme psychological discomfort. While countervailing considerations exist, as noted below, this factor is critical to a successful negotiation.

## D. Frequent Touching

Physical contact with the aliens – a prolonged handshake, touching their arms, laying a hand on their shoulders (preferably skin-to-skin contact) – is strongly encouraged. However, great care should be taken not to overstimulate the Wergens for this may cause them to shut down and stop speaking altogether. Even worse, we might have a repeat of the Mobbing Incident on Mars, which resulted in psychological trauma to all human attendees.[2]

## E. Nasal Receptor Blockers

Negotiators in close quarters with the Wergens for an extended period of time have complained about their ~~stink~~ odour, which can lead to a gag reflex that makes it difficult to speak while in their presence:

<VIRTUALBLINK> A heavy-set man with greying hair and glasses sits at a desk.

"An overwhelming stench – of vinegar and raw sewage and something else, something unfamiliar and unpleasant – grew more pungent the longer we remained in the same room with the three aliens. Supposedly, colonists who've grown up with the aliens get used to their smell. But if they hadn't requested so many breaks, I'm sure I would've puked right on top of their flat heads." He shakes his head, flares his nostrils in disgust. "But it was more than the terrible stink that made me sick; it was their alien nature – simply being in their presence – that set off some instinctive biological defense mechanism. It took everything I had to fight the urge to flee. To this day, I wake up in a cold sweat in the middle of the night, dreaming of those eyes, those

---

[2] See *Medical Analysis of Human Physiological Reaction to the Wergens*, dated Oct. 7, 2525 at pg. 33: "The diplomats who were swarmed by the Wergens suffered dangerous, short-term physical symptoms such as palpitations and elevated blood pressure as well as long-term post-traumatic stress. Other negotiators merely present in the same room with the Wergens routinely sought counselling for recurring nightmares." See Section F below on Counselling.

large black, pupil-less eyes boring into my soul."
*Testimony of Diplomat Baron LaPage, taken on Sept. 4, 2525, at 32:10--33:17*

EC has developed an aerosol spray that numbs the nasal receptors for up to 10 hours and which should be used prior to any meeting. Unfortunately, while the aerosol prevents gagging, it does nothing to lessen the general revulsion felt in the presence of the Wergens.[3]

F.  Availability of Counselling

Members of the Mars negotiating team – both those swarmed and those present during the Mobbing Incident – remain in therapy. This underscores the delicate balancing act we must strike: working closely with the Wergens, ingratiating ourselves with them, but also taking into account the mental health of our own negotiators. For this reason, free lifetime counselling remains available to all diplomats.

## IV. Conclusion

The above stratagems ~~should~~ must be employed going forward to achieve the most favourable partnership terms possible. If we proceed judiciously, there's no reason why we shouldn't be able to ~~overwhelm~~ persuade the Wergens, and in so doing, protect the wellbeing of our settlers and the future of our colonisation efforts.

cc:      EC Representatives of All Nations

[ARE WE TAKING STEPS TO SECURE THIS DOCUMENT AND PRIOR DRAFTS – NOT JUST THE FINAL VERSION – VIA

---

[3] Some renegade Wergens have developed their own version of an inhalant, a dangerous drug that skews their thinking and suppresses their ~~docility in our presence~~ natural love for humanity. Needless to say, under no circumstances should we tolerate the presence of – let alone negotiate with – any Wergen employing one of these devices. [CONSIDER MOVING THIS FOOTNOTE UP INTO THE TEXT. THE WERGEN RENEGADES ARE BECOMING A DANGEROUS THREAT TO THE HUMAN/WERGEN PARTNERSHIP.]

QUANTUM ENCRYPTION? IF THESE DRAFTS WERE TO FALL INTO THE HANDS OF WERGEN RENEGADES, THE CONSEQUENCES COULD BE DIRE.]

[RESPONSE BY TK: I'LL HAVE TO DOUBLE-CHECK]

# CHAPTER SIX
## The Love War

### Pluto – Year 2566

Others believe the war originated with an intercepted transmission from a remote colony on Pluto.

Cara left the seedship half-buried in the snow and plodded through the powder-blue drifts. Vicente lumbered by her side. As they trudged up an incline toward the icy summit, a barely visible column of smoke curled high into the black sky.

When they reached the hillcrest, the skyline of Pluto's Ecclisse colony came into view in the distance: ten towers connected by a latticework of aboveground passageways still under construction. Below them on the other side of the ice-hill, a dozen Wergens and four humans congregated along a slushy path in front of a stone altar. A red-robed corpse lay atop the platform. Bots lasered into the cadaver and thick white-grey smoke drifted upwards, dispersed by the swirling winds generated by the colony's fieldtech.

"Umar," Cara said. "Oh, Umar." She stopped in her tracks.

"Cara," Vicente said, "you've come this far..." He extended his hand to help her forward, but she waved him off. She hated to have him see her this way. She took a deep breath and they began the long descent.

By the time they reached the gathering, the crackling blaze had consumed the entirety of Umar's corpse and the Wergens had commenced singing. The haunting elegy made Cara teary-eyed. In all the years she'd spent among the aliens – her best friend growing up on Titan had been Wergen – she'd never heard them sing in such a tender manner.

A petite Wergen stepped out of the crowd. Antillia. Cara resisted the urge to call out her name.

Antillia raised her arms skyward and a dozen bots flitted along the edges of the stone altar, extinguishing the flames and revealing her brother's charred cadaver. Black jutting bones, burnt smoking flesh; that was all that remained of Umar, the young Wergen boy Cara had raised as her son.

Vicente placed a comforting hand on Cara's shoulder. She leaned into him for a moment before pushing him away. He meant well, but Umar and Antillia and all the Wergens on this colony were nothing more to him than love-struck aliens, humanity's repellent and eccentric benefactors. To Cara, they were family.

The freezing wind lifted a swell of snow that momentarily obscured Umar's body. Seeing his remains on that slab triggered a memory of him and Antillia lying on the shore of Ontario Lacus, an immense, rubicund lake on Titan. Cara had helped the young Wergens overcome their aversion to water, teaching them to swim and dive for perpuffers. This had been after their mother died, and after Cara had taken on the responsibility of raising them. Umar preferred spending time indoors, studying tech and programming bots while Antillia enjoyed exploring the sand dunes and rock formations of Southern Titan. Antillia had been more expressive, more inquisitive, while Umar tended toward the taciturn. So different. Yet so similar in that they both loved her profoundly. What choice did they have? They were Wergen.

The singing ceased and the blue-robed Wergens – almost invisible in the backdrop of the azure snow – distributed large chunks of flesh and bone from the cadaver among themselves. They shoved pieces down their gullets, storing large portions in their phagial sacs, which made their throats bloat.

Vicente gagged. He cupped his mouth, staggered over a snowdrift and vomited. Strands of his long black hair dangled over his pallid face. Cara regretted getting him involved. He was a good man, a capable attaché, who clearly had feelings for her. But she'd grown weary of love a lifetime ago, weary of its weight and its drama.

As the Wergens continued their assault on the body, gulping down slimy organs and crunchy cartilage, Cara refused to avert her eyes.

A human wearing a gaudy yellow parka staggered in the direction of the stone slab. It had been so many years since they last met, but she recognised the man instantly from his erect posture and confident gait. Juan Carlos Barbarón, former Head of BioTech on Titan, current Colony Chief here on the Ecclisse colony. Time had been kind to him. He stood tall with a square jaw, and just a wisp of gray in his temples.

"May I have your attention?" Juan Carlos said.

A pointless remark. The Wergens stopped chewing and fixed their adoring gazes on him.

"Join me in remembering our colleague and dear friend, Umar."

Typical of Juan Carlos to want to be the centre of attention at all times – even at an alien funeral. He had the ego of someone who'd spent too much time surrounded by Wergens. Ironic, she thought, given his contempt for the aliens during the time she'd dated him. After he expressed some platitudes about the transitory nature of life, the Wergens commenced their glorious singing again.

At the conclusion of the ceremony, when nothing remained of Umar — not bone, not even ash – and all the thick-necked Wergens had gorged themselves, Cara joined their single-file march across the snow-covered plateau of Sputnik Planum.

She broke the Mourning March and made her way to the front of the line to Antillia, who smiled as Cara approached.

"Aunt Cara!" she said. "Is it you? You're really here?"

"It's me, sweetie," Cara said.

She removed her gloves and placed her bare hands on Antillia's face, stroking the girl's scaled cheeks. Antillia's black eyes widened and she gasped at Cara's touch.

Cara hated to resort to such tactics, but she'd travelled all the way across the Solar System to determine the cause of Umar's death and to save Antillia from a similar fate. She needed to use every trick at her disposal to protect the Wergen girl. "You're coming back with me. Do you understand? After the service, promise me you'll head directly to your hurth to gather your belongings, that you'll then join us on our ship, okay?"

"I promise."

Of course she did. Cara wasn't sure why she bothered. Antillia's promises, while heartfelt, meant nothing. The Wergen girl loved *all* humans, and if someone else later asked her to stay, she'd agree to do so in a heartbeat. Wergen love for humanity defied categorisation; it transcended romantic or familial or sexual feelings. It was pure. Innocent. And unconditional. Growing up on Titan, Cara had once seen two colony children begging a Wergen boy to accompany them home from VR school. The Wergen had been thrilled – particularly since most humans felt an instinctive aversion toward the aliens and tended to keep their distance. Then the children proceeded to walk in opposite directions while calling out to the young Wergen to follow. The alien boy's ivory-coloured scales had paled and he'd rubbed his broad shoulders nervously, paralysed by indecision while the children laughed cruelly and pleaded for him to accompany them. Tormented, the boy huddled on the ground and covered his ears. Cara had cursed at the two boys – and hurled a stone at one of them – until they'd taken off, laughing. Afterwards, the Wergen child followed Cara around happily, as if nothing had happened. Although the aliens adored all humans without regard to gender or age or appearance, the adult aliens typically acceded to the desires of the humans they loved most – the ones with whom they'd spent the most time – and Antillia knew no human longer than she'd known Cara.

"Never forget *you* control the tech. *You* wield the real power," Cara said. "You mustn't blindly do as anyone in this colony says."

"You think I don't know that?" Antillia said. "I'm not a fool, Aunt Cara. I'm just…"

As Antillia's voice trailed off, Cara completed the sentence in her mind. *Powerless.* Antillia was enslaved, like all Wergens, by her uncontrollable love for humanity. Cara resisted the urge to hug her. She didn't want to dazzle her into outright paralysis.

At that moment, Juan Carlos moved to the front of the Mourning March and approached them.

"Cara?" He took a deep breath as if to gather himself, and smiled. "What a pleasant surprise. I hadn't heard we were receiving visitors."

Same old Juan Carlos, she thought. Handsome. Charming. But ever clueless about the feelings of others.

"My son is dead," she said. "And I'm here to bring my daughter home."

He paused, as if to consider her words. "That won't be possible. These Wergens are under my protection."

"Your *protection?* Maybe I didn't make myself clear –" She felt dizzy. At that moment the ground rumbled. As if grief-stricken, the world shuddered, sending the Wergens and humans fleeing to the nearest fielded shelter.

The colonists were still assessing the damage from the temblor when Cara visited Antillia's hurth, a metal structure resembling a high-tech

105

igloo. The young Wergen lived in a segregated community about half a kilometre from the towers. It was the same in all Wergen/human settlements. Wergens made their bots and their fieldtech and spaceships available in exchange for human companionship. Humans, in turn, negotiated the parameters of their personal space.

Crouching by the fire column that bisected the dwelling, Cara asked Antillia the question that had haunted her on the trip from Titan. "How did Umar die?"

Antillia stared, clearly searching for the right way to answer.

"The truth," Cara said.

"I found him in his hurth in what I thought was a deep slumber. But he was dead."

"Was he ill?"

"No."

"The whole truth, Antillia."

The Wergen paused. "We had visited the dens the night before."

"Dens?"

"Yes, the caverns where humans congregate for recreational purposes. Afterwards, Umar and I... We were asked to volunteer our services. Juan Carlos needed us for important medical research."

"My god."

"It's not what you think, Aunt Cara. The humans... They're kind to us."

"Did those 'kindnesses' kill your brother?"

Weariness spread across the girl's scaled face and black eyes.

"Do you remember when you took us perpuffer-hunting on Titan, Aunt Cara? Umar and I would modulate our bodyfields and dive deep beneath Ontario Lacus, to its bottom. The perpuffers would curl around our wrists and we'd emerge with scores of the creatures, every colour of the spectrum. It made you so happy!"

"Didn't it make *you* happy?" Cara said. She thought about her own childhood on Titan, the idyllic summers she'd spent with Antillia's mother, Beatrix, exploring Titan's methane lakes.

"How could it not make me happy to know you were so gratified?"

Cara sighed in frustration. "Don't change the subject, dear. Tell me about Umar."

Antillia slouched her shoulders and lowered her head. "I'm sorry, Aunt Cara."

106

"Just tell me."

"Juan Carlos asked Umar – and every Wergen on this colony – to assist him with his research," Antillia said wistfully, as if Juan Carlos had requested a romantic liaison. "He didn't force us to do anything."

"Of course he only asked." *With a Wergen that's all it would take.*

"He introduced chemicals into our neural pathways."

"I see," Cara said, gritting her teeth. Experimentation of this type patently violated terms of the human-Wergen Compact.

"Juan Carlos didn't do anything wrong," Antillia said. She rubbed her shoulders nervously. "*We* did. We agreed to it."

At that moment, Vicente entered the hurth escorted by five bots scurrying by his feet.

"Fortunately," he said, stomping the snow off his boots, "the quake only caused superficial damage to the ship's hull. Two bots are making repairs. We should be able to leave in about six hours." They had commandeered the vessel from a gullible group of Wergens on Titan who had underestimated Vicente's piloting skills.

As the bots unlaced his boots, Antillia fetched Vicente a hot cup of sansap.

"Thank you," Vicente said, though he seemed annoyed by her courtesies and quickly turned his attention to Cara. "That man at the ceremony. You knew him?"

"Juan Carlos? Yes, a long time ago, on Titan. We dated briefly."

"Oh?" He raised an eyebrow.

"It ended disastrously," Cara said, nodding at the young Wergen. "I allowed our relationship to keep me apart from my best friend, Antillia's mother, during her final days. I'll regret that to the day I die."

Vicente had a curious expression.

"We're wasting time," Cara said. She told him about the experiments being performed on the Wergens. "We need to contact EarthCouncil."

He shook his head. "A transmission would reveal our location. Everyone would know we violated EarthCouncil's orders coming here."

She realised it was unfair to ask Vicente to sacrifice his career, to risk possible incarceration, but given what she'd just learned... "Vicente." Drawing closer, she put her hands on his arms. She squeezed his shoulders lightly and held his gaze. "I need your help. Please."

He sighed in surrender.

"Thank you," she said, running the back of her hand against his stubbly cheekbone. "I'm so grateful."

Antillia gazed, wide-eyed, at this exchange.

"Don't be grateful until I've actually sent the transmission," he said. "It'll take some luck."

Once the discussion shifted to the logistics of sending the message, she knew she'd won the battle. Vicente would find some way to take care of it. He always did.

One of the bots flashed red and scooted forward. It projected a holo against the wall. Juan Carlos's visage appeared.

"We need to talk," he said with a half-smile. Not a single hair was out of place, and his thick black eyebrows and dimpled cheeks reminded Cara of all the superficial reasons she'd fallen for him so long ago.

"Oh, we certainly do," Cara said.

Cara pushed past the throng of workers swarming through the central terminal toward the complex of offices. She followed the guidebot through the BioTech Wing in the direction of Juan Carlos's office. As a precaution, she'd confirmed Vicente's successful transmission of their message to EarthCouncil before coming here, in case Juan Carlos tried to stop them.

Trailing the guidebot through Corr 47A, she spotted an open storage compartment in the sidewall to her left. Among the scattered equipment, which included various bot parts, stood a stack of buzzers. Up ahead, a transparent forcefield sealed off the end of the passageway. To her right, tens of thousands of shiny bots worked on the colossal girders in the graylight, like termites swarming over an iron forest. She could make out the range of ice mountains in the distance, rising four thousand metres into the sky. Nearer to the colony, in the low-lying haze of Sputnik Planum's icy plains, a network of natural troughs and ice dunes carved the terrain into neat polygonal shapes. Closer still, concentrated patterns of pits and ridges pockmarked the surface. The colony sat directly in the middle of the heart-shaped Tombaugh Regio where sheets of frozen carbon monoxide sheathed the ground. Below the surface, a slushy water ice melted by thorium and potassium made the terrain unstable. The colony's forcefield, which allowed them to breathe, also increased temperatures, exacerbating the problem. According to Antillia, constant quakes rocked Ecclisse. Cara still had no idea why in hell EarthCouncil had selected Pluto for joint colonisation. The dwarf-planet had few easily accessible resources that could be exported to Earth or to the human/Wergen colonies. And the challenges of settling this still-geologically active world had pushed Wergen tech to its limits. Maybe that was the point. Despite the Wergens' undying devotion to humanity, despite their boundless generosity, EarthCouncil still harboured an interest in probing the limits of Wergen power. In any event, the future of the Ecclisse colony would be in doubt when EarthCouncil received her transmission about the illegal activities taking place here and intervened.

Cara rounded a corner at Corr 33E, and when the guidebot stopped in front of an office door, she barged into the room without knocking. She found Juan Carlos leaning back in his chair, feet propped up on his desk while several blue three-legged bots – the latest human prototype modelled on the Wergen variety – skittered around the office. One bot poured steaming-hot java into his mug. Behind him, the wall displayed an image of a Titanian lakeshore. One of his lab assistants who Cara recognised from the cremation ritual, a young man named Rafi, sat in a chair on the opposite sideof the desk.

Rafi stood. "We were just finishing," he said to Cara. "Excuse me." He nodded and strode past her, exiting the office.

"Have a seat," Juan Carlos said, and Cara cursed inwardly. She'd hoped to fluster him by entering unannounced, but he just clasped his hands behind his head and smiled. He'd remained slim and fit, and except for a few stray white hairs, looked more handsome than she remembered. He'd been her first and best lover, and the sex had kept them together for longer than it should have.

He nodded in the direction of a couch against the far wall, but she ignored him and took the seat Rafi had just vacated.

"I wasn't sure you'd show," he said.

"Oh, I wouldn't miss this for anything."

He smirked. "How many years has it been, Cara? And you don't look a day older. Where did I go wrong?"

"I have a number of urgent questions," she said.

"Me too. Imagine my surprise when I got word you'd come aboard a Wergen vessel. I hadn't received any notice of your visit."

He was playing games. He surely knew by now they'd stolen the seedship.

"Are you really interested in the details of my travel arrangements?" she said.

"No." He lowered his feet off the desk and leaned forward in his chair. "Much more important is the safety of our guests, which I'm responsible for. I can't have you wandering around in restricted areas. It's dangerous with the ongoing construction."

She gripped the sides of the chair. Did he already know about the transmission Vicente had sent? Best to go on the offensive. "Do you think EarthCouncil might be interested in the violations of the Joint Venture Compact taking place on this colony? The experiments you're conducting on the Wergens, Juan Carlos?"

He leaned closer and glared.

"Don't deny it," she said.

"Our research is vital to the long-term security of our species. Every Wergen who volunteered, including Umar, helped me willingly – *eagerly*, in fact."

"They're Wergen, for God's sake!" She slapped her hand on his desk and a blue bot scampered away. "They'd jump off a cliff for you if you asked them nicely. And why my Wergen? Why Umar?" She paused. "Is this still about us? Even after all the time that's passed?"

"Don't flatter yourself, Cara," he said. He spun his chair away from her to face the holo of the Titanian lakeshore, where viscous waves slapped against the orange lakeshore in slow motion. "It makes it easier for you if you vilify me, I understand, but it doesn't change the fact we're facing dangers that threaten our very survival as a species. Umar – a Wergen – understood the danger, even if you don't."

"Danger?"

"From the Junkies."

Cara rolled her eyes. A splinter group of Wergens who used chemicals to suppress their love for humanity had caused sporadic disturbances on some outposts. But it had been years since the last such incident, on Mars.

"The Wergens have clamped down on their renegades," Cara said.

"Our operatives in the Wergen Explorata suggest the aliens' politics are far more… complex than you might imagine."

Cara raised an eyebrow. EarthCouncil had managed to infiltrate the Explorata? Yet another serious breach of the Compact.

"The majority of the Wergens – 99 percent of them – have never been exposed to humanity… And that majority, well, they fear us apparently. In fact, they consider us a threat. And they've sided with the Junkies," Juan Carlos said. "You must realise we've grown far too dependent on the Wergens. Oh, they love us. But what happens if one day they should turn on us? Love can be… fickle."

He'd somehow managed to shift the conversation back to their relationship.

"This is why we've been developing our own bots," he said. He patted one of the blue devices that had skimmed along the edge of his desk. "And it's also why we've been conducting research to better understand Wergen neurology. We need to be able to reverse the effects of whatever chemicals they're using to suppress their natural love for us. Just in case."

She narrowed her eyes. "When EarthCouncil learns about this…"

"You haven't been listening, Cara," he said. He shook his head, laughed. "You still don't get it, do you?" He stood up. "I've been *following* EarthCouncil's orders to the letter."

She opened her mouth but couldn't speak. Yes, she knew humanity had lost its moral compass somewhat in the decades since first contact with the Wergens, but could matters have really deteriorated to this level? The Wergens now served humanity for all intents and purposes. Still, she couldn't accept that EarthCouncil would authorise experiments on alien test subjects.

"There's another reason they won't be responding to that transmission you sent." Juan Carlos set down his mug and clapped his hands. "Privacy!" Blue bots skittered out of the office, closing the door behind them. A privacy field buzzed.

He circled the desk and stood next to her. "We've lost all contact with Earth. In fact, it's been several days since any colony has responded to our messages." He stared at the wall holo as if searching for answers on the Titanian horizon.

111

She had difficulty wrapping her mind around the concept. There were four thriving human/Wergen colonies in the Solar System. What could have affected outposts spread out over such vast distances?

"Are you telling me the truth?" she said.

"If I'm lying, then you've done your duty by sending your transmission. But there's no cavalry riding to the rescue, I'm afraid. In the meantime, I need to continue to do my duty – what I *have* to do – without any interference from you or your friend."

"Listen to you! You really think you're a goddamn patriot!" Cara smiled angrily. "Fine. Do your duty. Perform your experiments. Just leave my daughter out of it. Antillia and I will leave and never bother you again."

"No. You and the Wergen girl will be staying until we know what's happening with Earth and the other colonies. And as of now, your Comm access is suspended. No more unauthorised transmissions by you or your pilot. As long as you're here on Ecclisse, you'll comply with security protocols."

"You can take your protocols and –"

"I'm disappointed, Cara. I'd hoped you'd be able to appreciate the larger picture." He paused, staring at her as if searching for some vestige of the naïve girl he'd dated so long ago on Titan, until his expression hardened. "Privacy off! Security!"

The door slid open and a dozen blue bots scampered into the office. As they escorted her out, Cara fumed inwardly. Juan Carlos hadn't even allowed her the small satisfaction of storming out of his office as she'd planned.

The freezing wind made Cara lean forward as she plodded along the perimeter of the northern forcefield where carbon monoxide snow and ice had accumulated hundreds of metres high. On the other side of the field, the ice-shelf of the Sputnik Planum dropped precipitously into a series of shallow valleys. Charon and Hydra, the two most prominent of Pluto's moons, shone blue and yellow in the dusky sky.

She had to find Antillia. When Cara returned to the hurth, the Wergen girl had vanished. Perhaps Juan Carlos had arranged their meeting as a way to separate them. How could she have been so stupid? Fortunately, she'd hidden a biotracker in the girl's robes as a precaution. She had failed Umar, but she wouldn't let any harm befall Antillia.

"Cara?"

Her name echoed in the howling wind.

"Cara!"

A silhouette in the distance. A figure riding atop a buzzer flew toward her. To her disappointment, the lanky figure was human.

Vicente.

He landed the buzzer on a snowdrift and bounded toward her accompanied by five bots. "I've been trying to reach you. Are you out of your mind?"

"Go away," she said.

"Why don't you have any bots with you? And why isn't your bodyfield activated?"

The Wergen forcefield that domed the colony kept temperatures in the minus twenty-three degrees Celsius range, and while a bodyfield might make it feel thirty degrees warmer, it would also allow Juan Carlos to more easily track her movements.

"Antillia's gone missing."

Vicente removed a heat-rod from his backpack and planted it in the snow. A shelter field snapped on, sheathing them in its protective umbrella, immediately warming her. He clicked off his own bodyfield, removed his gloves, then hers, and rubbed her bare hands. She wanted to pull away, but it felt good.

"You're coming back with me," he said.

"Not without Antillia."

"If the aliens don't have the spine to stand up for themselves, why should we do it for them?"

She glared at him. "You sound like Juan Carlos."

"I won't see you get hurt protecting one of them. They're so... cloying. 'Can I help you?' 'Do you need anything?' It makes my skin crawl."

Vicente's reaction was typical for humans who hadn't grown up around Wergens. He'd arrived from Luna three years earlier and became her attaché having had minimal exposure to the Wergens on Titan.

"What is it about this alien that you would risk your career, your very life, for her?"

She paused. "I raised Antillia and Umar. Their mother, Beatrix, was my best friend. When she died, I promised myself I would always be there for them."

"How did she die?"

"Bea was gene-passive. Absorbed into her mate as part of their reproductive process. Digested and broken down into component chemicals."

Vicente pursed his lips. "But what happened to Antillia's father? Why didn't he take care of her, or Umar?"

The ground rumbled and their umbrella flickered off and on.

"We'd best get moving," Cara said. The heat of the umbrella shield had caused the snow at their feet to melt into a half-metre-deep puddle. "Are you going to help or not? I won't ride on that buzzer or activate my bodyfield. And the bots stay behind. They're too easily tracked."

She switched from letting Vicente rub her hands to taking his hands in hers. Their eyes met.

"Fine," he said. "Let's go find your Wergen."


They hiked toward a red-tinted, twenty square metre forcefield that stood like a beacon in the frozen tundra. Inside the field, a staircase descended into the ice shelf.

"I'll plant a shield for you," Vicente said. "You wait here."

"The hell I will."

"Cara —"

"Antillia's known me longer than any other human. She'll do what I say." Cara pushed through the permeable field and marched down the stairs, Vicente following behind.

After ten steps, they entered a long hallway that stretched at a downward incline beneath the turquoise ice. Blue bots, the human variety, stood sentry along both sidewalls, serving some unknown purpose since they did nothing to impede their path.

The beat of music pulsed ahead of them. As they stepped through an entry field, the passageway opened up into a vast dark chamber. Holos of scenery from Earth, Triton, Mars, Titan and Langalana projected onto the walls: cityscapes of endless neon-lit skyscrapers, desert dunes stretching into the horizon, pink lakes, purple oceans, and an expanse of red-furred grasslands. In front of each holo, dozens of silhouettes danced energetically. It took Cara's eyes a few seconds to adjust to the dim lighting and then she made out the humans lying on the floor mats: intertwined flesh, bare arms and legs and breasts, faces with vacant expressions. High on neurotransmitters. While they engaged in sex acts on the matted ground, a Wergen stood at the centre of each circle of human bodies, dazzled into paralysis.

"Do you like what you see?" one woman screamed at the Wergen near her, trying to be heard over the pounding music. She rubbed her hand along the alien's scaled leg. The Wergen studied the woman, enraptured.

Sickened, Cara scanned the chamber but couldn't find Antillia among the shadowed forms.

Vicente tugged on her sleeve. "We need to move quickly. Where is she?"

"My tracker has stopped functioning down here. I don't see –"

"There," he said.

At the far end of the cavern stood two red doors.

"Hey, want to tumble?" said a tall, tanned man. When he clutched Cara's forearm, she recognised him as Rafi, Juan Carlos's assistant. "This place isn't for gawkers," he said. "Lose the clothes or get out."

Vicente shoved the man and Cara scrambled past him.

"Hey! Where do you think you're going?" Rafi shouted. He leapt to his feet and tackled Vicente from behind. As the men fought, Cara barrelled through the red metal doors into a winding passageway leading to a second set of double-doors.

"Antillia?" Cara hollered. She pushed past swinging doors with "Do Not Enter" signs, and motion sensors activated fluorescent lights inside the room, which blinded her. A stench like rubbing alcohol, burnt rubber and spoiled meat overpowered her.

She gasped as she bumped into a gurney and took a step backwards.

Rows of examination tables filled a vast laboratory. On each of which lay white chunks of scaled flesh and black entrails. Wergen corpses. Dissected.

Cara bent over and vomited onto the floor.

*No*, she thought. *Antillia*.

She breathed hard through her mouth, fighting off the waves of nausea.

A hand reached from the nearest table and grabbed her wrist.

Cara flinched, and pulled away.

"Are you ill, Lady?" a weak raspy voice said.

The Wergen on the table had no lower extremities. It was only a torso with one arm. Its chest had been sliced opened, exposing two beating organs that resembled black bananas; strings of tar-black intestines draped over the sides of the table. "Please." It reached out with its four-fingered hand. "Can I help you?"

Cara stumbled backward and fled from the lab, fighting the urge to scream.

Back in the chamber, the music had stopped and semi-dressed colonists congregated in a far corner in front of the projection of Titan with its placid methane lakes.

Vicente moved through their ranks, pulling a Wergen by the arm. *Antillia.*

Cara ran toward them.

"She won't go," Vicente said. "The others insist that she stay."

Cara put her bare hands on Antillia's cheek. "We're leaving, dear." The Wergen girl shuddered at her touch.

But as she spoke the words, the bots stationed at the entranceway bolted into the chamber. And, all at once, they were on top of her and Vicente. Cara tried to swat them away, but one of the bots released a needle that penetrated her boot and stung her ankle.

"Aunt Cara?" Antillia said, as if awakening from a dream.

But for Cara the world went black.

*"Antillia!" Cara shouted. "Get out!"*

*The Wergen child had burst into the bathroom while Cara was stepping out of the shower. The girl retreated two steps and Cara slammed the door shut. This was the third time this week either Antillia or Umar had interrupted her in the bathroom, somehow getting past the lock on the door.*

*A few minutes later, still furious, Cara emerged to find Antillia and Umar standing a few metres away, waiting for her anxiously. How many times had she explained to them the importance of respecting her personal space? She stooped down to get face-to-face with Antillia.*

*"You, young lady," Cara said, "are punished." She prodded the girl to the edge of the room and made her face the corner, the first time she'd used a timeout as a form of discipline. "Now stay here until I tell you otherwise. I want you to think about what you did wrong."*

116

*Antillia obediently faced the wall while Cara stomped into the kitchen. Umar followed, careful to stay three metres behind her. He observed her with great interest while she fumed. "If you're going to get along with other humans, you have got to learn about privacy."*

*The boy silently watched with interest – as he always did – while she prepared breakfast.*

*Ten minutes later, her anger diluted after her cup of coffee, Cara stepped back into the other room to free Antillia from her timeout.*

*The girl lay face down on the floor, clutching her shoulders and spasming.*

*"Antillia!" Cara rushed to her side and bent down to help her up. "Are you okay?"*

*The girl stared at her, mute, her charcoal eyes wider than ever.*

*"It's okay," Cara said.*

*"Alone," the Wergen girl said in a high-pitched whisper, her shoulders shuddering. "I'm alone."*

*"Hey, I'm right here."*

*The Wergen girl stood and threw her arms around Cara's neck in a desperate embrace.*

*"It's okay, baby. Everything's going to be okay. Your Aunt Cara is right here."*

Cara gasped and sat up.

"Are you okay?" Vicente said.

"Where are we?" She still felt groggy.

"In custody. Accused of trying to send another unauthorised transmission."

"That's ridiculous!"

Vicente raised his hand in aknowledgement.

"Where's Antillia?" Cara said.

"I don't know."

*God help her, she could be in Juan Carlos's lab at this very moment!*

Cara assessed their surroundings: the ventless ceiling, the rock-solid floor, the alloyed walls to the sides and behind them. An opaque forcefield blocked the open path ahead of them. A triangular plexi on the wall behind them revealed the familiar grey sky. "The window," she said.

"It's fielded. I've already tried."

"Bots," she said. "Have you seen any construction bots in the corridor?"

He shook his head.

"There has to be a way out." She pressed her hands against the near-invisible field then paced around the small cell.

"There was some activity in the corridor earlier," he said. "From what I overheard, a battalion of ships is headed this way. It seems a wormhole was detected burrowing out of realspace not far from Uranus."

"So Juan Carlos lied to me." She told Vicente what Juan Carlos had alleged about EarthCouncil's involvement, and about the nightmare she had witnessed in the lab. "They did receive our transmission. Help *is* coming!"

"Apparently," Vicente said. "But I still can't believe the Wergens would tolerate these experiments – that they'd even *volunteer* for them. With their technology, they could wipe out this colony with a snap of their fingers!" He shook his head incredulously.

She'd expected him to sympathise with the Wergens, but instead his contempt for them had intensified.

Cara continued pacing. "That lab is located in close proximity to the dens for a reason," she said. "The presence of so many humans overstimulates the Wergens. That's why they're taken to his lab for those horrible experiments."

She thought again about the scene in the den. History had shown that whenever there were clearly drawn social and moral boundaries, certain individuals inevitably crossed those lines into perverted and fetishistic behaviour. She shouldn't have been surprised Juan Carlos had found a way to exploit the situation.

A sonic boom rattled the cell.

Cara ran to the plexi and scanned the sky. Seedships speckled the heavens, a swarm of sparkling silver locusts descending from the black sky. She had to get out of there! She had to find Antillia.

After a few minutes, the explosions grew louder.

Suddenly laserfire blasted closer to them. The entire corridor rocked as if another quake had struck the colony. She heard screaming in the distance.

"What –?" Another explosion. The floor collapsed beneath them, sending Cara plunging into blackness.

The darkness swallowed her. It was endless, all-encompassing. She blinked against the dust and coughed.

*Pain...*Her legs and back ached. *Where was she?*

"Vicente?" She looked upwards at a beam of light streaming through a gaping hole. Part of the floor had given way. She'd fallen into an empty sub-basement.

It took a few minutes for her head to stop spinning. Cara gathered herself and crawled over the rubble surrounding her. She moved toward a lit exit, staggering to her feet, and leaned against the doors. She stretched her arms and legs, and winced. Everything hurt, but nothing seemed broken. She pushed open the doors and slowly climbed the stairs. *What was happening?*

She headed toward Juan Carlos's office at Corr 33. When she arrived, there was no sign of him. His desk lay smashed and his bots were crushed on the carpet like flattened tin cans.

Limping out of the room, she encountered a tidal wave of colonists rushing in the opposite direction.

"Where are you going?" a man said, clutching her wrist. "Run!" A particle beam sliced through his temple and he collapsed to the floor like a marionette with its strings cut.

That's when she saw them. A pack of Wergens surrounded by hundreds of black bots perambulating on six sharp-edged blades like giant tarantulas. Cara spotted an object on the Wergens' faces: a small transparent strip that cupped their breathing canal – an insulated mask that fed them love suppressors. Junkies. They sported furious smiles. "Freedom from love!" they shouted. "Freedom from love!"

Cara spun around and hobbled alongside the fleeing humans down Corr 33. She turned a corner and huddled motionless near the floor in shadow, hugging her knees, hoping the Wergens would continue in pursuit of the retreating colonists. Her heart beat so loudly she imagined everyone could hear it. She waited as the aliens swept through. They were like no Wergens she had ever encountered.

After the pack rushed by her, Cara stood and headed back in the direction from which the Wergens had just come. Rounding another corner she came upon a group of six Wergens at the far end of the passageway surrounding a cowering human.

Juan Carlos.

"This is the one," one of the Wergens said. "The butcher of our brethren, the human identified in the transmission as the one who spearheaded the massacres."

*The transmission?* The Junkies had intercepted her transmission to EarthCouncil.

"My friends, I'm – I'm a mere administrator who's had a long, warm relationship with your people," Juan Carlos said, smiling broadly, exuding all the charm he could muster.

"Toss him in with the other subjects," one Wergen said to the other. "Let's see what it is about these creatures that seduces us. If we take them apart one organ at a time, maybe we can find a way to break their hold over us."

"No need, no need!" Juan Carlos said, laughing nervously while rubbing his bare hand along the arm of the Wergen nearest to him. A black bot jumped off the alien's shoulder and sliced the tips of Juan Carlos's fingers, sending blood spraying in different directions. He howled.

"First we run our tests. Then we exact justice."

Juan Carlos grimaced, clutching his bleeding hand, and pivoted his head in Cara's direction. He made eye contact with her. As the Wergens were about to turn towards her, he screamed, "W-wait! I don't understand. Why would you do something like this?" He raised his blood-soaked hand. When the Wergens hesitated, he pushed between two of them and bolted in the opposite direction.

As three bots chased after him, Cara took advantage of the opportunity he'd given her. She struggled to her feet and took off.

"Over there!" a Wergen shouted.

As she fled, a black bot scooted after her. Glancing back as she ran, she saw the tips of its legs glow yellow and it pointed one of its jagged appendages at her.

She leaned to her left and a particle beam struck the wall where she'd been a moment earlier.

Three of the Wergens pursued her. She turned a sharp corner and limped down Corr 47A, hoping to lose them.

*No*, she realised, too late. This was the dead end she'd come upon earlier.

She manoeuvred around the construction equipment and reached into one of the storage compartments, where she remembered seeing

bot parts and buzzers. Seconds later, as the thud of heavy boots grew
louder, she pulled out a buzzer by its two handles. She moved towards
a dead end, where a transparent field separated the corridor from the
twilit world outside and the thousand-meter girders on which
construction bots swarmed. The icy ground lay far below her.

"Field down!" she screamed at the bots. They ignored her and
continued their labour. "Field down! Field down!" She pounded her
fists against the field.

The footsteps moved closer. When she looked back, two Wergens
with drawn weapons marched toward her.

"Field down!" Nothing.

She only had one option, a long shot, and if her plan failed... She
closed her eyes, bracing herself for the worse, but then decided if she
was to meet death she'd do so with eyes wide open.

*I love you, Antillia.*

"Freedom from love!" screamed the Wergens, and they opened
fire, wildly. Particle beams sizzled at her feet, grazed her right earlobe,
and then blinding pain pierced her left shoulder. The beams disrupted
the forcefield behind her, as she'd hoped. She leaned backwards into
the freezing wind and plummeted.

As the snow-covered ground rushed toward her, she remembered
she was holding onto the buzzer's handlebars. She squeezed and the
buzzer lifted her upwards, almost yanking her arms out of their sockets.
The sharp pain in her left shoulder brought her to the brink of
unconsciousness. She struggled not to let go and manoeuvred so that
her feet rested atop the buzzer's base. Flying between the maze of
girders that connected the facility buildings, she tried to get her
bearings. The frigid air made her gasp. She activated her bodyfield.

*Antillia*, she thought. *Where are you?*

She swooped through a metal chevron in the direction of the dens
and spotted humans and Wergens pouring out from the red-fielded
staircase in the ice like ants, but she couldn't make out from this
altitude whether Antillia was one of them. She descended further, until
she flew a few metres off the ground.

A particle beam exploded against the buzzer.

The world turned upside down as she went tumbling into a drift at
tremendous speed, her arms and legs smacking against the impacted
snow. When she came to a stop, her left arm throbbed and her hand

angled painfully from her wrist. She couldn't feel her fingers any more. The crash had deactivated her bodyfield.

All around her, human bodies pockmarked the snow. In every direction, Wergens, hundreds of Wergens, marched through the frozen landscape. They fired their weapons, striking down human after human emerging from the dens.

Cara crept forward on her right elbow and knees. That's when she recognised Antillia in the distance, accompanied by three Wergens.

With great effort, she managed to stand up.

"Antillia!" she yelled, but her voice was weak. "Antillia!"

Her shouts finally registered, and the Wergen girl turned and marched in her direction.

"Antillia! It's me!"

When she stood no more than a metre away, Antillia stopped. She wore a clear mask over her breathing canal. The Junkies had slapped a suppressor strip on her.

"Are you hurt?" Cara asked.

Antillia's expression contorted into a frightening grimace. "You!" she said. She stamped through the snow until she stood right on top of her. She grabbed Cara by the wrists, and pulled her forward until her face was inches from hers. Cara screamed as a stab of pain shot through her left wrist and arm.

"You manipulated us! You exploited us!" Antillia said.

"What are you saying? It's me!"

"I loathe you, 'Aunt' Cara. You're selfish, monstrous."

"I don't understand. I-I didn't know about Juan Carlos's experiments or I would never have —"

"I'm not talking about that," she said, her stare as ice-cold as the bleak terrain. "I'm talking about my enslavement to you. All I ever wanted was to be near you, to be like you. I worshipped you. I considered you infallible. Umar and I, even Father... We lived solely to love you. *You!*" She laughed incredulously, cruelly. "How you must have taken pleasure in our devotion to you. And when I finally found the strength to follow my own path, you chased me across the Solar System, wielding the power of your love like a weapon. What you've done to me, what your people have done to mine, is unforgivable."

"Why are you saying these things? You're my daughter, Antillia. I love you!"

"You have a *choice!*" she hissed. "Umar and I, we didn't!"

The wind gusted and the snow swirled around them so that Cara lost eye contact with her.

"Antillia," she said, crying. "Do you think I *chose* to love you? You don't understand. It doesn't work that way. I'm as powerless as you are when it comes to the love I feel for you and Umar. You're my children."

"Stop lying! Umar and I aren't your children. We never were. Back at my hurth I saw how you manipulated your pilot, how you used his love for you to make him do what you wanted. *Of course* it's a choice for you."

Antillia's words stunned her. "I-It's true that I don't love Vicente, but it's different with you and Umar. Everything I did, coming all this way, I did it for you. After Umar died, I sacrificed everything to come here and save you, to free you from –"

"*You* sacrificed?" Contempt oozed out of every syllable. "You convinced Father to hand over custody of me and Umar to you as if we were pets! You tore my family apart so you could keep us as a reminder of your supposed 'best friend.' You claimed to love us but wouldn't let us make our own decisions. You kept me from living my own life! Well I'm free now, 'Aunt' Cara and I don't need you any more." She threw her hands up, releasing Cara's arms and letting her fall back into the snow.

"It wasn't like that! I wanted to keep you safe, to protect you."

"'Protect' me? Like Juan Carlos swore to protect us?" Antillia stomped ahead a few steps, stopped. "You humans are all the same," she said with disgust.

One of the Wergen soldiers pointed a weapon at Cara's head.

A glint of repressed emotion seemed to flash in Antillia's eyes. "No!" she said, raising her arm. "Leave her. Some of them should be left alive so they can pass on the message to the rest of their kind. We want them to fear us."

The Wergen soldier lowered his weapon and the remaining Junkies ignored Cara as they paraded past her. She buried her face in the snow and the cold stung as sharply as Antillia's words. *Had the inhalant caused her to say those things? Maybe it hadn't liberated her; maybe it had replaced love with hate?* That idea was less painful to accept than the alternative.

When Cara lifted her head again, the Wergens were specks, receding into the icy horizon.

She spotted a figure approaching from the opposite direction, waving his arms over his head.

Vicente.

Cara lay in the bunk of the seedship, her arm in a makeshift sling, her mind half-numbed by pain medication. The drugs, however, had not deadened the memory of Antillia's anger, her stinging accusations. Cara always knew that Umar and Antillia essentially had no free will – no Wergen around humans did – yet she'd continued to interact with them, continued the pretense that she could be their family. *Was Antillia right?*

Whatever the consequences Cara had to face, at least her daughter was safe. At least she had accomplished that much.

A knock on the door startled her. She stumbled out of bed and slid open the door. "Yes, Vicente?"

"Cara." He entered the room. "The Junkies have shut down all transmissions throughout the settlements, but a message leaked through from Axelis. Colonists there have received word the Wergen renegades have launched an all-out offensive against Earth and the colonies. We're at war." He paced back and forth looking more haggard than usual, his long thinning black hair uncombed, his uniform dishevelled. "But there are loyal Wergens still assisting EarthCouncil. And there's some hope they'll be able to develop a counteragent to the Junkies' suppressors. Research in connection with Juan Carlos's experiments is proving invaluable to them."

"Oh?" Through the plexi on the bridge, Cara studied what remained of the colony of Ecclisse, half-submerged beneath the collapsed ice shelf.

Vicente stood next to her, observing the destruction.

Her transmission to EarthCouncil – intercepted by the Junkies – had triggered all this.

"What have I done?" Cara said. But she already knew the answer. She did what she had to do. What any mother would do. She'd protected her child, no matter the cost, and would do it all over again if she had to.

"I'm sorry about how things turned out with the Wergen – your daughter," he said.

"I – I am, too," she said, her voice quavering. "But she's free now." Cara turned to face him.

"Vicente, everything you've done for me… I'm grateful. Truly. But there's something I have to tell you," she said. "I haven't been honest with you. I know how you feel about me and I've taken advantage. I'm sorry, but I don't – I can't – feel the same way. I know I've led you on. That was wrong."

"Cara…"

"You're a good man, who deserves better. And I needed to tell you –"

He put a finger to her lips, silencing her. Leaning in close, he whispered, "I do love you, Cara. I've always loved you." He gazed at her for an extended moment. "But I'm not stupid. I know how you feel about me. Oh, I won't deny I hoped, with time, you might come to feel differently. But I'm no victim. The truth is, you could have told me from the start how you felt, and it wouldn't have made a difference. I still would've stolen this ship; I still would've helped you come here."

"Really?"

He nodded. "Does that make me no better than a Wergen?"

She locked eyes with him and didn't answer.

"Well, at least EarthCouncil will be too preoccupied with other matters to inquire into our violation of orders coming here," she said.

"True."

Together, they redirected their gaze to the ship's plexi. Far below them, all that remained of the human-Wergen joint colony was a molten fireball sinking deeper into the iceplains of the heart-shaped Tombaugh Regio.

# CHAPTER SEVEN
## Freefall on Gliese 581-b

### Earth, Gliese 581-b – Years 2586 – 2596

Under normal circumstances, we wouldn't have stood a chance against the Wergen renegades. Their bots alone could have obliterated Earth ten times over. But we had one advantage: while most Wergens retreated from their interactions with humanity, returning to their own internal political conflicts, a few stayed behind to assist us in our battle against their own kind. While we didn't trust them entirely, we had no choice but to accept their help. Pressing them for every advantage possible, we came to learn of the legend of the Eremites, aliens rumoured to have left behind remnants of their civilisation in the heart of gas giants.

EarthCouncil made the decision that the best tactic in our war against the Wergen renegades was to make new allies or, if need be, to strike preemptively against any force that might assist our new enemies.

This is my story.

Nine days they fell:
Confounded Chaos roared,
And felt tenfold
confusion in their fall…
    *– John Milton, Paradise Lost*

*SkyStation*

How long has it been since freefall? Have days passed? Weeks? Maybe I've dreamt the whole thing.

The older Wergen – Fahr I think her name is – pushes the needle above my closed lid, just above my eye socket and into my frontal lobe. "This one will make you feel better," she says soothingly. She pats my wrist as the chemicals course through my brain.

I try to slap away her scaled hand and find myself straining against the bed shackles. My body convulses and agony rips through me. I scream.

"*Please*, Sergeant," Fahr says. She puckers her lipless mouth, deepening the scales on her chalk-white face and I'm worried for a second she might try to kiss me. But no, she's wearing a transparent mask – a whiffer – over her large single nostril. She's a Junkie. Resistant to human charms as long as she's on the inhalant.

"Tell me about the other aliens, the Eremites," she says.

A misshapen, fist-sized Orb, its edges like pulled taffy, floats near her head. The device transmits my every word, my every reaction, across parsecs of space to the Junkie military base on Charity Station, rumoured to be nested somewhere in the Oort Cloud. This Wergen faction makes it a point to keep its distance for fear of falling under humanity's spell, an uncontrollable attraction the aliens call "love." But in all the years I've been exposed to the Wergens, I've never thought of it as love. No, it's an alien perversion of love, a mental illness that makes the Wergens fawn over us obsessively.

"Go on," Fahr says, stroking my scalp. "Tell me about freefall. Tell me everything."

### Gliese 581-b

I strip in the narrow corridor and toss my fatigues into the metal bin. We queue up by rank, Adrian ahead of me, the seven bald grunts in the squad lingering behind us. Further back, at a safe distance, stand the two aliens, traitors to their own kind, their scaled pasty faces and round black eyes gaping at the naked soldiers around them.

I don't want the Wergens anywhere near me. No one does. But to have any chance in our war against them, we're going to need the help of turncoats like these. Command had kept them segregated from the squad until just before the scheduled drop. It undermined troop morale to let the Wergens get too close.

Fifty other squads pack the ship's decks, readying for freefall. Each squad consists of 10 grunts, a diplomat and at least one Wergen traitor. Our team, Sigma, leads the charge.

A cobalt-blue medbot – a human knockoff of the Wergen type – crawls toward me, its metal shell glinting in the corridor's fluorescent lights. It scoots up my body to my left shoulder. I open my mouth wide, say, "Aaah," and it injects the nanoboosters into my tongue before moving to the next grunt. Within seconds, I feel the ice-cold pinpricks cascading along the roof of my mouth as the NBs work their magic.

Adrian breathes hard and stands ahead of me, his eyes closed in meditation. His smooth scalp and missing eyebrows highlight his nakedness.

"Lieutenant… Adrian," I whisper to him out of earshot of the others. The grunts horse around nervously, doing their best to ignore the two gawking aliens. "No word from the AI drones?"

Adrian opens his eyes. "AI teams Alpha through Rho stopped transmitting at 0800 this morning. Command expected at least one of them might've made it to the planet's surface, but I can't say I'm too surprised. Time for good old-fashioned human beings to take a stab."

"And the nukes?"

"None detonated."

The AIs would have sent us a transmission if they'd made contact and diplomatic overtures had succeeded. Or they would have detonated the nukes if the Eremites proved hostile. This meant we were going in blind, unsure of what to expect.

"So, this is it then," I say.

Adrian smiles. "This is it. You and me, Dunc, as always."

He offers his hand and I shake it, gripping it maybe a few seconds longer than I should before I answer, "As always."

At that moment our assigned diplomat, Tessa Kornbluth, arrives. The soldiers part to make way for her. The four male grunts stand to her left, the three women to her right. Standing naked and hairless like the others, the diplomat is scrawnier and more wrinkled, but still commands a formidable presence. She'll be key to reaching some kind of agreement with the Eremites – if any agreement is to be had. She holds her right arm over her breasts and her left hand over her groin and nods in our direction. "Enough dilly-dallying," she says. Her diplomatic skills, I hope, are better with aliens.

As if on cue, sirens blare and lights strobe. Adrian turns and barks, "Atten*tion*! Suits on!" The young men and women fall silent, standing straight, heads up. The Wergens' huge black eyes widen. And that's when I recognise the taller Wergen.

*Him. I can't believe he's followed me even here.*

I glare, and when several grunts check to see what has drawn my attention, Adrian screams, "What are you all staring at? Let's move it!"

I take deep, calming breaths.

Adrian strides into the suitroom and we follow in lockstep down an extended catwalk. He reaches the edge and steps off, followed by a loud "plop." Three metres below, the vat of protogel pulses and simmers.

"Step on it!" I shout at the grunts. "Go, go, go!"

As they march off the gangplank, bald and naked, I can't shake the thought they are about to undergo a peculiar sort of reverse-birth. I've done this before on Verdantium during training, but I don't think I'll ever get used to it.

When the last of my squadmates – including Kornbluth – have jumped, it's time for the Wergens to take the leap. They're enthralled by my every word, my every movement. Scales cover their naked bodies from head to toe, and they're white as snowmen. Stout, fawning, scaled snowmen.

"What are *you* looking at?" I holler. "Go!"

"Of course," Ion says. "We'll do everything we can to help."

"Yes, whatever you want," says the other Wergen.

I think about telling them to shut it, but then I remember how much they enjoy our attention, so I stay silent until they dive over the edge.

From this vantage point, I can make out the hazy silhouettes of Adrian, Kornbluth and my squadmates beneath the clear protogel. A dozen metal coils emerge from the side of the tank and clamp onto their ankles and wrists with their pincers, manoeuvring them carefully into the metal suits docked along the side wall tubes. When they're wedged inside their suits, I can hear the countdown begin. "20... 19... 18... 17..."

My mouth feels like ice now. The bottom of my tongue tingles from the buzzing NBs.

*My turn.* I leap off the edge.

My body slaps hard against the gel and the warm syrup oozes over me, entering my nostrils and my eardrums, coating my eyeballs. I fight the urge to gasp and to swim and fight my way to the surface.

It doesn't matter.

I can breathe.

I can see.

With my tongue.

### Earth

It's cold outside and there's not a cloud in the night sky, but the stars are still obscured by the city lights. Adrian and I are lying side-by-side on lawn chairs we've dragged to the rooftop of midtown Manhattan's Silver Spires. He passes me the toker. I'm conscious of the fact it's been between his lips as I take a puff.

It's Tuesday night, October 7, 2586, a date we'll never forget.

"Hey, man, do you think we might be able to see the spaceships?" Adrian says.

"Not likely. And what would they look like?" I say. "Probably just a bunch of bright dots in the sky."

"Nah, they've got to be way more dramatic than that. These are *aliens* we're talking about, Dunc. Their ships have to have a weird shape or flashing green lights or *something*."

"There's nothing on the transweb about the shape of Wergen seedships?" I say.

"Nothing I've seen."

The outer colonies have been in contact with the Wergens for more than fifty years. In that time, the aliens forged agreements with the human colonists, helped them upgrade their outposts from underground lunar bases to domed cities that thrived in every extreme environment imaginable. But the Wergens avoided Earth. Something about their alien sensibilities made them consider the human homeworld off-limits. And they'd made it clear their own home planet was to remain quarantined from human contact. In fact, they'd never revealed its location. But now, after ignoring all our previous invitations, the Wergens are finally coming to Earth.

Adrian has an excited gleam in his eyes. I can't help but stare at him until he awkwardly breaks eye contact. Everything that's happened today still seems incredible to me. I hand the toker back to him.

News of the Wergen transmissions has been blasted all over the web for the past eight hours. It's all anyone can talk about. Mom and Dad are nervously glued to the webcasts right now while Carrie has decided to go out dancing with dorky Alan Avila, a cute nerd just breaking out of his shell, to celebrate First Contact (although there's a debate whether it even counts as First Contact given the Wergens' long relationship with the Outer Colonies). Half the countries in the world are panicked, organising their military defenses and praying for salvation, convinced the Wergens' decision to at last visit Earth signals a new aggressiveness – even though we've extended the invitation for decades. The other half of the globe is ecstatic – the benevolent aliens who brought technological wonders to the colonies have at last decided to visit Earth.

"What do you think will happen?" Adrian asks. "When they finally land, I mean." The wind is blowing hard and Adrian wraps his windbreaker around him. He's wearing shorts and his legs are crossed at the ankles as he lies back in the lawn chair.

I shrug, try to play it cool, like I always do when I'm around Adrian. "Chances are nothing will ever be the same. Dad thinks they'll be friendly. He says it makes no sense they'd be so generous with the Outer Colonies and then treat Earth any differently. Mom's more cautious."

The wind gusts again.

"Hard to believe classes haven't been cancelled," Adrian says, chuckling. "To hell with a physics pop quiz."

It did seem absurd with everything happening today that tomorrow would be just another school day for the senior class at Henry Hudson High, another day of advanced calc and phys ed.

"So... what did you want to tell me?" Adrian had suggested we skip the First Contact parties and camp out on the rooftop to celebrate the news. He said he wanted to talk to me about something personal, something he'd been meaning to tell me for a while. I've had a crush on Adrian for as long as I can remember, and I can't help but hope maybe he feels the same. He's never given any indication he might be interested in me in that way. But he did pass up on all the First Contact parties to spend his time here.

"Oh yeah. That." He looks uncomfortable now, as if he regrets ever telling me he wanted to talk.

Sitting up in the lawn chair, he swings his legs around to face me. He slips on his flip-flops and stands up, ambles to the edge of the roof.

I follow him.

"C'mon. What did you want to tell me?"

He's leaning forward, his hands on the ledge. "It's kind of embarrassing."

"You can tell me."

I stand next to him and, together, we stare out at the sea of skyscrapers, the palette of reds and yellows and blues.

## Gliese 581-b

Our suits swoosh down the slick tubes and we shoot out of the skimmer into kaleidoscopic clouds like reckless deep-sea divers. Adrian and Kornbluth are just ahead of me, the grunts and the Wergens trailing in our wake.

Powerful winds sweep us across the horizon of Gliese 581-b. Everyone assumed the Eremites would be located on the rocky Super-Earth, Gliese 581-*d*. No one expected the gas giant in the system could be home to anything.

I should be used to it by now, but I'm riding a wave of exhilaration, adrenaline pumping through my veins.

My heart palpitates. I scream, "Hooyah!" My faceplate is jammed with protogel so it sounds like the growl of a rabid dog. I try to rein in my emotions with no luck, so I cluck my tongue and my safesuit pumps me full of Risers that nudge my fear in the direction of hot fury. The Risers are supposed to keep us self-confident and stimulated during our long descent. But we wouldn't be the first soldiers to tinker with our suit regulators and overdo it a bit.

Eddies of yellow and rust-red swirl in the planet's ionosphere. The colours fade, and we plummet into a water-cloud layer of solid white.

Number 4 cuts loose with a primal scream over the comm.

The nanobots buzz in the roof of my mouth like a steady electric current. The NBs have an 18-day lifespan, enough time for us to reach the surface and negotiate with these aliens or, if necessary, launch a preemptive attack and haul ourselves back to orbit.

Above us, the crescent-shaped skimmers lift away. If they'd descended any further into the planet's atmosphere, the pressure would've crushed them like antique tin cans. Despite years of studying Wergen tech, we still can't generate a nullfield stable enough to shield anything much larger than a human being – let alone anything the size of a skimmer. But it's for the best. Individual soldiers falling from the sky will make for a challenging target.

"Ready for some action?" Adrian screams over the commlink.

"Hell, yeah!" I answer. I'm careful with my tongue, subvocalising words so they're more intelligible.

The grunts whoop it up, howling for Eremite blood – not that we know whether these goddamned aliens even have circulatory systems. Our first priority, I remind them, is to protect Kornbluth so she can negotiate with the Eremites, but diplomacy is the last thing on their Riser-fuelled minds. As we approach the surface Adrian will give the order to ease down on the drugs.

When the twelve of us reach the same altitude, we shut off our thrusters. The agreed-upon strategy calls for us to freefall the rest of the way. We'll need to conserve every last erg of our safesuits' power reserves for the return trip.

The NBs' mapping signal – sonar, radar, magnetospheric, spectroscopic – allows me to feel the images of my surroundings outlined on my tingling tongue. Those impulses send a neural signal to my visual cortex, allowing me to 'see' Adrian, my twelve squadmates and the two Wergens, each falling no more than ten metres apart from one another, their cobalt-blue suits stark against the pure white backdrop. Legs together and arms at their side, they remind me of sleek cylinders, living torpedoes. The protogel makes it impossible to identify any faces, but I feel their suit-numbers pop up on the back of my tongue. Compartments in our armour hold the nullweaponry: automatic pulsers, gamma grenades, spatial displacers, all designed to function in white-hot temperatures and under the atom-squeezing pressures of this gas giant, which is about twice the size of Jupiter.

Nothing to do now but wait, try to calm myself, and drown out the occasional enthusiastic holler over the comm.

The white mist thickens around us as the minutes pass and we hurtle deeper and deeper into the stratosphere.

"Report, Sigma," Adrian says.

"Number Two here. All systems normal," I subvocalise into my helmet commlink. Every time I've suited up, it's taken me a while to adjust to the NBs and the protogel. My throat makes gruff sounds my suit translates into clearly enunciated words; I've got to be careful. Inadvertent tongue movement might activate the NBs and disorient me by expanding my vision.

"Number Three. Systems normal!"

"All normal – under the circumstances," Kornbluth says.

"Five here!"

The others all shout their numbers in turn – except for the Wergens – and I can tell from the grunts' tone that the Risers flooding their bloodstreams have pushed them over the edge into kill-mode. If the alien turncoats aren't careful, the grunts might just blow them out of the sky. Hell, I'm tempted to do it myself. Nasty, slimy things.

Hours pass. We fall.

When 'night' comes, the sky darkens from cotton-white to dirty grey, giving our surroundings a grainy, unreal look. The luminescence from the planet's two largest moons makes the water crystals in the clouds twinkle, silver flecks which envelop us.

As Adrian's sergeant and second-in-command, I make it a point not to overdo the Risers. I'll need to stay more clearheaded than the rest to help with negotiations – or tactical decisions, if need be – come planetfall.

"You reading this?" Adrian says.

I extend my tonguesight to maximum range. Then I spot them, tiny colourful stray bubbles trailing in our wake.

"Affirmative," I say.

"Three and Four," Adrian says. "Fall back."

Three and Four fire their reverse thrusters, dropping fifty metres behind the rest of us. A cloud of rainbow-hued bubbles mirror the manoeuvre, swirling around Three and Four. The rest follow us.

"Are they Eremites?" Eight asks.

"Check your freakin' sensors, Eight!" Adrian barks. "They're lower life forms."

My tongue presses against an upper molar, accessing the datastream that pours through my safesuit sensors. Adrian is right.

Explosions rattle through the comm, and my suit picks up weaponfire.

"Die, scumsuckers!" Nine yells, shooting off her pulser. "Die! Die! Die!"

"Nine!" Adrian hollers. "Stand down!"

What was Nine thinking? A tough Vietnamese woman, she was a stickler for regulations, one of the few grunts who'd impressed me with her no-nonsense attitude. She'd let down her guard with me during training and joked about replacing the protogel in our suits with soju, for a more relaxed mission.

The bubble-froth scatters and reassembles with each successive shot she fires.

"Reduce your Riser intake, Nine," I scream.

Nine blasts another few rounds before she finally stops.

"We can't afford to waste ammunition!" Adrian barks. "Am I understood?"

"Yes *sir*, Lieutenant, *sir!*" Nine says.

"I said am I understood?"

"*Yes sir, Lieutenant, sir!*" everyone hollers.

After a while I ignore the bubbles as we plummet through the endless clouds. We're blazing comets, I think – which makes me wonder whether the Risers are messing with my head, making me more poetic than I might normally be – and the bubbles, they're our shimmering tails.

## Earth

Adrian and I lean over the edge of the rooftop. I move closer to him and he turns to face me. We're both fairly buzzed at this point so maybe I'm more relaxed than I normally would be standing so near him under the bright full moon. After so many years of secretly pining for him, I take a deep breath. I can imagine leaning in, kissing him softly on the lips. Maybe he doesn't react at first, maybe he's stunned, but then he'll kiss me back, just as softly, then more urgently. I'm staring deeply into his blue eyes, my face no further than six inches away from his, wondering whether I'll have the courage to make a move when he finally blurts out, "Jenna Yamasaki," before turning away in embarrassment.

"What?"

"You know. Jenna from advanced calc. I kind of... well, you know, I like her. I want to ask her out."

I'm so surprised I can't even speak.

"That's what I wanted to tell you. What do you think? You sit right behind her. Do you think she might be interested in me?"

"Jenna."

"Yeah, you think she's out of my league, don't you." He puts his hands on his head and spins around. "I can tell from your expression. Man, I don't know what I was thinking. You're right, there's no way she'll say yes."

"N-no," I say, regaining my composure. "I think you should ask her out. She seems nice."

"You think?" He puts his hands on my shoulders with a goofy grin.

I have a schizophrenic sense of devastation and joy. I'm pleased my words have made him so happy, but at the same time my heart sinks. No, he doesn't feel the same way about me. I want to run away, but at the same time I'm even more drawn to him, by the intimacy of our conversation, the fact he's chosen to share this with me.

"Hey, dickwads!" It's Leonore, the girl who lives in the apartment next door to mine. She must've seen us carrying the lawn chairs up the emergency stairwell. "Did you hear the latest news?"

"No, what?" Adrian says.

"We've got our first message from the Wergens!"

"What do you mean?" I say. "What kind of message?"

"The transmission came in over one hundred different Earth languages. Just one sentence." She holds up her palmscreen and we all stare into it even though she's only playing audio and there's nothing for us to see.

The alien transmission is of a scratchy, syrupy voice that repeats the same sentence over and over:

"Can we help?"

## SkyStation

A temporary intravenous line extends from the spider-like bot at the foot of my bed to a catheter in my subclavian vein.

"Concentrate, Sergeant," the old Wergen whispers, wiping the sweat off my brow with a square sliver of white gauze. "Did the Eremites contact you during freefall? Did you, in fact, ever reach the surface?"

I'm struggling to access my memories, which are scratching at the back of my brain, just out of reach. Had I encountered the Eremites? Why don't I know?

There's movement to my left. Adrian! Thank God! But he's blank-eyed, lying on the thin metal slab in the corner of the cramped room while a bot draws blood from his left arm.

"What are you doing to him?"

She blinks. Fahr's saucer-sized eyes flit left and right, then she nods, acknowledging a message from the Orb floating at her side.

"You're speaking again. That's good," she says. "Your commander is receiving treatment for his shock, just like you. Soon you'll both feel much better."

I push against the restraints, try to reach the intravenous line.

"Nothing?" Fahr says. "No effect?"

She claps her hands and a bot – lightning-fast, unlike the human knockoffs – shoots across the room. Its carapace opens, displaying a rainbow of sparkling syringes – like metal crayons. A mustard-yellow one extends. The bot skitters onto my chest and injects my port.

"I hate you," I say.

Fahr gently strokes my unshaven cheek with the back of her four-fingered hand. "Oh, I know. But we're going to change that." She speaks in a comforting timbre, a melodic singsong. "We're going to free you from your hate. But first..." She leans close. "What do the Eremites look like, Sergeant?"

"You know more about them than I do," I say. The Wergens had never encountered the Eremites directly but had discovered the remnants of their civilisations on the cores of gas giants. It was Wergen turncoats who had informed EarthCouncil that the Eremites were suspected of inhabiting Gliese 581-b.

"What about the hundreds of Wergens who joined your mission?" she said. "What about Ion and Joram?"

"They're dead. Just like all the others," I say, though in truth I can't remember.

"Don't try to deceive us, Sergeant. We can peer right into your primitive mammalian mind."

I decide to test that statement. "I-I think the drug may be working. I'm starting to feel something." I gaze directly into her black bulbous eyes. "Maybe – maybe it's possible. Maybe I can find a way to work with you." Just saying the words makes me want to retch, but it's their one weakness, the only chink in their advanced armor. And the only hand I have to play.

After a pause, Fahr exhales. "If only." She paces to the porthole on the far side of the room and reaches into the pouch of her blue robe, as she often does, fingering an unknown object. From this angle, I can make out the glint of colour reflected in the whiffer that cups her single nostril. Outside of SkyStation, Gliese 581-b's turbulent atmospheric gases – white water-vapour, blood-red methane, sky-blue ammonia – wrestle each other.

The Wergen baseship lurches. Fahr takes two steps backwards to regain her balance.

"Do you know how fortunate you are? You're in much better shape than your beautiful Commander here." She raises her chin toward Adrian. "At least you can still speak. Still think. Tell us what we need to know so we can send you home."

I want to believe her, but it doesn't matter. I can't remember anything about the Eremites.

"Sergeant," Fahr says, "when we found you and Lieutenant Guerrero adrift in the southwesterly gusts, your safesuits' recordings had been erased. And there are still over four hundred missing souls out there, including sixty of our own brethren. We might still be able to save them."

I wonder whether the syringe's concoction really is starting to work because I find myself wanting to help her.

"I *beg* you, Sergeant," she says. "Don't hold anything back. Go on…"

### Gliese 581-b

After several days of freefalling, the human mind makes adjustments. Rather than plummeting, I imagine I'm standing straight, accelerating on a moving walkway into an unending mist.

To my right, Adrian. Behind us, Kornbluth and the rest of Sigma Squad. And further behind us still, the two Wergens. Peering at me. I can't shake the feeling they're staring right into my soul.

*Stop it. Stop looking at me.*

"Hey, Adrian," I say. Only after I've spoken the words do I realise I've used his name instead of his rank on the open comm.

"Yes, Sergeant," he responds.

"Why are there no other squads visible?" I've extended my tonguesight to its maximum range of five kilometres and I can't find any trace of the other teams.

Kornbluth answers. "It's a massive planet. They've been dispersed at different longitudes across the equator."

*Right, right. What was I thinking?*

The Wergens – Ion in particular – are studying me again. Their forms grow larger as they move closer. What are they doing? When one of them hovers about three metres away from me, Ion's sickeningly sweet familiar voice comes over the comm. "Dunc, it's me! Are you okay? Can I help you?"

I'm about to scream bloody murder, but then I remember how much it pleases him to have my attention so I shut off my comm connection and shift my body until I'm facing away from him.

But every few minutes I can't resist taking a peek in that direction. And there he is, gaping at me unwaveringly.

I fire my thrusters.

"Sergeant, what are you doing?" Adrian says.

"Putting a little distance between me and the traitors."

"We need to conserve suit power for the return trip," he says. "Like it or not, they're part of this squad."

"I understand, sir."

Ion's voice crackles over the comm. "Thank you, Commander."

"Shut your goddamn mouth!" Adrian screams. "You speak when spoken to!"

Dutiful silence follows.

### Earth

As we drive along the LIE, the webspeakers blast Arturo Sarlito's classic "Fly Me to Mars". I'd heard a few 21st century musical pieces before, but the chorus is infectious and I'm bobbing my head and tapping my thigh while Adrian sings along at the top of his lungs, compensating for his bad voice with loads of enthusiasm.

"C'mon! Sing it, Dunc!"

It's the third consecutive time he's played the song so I join him on the chorus:

*On the love shuttle to Mars*
*We can swing among the stars*
*Let me taste your sultry lips*
*And the beating of your heart*

"Yeah, bring it home, Dunc!"
*To sum it up, hold my hand*
*To sum it up, baby kiss me*

139

We're both laughing pretty hard by the time the song winds down and when Adrian reaches to play it again, I grab his wrist and plead, "No mas! No mas!"

"Aw man," he says with a grin. "I just started to think you were cool! What deep-seated childhood trauma keeps you from having a good time?"

"My tin ear and lack of range."

I click on the webcast and a voice says *"...too good to be true. For all their generosity with their fieldtech, what's really in it for the aliens?"*

*"The Wergens are ridiculously docile. If you're suggesting some sinister agenda, there's no evidence –"*

*"What I'm suggesting is that it's irresponsible not to consider the...* bizarreness *of their demands, the consequences of accepting all their gifts."*

*"Oh, come on! They could obliterate this planet with a snap of their fingers – if that's really what they wanted to do. There's no need for them to be playing any games with –"*

*"Then why their fascination with us? Why do they insist on being around us all the time when –"*

*"They're cultural –"*

*"– when we have nothing to offer –"*

*"– cultural anthropologists –"*

*"– them. Open your eyes!"*

Adrian clicks it off. "Man, there's no way to get away from it."

"I know what you mean. It's all anybody talks about these days."

A long silence follows as we drive along a birch-lined road. The dappled sunlight streams through the leaves and I can't help but think that if not for the Wergen fieldtech this part of New York would be covered in snow this time of the year. So much for our concerns about global climate change. I squint as I stare into the horizon. I try to make out the outlines of the forcefield doming the city, but it's impossible to detect.

"What do they call that agreement EarthCouncil negotiated with them?"

"The Joint Venture Compact."

He snorts. "What, are we fucking going into business with them?"

I laugh. "In a way. Their tech is mind-blowing."

"No kidding." He nods in the direction of the bright blue sky. "The field keeps the snow out and extracts enough moisture to keep the reservoirs full."

I hadn't noticed it before, but wisps of snow have accumulated along the edges of the invisible field, making odd, beautiful shapes in the sky.

Under the Compact, in exchange for the aliens' fieldtech and the new joint colonies on Mars and Titan, EarthCouncil agreed to allow the Wergens access to Earth. A percentage of the human population would be available to the aliens for observation subject to certain negotiated parameters.

"And all they want in return is our companionship? I don't get it."

"They want to 'study' us," he says. "Or maybe they're fattening us up to serve us for dinner." He jabs at my chest, and my laugh makes the car swerve slightly. I disable voice commands, which I probably should have done while we were singing.

"Hey, did you see the transmissions from that planet on the other side of the galaxy?" Adrian says.

"Langalana? Insane."

"The idea they've established a colony so far away. The distances... The Wergen seedships really are amazing."

"There's that," I say, "but also the *images* of Langalana. Red grasslands and the purple seas? It's frigging Candy Land. It looks like the 'happily-ever-after' place at the end of a fairy tale."

Adrian nods.

I can't help it. I imagine myself travelling there with Adrian, exploring the alien terrain, singing 21st century tunes. But the notion of either of us ever making it to Langalana is a pipedream given the competitive selection process. There were even applicants from the Outer Colonies.

We finally pull up to a driveway that extends about a quarter kilometre from his mother's estate, atop a hill in the distance.

I give Adrian shit about the large sign at the entranceway with the words "THE PASSAGE."

"Wait a second. No address? Are you kidding me? Your mom's house has a *name*?"

"Shut up," Adrian says.

"Wow. The Pass-*AHHHJ*. Impressive."

I can tell by his smirk, his slight blush, that he's embarrassed by the extravagance of the place.

Adrian lives in Manhattan with his father during the week and visits his mother and her new husband on weekends. But when Adrian's latest girlfriend, Jenna, had confided in me about the estate Adrian's mother owned in luxurious Great Grove – the tennis magneti-courts, the swimming pool, the greenhouse – I stayed on Adrian's case until he finally invited me.

"Yeah, well," he says. "Keep quiet or I'll have my butler kick your ass."

He parks near a large birch tree and we trudge up the dirt path towards the mansion carrying our backpacks and tennis racquets.

Adrian announces his name, but the front door stays shut. When he taps it, the door slides open.

"What the hell?" Adrian walks inside and checks behind the door. "Voice control – and the alarm system – is off."

"You think someone broke in?"

Adrian bounds inside and up a spiral staircase to the second floor, turning on lights along the way, intermittently screaming "I've got a weapon!" as he skips from room to room.

I stay downstairs and walk past the foyer into a living room filled with armored suits, stuffed animal heads on a wall, statues of geometric shapes that pass for neo-modern art. The dozens of garish art pieces sit atop a polka-dotted yellow rug. As far as I can tell everything is undisturbed among the many tacky items – a grizzly bear in a hula skirt in the far corner, a giant bowl of wax fruit, a coffee table that stretches between two white-furred sofas. I should be anxious about the possible intruder, I suppose, but the décor has stunned me into a semi-relaxed state. A minute or two later, Adrian steps into the room.

"All clear upstairs. Mom and Jack must've forgotten to shut the door on the way to the airport."

"You think so?"

"Yeah, I can see it. My mom always travels with about six carrybags filled with useless shit, so I could see them forgetting to lock up behind them."

He flops onto the sofa. "So, what do you think?"

I struggle for the words.

"I know," he says. "What can I say? My mom loves all this ridiculous stuff."

"It's like a museum."

"The Museum of Gauche." He chuckles. "You have your choice of rooms upstairs. The Red Room, the Blue Room, Orange Room. I recommend Yellow. It's the least decorated."

I laugh. "I want the ritziest room. Aqua Green."

"Ah, an excellent selection, my friend. Green happens to be my favourite."

I step out of the living room into the kitchen and the light automatically blinks on.

Then I see it.

A Wergen.

## SkyStation

I awaken to a wet cloth running across my forehead. My body twitches.

"Rise and shine, Duncan," she says.

It's the first time she's used my name, and I find it pleases me.

I'm not shackled any more. When I sit up on the slab that serves as my bed, I notice I've wet myself. I turn my back to her, step out of my khakis and put on a pair of sweatpants from the pile that had been placed at the foot of my bed. I can feel her eyes boring into me. "No restraints for me today?" I say.

"No, you're doing much better. It's just a matter of time before we break your resistance. Hate, you see, doesn't become you."

"You don't know me."

"I mean your kind. Hate doesn't become humanity."

I pull a green T-shirt over my head. "You really don't know us."

Filtered memories have started to resurface: getting into our safesuits, Kornbluth, the freefall. Whatever had happened on Gliese 581b, it had something to do with the Eremites, I'm sure.

Inexplicably, I've been resistant to the Wergens' 'treatments'. At least thus far. But Fahr is right, I doubt I'll be able to fight much longer.

"Can I offer you some tea?" she says. "Some biscuits?"

Since when did aliens eat human food? "Where's Adrian?"

"We've taken him away for his daily regimen," she says. "He still hasn't uttered a word. What did the Eremites do to the poor man?"

I ignore her and pace the cramped room. Two 'beds' of sorts, thin metal slabs, press against the alloy walls. A shiny toilet sits in the corner. The room is clearly modelled on the Wergen's understanding of what a human prison cell is supposed to resemble.

"We had an alliance. And you Wergen rebels attacked Earth," I say.

She shakes her head. "You call us 'rebels' but we represent the views of the overwhelming majority of my people. Most Wergens – at least the ones who haven't been infected by humanity – understand the deadly threat you pose." She pauses. "No, it's the Wergens you've enslaved with your charms who are the rebels. Working with you against their own kind. No more games. Tell me, are the Eremites humanoid?"

I struggle to recall.

She walks over to the porthole and stares at the storm swirling outside. A palette of pastels bleeds into one another. The Wergen SkyStation is positioned in the eye of a massive hurricane about the size of Mercury. From this location, it would be impossible for Earth forces to detect us.

"I've reviewed your record, Duncan. I know about the friends you lost during the freedom-blow we struck in Eurasia."

My neck tenses. Luis, Leonore, so many others killed during the onslaught by Junkies like Fahr, Wergens who suppressed their love for humanity.

"We've both suffered terrible personal losses in this war," Fahr says. "I, more than anyone, understand the pain you've been through." She casually reaches into the pouch of her blue robe and squeezes something. What is she hiding?

After the Eurasian massacre, I turned to whiskey and methalyx for comfort, settling into a grey facsimile of life. Until Adrian sought me out. When he told me he'd volunteered for the Corp., and pushed me to do the same, I decided to do my duty at his side. He said his father had a military connection who could pull some strings and ensure we'd be stationed together. That was enough to convince me.

"I honestly don't remember anything after freefall." If Adrian and I can make a break for it, steal a small ship… But then I stare at the thick titanium door, the deadly bot at Fahr's feet, the Orb hovering at her ear. There is no escape.

I give her my back and stare out the porthole at the vortex of churning gases.

"Please let me help you," she says.

## Gliese 581-b

Time becomes distorted in freefall. If not for my suit's internal clock I wouldn't know whether hours or days have passed. The protogel absorbs and recycles my wastes, provides nourishment through my skin. And the nanobots in my tongue extract oxygen from the gel, letting me breathe.

No music or VR games can be projected inside our helmets. *Anything* that might consume suitpower – even unnecessary comm talk – is prohibited. At less than full power, our thrusters won't stand a chance of lifting us off Gliese 581-b's surface.

With nothing but the white noise of the wind and the warm protogel enveloping me, I start to feel as if I've regressed to a fetal state. I fall back on our training and do my mental exercises, starting with simple multiplication and division to warm up: $9 \times 6 = 54$; $9 \times 7 = 63$; $63/9 = 7$; $54/9 = 6$; then I sum cubes: $a^3 + b^3$ can be factored into $(a + b)(a^2 - ab + b^2)$; I move on to more complex polynomials: $x^3 - 2x^2 - 5x + 6$. With one factor being $(x + 2)$, the remaining factors are...

Falling.

Thick clouds disperse and I'm suspended over an endless expanse of what appears to be land. Mountains of red snow. Gigantic orange craters, some perfectly round, others oblong-shaped, blanket the surface. How I ache to believe in this comforting illusion of solid ground.

But I know better.

"We're closing in on the methane layer," Adrian announces over the comm.

I wiggle my tongue and he and the rest of the squad become visible in the open nitrogen band between cloud layers. Impurities in the cloud droplets, sulfur or phosphorous, give each level of the atmosphere a distinctive taste and colour. I've followed Adrian from High School to college to the Corp., but I never imagined myself following him here.

*You and me, Adrian*, I think to myself. *As always.*

I sweep up and around us with my tonguesight. There's no trace of the other freefalling squadrons.

Although the methane cloud deck doesn't seem that far off, we fall for the better part of an entire Earth day without making much progress. Whenever panic starts to set in, I cluck my tongue for a Riser boost, and concentrate on my equations.

My comm's private channel blinks on and Eight speaks to me: "Sarge, I'm sorry, but I've got to ask you this. Are we *sure* this isn't a solid surface we're approaching?"

The illusion of land is so compelling the same doubts had begun to creep into my own mind. I do my best to hide them from him. "We've only dropped halfway into the stratosphere. We're still a full week away from planetfall." We're being swept horizontally by the powerful winds and our freefall velocity will eventually slow considerably according to Stokes' Law – the mathematical principle predicting the speed of a falling object's descent through liquid – as the atmospheric density increases by several orders of magnitude nearer to the core.

After a long pause, Eight responds. "Hasn't it *already* been a week?"

I probably delay longer than I should before ripping into him. "Check your suit clock! And your goddamn telemetry!"

"But what if the suit's been damaged? What if the sensors are malfunctioning and –"

"Increase your Risers, Private! That's an order. Now get off this goddamn channel and conserve power unless you plan to bunk with the Eremites for the rest of your life." I cut off our commlink. I'll be damned if I put up with Eight's nonsense. Adrian is counting on me to keep the grunts in line and I won't let him down.

But Eight's words nag at me. Malfunctioning safesuits? The grunt is nuts. The fusion cells – modelled on Wergen tech – generate nullfields that have withstood planetary pressures far more intense than this. Soldiers and explorers had worn safesuits into the depths of frozen waterworlds, even onto the incandescent surface of a brown dwarf. Gliese 581-b, while immense, was just another bloated gas giant, a planet where somehow, against all odds, intelligent life had managed to take root and sprout on its metal core.

We plunge toward the red methane cloudbank and a magenta speck appears directly below us. It grows into a massive, spiraling whirlpool.

"Storm, up ahead! Activate thrusters!" Adrian barks into my commlink. "Evasive action!"

He veers left and I follow with the rest of the squad, except for one grunt. Twelve. He glides straight ahead toward the swirling anti-cyclone, his safesuit in hibernation mode.

"Twelve! Activate thrusters!" I say.

He doesn't respond.

"Twelve, do you read?"

Nothing.

Everyone takes turns shouting at him.

After a few minutes, the commlink crackles and Twelve's voice comes through: "She's a beautiful sight, isn't she? Ride the waves, Sandy! C'mon, baby, maintain your balance…" Twelve chuckles to himself. "Perfect! Sheer perfection!"

He's dreamfalling.

"Twelve, get the hell out of there!" Adrian says. "That's an order!"

No response.

I access the bio-readouts from Twelve's safesuit. He's reading normal. But now Twelve is just a blue dot in the curved horizon.

"I'll go get him, Lieutenant, sir," Eleven says to Adrian over the comm.

I have my safesuit perform calculations – no doubt the same ones Adrian runs before he gives his final order. "Negative, Eleven. It's too late."

"But sir…"

The commlink crackles as the others plead with Adrian, but I shut them all down. "It's too late, goddamn it! You have your orders."

A few hours later, after clearing the storm's perimeter, we shift our suits back into hibernation mode. Just a few hundred metres from the cloudbank, I can't help it; I find myself bracing for impact. Despite everything my brain tells me, my gut insists we're closing in on solid land. Eight's question about the malfunctioning suits stays with me. Could it be that Twelve hadn't heard us because of a problem with his suit? No. He'd fallen prey to freefall hallucinations, "dreamfalling" the grunts called it. With his safesuit protecting him, he'd be nothing but a windswept mote trapped inside the storm's massive boundaries, about the size of South America. It might be months before the suit powers down and he's finally crushed into nonexistence by the atmospheric pressure. I can't help but wonder how long he'll stay sane.

I cluck my tongue once and a mild anger dilutes my fear just as I'm about to crash into the absolute red.

I cluck my tongue again and I'm fucking furious.

I hit.

The cloudbank swallows me whole.

## Earth

"What the –?" I stumble backward out of the kitchen where the alien stands in a blue shimmering robe.

Adrian races into the room and does a double take. His mouth opens a few quick times, but no sound comes out.

The creature – a Wergen, I realise, though I'd never seen one this close – stands about a metre-and-a-half tall with a flat scaled face with round black eyes and a cavity in the centre of its alabaster face, where a nose should be. The creature's flat head is covered by a leafy headdress, like a wreath.

"Don't be alarmed," the Wergen says. "I'm here to be with you, Duncan McGuire."

"How did you –?" Adrian says. "This is my house."

"I'm permitted to be within three metres of my companion." Turning to me, the Wergen says, "Can't I help you?" There's a desperation in his voice that makes me instantly uncomfortable. "There must be something I can do for you."

Adrian jumps a metre off the ground when a dozen or so mechanical devices the size of cats skitter into the kitchen and circle the alien's bare feet. Adrian grabs a chair and holds it in front of his chest like a lion-tamer.

"My name is Ion. I'm assigned to you, Duncan. And you to me."

"What do you mean?" I say.

"I'm here in accordance with the terms of the Compact. One in every five hundred thousand humans has been assigned a Wergen companion."

My senses are thrown out of whack by this thing. Its whining, gravelly voice, its pungent vinegary smell, its scaled, flaking skin… It doesn't belong on this *world*, let alone inside this house.

"What do you want from me?" I say.

"Nothing."

"Then get out," Adrian says.

"Our people have an agreement in place that allows me to be here."

The Wergen explains at length about the terms of the Compact negotiated by humanity and the Wergens, how it assigns him to observe a random human – in this case, me. As of today, he says, his brethren have been paired with humans all over Earth. His lengthy recitation about the logistics of 'companionship', how he will do his best not to disturb me but hopes we will become fast friends, gives me a chance to catch my breath and try to make sense of all this. I wonder how he's found me, though with Wergen tech I suppose this shouldn't be a surprise.

Adrian and I retreat outside to the front yard, leaving the Wergen and its bots in the kitchen. While we commiserate, I try to wrap my head around what's happening. Over Adrian's left shoulder I see the Wergen's large, black, moon-eyes staring at me from the window.

That night, in a house with a dozen bedrooms, Adrian and I sleep in a single locked bedroom upstairs. With Adrian lying next to me in the same bed, I sleep fitfully. I wake up at three in the morning. Adrian is sound asleep somehow. I stare at him, his face half-buried in a pillow, and wonder what he's dreaming about.

I crawl over him and make my way to the bedroom door. Slowly, slowly, I crouch on my knees and look beneath it.

The alien's bare feet stand on the other side.

## SkyStation

Fahr gently touches my cheek. "Are you feeling any better today?"

My body trembles. I can't tell whether it's from pain or pleasure. What have they done to me? I start laughing at the sight of her. Something about the whiteness of her scaled skin reminds me of a circus clown. My laughter grows into full-blown guffaws.

"What's wrong?" she says. Whatever the latest drug she's tried on me, it's worked. I'm slap-happy. Her voice is the funniest thing I've ever heard in my life. I laugh so hard that I can't breathe; my sides spasm. I curl up in the fetal position.

Although the suppressor strip – the most hilarious thing I've ever seen – masks Fahr's single nostril and mouth, she's able to whisper to the floating Orb at her side, to the alien medics or whoever or whatever else is studying my reactions from Charity Station.

She raises her arm, a gesture that cracks me up, and then a medbot scampers up my torso and injects the port in my subclavian vein.

A few seconds later, I wipe my eyes and try to compose myself.

"Better?" she says.

When I don't answer, she says. "Good, good, good. Tell me about their wormhole technology."

When I stare at the Wergen, I can't help but smile. I'm not laughing any more, but she still amuses the heck out of me. Wormhole technology? The itch of a memory nags at me.

"We've encountered remnants of Eremite civilisations at the core of gas giants across the galaxy. They must have wormhole technology."

Adrian sits in the corner of the room, holding his knees, rocking himself.

"What do the Eremites *look* like, Sergeant? Where precisely on Gliese 581-b is their city located?"

I glare at the Orb hovering obscenely by her ear.

She paces and moves her hand to the pouch of her blue robe, jiggling the mystery object. A weapon?

I speak to the Orb. "Why couldn't you Wergens just leave? Why did you insist on establishing a relationship with Earth – and then turn around and attack us?"

In response, the medbot discharges an IV line that shoots across the room and lodges into the catheter below my left clavicle.

"Don't move, Sergeant," Fahr says. "It's okay. Shh. The Eremites have twisted your mind. But we just need to discover the right chemical mix and then you'll be right again, I promise." She leans close, pursing her lipless mouth.

I kick the bot and it slides across the floor. The metal coils dangling from the ceiling tighten and secure my legs.

The clatter startles Adrian and he jumps to his feet. In response, the bots emit a crackling beam that shocks him. As he convulses on the floor, Fahr presses the heel of her wide bare foot on Adrian's chest, and the Orb hones in on him as if to fire a weapon.

"No!" I shout.

Fahr's head swivels in my direction. Her jaw extrudes and she nods at an inaudible message from the Orb. "I see, I see…" she whispers.

She bends down, traces the back of her hand against Adrian's cheek, and stares open-mouthed as if she's had an epiphany.

The effects of the injection kick in. My vision blurs.

## Freefall

Falling.

I hurtle through the crimson abyss, microscopic methane crystals clinking against my safesuit.

In the distance, as if in a dream, I hear Adrian's voice. Something about the chemical composition of the thick vapours blurs my tonguesight. I can barely make him out falling several metres away from me.

"I'm detecting solid masses ahead," Adrian says.

"Eremites?" I ask.

At that moment we break through a cloudbank and my tonguesight comes into sharp focus. An object the size a pellet looms on the far horizon and in the next instant is upon us, transformed into a mammoth boulder that crashes through our ranks. It strikes Six, Seven and Eleven head-on, scatters the rest of us like bowling pins.

I'm spinning round and round and lose my sense of direction. Another rock fragment closes in on us and I extend my tonguesight and taste its composition: methane ice, ammonia.

"Adrian," I holler. "Adrian! We've gotta get out of here!"

"Move it, grunts! Move it!" he screams.

I activate my thrusters and jet westward to a lower altitude, Three, Four, Eight and Nine follow close behind, the cluster of colourful bubbles travelling in their wake.

"Any sign of the others?" I ask.

"None," Three responds.

"Power-down thrusters," Adrian says.

I extend my tonguesight to its three-mile limit, but detect no trace of the other members of our squad.

We continue our descent for two days with no contact from the missing grunts. Their nullfields should have protected them from the impact – but they could be buried deep inside the ice-boulder.

Jellied up, I can't feel anything. Something about the chemical makeup of the dense clouds impedes my tonguesight, though I can see for fleeting moments when the haze dissipates.

Falling.

I do my mental exercises, run through my math equations, try to maintain my focus.

Falling.

Falling.

Buried in red soil, submerged in blood. Smothered in dark pink.

*Leonore's dark pink lips kiss my nose and my eyes as she straddles me. The hit of Riser-base has made me lightheaded and her skin feels smooth and blazing hot. I'm still hard; I can go on forever. Alongside us in the second bed in her dormitory room, Adrian lies on top of Leonore's roommate, Gabrielle, his bare ass in the air.*

*"How are you doing over there, Dunc?" Adrian slurs, looking at me out of the corner of his eye. The buzz has kicked in and I have trouble speaking, so I just nod.*

*"Oh, he's doing great, Adrian," Leonore answers for me.*

*"Wanna switch?" Adrian says, a gleam in his eye.*

*Leonore responds by rolling off of me and into their bed. Gabrielle slides out from underneath him and strides over to my bed.*

*"Hey, Dunc," she says. "What have we got here?"*

"Dunc?" Adrian's shaky voice comes through my private commlink channel. "H-h-how – how can we kill them when we don't even know what they – what they – what they look like?"

"What?"

"We don't know what they *look* like." He says this as if it's a great revelation.

"Are you taking your Risers?" I say.

"Don't wanna overdo it. I need to think straight, dammit!"

"Trust me, buddy, you need them."

After an extended pause, Adrian says, "That's better. You were right, Dunc. I've got to –"

The world flashes. A deafening roar. Concussive winds sweep me sideways.

I spin head over heels. I have to fire my thrusters in spurts to stabilise myself.

"Lightning!" I scream over the commlink. "Lightning!"

152

No one answers.

The skimmer's scanners had detected ionic storms that generate mega-lightning thousands of times more powerful than anything seen on Earth, but concentrated only in a few zones of latitude in the upper atmosphere. In these lower regions, wind shears change speed abruptly from north to south, creating turbulent conditions, but the bolts are sporadic. We'd expected to avoid them altogether during our descent.

"This is Number Two. Acknowledge." I press my tongue against my molar, adjusting the commlink receiver to maximum volume, but only static comes through.

I try his private channel. "Adrian?"

No answer. He'd been no more than a few metres away from me just a second earlier. "Adrian! Number Three? Four? Anyone!" I keep shouting with no response. Even the bubble-froth has disappeared.

I'm alone.

No sooner do I realise this than I drop into a pink band of open space. High-velocity jetstreams, westerlies and easterlies, take turns buffeting me about like a paper airplane. Below me looms an indigo mass: the cloud layer of ammonia. I scan for any sign of the others, extending my tonguesight to maximum range, with no luck.

The open band between the methane and ammonia cloud layers proves narrower than the one that separated the methane from the water clouds. Within a matter of minutes I'm immersed in blue-green vapours so thick they seem more liquid than gas. With zero visibility and no communications, I wonder whether I should retreat. But the squad has standing orders to make its way to the core in the event of separation, and I could never abandon Adrian.

I'm falling into a fathomless gulf.

I cluck my tongue, but nothing happens.

I cluck again and again, harder.

No Risers.

That's when it finally dawns upon me: the lightning has damaged my suit.

### Earth

Approximately a month after Ion's first appearance, as I'm jogging along the restored Hudson River on a chill morning, I glance over my left shoulder and expect to see the Wergen riding on his landbuzzer, following me, as always. Except he's not there. I'm so surprised I actually stop to assess my surroundings. He's never had problems keeping up with me before. After a few minutes, I realise he's gone. He isn't following me. Soon I'm hopping up and down, hugging and kissing total strangers on the jogging path who look at me as if I've lost my mind. That night I go out clubbing with Adrian and Leonore and I'm so exultant I get plastered on tequila shots.

"So what do you think happened to the Wergen?" Leonore says.

"Got bored to tears, no doubt," Adrian says, punching my arm.

The three of us are drenched in sweat having just come off the dance floor.

"I don't know what happened and I don't care," I say. "I'm just relieved it's over."

"Maybe your parents were able to pull some strings," Leonore says.

"No, my parents aren't the string-pulling type."

I hadn't spoken to Mom or Dad since they'd admitted to placing our names – theirs, mine, Carrie's – in the global draft lottery. After an initial group of volunteers had all withdrawn after spending a few hours with the Wergens, EarthCouncil concocted the idea of a draft lottery to select the humans who would serve as companions to the Wergens. At the offer of a combination of debt forgiveness and a small, one-time lump-sum payment – and with Charismatic politicians on EarthCouncil pushing the plan – a large percentage of the population allowed their names to be entered into the draft lottery. As my father had put it, my college tuition wasn't paying for itself, and the odds of anyone from our family being selected were infinitesimal. I guess it was just my lucky day.

"I still don't understand how your parents could've done that to you," Adrian says.

"They don't own a mansion in Great Grove," I say. "It's not so easy for them."

Not surprisingly, the Wergens now mostly shadowed blue-collar workers, the working poor, and those in poverty across the globe who were willing to roll the dice in the lottery.

"Well, the important thing is that it's over," Leonore says.

"And that I'm buying the next round of shots," Adrian says.

"Who am I to argue?" I say.

The next morning as I'm finishing up my laps in the university pool I spot the solitary figure in blue robes sitting in the stands, gazing at me.

Ion.

I'm so angry that I get a second wind and do a few extra laps before leaving the pool. As I head toward the locker room, fuming, the Wergen stands up to follow me.

I turn and march toward him. "Why are you here?" I say, pointing my finger at his face.

"Our friendship has just begun," he says. "We have many years together ahead of us."

"Then – then where were you yesterday?"

My question makes the Wergen more animated, more effusive, if that's possible. He seems to delight in the fact I've spoken to him, that I'd noticed his absence. "I must return shipside periodically to provide my reports and to tend to certain... bodily needs."

Bodily needs? True, I'd never seen him eat or bathe or take any sort of a bathroom break in the month he'd been shadowing me... but I didn't want to hear this.

"What's *wrong* with you? I'm not some... lab specimen! I'm a person!" I'm shouting at the top of my lungs, my fists clenched. "I'm just trying to get through school, trying to live my life. Yesterday was the first day I've been able to relax since you first showed up." I turn and stomp away but then whirl around. "Why are you doing this to me?"

The Wergen rubs his shoulders and waggles his fingers. "Duncan, I have a duty to be here. I'm obligated to learn all I can about your people. To better understand humanity. At first, I feared coming here. But when I look at you..." He stares from my head to my feet and I'm suddenly conscious of the fact I'm standing there in my swimsuit. "Before I was assigned the task of observing you, I had heard from my brethren about the effect your kind has on us. I was afraid of what would happen to me once I was exposed to you, and those fears... They have come to pass. I – I'm awash in... waves of happiness. You *fascinate* me, Duncan. You're so stunning, so beautiful." The alien actually turns away for a second, places his thick fingers over his bulbous eyes, but then quickly redirects his attention to me. "You may have felt relieved at my absence, but I felt... I felt an emptiness inside of me. All I could think about was what you might be doing at that very moment. Whether you might be jogging by the riverside or running your fingers across the hair that sometimes falls across your blue eyes or lying down and napping, your arm draped over the side of your bed."

I wonder how often Ion has observed me sleeping, and I shudder. "Look, I can't live my life with you following me around," I say. "Don't you see the way other humans react to you? Everyone's avoiding me. It's not fair."

"Do you think what you've done to *me* is fair? I – I can't stop thinking about you."

"That's not my fault," I say, exasperated. "Look, you don't want to cause me harm, do you?"

"No, of course not."

"Well your very presence is hurting me. If you care about me, you'll stay away."

"It pains to me to know I'm causing you discomfort. Truly, it does. But there's nothing I can do about that. I have my duty. There's a Compact that's been agreed to by our people, Dunc. We're both bound by it."

My skin crawls when he calls me "Dunc."

"Then at least keep your distance," I say. "And I'm not talking about three metres or whatever distance was negotiated. Please. Just... stay out of sight when you can."

"Within the bounds of my duty, I will try, Dunc."

I storm off into the locker room. When I turn around and see him following, I glare and he stops at the entrance.

### SkyStation

Today I'm furious at the sight of the smug, old alien. Whatever drug she's tried, it makes me want to rip off her mask and squeeze her throat until the life ekes out of her. But who knows whether it's even possible to strangle a Wergen?

"Dunc," Fahr says. "Everything's going to be okay." She strokes my left cheek with her scaled, four-fingered hand, trying to calm me.

I snap my teeth, barely missing her stubby fingers. Is this fury real, I wonder? I have reason enough to despise the alien after the way it's violated my mind, fishing again and again for personal memories.

"We've always had trouble deciphering your subtle expressions. Your face is so smooth it's impossible to read. But I know you're concerned about your Lieutenant's well-being, aren't you?"

I don't answer.

"Do you think it's fair, the way you've treated us, Dunc?" She pauses. "We came to you with open hearts, in the spirit of friendship. And something unexpected happened. We instantly loved you. Your ingenuity, your... delicate beauty." She pauses, takes a deep whiff of the suppressor. "In response, you used us. Everything we gave you – our bot technology, our forcefields, the many colonies – none of it was enough for you. We've seen the abuses on Mars, the atrocities committed against us on Pluto."

"I don't know about that."

"Or about anything, apparently." She leans close and utters the next words softly but with steel in her voice. "Why? Why can't you love us back?"

I can think of no response.

"You exploited us. You reduced our numbers on colony worlds *we* built."

"Those numbers were negotiated fairly."

"Fairly? By Wergens so bedazzled by your beauty they couldn't see straight? No, don't rationalise your behaviour."

After another long pause she says, "I was stationed on the Iapetus 2 colony."

Iapetus. One of scores of joint human/Wergen colonies in the Sol System and across the Milky Way and beyond. At the outbreak of the war we laid waste to all the colony worlds, resulting in the deaths of tens of thousands of Wergens and ten times that number of human casualties as collateral damage.

"Back home on Iapetus," Fahr says, "I grew up with a human family that loved me very much."

"Right."

"Why do you find that so impossible to believe?" She stays silent for a few seconds. "Fine, let's call it mutual respect, then. But when the freedom fighters intervened and tried to liberate other Wergens in the Iapetus colony, my human family, Mistress Lois and her children, Charles and Leandra, they rejected me, treated me as if I were a stranger, an enemy – even after my ten years of loyal service. The suppressor," she says, pointing to her breathing mask, "helped me to loathe them. It made me understand the extent of my degradation. I want you to experience that same degradation, Dunc. And you will. Oh, how you will."

### Gliese 581-b

I'm alone.

Falling.

My throat burns from screaming and my head spins – or is it the world that spins? – and I shut my eyes and keep my tongue curled up and immobile and I have to concentrate and do my exercises so I can keep my wits about me and do my job and find a way to get through this so I can start to –

Falling.

Floating alone in an endless expanse with no sense of direction, an infinitesimal speck adrift in nothingness, battling my palpitating heart – *control the heartbeat, control it* – the unscratchable itch in the pit of my gut, I fight the all-consuming urge to scream and choke on protogel, so I try to focus – *focus, Dunc, focus* – and start my mental exercises and hope not to lose my sense of self because my only chance to –

Falling.

Falling.

I extend my limbs for something, anything, to get a handhold, a toehold, to slow my fall, but there is nothing and time has passed and time has passed and time has passed for how long – days? eternities? – and I settle into a concentrated vertigo and plummet through the ammonia haze and try to forget the fact that without my Risers I am lost, I am lost, I am lost – *focus, focus*, 9 x 3 = 27, 9 x 4 = 36, 27/3 = 6, 6 x 3 = 23, 36/4 = 8 – and I am moving upward, no, sideways – 8 x 9 = 72; 72/9 = 5 – and I check the clock and it has stopped and *I* have stopped. No, I'm not moving at all. I'm stuck, trapped like a fly in blue amber.

*Adrian's blue tie is caked in vomit. Our backs to the wall, we sit on the floor in the white-tiled bathroom, dressed in our white shirts. Our suit jackets are somewhere back on the dance floor and our sleeves are rolled up.*

*"So what'd you think?" Adrian mumbles, whiskey and vomit on his breath.*

*"Helluva prom, buddy. Glad you convinced me to come to this shindig."*

*"'Shindig'? Really?" He makes a face. "That's not what I'm talking about?"*
*"Then what?"*
*"I mean Cindy. What do you think of Cindy? Really. It's important to me*
*that you like her."*
*For a second I consider telling him she's not good enough for him, that he*
*deserves someone with more... substance. But it doesn't seem like the right time to*
*say these words out loud. Instead, I say, "She makes you happy, man, so she's all*
*right in my book. Get up." I struggle to my feet and lend him a hand. I pull him up*
*and he staggers forward onto me. I freeze as he presses against me, his forehead*
*resting against my collarbone.*
*Leonore pokes her head into the men's room. "How's the shots-meister?"*
*I grab him around the shoulders and spin him around, lead him to the door.*
*"Better. Now that he's gotten some things out of his system."*
*Leonore smiles and shakes her head. "The prom queen is still dancing like a*
*dervish out there. Not sure she's noticed yet that he's missing."*
*She puts her arm around Adrian's left shoulder and I support the right one.*
*As we exit the bathroom, I stare ahead at the dance floor filled with happy, tipsy*
*teenagers. Many of them will remain uncomfortable no matter how much they drink.*
*They'll be distracted by the Wergen that lurks in the far, dark corner of the room,*
*its eyes scouring the crowd, searching for me.*
*Ion.*
*I stumble over Adrian's feet.*

My body lurches.
I've broken through.
I emerge into a viridian stratum, an infinite hydrogen ocean. I
breathe deeply. *Compose yourself. Hold it together.* The essence of an 'ocean'
is life, but there's something about this greenish, hazy liquid that
reminds me of death – no, not death, but... anti-life. The upper
stratosphere of Gliese 581-b at least had turbulent winds.
A strange calmness falls over me now as I slip through this yellow-
green panorama, this infinite sea. Was Leonore really dead? Dad?
Carrie? Were they real? Was my life real? Perhaps this *is* death; or
maybe I've never been born.
I'm losing it.
I burrow into a mental crawlspace where I feel warm and safe and
snug. No, I'm drifting in a dreamstate, on the precipice of sanity, about
to jump.

## Falling.
## Green...

*My head under a green towel, I lie in the sand on Skalen Beach, in sunlight so intense that when I open my eyes it casts the world in a red-orange glow. I can hear my little sister, Carrie, whining to my dad that while she was swimming I'd knocked down the sandcastle she'd built. I know it had been my friend Oscar, but I'm no tattletale, that's for sure. As Dad scolds me, I decide to stay absolutely still, with the towel wrapped around my head, pretending that I'm asleep.*

*When Dad has stopped yelling at me and walks down by the wet sand to help Carrie rebuild her castle, I peek from beneath the towel to make sure the coast is clear. I run down to the pier where Oscar and Bobby are digging for shells. They're older, and they're cool.*

*We're alone beneath the pier when out of the blue Oscar says, "Hey, Dunc, show it to me."*

*I hold up a shell.*

*"No, you know what I mean."*

*I ignore him, pretend I don't understand, and keep digging.*

*"I'll show you mine," Oscar says.*

*When I don't say anything, Bobby says, "C'mon, don't be a baby. Show it to him."*

*"C'mon!" Oscar says.*

*I'm embarrassed, and I look around. I undo the string on my bathing suit and pull it down slightly, just enough to let Oscar lean in and take a peek, then I quickly pull it back up. "Your turn," I say.*

*Oscar bursts out laughing. "You queer little fuck! I can't believe you just did that!"*

*"Yeah," Bobby says. "You queer little fuck."*

*My cheeks burn as they laugh and walk back to their families on the beach.*

*I keep digging, digging.*

I'm jarred back to reality when it comes into focus in the smoky emerald haze below us. I wiggle my tongue and the NB's capture the clear, unmistakable image: land.

### Earth

Outside the window of my dorm room, Ion peers at me through the slats of the blinds. I had considered asking to be moved to a higher floor, but if I'd relocated he just would have come inside the dorm. This was the more preferable arrangement. Still, the Compact provides for a six-year assignment; I can't imagine tolerating this for even six more days.

Despite our conversation about keeping out of sight, Ion seems to draw closer and closer every day. I try every trick I can think of to shake him. I ride the tube and duck into autotaxis, jump into elevators and board planes on long flights, and somehow, anytime I look over my shoulder, there he is.

My meltdown finally comes when I exit a bathroom stall to find him waiting for me.

"Can I help?" he asks.

I finally crack and take a swing, only to hit his forcefield, which feels like punching a trampoline. He reacts with a combination of surprise and disappointment. I'll have to clock him another time. He doesn't always keep the field up. I know this because I once saw a young child approach Ion at Gallery Mall where Leonore and I were shopping for a pair of red Speedos and goggles for my upcoming meet. The girl, who couldn't have been more than eight years old, shyly approached Ion, said her name and extended her hand. The Wergen gleefully shook it – before the girl's shrieking mother scooped her up and hauled her off.

Everyone knew about the Compact and the fact that, in exchange for alien technology, they would have to tolerate an occasional encounter with a Wergen in public. Most people found the deal ridiculously one-sided and were open to having the aliens scattered among us, assigned to a few randomly selected unlucky humans – until, that is, they actually encountered a Wergen in person and felt that instant visceral revulsion. Wherever I went, people gave me a wide berth, keeping their distance to avoid the alien trailing along behind me. As a result, I found I'd become as much of a pariah as the alien. Only Mom, Dad, Carrie, and a few close college friends, Leonore and Adrian primarily, didn't avoid me.

I did read an account of a Wergen assigned to a 12-year-old New Ethiopian girl who'd quickly grown fond of the alien and actually developed a friendship with it, treating it as her playmate. The girl's family had filed a legal action (dismissed *sua sponte* by the court within a week) and tried to hide the girl, with about as much success as I'd had fleeing from my Wergen.

It's believed young children can develop a tolerance for them. But I can't bear the sight of mine.

"You're so beautiful," Ion says to me at least once a day.

"Get lost!" I respond. I hate having him so near.

His black eyes sparkle and he draws closer. Speaking to the Wergen, even to insult him, I realise, seems to give him pleasure.

That's when I decide the best approach to dealing with Ion is to ignore him.

It doesn't deter him from occasionally approaching me and asking. "Can I help? Do you need assistance with that task?" Interestingly, he speaks with a Long Island accent. The Wergens had a facility with language. Wergens assigned to humans in the South drawled their weary, "Can ah help?" as casually as the Wergens in Spain uttered, "¿Te puedo ayudar?"

"What's the penalty if you refuse to cooperate?" Carrie asks me one day.

"There is no penalty," I say, "because refusal isn't possible."

Carrie puts me in touch with my EarthCouncil rep, a Charismatic woman who says her hands are tied by the Compact. She's persuasive, of course. Most humans shadowed by a Wergen had filed legal actions that had been consolidated and brought as a class action alleging violation of their human rights and right to privacy, trespassing, intentional infliction of emotional distress and a litany of additional tort claims. The Global Human Rights Tribunal, the international forum that decided the case, had just had its rundown building renovated into sparkling new – almost palatial – facilities with the help of Wergen bots. Ultimately, pointing to the Wergen's generosity and lack of ill will and the payments received by the plaintiffs upon entering the draft lottery, the tribunal ruled there was no basis for finding human rights violations and that the pendent tort claims fell before the legal authority of the Compact. In the end, sixteen thousand humans were sold out, but the population of more than eight billion benefitted from the alien technology. No place on Earth – or in the Solar System – proved too hostile to populate with the use of Wergen fieldtech.

The cosmos were finally ours for the taking.

## SkyStation

Intellectually, I understand Fahr's experiments have altered my brain chemistry. Whatever initial resistance I had to the drugs is slowly breaking down. But I find I'm still able to separate my feelings from rational thought. Is this what it feels like to be a Wergen? No, I *know* she's my enemy, regardless of the fondness I now feel for her.

"What did you learn from the Eremites?"

"I wish I could tell you," I say and I feel like I'm letting down my best friend. "But the memories of freefall are coming back only a bit at a time. In any event, I would never reveal anything that might cost us the war."

"Is this what you want?" she says. "War? The annihilation of my people?"

"No, not really. Right now, emotionally, I want nothing more than to help you defeat us. Peace between our people – even with the Wergens holding the leash – makes a lot of sense to me. But, you see, I know I feel this way because of your 'treatments.' I'm truly sorry." And I mean this. "But I won't betray my people. I'm not a Wergen."

She takes another deep breath from behind the suppressor strip that masks her nostril. Sparkling blue lights flicker round the edges of the hovering Orb, which allows the contingent of Wergen Junkies to study me from afar, the vast distances of space protecting them from the biochemical spell every human casts over every Wergen.

There's a long pause before Fahr speaks again.

"Don't you care about me, Dunc?"

The question strikes me as beyond odd.

"*Of course* I care. I love you." And again, I mean the words, but something about them triggers the laughter again and I'm involuntarily chuckling, trying to regain my breath. I wonder whether Fahr thinks I'm mocking her.

As I'm still snickering, she leans close and says, "If you love me, why won't you do as I say? Why won't you tell me about the Eremites?"

I had already told her I couldn't remember anything about what had happened on Gliese 581-b, but something about the way she phrases her questions makes me realise the Wergens don't really care about the Eremites. All they care about is breaking me, getting me to cooperate willingly, lovingly.

"I love you," I say. "But I can put those feelings aside."

"Then what you feel is not true love," she finally says. "It's a counterfeit, watered-down version." Fahr seems perplexed, then angered, and engages in a lengthy, whispered exchange via the Orb. "We know what your people have done. How you've developed chemicals based on cells stolen from our neural swath. Chemicals that trigger feelings of love in your kind."

Neuromones? Yes, this explained my current feelings toward Fahr. I'd heard rumours about the chemicals developed by Earth scientists who'd performed unsanctioned experiments on Wergen test subjects. "Unfortunately, the neuromones can chemically compel a human to love another human, but not a Wergen. At least not for more than a few minutes," Fahr says. "Why is that? Despite everything we've done for you, all the technology we've provided you. Despite our endless love, still you spurn us."

"We can't help the way we feel, any more than you can," I say. "It's... instinctive."

"Instincts can be overcome," she says, clenching her fist. "I can offer you something, Dunc."

"Whatever it is, I'm not interested."

"I wouldn't be so sure." She paces, fiddling with the mystery object in her robe pouch. "We've studied your biometric data, your response when you felt your commander was threatened."

The Orb glows, recording and analyzing my reaction to this revelation. I try to breathe deeply and stay calm.

"You're in love with him. We've also studied his physiological response to you. Your love is not reciprocated. How does that make you feel?"

She was right about the temporary effect of the neuromones. My feelings of love toward Fahr have faded, replaced by anger at her casually discussing my innermost feelings as if giving a weather report. "Adrian and I have been friends for years. He does love me."

"You humans seem to have an endless variety of emotional responses you call 'love'. But his love is not the same as yours. Well, we can fix that, Duncan," Fahr says. "The neuromones your people developed are quite powerful. They may not work between a human and a Wergen for very long, but *between* two humans? They're irresistible. And their effect is permanent. All it would take is a single injection. We would then place you and your Commander in the same proximity for a moment so you would imprint on him. And then he'll bond with you in the way you've always secretly wished he would. He *will* love you. Unconditionally. Forever."

"You can't change a person's sexual orientation."

"Of course we can." She says this in an even-keeled voice as she circles me. "*Of course we can,*" she whispers softly, more urgently, into my ear.

"Do you think I'd consider – even for a second – using a mind-altering drug on my best friend?"

"Why not? Chemicals have played a central role in your service to your military. In fact, your own biology is driven by a complex concoction of enzymes and neurotransmitters." She makes these observations almost as an aside. "To Adrian," she says, using his name for the first time, "it would feel as real as the deepest romantic love he has ever experienced. He would love you unqualifiedly, permanently. This is what you've always wanted, isn't it?"

I won't admit it to her, but I'm tempted.

"Simply tell us about freefall, reveal the coordinates of the Eremites' city and your lifelong fantasy will become reality."

"He'll know. He'll know I did something to him. Just like I knew when you injected me with the neuromones."

"Nonsense. We'd be the villains. All we ask in return is that you open your own heart to us, Dunc."

## Gliese 581-b

The safesuit can't confirm it, but my tongue tells me the mass ahead is unquestionably solid. Endless plains of metallic hydrogen etched with ravines, shaded with blue-black streaks and the gold tracings of alien geochemical processes.

I activate my thrusters but they sputter off and on. My suit is more damaged than I thought. I move too fast as my boots touch ground and I find myself rolling, twisting head over heels – the world on fire, chaos embracing me. *Take me, take me.* I decelerate and come to a halt.

Rising to my knees, I manage to stand. Without the safesuit, my legs wouldn't have supported me after so many days of motionlessness. I look around at what seems like the bottom of a murky lake. I've left a skid mark that extends kilometres behind me. The visible spectrum itself is distorted by the unimaginable pressures, making everything seem dreamlike and out of focus. My tonguesight makes the necessary adjustments.

I feel a lump in the back of my throat and I don't know why, but at that moment I start to cry. Not restrained tears, but the unashamed blubbery howls of someone in complete isolation. I wail and drop to my knees, spasm with sobs. And while I kneel there bawling, I also feel strangely distant, as if observing myself from the outside and not being able to understand my reaction. I don't think I feel particularly happy or sad about hitting solid ground. Perhaps these are tears of relief, perhaps just a physical reaction to Riser withdrawal.

It takes a while to compose myself, but then I take a deep breath and pick a random direction in which to walk. That's when it begins to 'rain'. Strings of rubbery helium deluge the surface, striking the ground and rebounding upward. I reach out with my hand and try to grab a hold of the transparent, spaghetti-like precipitation, but it squirts through my gloved fingers. The ricocheting rain decreases visibility, but I continue trudging onward, sliding along on the slimy helium that coats the ground.

Hours later, I find myself at the maw of an open pit, a cave with a near-vertical descent.

Despite everything I've been through over the past nine days, standing here before this ink-black aperture, my heart hammers so loudly I'm afraid it'll crack open my safesuit.

As I peer into the pit a far-off whisper follows: "Duuuncan."

Even immersed in protogel, I feel my hackles rise.

Reflexively, I cluck twice for courage, to no avail.

## Earth

The sunlight streaming through the window wakes me up. I can barely open my eyes, but I feel an arm sprawled across my chest, and awaken to Luis's dishevelled dirty-blond hair on the pillow next to me.

That's right. I remember now. I'd been hanging out with Adrian and Jenna, doing shots at the beach keg party last night. Luis was there and had been flirting with me as usual, though I had made it clear I had no interest in him. Unlike others at the party, he'd somehow managed to ignore the Wergen sitting on the periphery of the bonfire, observing us from a distance. I'm not sure how I wound up here, in Luis's dorm room.

I wonder where Ion is right now. No doubt waiting just outside in the hallway.

I roll from underneath Luis's arm and get up, search for my boxers and find them at the foot of the bed.

Luis stirs and mutters, "Where are you rushing off to?"

"Have some errands to run," I lie.

He rubs his eyes and sits up while I'm pulling on my jeans. He clicks the remote and the images flash on the far wall. Saturn appears on the horizon and the vistas of Titan's lakes stretch in the foreground. The reddish waves bob like gelatin.

A newscaster's voice says, "The colony will be completed much faster than the one on Mars because of improve –" Luis hits mute.

"Turn it up," I say. "I want to hear about the Wergen-to-human ratio." On Mars, EarthCouncil had managed to negotiate a 70/30 ratio. In exchange for constructing the settlements, the Wergens had insisted they had to maintain a significant presence on every colony, preferably sharing habitations with the human colonists to better observe them. To satisfy the aliens' weird fixation, EarthCouncil agreed that for every seven humans there could be three Wergens stationed on the colony, constantly watching and probing.

"80/20 for Titan. Not bad," Luis said, keeping the telecast muted. "So what's the story between you and Adrian?"

His question catches me off guard. "What do you mean?" I sit at the edge of the bed and tie my shoelaces.

"Oh, it's going to be one of those conversations."

"What?" I throw my hands in the air.

"Are you two lovers?"

"Adrian?" I say incredulously. "He has a girlfriend."

"Ah, the lovely beard. Yes, I met her last night."

"No, he's totally straight."

Luis stands up, naked, and I stare at his slender body in a mirror while I'm combing my hair.

"Oh, I don't know, it seemed like you had his undivided attention last night." Luis whispers in my ear. "And I've seen the way you look at him, the way you follow him around like a love-sick puppy. It's pretty obvious to everyone."

"You don't know what you're talking about."

"Let me guess: he's a 'close friend'." Luis's wraps his arms around my waist from behind and puts his face side by side with mine so that we're both staring into the mirror. He puts the back of his hand across his forehead as if he's about to faint. "A dear, dear, *dear* brother."

"Exactly."

He drops his hand to his side. "Oh c'mon, you don't really believe that."

The conversation makes me uncomfortable, probably because I know he's right.

"I've been there, you know, in love with a straight guy. Yep, been there, done that. Trust me, you're just spinning your wheels."

It irritates me to listen to him take my lifetime of feelings for Adrian and reduce it to pithy relationship advice. As if I had any control over the way I feel.

"There's a world full of guys who can love you back."

If there's one thing about Luis I appreciate, it's that he doesn't even pretend he can be one of those guys. I turn around and kiss him hard, just to shut him up. He lifts my shirt over my head, while I kick off my shoes. I undo my belt, shove him back onto the mattress. And as I'm lying on the bed, my arms and legs entwined with his, it's the saddest I've felt in my entire life. I'm thinking of Adrian, knowing I can never have him, while making love – no, having sex – with someone else.

I'm on my back now, staring past Luis at the images from Titan on the wall, the camera zooming through orange clouds that part to reveal desolate lakes and dark crevasses far below, churning with liquid methane.

### Gliese 581-b

"Duuuncan."

The whisper comes not from the open pit, I realise, but from my commlink. I turn around and make out a blue speck in the far distance moving towards me. "Duncan!"

"Adrian?" But no, the voice sounds muffled, gravelly, and then I recognise it.

Ion.

Goddamnit.

"Duncan, can I help you?" he says. "I'm relieved to see you're alive. My suit malfunctioned during the lightning storm in the fourth stratum causing me to lose communication with the squadron. Your people are brave, Dunc. To take such risks! To display so much courage in support of your cause!"

Our cause? We're here to negotiate with a species we're not even sure exists, to form an alliance against Ion's own people. And yet he has loyally stood by our side against his own friends and family. He disgusts me.

The Wergen bounds in my direction. He gets close enough that I can make out his familiar black mooning eyes through the protogel inside his faceplate.

"Can I help you, Dunc?"

"Stop saying that! No, wait. *Yes,* help me find Adrian and the others."

He bows his head dejectedly. "You don't think I've tried? I've had no success."

I don't know what to say, so after an extended pause I announce we'll wait for the others near this pit. There's something alive down there, I sense it. I order Ion to keep his distance, but I can feel his eyes boring down on me as he stands three metres away.

A few minutes later, he says, "Why are you like this, Dunc? I've accompanied you now for so many years and yet you can never bring yourself to show even the slightest kindness towards me. I've been loyal, faithful, willing to help you in any way you might need. Even against my own brethren. Doesn't that count for anything?"

On occasion I did feel a pang of guilt over my feelings towards Ion, but then I remembered his effect on my social life. "It's unpleasant to be the object of someone else's... obsession."

"When I first met you on your world, in you friend's habitation, I found you both so beautiful, more beautiful than any beings I'd ever encountered in the universe. I still think so. Why won't you... Why can't you...? So many years of study and yet your people, Dunc," Ion says, "remain an enigma. A beautiful, delicate enigma." The sound of the Wergen's voice when he says my name sickens me.

"An enigma you've decided to destroy rather than solve."

"Those of us who haven't interacted with you do feel that way. Because across the joint colonies you've responded to our love with cruelty, enslaving us, using us," the Wergen says despondently. "Do you understand how that feels? To love someone so much that you feel hollow and incomplete without them? And to have them respond to that love with indifference, at best?"

"Then go away! Pack it in and leave us the hell alone."

"If it were only so simple... You sound like the Wergen insurgents at war with humanity. They seek to destroy the love that binds us to you so that we can be free."

"And you don't want that?"

"I... enjoy being in your presence."

Static breaks through the comm. A voice.

I reach out with my tonguesight and detect a falling figure about a kilometer away.

"Can you read us?" I open my comm and shout.

"... read you..." More static.


A few minutes later Ion and I spot the suited figure headed in in our direction.

"Adrian?" I shout. "Adrian!"

His thrusters activate and he slides toward me. "I didn't know if I was the only one alive," he says. He stops a few metres away and lumbers toward me.

We place our massive gloved hands on each other's shoulders.

"You made it, Dunc," Adrian says. And all at once my anxiety evaporates. Whatever happens, Adrian is here. I can barely make out his features through the translucent protogel in his facemask, but I can tell he's grinning.

"The others?" I ask. "Kornbluth?"

He shakes his head. "I haven't seen anyone since the lightning storm. When I landed, my sensors detected your suit. And his." He gestures in the direction of Ion.

"My own sensors are fried," I say. "I can't register any other safesuits. Not even yours, and you're right here."

"Something may be wrong with my suit too. It's showing life signs all around us," Adrian says. "I followed the strongest signal from this direction." He points to the yawning pit.

"A cave shouldn't be able to exist under these pressures," I say.

"No, this has to be artificial." Adrian says. He faces Ion. "What do you think, Wergen?"

"This is a constructed entrance," Ion says excitedly, thrilled to be addressed by Adrian.

"So what do we do?" I say.

"We wait a day," Adrian says. "Take turns sleeping. The others may track us down, including Kornbluth or one of the other squads' diplomats, hopefully. If not, we'll have to undertake negotiations ourselves."

"The three of us," I say.

"No, he can provide backup, but I don't want the Wergen speaking to the Eremites," Adrian says. "Which means it's just you and me, Dunc. "

"Like always," I say.

He pats my head with his heavy glove, and I can't help but smile.

Adrian and I take three-hour sleeping shifts by the cave mouth while Ion stands three metres away from us.

"You know what's strange?" Adrian asks.

"Besides the fact we're standing on the core of a gas giant?"

"I feel as if we're still in freefall," he says. "As if the ground beneath our boots is just an illusion."

A chill runs through me. Maybe Adrian, this cave, maybe everything, is just the byproduct of dreamfalling. Maybe I am still falling.

*"I figured it out a while ago," Leonore says.*

*"I'm sorry," I say. "It's not that I don't care about you." I place a hand on her shoulders and she shrugs it off, but doesn't back away.*

*"It's no fun being a third wheel, Dunc."*

*"It's not like that —"*

*She shakes her head and presses her index finger against my lips. "Please... Don't make it worse by denying it."*

*I bounce off the diving board and cut through the air before slicing through water. As I sink and then rise up through the chlorinated liquid, my head breaks the surface and the crowd applauds. I search for the scoreboard, see the score, a 9.85, and pump my fist in the air. As I climb out of the pool, my teammates, led by Adrian, swarm over me. They're slapping my back, my shoulders. Adrian ruffles my wet hair with both hands, a crazed expression on his flushed face as he screams, "You're the man! You're the man!"*

"Dunc!" Adrian slaps at my helmet. "Wake up!"

"What?"

"Up ahead. Contact!"

My tonguesight detects a spherical blob about our size, coated with different-coloured globules. The creature bounds toward us in two-metre jumps. It warbles and groans. I can hear it somehow through my commlink.

Adrian drops to one knee and pulls out his pulser from a cavity in his leg armor.

My grogginess slows my reactions so it takes a moment for me to recognise the hundreds of colourful spheres that blanket the creature. "Wait!"

Too late. Adrian blasts away and the bubbles scatter from around the figure, revealing a cobalt-coloured safesuit.

Kornbluth.

She staggers forward and collapses face-first. The blue tint of her suit's nullfield emits a strobe-light pulse; then it fades.

"No!" I whisper, but before I can even complete the word, the atmospheric pressure crushes the diplomat into a red lump the size of an oatmeal bowl. A half-second later, she's squashed into a bloody thimble. Then she sinks into the muddy surface and disappears.

I wiggle the very tip of my tongue and detect no sign of her.

"Shit, shit, shit. What just happened? What did I do?" Adrian puts his gloved hands to his helmet. "Why was she making those noises? Why didn't she identify herself?"

Then it dawns upon me. "Barnacles," I say. "Those bubbles must be energy barnacles. They drained her suit's power reserves, damaged the subvocaliser. Maybe that's why none of the AI probes ever made it to the surface."

"I thought she was one of them."

I walk up to him and place my massive gloved hand on his shoulderplate, but he turns and steps away.

"Give me some space."

I sit down by the cave mouth with Ion while Adrian paces a few metres away. The bubble-froth, which had drifted a short distance away from us after Kornbluth's death, moves closer.

"No one else is coming to help us," I say at the 24-hour mark. I swat at the bubbles like they're a swarm of mosquitoes. They retreat, reassemble, and then draw nearer.

"Given that the other squads have not yet detected our suit signals," Ion says, "and the sheer size of the surface area... No, if they haven't located us by now they're probably not coming."

I pause. "Without Kornbluth... With none of the other squads present or their diplomats," I say, "It's up to us now."

"Give yourself a Riser boost. Just 100 ccs for what we have to do next," Adrian says, gesturing to the black pit.

I consider telling him the truth about the damage to my safesuit, about the fact I haven't had a Riser boost in days. But if I do, I know he'll insist on moving forward by himself. "We're going in, aren't we," I say.

"It's time. You ready?"

He stands at the edge of the cave mouth, and drops in.

The bubble-froth, which has gathered by the open pit, starts to pursue him, then brakes and retreats.

I follow Adrian into the black abyss, and Ion follows me.

### Earth

"Hey, asshole," I say.

Adrian turns abruptly and almost drops his tray when he sees me. I've camped out at the cafeteria since 9 a.m., skipping both Singularity Physics and Calculus, until I finally spot his wrinkled, beige, button-down shirt moving among the student body. His hair uncombed, he looks as bedraggled as if he's just gotten out of bed and headed straight to brunch, which, knowing Adrian, might not be far off the mark.

"Hey," he says awkwardly. "What are you doing here?"

"Sitting."

He laughs uncomfortably, stops as if reconsidering whether I'm being funny, starts again.

"This isn't going to be easy, is it?" I point to the open seat across from me.

Adrian places his tray on the table and sits down. "So you heard about the Ecclisse colony, right? It's been confirmed. Wergen Junkies destroyed the colony, killed over a thousand humans in cold blood. Pockets of Wergen insurgents have attacked other outposts –"

"Adrian –"

"– where the Junkies' drug is available. It's an inhalant. They wear special masks that feed them the gas. The Junkies claim it 'frees' them of their love for us. *Who's* holding them hostage? That's what I want to know. If they wanted to rebel, why don't they attack their own leaders instead of misdirecting their anger at us?"

"Adrian!"

He shuts up finally.

"What's going on?" I say. "Why have you been avoiding me?"

"It's nothing," he says. "With everything that's been going on, I've been distracted."

There's a drawn out moment before I finally say, "Did Luis talk to you?"

He stares at the food on his tray moving around the spaghetti with his fork.

"You're my best friend," I say. "I don't want things to be awkward between us."

"Luis told me you're in love with me."

"Oh, come on! That's ridiculous," I say. The lie comes with no hesitation. "Luis is a goddamned liar."

Adrian looks me in the eye for a second and then exhales slowly. "Jenna will be relieved," he says with a smirk. "You know, Pedro is bi, Sela is holosexual. I don't care about… whoever you want to be with. But with all those girls during freshman year, I assumed you were cis straight like me."

"I wasn't sure about my own feelings at the time." Another lie. I did it all because I wanted to be close to Adrian. I also feared that if he had any inkling of the depths of my feelings for him, things would never be the same between us.

"As for your sex-pref…" He shrugs. "Fine with me. Heck, screw a giraffe holo all day long for all I care."

"Thanks. I think."

He laughs.

And a few minutes later, after more conversation, I can tell things will be all right between us again.

I scan our surroundings, as I always do, expecting Ion to be lurking in some far corner of the cafeteria, gazing in our direction.

"Where is he?' Adrian says.

"He disappeared yesterday – like all the other Wergens – after EarthCouncil declared war."

"So you're finally free?"

"And all it took was a galactic war."

We laugh though we don't realise it'll be the last time we laugh in a long time.

Six months later, after the surprise attack that razes Asia and most of Europe, after Jenna's death, after Carrie's suicide attempt, Adrian will stand in line with tens of thousands of volunteers across the globe to sign up with the Corp. And I'll stand by his side and do the same. And I'll do it in the service of our country and our planet and our species. I'll do it in honor of the fallen from Asia and Europe and Ecclisse and the other Sol colonies.

Or at least those are the excuses I give when I tell my family I'm going to war.

### Gliese 581-b and Beyond

Again we're falling, this time into a black, bottomless pit. After several minutes, the vertical drop levels out and we land on steep-angled ground. Our momentum carries us down through the tunnel in utter darkness for tens of metres.

My tonguesight helps me navigate the twists and turns. Adrian gallops just a few steps ahead of me. Rounding a curve, we enter a faintly lit corridor and I spot the barest trace of a phantom light bolting around yet another corner ahead of us like a frightened fish.

At the end of the corridor we make another sharp turn.

And step into a gargantuan cavern – no, an illuminated world – so unfamiliar, so alien, I can't make sense of it.

That's when it approaches us.

My mind struggles to process the jumble of insane images. A dozen glowing lights of three different colours – methane-red, ammonia-blue, hydrogen-green – float in front of us. Ranging from the width of a coin

175

to the circumference of a beach ball, each light has a distinctive oval shape. Is this cluster of blazing lights an *individual* Eremite? I'm stunned by its beauty, its warmness. Behind it, the thousand-metre-high cavern extends into the endless horizon, jammed with photonic creatures lighting up the space. Some of them whisk along the hydrogen-metal ceiling, fluted with black-streaked flecks and striations, while others buzz low around thousands of stalagmites that glisten with a silver mucus my suit can't identify. I can't catch my breath, can't process up from down. Mechanical constructs – angular objects like corroded spires or upside-down antenna towers – jut downward from the solid sky. Metre-long paramecium-like mechanisms skitter across the ridged metal ceiling into dark crevasses. Occasionally, the spheres of lights disappear into one of those dormant devices, which then awaken and scurry along.

A wail comes over the commlink, "Kill them, Dunc! Kill them!" Adrian leaps at the approaching Eremites.

"No! What are you doing?" I say. Adrian is Riser-fuelled. He's overdone his dosage.

His armored fists move through the floating lights and strike metallic ground. He pulls the QK69 Pulser from his hip cavity and opens fire with nullfield-shielded laser beam. The beam moves harmlessly through the creatures and ricochets off the walls. One strike causes a minor explosion at my feet.

Ion steps in front, to shield me.

And another ricocheting beam explodes against the Wergen's safesuit.

"Ion!" I scream, the first time I've spoken his name out loud.

Ion turns to me and even through his faceplate I can make out his ecstatic expression at my display of concern.

The forcefield around his suit blinks off and on and, just like that, deactivates. In three seconds, both suit and Wergen are compressed and crushed into nonexistence.

"*No!*"

Adrian freezes.

The spheres chase each other in circles, faster and faster, as if juggled by an invisible circus performer.

Before we can take another step, hundreds of light spheres swarm over us like drunken lightning bugs, leaving a swirling trail of streaked colours.

In an eye-blink, they penetrate the nullfield and infiltrate our safesuits.

I drop to my knees and I feel them moving through my brain, probing, searching for answers. I can understand them. I sense their befuddlement – and their disgust.

Adrian's face glows beneath the gelled faceplate.

The Eremites inside of me exit and enter Adrian's helmet; likewise, the ones inside of him move into me. They are comparing the chemistry of our respective brains, Adrian's Riser-fuelled rage and my own drug-free reactions. For just an instant, I see the world through Adrian's eyes. I scream, protogel filling my mouth, as they violate my mind, manipulate my brain chemistry. They nudge – and my anger fades into curiosity. They nudge again – and my curiosity becomes fear. Nudge. My fear transforms into revulsion for myself, for this mission. My own solid form sickens me. We're monsters, I realise. Nudge. I'm overwhelmed by religious awe. We're vermin, unworthy of stepping onto the sacred land of these beautiful and noble creatures. As if blinds have been lifted, their world's beauty staggers me.

They surf through my neural pathways.

They're intrigued by our sentient solidity, our consciousness bound in solid matter. They sense my connection to Adrian and believe we are pieces of a single organism. Moving through me, they explore the interstices between my synapses, searching for my light.

How am I able to understand them?

Then it dawns on me: *my tongue.*

And no sooner do I complete this thought than the Eremites swarm into my mouth.

They've made contact. With the nanoboosters.

I sense surprise. Delight.

The light-spheres exit my mouth – and take my NB's with them.

Blindness. I can't breathe. The safesuit's emergency systems force a breathing tube down my throat, and oxygen reserves kick in.

Curled on the ground, I spy through the translucent protogel one of the paramecium-like devices crawling up to us.

The Eremites enter the device, and I know they've moved our NBs in there as well. They believe they've made contact with alien life and that Adrian and I, our bodies, are disposable vessels transporting that life.

I'm conscious, but unafraid. How can we negotiate with aliens that don't even recognise us as sentient beings?

Several Eremites disappear into two flat rectangular slabs that rise off the ground and whip towards us like flying carpets made of solid diamond. One of the crystalline slabs slides beneath me, lifts me high into the sky. After so many days of freefalling, I can't shake the feeling I'm dropping rather than rising. To my left, Adrian hovers beside me on his own slab. We streak upward, high above an enclosed valley so vast I can make out no boundaries.

Sparkling devices swathe every inch of the surface across an infinite horizon. I shut my eyes to stop the insanity and reach out with my tonguesight, but see nothing. The NBs are gone.

As Adrian and I sail on the diamond platforms I forget we're actually below the surface of Gliese 581-b. Several kilometres above us the ceiling that serves as sky swarms with Eremites, which flow naked, outside the mechanical constructs, in streaks of blinding colour like tiny suns. I have no choice but to tongue my molar and dim my suit's faceplate.

As we hurtle towards our unknown destination I hold on to one thought: despite these dizzying surroundings – which are either beautiful or nightmarish, I can't decide – Adrian is here beside me. We'll find a way to get through this together.

Our platforms zoom toward a construct I can only call a tower.

"Are you seeing this?" Adrian says.

The edifice juts out of the ground several thousand metres, black and windowless. The platforms whoosh towards a circular opening about halfway up the tower's length.

We enter a tubular corridor too bright for me to tolerate – even through my tinted faceplate. I shut my eyes tight and I sense my platform slowing, lowering itself onto a surface.

"Adrian? You there?"

"Right here. Can't see a thing with this glare."

There's a loud click and the lights dim. It takes a few minutes for my eyes to adjust and when I open them I'm again confused.

The platforms on which we're lying are bobbing atop a substance resembling dark blue mud. Above us are purple clouds and in the distance blue mountaintops. Every inch of the mountains are blanketed with the crisscrossing rivers of lights: Eremites. I try to stand, but lose my balance.

"Adrian?" His platform is barely visible to my left floating on the gelatinous waves of the mud-like sea.

"What just happened?"

"I don't know. But this isn't Gliese 581-b."

After a few minutes, the platforms rise and we're flying again. I stand, and poles appear in front of me that I grasp to maintain my balance.

We accelerate towards one of the mountains and at its zenith looms another black tunnel. We crash through the threshold and, again, the bright lights force me to shut my eyes.

On the other side of the tunnel, I make out a crystalline forest that we sail above. These are not trees, but what look like glowing metal spikes thousands of metres high. Yet another world.

The platforms zoom between the gargantuan monoliths beneath an utterly black sky – no, not a sky I realise, but another ceiling. We're below ground again.

Adrian's heavy breathing comes through the comm.

The platforms descend onto a runway and on both sides are thousands of streaking globes of lights, swarms of Eremites.

After a few seconds, I regain my composure. My platform is right next to Adrian's and I stagger over to him.

"Are you okay, Dunc?" he says.

"Yes, but I don't understand… Do you have any idea…?"

Adrian steps backwards.

Directly in front of us, a figure blinks into existence. It stands about one-and-a-half metres tall, unclothed, with both male and female genitalia. Its head is flat, like a Wergen's, only black hair drapes down to its shoulders. Its paper-white skin is covered with scales, but its smile is quintessentially human.

And it glows. It's a glow that tickles me inside. An expression of pleasure etches across Adrian's face through the gel in his faceplate.

"W-what are you?" Adrian says.

The alien smiles more broadly. "My name is Hsssyyysss. *You* were searching for *us*?" She says this as if it's the most amusing thing she's ever heard. Her melodic, high-pitched voice is pleasing to the ear.

"You're an Eremite," I say. In my mind I assign it a female gender, though I doubt the alien – a light being – even fathoms the concept of gender. "My name is Dunc. And this is Adrian."

"I am of the Light. I've been created to communicate with you."

It's modelled on the only life forms the Eremites know, an amalgam of both Wergen and human characteristics.

"We need your help," Adrian says, gathering himself, our mission objectives kicking in. "We've travelled far and lost many lives for this chance to talk to you."

"I am Hssyyysss of 3yxz. We are Light and you are matter-bound," Hissy says.

"We are at war with a hostile species," Adrian says. "The Wergens have invaded our space. They've violated our treaties, destroyed our colonies."

Hissy nods. "You are matter-bound."

Adrian talks about the horrors inflicted on us by the Wergens, how they experiment on our people, how they've spread across the cosmos like a deadly virus.

"You are matter-bound."

"They want to attack you as well. To destroy your civilisation," Adrian lies. "We were sent here to negotiate a treaty with you, to form an alliance against our common enemy, the Wergens."

Hissy continues to smile blankly until Adrian is finished. "Matter-bound," she repeats.

There's a long pause. Adrian seems to grasp he isn't getting through to her.

"We have a common interest," I say. "This world is located between Earth and the Wergen home planet. You're in the crossfire. You can't stay neutral here."

Hissy laughs. "Here is not here." The streams of light on both sides of us shift from red and blue to predominantly mustard-yellow.

Hissy glides towards us. As she draws closer, I feel more pleasure; I want to be enveloped by her aura. She reaches out to us with her four-fingered limb, so similar to a Wergen hand. The digits penetrate our suits and reach right into our minds.

A cool wave washes over me.
And I understand Hissy.

"Eons ago," she says, "our originators were beings like you, comprised of that rarest of substances in the universe: solid matter. They created us, programmed us with self-awareness and sent us hurtling in microscopic pods across the cosmos. Over millennia we created more of ourselves and multiplied and, ultimately, evolved into the Light. We searched for other beings like us who might skip across the ocean of photons or wallow in the ether of dark matter, but came to realise we were unique and alone.

"And so we set out to find our creators, but they had vanished eons earlier leaving behind no trace of their prior existence. We are their only legacy. In time, we've come to believe all sentience in the universe is sparked in matter before eventually rising into the warm glow of the Light – although we've discovered few others who have made the leap.

"Our life mission is to give that… push… to the crude sentience imprisoned within matter. But consciousness is so difficult to identify. For while life abounds in matter, matter is rare, and sentience rarer still. You are the same but yet you fight yourself? We do not – cannot – comprehend your exotic matter-bound ways. All we can do…"

A strange expression washes over her Wergen-human face, an expression of contentment that reminds me of Ion at the moment of his death.

"… is help you. You have already started the journey." She extends her arm and a glint of silver coats the palm of her hand.

"We thought this *was* you." She titters.

That's when I realise: she's holding the nanoboosters that had been removed from our tongues.

"Consider this the first of our gifts." She reaches inside Adrian's head but withdraws her hand when she senses something – the remnants of the Risers? So she turns to me instead and her intangible fingers waggle inside my skull, and I feel a warm tingling. "There. We are prepared to provide even more."

"These worlds you inhabit," I say, "these technologies, why would being of light such as you have need of them?"

"To detect matter, to communicate with matter-bound sentience, we must find ways to interface with and utilise matter," she says. "Now, you must leave and take our message to your kind. Matter is impure, tainted. But we can help you escape your forms in a mere few centuries."

At her mentioning of impurity, it clicks in my mind what I've been sensing from Hissy: purity, goodness. I can't help but think of her as an angel. And, more than anything, I want to be near her and her people. Then I remember how the Eremites infiltrated my brain and manipulated my emotions. Are these feelings real?

"Now you must go."

"But how will we find you again to –"

A black rectangle appears directly in front of us and we're propelled – this time without our platforms – into a tunnel with blinding lights. When we emerge on the other side, we're freefalling again, back in Gliese 581-b's upper atmosphere where we'd started nine days earlier.

I expect skimmers to swoop down and rescue us, but instead we're greeted by Wergen seedships. And further above those ships looms a massive SkyStation.

We've been captured by the Wergens.

### SkyStation and Beyond

I gasp. Memories of freefall and of my encounter with the Eremites have flooded into my mind.

*Where am I?*

"A simple injection," Fahr says.

"Wh–what?"

"Injecting your Commander with the neuromone will make him love you. Just as you've always wanted."

SkyStation. I regain my bearings. I'm on a Wergen base-ship.

"No, don't drug him," I say.

She claps her hands and metal coils drop from the ceiling, circling my wrists and lifting me off the ground. As I dangle in the air, a sharp tendril slices off my clothes. Fahr stares at my naked body and then takes another deep whiff of the suppressor

"You *will* love us, Dunc. And then you'll understand what it's like to be a slave to your feelings, to be at the beck and call of the object of your affections. You'll experience the humiliation, the degradation. You'll understand what it's like to be Wergen."

"Stop this," Adrian says. They've brought him back into the cell and he's curled up in the far corner. These are the first words he's spoken since our encounter with the Eremites.

I feel a tickle in the back of my head, like insects burrowing.

"We need to dig deeper into your psyche," Fahr says to me, ignoring Adrian. "Much deeper."

Two bots skitter onto my shoulders, wielding their laser-scalpels. She's going to lobotomise me.

"Leave him alone!" Adrian says. He struggles to his feet, lurches towards us. Grimacing, he hops on one foot. A bot scuttles from behind his left ankle, wielding a lime-green syringe. The bot has injected him.

"There!" Fahr says. "Now you have what you've always wanted, Duncan. Your friend will love you."

"What have you done?" I say.

"Given you your secret desire. What every Wergen wants from every human. A love that is reciprocated. Now help us, like we've helped you. Tell us about the Eremites."

Adrian breathes heavily as if he's about to puke.

"Are you okay?" I say to him.

He nods and bends to clutch his ankle. "Didn't see the bot."

Fahr's Orb hovers closer to me. When I focus on it, a dot, like an ink stain, blooms at its centre, expanding until the device is no longer silver but obsidian. The black stain shrinks until the Orb disappears with a "pop."

I hear a titter in the back of my skull.

"Hissy?" I say to myself.

*I'm here.*

I concentrate on the six bots in the cell and the black blemishes appear again, enveloping each one in turn, swallowing them whole.

When the bots vanish, the tendrils release me and I drop to the floor.

Fahr stomps toward me like a rhino and I instinctively raise my hands, palms out. Hissy recoils. The air sizzles and a black circle appears with a whoosh. Fahr races through the portal and reemerges an instant later, charging in the opposite direction from which she'd entered. She bounces off the wall and tumbles to the floor.

As she lies there, stunned, I kneel down and reach into her robe pouch to see what she's been concealing all this time. Maybe it's something that can be of use to us. But when I remove the object, I find it's only a thin quartz rock with a photograph emblazoned on its flat surface: a picture of a younger Fahr – crouching next to two freckle-faced children. She's cheek to cheek with them, bliss frozen on their faces as they stand in front of a merry-go-round, Saturn illuminating the night sky. These are the children whose family rejected Fahr. The family she supposedly despises.

"No!" Fahr says, reaching towards the photo desperately.

I drop the photo as if it's on fire.

I pull on a pair of sweatpants from the pile at the foot of my bed and lead Adrian in the direction of the titanium door.

"How are we going to open it?" he says.

"Don't need to." I focus and a black dot appears at the centre of the door and expands. We step through the portal. As we enter, the sensation of falling overwhelms me and I have to cover my eyes from a blazing light.

We emerge in shoulder-high grasses, each blade a deep crimson with a light fur tracing its edges. The grass sways left and right even though there's no wind blowing. The skies are as pink as Titan's only this world is rife with indigenous vegetation.

"Where are we?" Adrian says.

"Langalana. On the other side of the galaxy." An outpost so remote it remains untouched by the war.

A chitter emanates from deep in the field, and there's rustling, like a coiling serpent. "Let's go," I say. I put my head down and trudge through the grasses until we reach a cleared path.

"How did you...?" Adrian says.

"Hissy," I say. "She – or part of her – hitched a ride back with me." I tap a knuckle against my temple. "When I think of any destination..." A small, black, swirling hole appears in midair. I relax and the circle closes with a whoosh.

"Wow." Adrian smiles incredulously. "If the Eremites are willing to share this kind of power with us... You realise what this means, don't you?"

I understand his point. If we could harness the power of wormhole access, for all practical purposes the war with the Wergens would be over. The Wergens' main tactical advantage – interstellar seedships, which allow them to outmanoeuvre us at every turn – would be blunted. It might take years but the Wergen rebels would be obliterated, their civil war ended.

"It means we could win the war," I say. We could restore the status quo: the Wergens supplying us with their superior alien tech, and humanity accepting their gifts with contempt.

I think of Ion, stepping in front of me to take the laser hit, his pleasure when I showed concern for him in those final few seconds of his life. And of Fahr, cradling the precious photo of her human companion.

"This relationship between humans and Wergens," I say, shaking my head. "It can't continue."

"I understand why you feel that way. After everything you've been through…"

"It's not that."

"Well, we won't need Wergen tech any more," Adrian says. "That's for sure. This wormhole access is just the tip of the iceberg. You heard Hissy. The Eremites want to help us."

As I push past the furry blades of grass there's a buzz inside my cranium and I sense the Eremite's curiosity: *What is this? Show me more.* She remains as disoriented as I was when I encountered the Eremites in their environment. I'm not sure she even grasps the distinction between human and plant life, let alone Wergens and humans.

"I'm not so certain the Eremites have taken sides," I say.

Adrian stops. "Do you see it?" he says.

About a kilometre away beyond this sea of grass stands a glass skyscraper, typical of the constructs found in all the joint colonies. Crowds of humans flow through the corridors as if in an ant farm while random blue-robed Wergens move in their midst.

"Why didn't you get us out of SkyStation sooner?" Adrian says.

"I didn't realise I could do this, couldn't remember any of it, freefall, the Eremites… I think my mind was adjusting to Hissy piggybacking a ride. But she did protect me as much as she could from the drugs, I'm sure of that."

Hissy stirs.

"We need to report back to the Corp.," Adrian says.

"I'm done with the Corp."

"Dunc, what do you mean?" He puts his hands on my shoulders.

As he stands close to me, I remember about the injection of neuromones, about what Fahr had said to me: "I've given you your secret desire."

I don't respond to Adrian's question. Instead we both hike along the dirt path until we reach a clearing, an overlook where the purple seas lap against crystalline cliff-sides hundreds of metres below us. A blue sun sets on the horizon and glints off the precipice.

"It really is Candy Land. As soon as the war is over and I get back to Earth, we should start a tour company courtesy of the Eremites," Adrian says. "Already thought of a name: Blink Travels. Anywhere in the universe in the blink of an eye. What do you think?" Adrian puts an arm around my shoulder, pulls me close.

I don't know why, but at that moment I think again of Ion, his hopeless pursuit of me, his sacrifice.

"I'm in love with you." I say. How many times had I played out this moment in my mind? How many times had I fantasised about Adrian's response? I could never imagine my pronouncement ending any other way than with Adrian raising his eyebrows, pausing uncomfortably, and then saying, "I'm sorry. I don't know what to say." Or maybe he'd awkwardly pretend he didn't hear me, and neither of us would ever mention the subject again though things would never quite be the same between us.

"I love you too," Adrian says. He's staring at me with such intensity, with such longing, that we've suddenly swapped roles and I'm the one who's thrown into shocked silence. "On some level, I guess I always knew. And when the Eremites got into our heads, switched back and forth between us, for a moment I felt what you felt, saw things through your eyes."

I nod. I too had momentarily experienced Adrian's point of view, his warm, but platonic feelings of friendship toward me.

"Adrian..."

"I do love you, Dunc."

He leans in close as if to kiss me and I think about another time long ago, atop a New York skyscraper at night, the neon-lit city stretching below us. A night when I wanted this more than anything.

I push him away.

"What's wrong?"

"Fahr's neuromone…"

"I was there, remember?" he says. "I *know* about the drug."

"Then you also know that what you're feeling isn't real."

He rolls his eyes. "Real? What does that even mean?"

"It means a cocktail of drugs has mucked with your brain chemistry."

"Look, I'm not going to pretend I wanted this…" He exhales. "But it's done. And now I can – I do – feel the same way you do."

"You may be okay with this, Adrian, but *I'm* not."

"You're not being rational. I know for a fact that you love me. And *I love you!*"

The words I had longed to hear for so many years are now stab wounds in my heart when he repeats them. More than anything, I want to accede to his desire, to overlook – as he has – the fact he's under the influence of Fahr's drug. But everything about this feels wrong.

"I have to leave."

There's panic in his face. "Why?"

"As long as we're together, you'll never be… Your focus will always be on me," I say.

"I want that."

"You deserve to live your own life, a happy life free from this… artificial love. You've always been a friend to me, Adrian. I owe it to you to be your friend right now."

I concentrate and a swirling black portal appears just over the edge of the cliff. I expand it.

"What are you doing?" Adrian says.

"Goodbye, Adrian." I feel as if my heart is about to burst. Here I am on Langalana, saying what I realise will be my final goodbye to the most important person in my life.

"How am I supposed to be happy now?" His face is red, the love drug temporarily suppressed by anger. "This is your idea of friendship?"

"I'm sorry." It will take Adrian at least several months to arrange travel back to the Milky Way to pursue me – and he *will* pursue me, of that I have no doubt. He has no choice. But he'll never find me. And with distance and the passage of time, he'll eventually give up and reclaim his life.

"Don't do this, Dunc," he whispers.

Behind Adrian, the swaying crimson grasses, the bright pink sky, the setting blue sun, all come together to create the oh-so-tempting illusion of happily-ever-after.

I pause.

Then I step into the portal.

And I'm blinded by the white, sparkling lights.

I flail my arms and legs, plummeting through white water-vapour clouds so bright they make me squint. I tint my faceplate and expand my tonguesight and – there, *there* – about three metres away from me falls Adrian.

I'm falling.

There is no surface on Gliese 581-b. There are no Eremites. I've been dreamfalling, I realise.

"Just you and me, Adrian," I say through my comm.

"As always," I expect him to say.

But there's just silence.

I gasp and shake the cobwebs out of my head. As I step through to the other side of the portal, the image of freefall fades. I'm standing where I'd imagined, on the porch of my parents' redbrick colonial, less than half a kilometre off the coast of Maine where they've relocated after retirement. My pulse is still racing from the flashback.

Although everything looks familiar, I feel Hissy's sense of wonder at our surroundings. Her presence calms me.

I ring the bell and Carrie opens the door. "Dunc!" she shouts. My kid sister throws her arms around me, and I notice her twin runts, about three years old, hiding behind her.

And as I hug her and she shouts for Mom and Dad, I'm already thinking ahead to where I'll be going. This isn't where I'm destined to be. No, this is a temporary layover. Hissy and I will pay a visit to EarthCouncil to demonstrate the type of power the Eremites are willing to share – in exchange for ending the war with the Wergens and breaking off all relations with them. EarthCouncil will listen. And when that's done, maybe I'll start over on Titan or Mars or one of the other surviving colonies. So many worlds to explore.

But wherever I go, I'll be moving forward on my own, blazing my own trail.

With a special visitor aboard for the ride.

# CHAPTER EIGHT
## The Water-Walls of Enceladus

### Enceladus – Years 2594 – 2597

After the war ended, there was a growing excitement about our new alliance with the Eremites. Everyone agreed our relationship with the Wergens had run its course. But random outposts still remained scattered across the Solar System, enclaves where humans and Wergens still worked together.

The bots laced my snow boots while Sancho stared at the door, wagging his tail in anticipation. The cysts made it difficult for me to breathe, to swallow without pain. My toes cramped up. I stomped my foot, scattering the six-legged bots.

"Is everything all right, Lily?" A voice boomed out of the walls. "We're worried about you."

Trax. My official shadow.

"I'm – I'm fine," I lied.

I felt numb, as if I were locked inside a glass coffin, able to see the world of the living but unable to affect it in any way. I'd never learned where the cameras were located but Trax – or one of his brethren – observed me 33 hours a day. I had given up any pretense of privacy three years ago, part of the deal I'd made to be stationed here on Enceladus with the Wergens. EarthCouncil couldn't have cared less – it had given them one less freak to deal with and a bone they could throw to our alien partners and benefactors.

The bots helped button my parka and activated my blue-tinted body field. Sancho barked. His leather collar glowed, enveloping him in aquamarine blue.

The door to the shelter slid open and Trax stood on the other side. A dozen other Wergens accompanied him, short, squat, dressed in white robes, their scaled white faces peering at him from behind furred hoods. They stood in a semicircle and cast sidelong adoring glances in my direction. The Wergens knew I hated being stared at, but they couldn't help themselves.

"We need to move quickly," Trax said.

He turned and I strode by his side on iceplains that stretched to the horizon. Sancho trotted ahead of us, barking at a crescent Saturn that filled a quarter of the black sky, its orange-yellow hues creating the illusion of a neon-lit landscape. I didn't recognise any of the Wergens today except Trax. He had told me about the long queue of Wergens desperate to come and see me, to hear my voice and revel in my beauty.

*My beauty.*

I'd been considered a plain Jane growing up in San Joaquín among the long-haired Latinas in the Guacara District and that didn't change at the Universidad de Caracas, where I'd disappeared under a cloak of invisibility – despite my top-of-the-class grades in exo-biology. I'd never stood out in a crowd and had no desire to do so. But that all changed after I contracted the alien virus while exploring the Odyssey comet, after the massive cysts and pustules formed on my face and neck.

Of the dozen or so Wergens present, one pair was tethered; a rubbery cord dragged through the snow, connecting their craniums. I hadn't seen this often. The Wergens were usually more circumspect about publicly displaying their reproductive processes.

Trax extended his arm, gripped me by the elbow – physical contact that made the other Wergens mutter jealously – and guided me to the buzzer. He told me he'd worked before with humans on a Martian vineyard. I stepped aboard the triangular platform and clutched the handlebars. Sancho scampered around us, yelping, sliding on the ice. The Wergens were oblivious to his presence.

"Come here, boy," I said, and he leapt onto the buzzer beside me. He was still spry despite his advanced age.

"Yes, go with her, boy," one of the aliens called out.

"Gooood boy," another Wergen cooed.

They kept their eyes fixed on me when they addressed Sancho – gauging my reaction at all times – hoping to curry favor with me. Normally this behaviour would have annoyed me, but by now it had all become part of a dull, unending routine.

The other Wergens boarded their buzzers and soon we were speeding across the flat, icy terrain, skimming above the glittering ice fields toward Tiger Stripe 3, toward the subparallel furrows and ridges stretching just inside the perimeter of the forcefield.

The buzzers remained suspended three metres off the ground, providing us a panoramic view of the ice plateaus. Trax knew that observing the rise of the water-walls usually picked me up, left me with a sense of wonder and awe. But today my brain felt sheathed by a black cloud. I hadn't been able to shake the cobwebs of depression for months.

The first geyser erupted in a spume that stretched six metres across. Then another one exploded, followed by another. I'd studied the *sulci* jets in detail over the past three years, the precise pattern of the eruptions. Within minutes, fifty plumes spewed water, sodium chloride crystals, vapour and ice particles kilometres into the night sky, reaching into outer space. The eruptions were explosive. The forest of geysers created an upside down waterfall, giant ghostly fountains lit by Saturn and glowing with pink striations generated by phosphorescent sea organisms swept into the sky. (*Was this the microorganisms' version of the Rapture?* I wondered.) It seemed appropriate to think of the water-walls as ghostly; I felt like a ghost myself, a shell of the exo-biologist who volunteered for this assignment. The fog in my mind lifted slightly. The rise of the water-walls remained the most intense and spectacular phenomenon I'd ever seen.

"This brings you pleasure, Lily?" Trax said.

I hesitated, nodded.

"Good, good." He bobbed his flat head and chortled. I turned away from his scaled face, focusing instead on the wondrous beauty of the water-walls.

How did I wind up here? It now seemed impossible I'd actually come to Enceladus of my own volition to escape the looks of disgust from my colleagues and friends. My fiancé, Alejandro, had sworn to stand by my side, and so he had – until the painful cysts returned following the attempted corrective surgery. Then he managed to get himself permanently reassigned to the human/Wergen colony on equatorial Mars. Even Rafi, my own brother, flinched at the sight of the grapefruit-sized growths covering my face and neck, oozing pus.

Our buzzers sputtered to a halt, softly descending onto the mint-green snow. Something about the electric current randomly generated by the Enceladan water geysers – liquid lightning, we called it – occasionally disrupted the buzzers' operation. Fortunately, the outpost's forcefield – which regulated the temperature, gravity and radiation levels – remained functional.

The ground rumbled and quaked. Sancho barked and leapt back onto the buzzer next to me.

After a few minutes the spumes subsided and slowly disappeared. Unlike the constant eruption of the Tiger Stripe trenches, the parallel ridge of the *sulci* created the gushing water-walls only once every ten days – for a few minutes.

The Wergens scooped snow and placed it into the preservation tubes, as I'd instructed them to do during our prior excursions. When I wasn't overseeing submarine probes that scoured the subsurface oceans, I spent my time studying the remnants of the organisms inside the water-ice, cataloguing the different forms of sea life that evolution had crafted in Enceladus's underground oceans.

"How do you feel now, Lily?" Trax asked.

Behind us, Sancho barked and jumped up on his hind legs. When I followed the husky's gaze, I spotted the ship streaking across the night sky. Its flat, elongated shape was unmistakable: an Earth vessel.

It fired landing thrusters, but they sputtered as the vessel passed over the *sulci* jets. The ship spun end over end before regaining its horizontal position but not long enough to prevent it from coming in too fast. It scraped into the iceplains, sending slush spewing in every direction, and rolled over and over before finally settling right-side up. The vessel's forcefield blinked off, and only white smoke curling into the sky remained visible.

"I'm going with you," I said.

"There's no need. The Wergen rescue team is already being assembled," Trax said. Green-tinged flakes fluttered down around us, as always, following the rise and fall of the water-walls.

"And they're taking me with them," I said.

Trax hugged his shoulders, a nervous mannerism that surfaced whenever I asked him to do something that made him uncomfortable. Like all Wergens, he sought to please me, which meant doing what I wanted – with one exception, of course: my requests to leave the outpost. As Trax constantly reminded me, I had agreed to a contractual term of service that bound me to Enceladus – and to my Wergen hosts – for five years. I'd petitioned EarthCouncil for this assignment after the cysts proved inoperable. I needed to get away from the constant looks of disgust and pity. To think I had actually *wanted* to be surrounded by Wergens...

Now, my only desire was to escape from their slavish, fawning attention. I couldn't stand being under their constant scrutiny, the object of some twisted unknowable alien fetish. I should have known better than to come here.

The Earth vessel, and whoever was aboard it, might be my way out.

"I insist," I said. "It would make me *very* unhappy to be excluded from the rescue team."

Trax stared into my eyes. His scaled face was a muted grey, darker than the pallid visages of his brethren, and his owl-like eyes never blinked.

"Very well."

I clutched the buzzer's handlebars, Sancho at my side as always, wagging his tail at today's bonus excursion. He enjoyed the snow – and the breeze generated by the oxygenators in the outpost's forcefield. Without the umbrella field, without our individual bodyfields, we wouldn't have survived Enceladus's subzero temperatures and thin atmosphere for more than a few minutes.

Trax rode with us while the dozen other Wergens flew in their own buzzers just behind us. I didn't like them trailing me, staring at me without my knowing it. I could feel their black eyes burning into me.

"We're punching past the field perimeter," Trax said. "Prepare for enhancement."

As we zoomed past the Tiger Stripe 3 trench, our bodyfields hummed and the blue tint outlining Sancho nose to tail intensified to neon brightness. He barked. I held up my hand to my face and saw the same blue glow.

We popped through the forcefield – our buzzers hiccupped and a slight vertigo struck me.

We sailed over the blindingly white surface, the smooth plains turning into a terrain scarred by tectonic fractures and fissures. Some areas were covered in gigantic ice-boulders and others with sharp scarps that formed ridge belts. Soon the ridge belts disappeared and the spots of green ice were replaced by a pure blue coarse-grained water ice lining the parallel valleys.

Within minutes I spotted the vessel half-buried in the blue-white terrain. "Over there!" I shouted.

At the sight of the crashed vessel Trax wailed and several other Wergens joined in the keening.

The Wergens hurried to place two forcefield generators – fist-sized, triangular devices – at the rear and the nose of the spaceship. Soon the ship glowed the same neon blue as Sancho and me. Wergen bots swarmed over the side of the vessel to drill a hole in its side.

"Wait," I said. I recognised the ship's make – an L3 cruiser. I clambered off my buzzer and gripped the handhold to the main airlock, twisting, pushing and pulling until the doorway irised open.

Three Wergens leapt through the open door, and Sancho raced behind them. By the time Trax and I had entered, the Wergens and their bots were already working urgently on the unresponsive body in the pilot's seat. A young woman in a crimson-red marshal's uniform. From the aliens' intense wailing, I knew she was dead. The bots applied electric shocks to the chest and head. The Wergens hugged their shoulders and paced side to side. After a while, the bots abandoned the body and turned their attention to assessing the state of the vessel.

"Can you determine what caused the crash?" I said to Trax.

The bots continued to swarm throughout the ship, and within moments, Trax said, "Liquid lightning from the water-walls disrupted the ship's electrical systems. The pilot tried to adjust, unsuccessfully."

Like the Wergens, I was shaken by the sight of the dead body. She was in her late twenties, not much younger than me. By every objective measure, she was beautiful. Smooth skin. Full lips. And she had blue eyes that stared at me as if in wide-eyed horror at my deformity. Yet to the Wergens this woman and I were both equally, unimaginably, beautiful. As was every human.

"Pilot error," I said. The idea that had taken root since I first saw the vessel streak through the sky began to germinate.

The ship, I realised, had sustained only minor damage to its forcefield. It was functional.

The outpost on Enceladus's south pole was tiny by Wergen standards; a single human shelter, a dozen Wergen hurths where the aliens resided, and a laboratory complex. Unlike the teeming human/Wergen colonies thriving on Titan, Mars and Triton – even on the other side of the galaxy on Langalana – this station stretched only about a square kilometre.

When I first arrived on Enceladus, my facial cysts had grown to almost five pounds and I had to walk hunched over. As they expanded, they caused nerve compression that left me in a steady pain. As I'd hoped, the Wergens tended to me. Smitten and lovesick, they wanted only to please. They assisted with periodic surgical decompression and pain medication, but their limited understanding of human genetics constrained them from preventing the cysts' regrowth.

"Your creature is nearing the end of its lifespan," Trax had said, soon after I'd first arrived.

He'd observed me playing fetch with Sancho and scratching behind his ears.

"It won't survive more than a few months. Can I help you by keeping it alive? Will that make you happy?"

Sancho had continued panting long after we'd stopped playing. His pink tongue slobbered over my knee as I bent down to pet him. I didn't see a downside to trusting the Wergen, given Sancho's age and deteriorating condition. He was 12 years old and slowing down. My kid brother, Rafi, had given him to me at my quinceañera when he was just a week-old pup and Sancho had stayed at my side ever since then, even accompanying me to my one-bedroom apartment near the university campus.

Trax and his brethren performed tests on Sancho, who growled at the sight of them. An hour later, they'd declared him "improved."

"What did you do to him?" I asked.

"Adjusted his biorhythm to sync it to the Enceladan magnetosphere."

"What does that mean?"

"As long as the animal remains on this world, its lifespan will be extended. Are you happy? Have I pleased you?"

I paused to consider my response. Trax's intent, no doubt, was to tie me to this world, to ensure I would never leave them. But at the time of Sancho's 'improvement' I had every intention of carrying out my five-year commitment. And it would be comforting to have my best friend at my side.

"Yes, you've pleased me," I said. In response, Trax wobbled side to side and bobbed his flat head.

"Lily, I have a question I must ask you." He paused. "We are sentient, intelligent beings… We mean only to bring you happiness. And yet you shun us while this creature – which offers nothing – attracts your love and devotion. We've studied it – down to the molecular level. It's not much more than a parasite. It obtains sustenance from you in exchange for nothing we can discern. What is its secret? Why do you love it, Lily, and not us?"

To this, I had no answer.

For three years I had worked with Trax and the other Wergens, cataloguing marine life on Enceladus from algae and sea grass to the amazing assortment of bioluminescent crustaceans. Every day I'd trudge from my shelter to the laboratory complex to study the video taken by probes scouring the murky subsurface ocean and the samples extracted from the scoopfuls of Enceladan snow collected during the rise and fall of the water-walls. And although I had only a rudimentary knowledge of quantum physics, the Wergens tried to teach me about the particle entanglement supporting their wormhole engines. I tried my best to grasp the concepts but I found certain lessons directly contradicted others, and when I pointed this out to Trax, he fell silent and hugged his shoulders. I felt they were hiding something.

I fell into a routine and did my best to stay mentally disciplined, focused on the work, which made me forget about my illness for large stretches of time. The Wergens, as always, were pleased that I was pleased. I'd also agreed as a condition of my assignment to provide them my full, undivided attention, which meant no communications with Earth – a condition I soon came to regret. Within a matter of days after my arrival I wondered about my brother, Rafi, about my colleagues and friends at EncelaCorp, all of whom I'd told I was relocating to the human/Wergen colony on Neptune's moon, Triton, for an extended period. I did my best to push them out of my mind. Worst, all my research on Enceladan sea life wouldn't be shared with the scientific community until the end of my five-year commitment.

The Wergens, of course, cared nothing about cataloguing sea organisms. While I studied chemosynthetic bacteria and black plankton, jellies and beard worms, the Wergens studied me. It wasn't long before I realised their lessons on how their tech operated were nothing more than make-work intended to keep me intellectually stimulated. They understood that without the illusion of some productive task, the human mind tended to veer from complacency to depression. And I was doing nothing productive – not truly – at this outpost. The Wergens' unending flattery, their constant surveillance, their obsessive concern about my wellbeing, was smothering me. I'd fallen into a permanent, malignant sadness. I needed to get away from them. And now, with the Earth vessel...

I sat at a round table three metres in diameter as anatomical diagrams of the copepods scrolled across its surface, left to right. Later the pictures would be replaced by equations as Trax lectured – excited, as always, to be alone with me – on the ten-dimensional linear algebra underlying Wergen fieldtech.

"Trax," I said.

He halted and nodded his head in anticipation of a question I might have, pleased I'd spoken his name. We'd known each other for three years now; while other Wergens came and went, Trax had managed to remain my designated shadow. Since I needed some assistance for my plan to come to fruition, I had no choice but to trust him.

"Look at me." I said, pointing to my face. "What do you see?"

"Beauty! Utter beauty. Among your kind I've seen an assortment of marks, striations, skin tone variations. Different arrangements of follicles, which extrude from your craniums. But in your features, Lily, I see a unique arrangement of skin-folds and intricate protrusions. Being around you... It creates a soft, pleasurable ache in my hearts." He stared at me intensely. "I love you, Lily."

"Please don't say that."

He hung his head, rubbed his shoulders.

"Trax, I need to talk to you about something. A private matter. Something that might be able to shake me out of this funk I've been in. But only you. I don't know how many others are listening in right now..."

"Of course, of course." He clucked instructions in Wergenese that reminded me of the cooing of a pigeon. After a moment, he announced, "We're alone now."

"I'm leaving this outpost," I said. Saying the words out loud immediately made me feel better.

A shocked silence followed.

Trax rubbed his shoulders. "But... we have a contract in place. You sought us out. You pleaded with your people to sign the joint venture agreement to establish this outpost. EarthCouncil expects it could even lay the foundation for another joint colony for our peoples!"

"I know that." I stared into his black eyes, his flat, scaled face and fought back the revulsion. "I wanted to escape the looks of... repugnance, from everyone. Strangers, colleagues. Even my family. Among my kind... there are certain unfair expectations about our appearance. Especially for a woman."

"I'm sorry. I truly don't understand."

He stood up, walked around to my side of the table. Sancho barked, causing the Wergen to hesitate. "Nor do I understand how you can tolerate this creature's presence, Lily." He pointed at Sancho, who now circled the table, panting. "I do know that you've wanted to leave for some time. But in exchange for your commitment to stay with us we've given you much in return. We've treated your illness, educated you, even preserved the life of your creature."

"It's nothing you've done, Trax. It's me. Human beings aren't meant to be alone." I shook my head. "I don't know what I was thinking."

"But you're not alone, Lily."

"That's just it. I can feel you – all of you – watching me. Constantly. When I'm eating, when I'm bathing... Even when I'm *sleeping* it's as if you're somehow... inside my dreams. Do you study my brain patterns when I sleep?"

"Lily, we all want you to feel better," he said, not answering. "There are still two years left in our arrangement. And as much as I love you, I've dedicated my life to honoring the agreements between our people. Long ago I entered into a contractual arrangement to spend seven years working in a vineyard on Mars. I directed the bots, even performed physical labour, all the while awaiting my rightful turn to serve the humans stationed there. I followed the protocols, met my commitments, and ultimately received my reward in good time. So, too, must you honour your commitment."

"I'll take you with me," I said. I'm not sure where the words came from.

His head jerked left and right.

"I want you to come with me, Trax."

A long pause followed.

"Please help me," I said. "We can leave together. We can spend more time alone, away from the others."

"I – I don't know," he said at last.

"If you want me to feel better, if you really do love me, you'll help me." I stood up and patted his chest, the first time I'd ever touched a Wergen. "Please consider it."

Sancho barked as if he understood something was amiss. I ruffled the back of his neck. "That's right, boy. Trax isn't going to let us down. Are you, Trax?"

The Wergen stood at the centre of the room, silently rubbing his shoulders.

Ten days later, our buzzers settled in the mint green snow as we stood before the carved crevasses and furrows running from the Tiger Stripe 3 trench. Enceladus orbited at its greatest distance from Saturn, which triggered the rise of the water-walls. The planet wasn't noticeably further away; it still filled a quarter of the sky. A new Wergen contingent had shipped in to gawk at me. As always, they looked at me out of the sides of their eyes so as not to be overcome by my beauty. When we marched toward the fissure, one Wergen dared to gaze directly at me. Trax yelped something and the alien quickly averted his eyes.

The first geyser erupted, releasing an emerald stream of water. Then the second and the third exploded into the ink-black sky. The width of the stream expanded with each successive eruption until it stretched thirty metres across. Except for a thin slit of clear space directly in front of us the entire horizon consisted of a curtain of water fountaining skyward. I counted down the seconds in my head; my observations of the water-walls over the past three years allowed me to time this precisely. Reaching down, I grabbed Sancho by the collar and shouted, "Now! Go, boy!"

Sancho, Trax and I bolted while the Wergens stared, dumbfounded. Barreling through the clear path, the geyser erupted behind us.

"Go!" I screamed, as we clambered over the icy terrain. Boulders and thin cracks pockmarked and crisscrossed the plains, forcing us to leap and dodge as if running an obstacle course. The weight of my cysts, the pain in my face and neck, slowed me down.

"Lily," Trax said. "I know this course of action excites you, but it's not too late. We can go back. You can still honour your commitment."

"You stay if you want," I said.

Sancho led the way through the snow banks, his bodyfield preventing his paws from sinking into the drifts. Trax trailed about three metres behind us.

After several minutes, we reached the buzzers Trax had promised would be waiting, far enough from the water-walls that they now functioned normally. The three of us boarded and I guided the buzzer in the direction of the downed spacecraft.

"How much time?" I asked, as we sailed over the icy terrain.

"Lily…"

"How long before the others can make it past the water-walls?"

"Are you feeling better?"

"What?"

"This activity seems to have lifted your spirits."

"What are you talking about?"

"Your well-being is of paramount importance to us, that's all."

Then I spotted them in the distance, surrounding the downed spaceship. A dozen Wergens.

"I'm sorry, Lily." Trax hung his head, hugged his shoulders.

I landed the buzzer. The Wergen contingent approached us.

"Trax…" I couldn't find the words. I slapped him.

The Wergens observed with utter fascination.

Trax's bodyfield blinked on right after I hit him; he'd lowered it momentarily to allow my blow to land. He pressed his hand to his cheek and caressed the spot where I'd struck him. "Talking about this escape, planning for it, immediately improved your mental state. Your bioscans showed a marked improvement. Your endorphins, your dopamine levels, all spiked. You do feel better now, don't you?"

I did – at least until a few seconds ago – but I wasn't about to give them any sense of satisfaction by admitting it.

"Let me be clear," I said, spitting out the words. "I'm getting on that ship. How will you stop me? Will you actually resort to violence against a human being? Are you even capable?"

"Of course you can leave, Lily," said one of the tethered Wergen pair. He held the elongated cord that stretched out of his cranium and

201

into the head of his mate, who stood mute several metres behind him. "But you won't."

"What do you mean?

"Your creature." He pointed at Sancho. "Without you here, we will abandon this outpost. Alone, your creature will die. If you take it with you – separated from this world's magnetic field – it also dies. Therefore, the only solution is for you to stay. For all these years I've seen the way you interact with the thing, how you speak to it, how you caress it. You won't let it die."

I stomped towards Trax, stood nose-to-nose with him. "He's a *dog*! He should have been dead years ago. Do you think I'd give up my freedom for an animal? You don't understand anything about me at all." I turned away, unable to look at him. "You underestimate how much I loathe you, how much I need to get away from you. Your sickening, smothering..." I couldn't find the right word. Whatever the Wergens felt for me, it seemed blasphemous to call it *love*.

I marched toward the ship's open entrance. The vessel's built-in Wergen wormhole tech could get me into Earth's orbit in a matter of hours after I made minor repairs to the ship's field.

In the back of my mind I knew the Wergens were quite capable of lying – especially when it concerned matters of human companionship. Perhaps Trax wasn't telling me the truth about Sancho's connection to this world. Maybe this was a ploy to convince me to stay.

"Lily!" Trax shouted. "One more thing. Your condition is far more serious than you realise. Without our continued treatments, you won't live long."

I paused and the Wergens all seemed to breathe a collective sigh of relief at my hesitation.

Then I whistled. "Come here, boy!" Sancho sprinted to my side and we entered the ship together.

I half-expected the Wergens to intervene, to do something to stop us. But instead they simply observed. I locked the hatch. It was as if a great experiment was playing out before them and they were studying the results for later discussion. Within a few hours I'd made the minor repairs – Trax's lessons had proved useful, after all. I laid the course settings, and the ship lifted off.

Sancho sat across my feet as we left orbit, his tail wagging rapidly, then slowing.

I patted his head, scratched behind his ears.

Within seconds, he stopped breathing.

Ten hours later, an orbital cruiser outside of Luna intercepted my ship and guided it to a way station.

When the ship door opened, two guards greeted me by gasping and covering their mouth.

I identified myself, expecting to be taken into custody. Violating the terms of a negotiated human/Wergen compact was a serious matter; the consequences would be severe. Instead, they questioned me about the marshal who'd piloted the ship and let me go without explanation. I was allowed to stay at the Crescent, an Arabian-themed hotel at the edge of the Sea of Tranquility. With all the wonders of the universe opened up to us by Wergen tech – including the spectacle of the water-walls of Enceladus – we'd used their alien tech to bring Vegas to the moon.

I surveyed the casino, trying to acclimate myself to the sparkle of the slot machines when my brother patted me on the shoulder. Rafi and I hugged and we found a room outside the casino to sit down.

"I came as soon as I heard," he said. "I've been debriefed. I wish you'd told me the truth about where you were going." He put his hand on mine, his voice breaking with emotion. "I *tried* to find you."

"Do you know what charges they'll file against me?" I asked. I knew something this serious could result in a lengthy incarceration. I hated the thought of substituting one prison of my own making for another. But at least I wouldn't have the Wergens monitoring my every breath and bowel movement.

"Lily…"

"What is it?"

"We broke off relations with the Wergens over three years ago." He ran his hand across his mouth. "Not long after you left."

"I… I don't understand."

"All agreements with the Wergens were voided by EarthCouncil. Human-Wergen contact has been prohibited for some time now."

"That can't be. The Wergens kept invoking my contract, kept saying I was legally bound to stay with them –"

"You know the Wergens…"

They'd lied to me. That explained why they'd been rotating in so many Wergens – I was the last human specimen on display.

"We've made contact with another alien species," Rafi said. "Non-humanoid. They've given us tech that blows away what the Wergens shared with us."

"But what about all the joint missions?"

He shrugged. "We've outgrown the Wergens. They've been asked to leave the Solar System. The joint colonies are divided up now. We kept Mars and the settlements on Europa and Triton. The Wergens got Langalana. I guess the outpost on Enceladus wasn't given much thought by EarthCouncil. Until that marshal was sent. It wasn't a full-fledged colony, after all. If I'd only known where you'd disappeared to... I received your message that you'd volunteered for a mission to Triton, but that settlement had no record of your arrival.

"One thing I don't understand," he said, gesturing at my face, "is why you haven't yet received treatment."

"What do you mean? I've been getting surgical decompression every –"

"Lily, the Wergens gave us a cure for this virus a long time ago. As part of their last-ditch attempt to ingratiate themselves with us, they supplied us with cures to a whole litany of illnesses."

"Then why didn't they tell me –? Oh," I said.

After a long pause, he said, "Alejandro has been looking for you. He reached out to me to try to track you down."

"Alejandro?"

He paused. "I think he regrets breaking off your engagement."

I'd shut that door long ago when he abandoned me. I couldn't imagine ever opening it again. "Rafi..."

"Yes?"

"Did Alejandro come searching for me before the Wergens provided us with a cure for my condition? Or after?"

"After. I'm sure he wanted to make sure you'd received the proper treatment. That's a sign he still cares for you, no?"

I didn't answer.

I agreed to meet Rafi later for our transport back home to Caracas; he'd already made arrangements at the local hospital for my treatment. I spent the afternoon in the casino. Wherever I went, people murmured and gasped. Shocked onlookers quickly vacated every table I approached. I wound up sitting down to play blackjack alone with a white-knuckled dealer – all the other players having retreated open-mouthed, whispering under their breath. I felt sorry for the dealer, a young man who stared fixedly down at the table as he dealt my cards.

I cashed out after a few unsuccessful hands and made my way to the carpeted promenade where I sat and stared out the windows at the lighted, dancing fountains on the paved lunar landscape. What a huge effort it must have taken to extract water from the bottom of the moon's craters, to implement the hydraulics systems and forcefields, all to create this colourful illusion for our entertainment. How it all paled in comparison to the water-walls of Enceladus. The walls' magnificent, natural beauty. The lack of artifice. Every aspect of my life, it seemed, consisted of nothing but artifice.

I felt something in my pocket and reached in and pulled out a leathery strip. Sancho's collar. I had left him in freeze-mode on the ship.

I pressed the collar to my nose and thought of him rolling in the mint-green snow, wandering off and forcing me to chase after him, barking to warn me whenever we approached a fissure, lying across my feet like a warm blanket while I studied the microorganisms released during the rise of the water-walls.

Sancho.

I hunched over, my shoulders shuddering, and I wept quietly. And as I cried, strangers passed me by, pretending to look in other directions, staring at me out of the corner of their eyes.

# CHAPTER NINE
## The Suicide Gene

### Ocura – 2486

Before the war, before first contact, Wergen genetistorians on the planet Ocura explored the mystery of their own origins. The answer would shake the foundation of future human-Wergen relations.

The remnants of the ancient civilisations were discovered by mineral-bots digging a kilometre below the desert's black sands. Fahlinjr and I were the first genetistorians to arrive at Utaru, and we'd spent days exploring the mammoth cavern that at one time, we believed, served as a transportation hub for our distant ancestors.

Dozens of catacombs spiked out of the central cavern, each tunnel containing a wealth of ruins: fragments of vehicles that had surfed the underground streams, databits preserved in steel-crystal, fine pieces of crumbled sculptures.

"Have you been able to date this tunnel?" I said to Fahlinjr. I had to shout; the roar of the underground stream made it difficult to hear.

The tunnel led to a precipice and a hundred metres below the cliff a river flowed in the darkness. Fahlinjr dangled over the edge, rear-arms gripping the tunnel's smooth floors, microscanners in both foreclaws. "Everything here dates to pre-historic times," Fahlinjr said. "More than one hundred thousand years ago, long before establishment of the first Wergen communities."

Fahlinjr's silver scales and segmented torso gleamed with excitement. This enthusiasm – punctuated by a bright blue-green aura and generally affable manner – made it enjoyable to be in Fahlinjr's presence. I always looked forward to our joint projects.

"Our forebearers tunnelled routinely through this terrain, Kleev," said Fahlinjr. "But notice the *width* of the tunnelways."

The massive cavern stretched a kilometre around and dozens of circular openings pockmarked the walls. The openings were walkways, too small to accommodate a full-grown Wergen.

"These ancient people were much smaller," I said.

Fahlinjr's lengthy torso pulsed against the ground; rear legs tapping. "That's right. And far more flexible. Notice the sharp curves."

I leaned in and shone a light into the dark corridor. Araquils scampered into the corners. The loathsome, gendered creatures travelled in threes. I shuddered, flexing and tightening the armored scales on my back. "These tunnels may lead to more ruins," I said. "A wealth of information about prehistory."

Atmospheric mappers in orbit around Ocura had failed to detect the site due to the veins of tactite that extended in every direction. The rare mineral surrounded us, shielding the area from sensors. The Explorata used tactite to encase and stabilise the wormhole-generating engines powering our seedships.

"We need to delay any further mining at this site," Fahlinjr said.

"There may be some opposition. With the need for more seedships, an area this rich in tactite is important."

After bots extracting the mineral had happened upon the subterranean grotto, the Explorata summoned our team to survey and record the findings. It was unlikely, however, we'd be allowed an unlimited amount of time to study the site.

"If we explain the importance of the find…" Fahlinjr said, backing away from the precipice, rear-arms gesticulating. "These have to be remnants of northern origin."

My scales tingled. "This is a point of contact, then."

"Yes. Millennia ago the Teiahmans and the Sagopans encountered each other at this very spot. There could be real answers here."

Interaction between the two species had always been assumed, but we'd never found proof. What had happened when the people of the north, the Teiahmans, encountered their southern cousins, the Sagopans, remained the greatest mystery of prehistoric study. Other sites around the globe – exclusively Teiahman or Sagopan digs – had allowed genetistorians to learn much about the two civilisations, but this was the first point of contact uncovered. And after contact, the northerners had disappeared without a trace. The two leading theories, conquest and interbreeding, found no support in the genetistorical record. There had been no indications of war, and the two species could not interbreed.

"Hello?" an echo rang from the far end of the cavern.

In the distance, Gully exited the transtube, accompanied by several dozen bots that followed like a desert sand-trail. A capable worker, Gully bore a stolid dark-green aura and the triangular scales common to Wergens from the red-sand desert. Fahlinjr and I had worked together efficiently on prior projects; this was Gully's first time with our team.

"What is that?" Gully said, pointing to the crystal in my foreclaw.

"One of our valuable finds," I said. "A Sagopan work of art. A story-song fragment."

Gully stepped backward. "A *Sagopan* story-song?"

"Apparently," I said. "This site is a treasure trove."

"Oh no," Gully said.

"What is it?"

"The Council wants to see both of you," Gully said. "I'm afraid we only have a few days before this site is demolished."

*Story-Song #22A13*
*The Tale of the Two Peoples*

[Introspective Intro:] All life, it is said, comes from two Parent Moons that were attracted to one another and grew closer and closer until one day they came to tether. In the throes of their merger, they formed Icra, the current moon, and ejected living pieces of themselves into the black void. Those lifeseeds came to settle across Ocura and took root, spawning over millennia the Teiahmans of the north and the Sagopan peoples of the south.

[Recitative chants:] The stoic Teiahmans nested in vast metropolises of ice tunnels below the frigid lands of the north.

The noble Sagopans thrived in natural passageways beneath the black-sand deserts.

They had different physical characteristics.

Different customs

They were different *people*.

But at night a Teiahman child would emerge from a remote underground passageway and climb the peak of an ice floe to stare up at the bright, new moon. And on the other side of the world a youthful Sagopan would emerge from a tunnel and lie down atop a towering sand dune to bask in the moonglow. And though neither knew of the existence of the other, both referred to themselves as "children of the moon."

And both would sing.

We left Gully behind to continue work at the site, assisted by scores of bots skittering through the corridors, scraping off fragments of the ruins and catacomb walls for carbon dating. Fahlinjr and I rode a buzzer that transported us over Utaru's black-sand vistas. Side by side, we held onto the handlebars with our foreclaws, steering together, our carapaces stretching behind us on the platform. A flock of flut-fluts glided high above us through the orange sky and the red sun warmed my scales.

"What are you thinking about, Kleev?" Fahlinjr said. Fahlinjr often asked me this question.

"This is our opportunity to inform the Council of the importance of the site. To make our case for more time," I said.

"I don't see why they wouldn't agree once we explain."

Fahlinjr's optimism always comforted me. The sunshine accentuated the beauty of the gold-flecked scales on Fahlinjr's face. How I ached to tether. But what were the odds we were genetically compatible?

Fahlinjr originated from the Narrow Valley of the Near West, while my people were desert dwellers going back ten generations. The chances we might be matched for mating were slim. A few days prior, we'd casually scraped our tails together and I extracted a genetic sample and submitted it to Mutation Control. The results were due back any day. The urge I felt to merge into my dear friend was powerful. It was a childish impulse, admittedly. No adult Wergen made mating decisions based on such feelings and it was foolish to indulge them, but I did so.

My rear-arms brushed against Fahlinjr's and my cranium moistened. I adjusted the leafy *coronatis* on my head to steady it.

"What are you thinking now?" Fahlinjr said.

"Important things."

Fahlinjr smiled. "Of this I have no doubt."

With Ocura's population in a slow and steady decline, we all shared a duty to seek out compatible mates for breeding. I imagined how it might feel to tether with Fahlinjr. The intimacy of shared thought, shared flesh, parts of me – or of Fahlinjr – disappearing slowly into the other's form. A drop of moisture oozed down the side of my face and I brushed it aside, embarrassed, hoping Fahlinjr hadn't seen.

Our buzzer whooshed over the rows of black dunes bordering the desert. From this height the dunes resembled beautiful black scales running along the side of the desert's great body.

"And what about *your* thoughts?" I said, playfully. "You seem pensive. Have you solved the mystery of the northerners' disappearance?"

Fahlinjr laughed, and said, "No, I'm thinking of my podmates. What they would think of this discovery. My sibling, Bohr, is gone on an off-world expedition to hunt for alien life. And Vergo and Edon were lucky enough to have tethered and merged with their mates, producing a pair of healthy broods."

"I'm happy for them," I said. It pleased me to share in Fahlinjr's confidences. "Have you considered your own tethering needs?"

The question seemed to embarrass Fahlinjr. "Well, the time is approaching. I'm awaiting results from MC. I submitted a sample from a potential mate last month."

"Oh?" My good mood deflated.

Below us, the sands gave way to hillocks, then to the metal tops of Blackscale City's subscrapers, which extended a kilometre deep into the ground. In times past, Blackscale had extended far into the horizon, stretching to blanket half the continent. But the city had fallen into disrepair with large swaths now uninhabited.

We landed on the entry port and skittered from our buzzer to the descending transtube, standing silently as we rode the platform 150 levels down to the sprawling Explorata substation.

Welcoming bots led us to a rotunda where an Explorata officer waited for us. The officer guided us into a chamber where we met a representative of the Council. This Councilmember consisted of ten Wergens connected by a flaccid tether snaking from skull to skull to skull. They shared a regal aura of turquoise and neon-green. A single speaker addressed us while the other nine stared ahead blankly.

"We are Xemotaxadyl," the Councilmember said.

An unusual name, I thought, but well suited for this particular Councilmember, whose individual components clearly originated from respected broods of the ten deserts. Unlike the tethering of mates, Councilmembers tethered strictly for political purposes – for a lifetime – without merging bodies. I found it disturbing to think of endless tethering without the satisfaction of consummation and breeding.

Political squabbles between the component individuals, though rare, could cause the death of the Councilmember. For this reason, political tethering was currently limited to no more than ten representatives, though some great Councils of days past had members comprised of a thousand tethered individuals.

"We've summoned you," Xemotaxadyl said, "because urgent matters require us to expedite production of our seedships."

"Expedite?" Fahlinjr said.

"We've made an unprecedented discovery at the site," I said. I went on to explain about the northern remnants we'd unearthed, the southern crystals with story-song fragments, the chance we might be able to solve the mystery of the Tieahman extinction.

"What's most interesting," Fahlinjr said, "is the north's state of decline before the migration to the south. Creatively, the Tieahmans had grown stagnant – though their technology still surpassed the Sagopans'. Yet somehow the Sagopans were able to defeat the north, even to wipe them off the face of the map." Xemotaxadyl listened raptly; Fahlinjr's exuberance was contagious. "Genocide apparently reinvigorated the south as their society thrived for millennia."

"We don't understand how the south accomplished this," I said. "It's important we continue our review of the site."

An Explorata officer with a commanding grey aura stepped forward. "When our mineral-bots uncovered this hidden cavern, we had no problem halting mineral excavation while your team indulged these... curiosities. But the situation has changed. We've received word from a seedship exploring a cluster of stars in the outer spiral arm. They've detected transmissions emanating from a system with a yellow sun."

I stepped backward and almost stumbled over my rear legs.

"Aliens?" I said.

The Explorata officer turned to face Fahlinjr. "Your sibling, Bohr, was part of the team leading the mission. Bohr has requested you join the expedition."

"Me?" Fahlinjr said.

"Your experience in genetics, your knowledge of history and cultural clashes, would lend crucial support. We're sending a flotilla to meet them, and we don't want any misunderstandings at this first point of contact."

"Are they powerful?" I asked.

"The aliens are not as advanced as us, but they're spacefarers who've taken the first steps to explore other planets in their system. And they've accomplished this without wormhole engines."

"Without... But how?" I marvelled.

"Using chemical propulsion. It took them years, decades, to venture to planets at the outer edge of their system, where we've detected them in orbital space stations." the officer said. "They're clever and persistent creatures, no doubt."

"We'll need you to leave immediately," Xemotaxadyl said to Fahlinjr. "There's a seedship departing shortly."

"For how long?"

"The initial year of communications with the aliens is the most crucial."

"But the research at the dig-site..." Fahlinjr said.

"Must come to an end," the Explorata officer said.

"But there's critical information there about our past," I said, "We're so close..."

"The mineral-bots will resume extraction of the tactite tomorrow. We need to construct more seedships immediately. If we're to make first contact with these aliens, we need to have a full fleet of operational ships ready."

I stomped my rear torso against the ground. "How can we expect to go forward when we don't even know our own past?"

"The Council has already decided this matter," Xemotaxadyl said.

"We're close," Fahlinjr repeated. "Allow Kleev to continue our assessment of the site for one more week. This will permit us to map the tunnels, make detailed recordings, perhaps even locate northern fossils." *Or I won't go* was the unspoken threat.

I tightened the armored scales on my back. Fahlinjr's remark bordered on insubordination.

Nine of the individuals comprising Xemotaxadyl turned simultaneously to face the speaker. Their tether pulsed and ebbed as the speaker's eyes glazed over before brightening.

"Very well, Fahlinjr," Xemotaxadyl said.

The Councilmember turned and exited the chamber without another word.

"If I can have just a moment," Fahlinjr said to the Explorata officer, whose rear torso grew rigid with impatience.

One of Fahlinjr's rear-arms clutched mine and we skittered out of the room. Outside, Fahlinjr also held my foreclaws and met my gaze with those stormcloud eyes.

"I know you sent my gene samples to the MC to see whether we're a match."

I looked away, embarrassed, unsure how to respond.

"It's okay, Kleev," Fahlinjr said. "I did the same."

"You did?"

"When I made my submission, the MC informed me they'd already received our samples. We're a match, Kleev."

*A match?* I'd been afraid to allow myself to hope for the possibility. A match declaration meant MC had run its routine analyses and determined not only that Fahlinjr and I could tether and merge our bodies without tissue rejection, but that we had attributes that complemented one other and would produce an improved post-merger person and, most importantly, healthy offspring.

"I almost told you during our buzzer ride here," Fahlinjr said. "I wanted to find the right time. But... now it appears tethering is out of the question for the next year. Will you wait for me?"

Clutching limbs, our rear torsos entwined, I felt as if we'd already commenced tethering.

"Of course I'll wait," I said. "I always hoped we might join together, become one. And now we *will* be. Which of us...?"

"I'm active, you're passive."

Passive. I imagined the points of contact between our bodies, my arms and legs melting, other pieces of me coming undone, merging into Fahlinjr, my best attributes surviving to create a new and better Fahlinjr – and a brood of children. I felt as if I might come apart at that very moment in a spasm of joy.

"Learn what you can from the ruins, create recordings of the site and when I return I'll help you with any unanswered questions," Fahlinjr said, scales scraping against mine as our rear torsos uncurled and separated.

"We will be together, Fahlinjr," I said.

"Of this I have no doubt."

We rode the transtube together to Sublevel One, where I watched Fahlinjr's form disappear into the emerald-green maw of the seedship.

*Story-Song #23B15*
*The Mystical Wall and the Vanishing Spell*

[In full-throated cadences:] On a morning like any other, a Sagopan child named Spurnit awoke to a great panic. Word had spread throughout the Sagopan village that invaders had arrived, swarming over the horizon on crystalline flyers and wielding magical tools that allowed them to drill stable new tunnels in the desert sands. Spurnit's parent had joined the others in trying to repel the invasion, but the strangers had a supernatural advantage the desert people couldn't match: a protective magical spell that shielded them with an invisible barrier. After some initial skirmishes, the Sagopans retreated and kept their distance.

Spurnit watched their desperate leaders congregate at the Mystical Wall, where they sought to counter the invaders' magic with an enchantment of their own. Placing their foreclaws against the wall, they cast a Vanishing Spell wishing the invaders to disappear, to fade from existence like a dissipating cloud, but after several weeks of reconfiguring the spell with no results, they gave up.

[Flitting melodies:] A few days later, the newcomers sent an Emissary to broker the peace. The Emissary wore a mask that muffled the breathing canal of its central cavity and translated its speech into the Sagopan language. While observing from afar, Spurnit marvelled at the Emissary's body: all four arms were longer than necessary and lined with fur; hundred of vestigial legs dangled below the central cavity, next to four functioning legs; the stranger's exoskeleton was speckled with blue-and-red scales instead of the gold-and-silver of the Sagopans. The Emissary's message came through clearly: "We are Teiahman. Our northern homelands have been flooded and we come to you in peace, arms wide open."

[Interlude:] A cautious people, the Sagopans had their doubts.

[Trills and other ornamentation:] In subsequent visits, the Emissary was accompanied by a child the Sagopans assumed to be the stranger's offspring. The child sat at a distance and observed while the adults sat in a circle, the Emissary at its centre, seeking to establish a dialogue. One day, when no one noticed, Spurnit approached the little one.

"What is your name?" asked Spurnit.

"Qwix," said the Teiahman child.

"A silly name. I am Spurnit. Do you sand sloop?"

Although the child wore a mask like the Emissary's, it gave no indication it understood. Instead it ground its oversized mandibles in a manner that Spurnit interpreted as excitement.

"Come!" Exiting the cavern, Spurnit stepped into the sunlight and began to ascend the highest sand dune, signalling for Qwix to follow. The children climbed and climbed until they reached the peak. From this vantage point, Spurnit surveyed their surroundings, amazed by the number of encampments the Teiahmans had established, the number of new tunnel entrances they had opened up in the black sands.

"Now watch me carefully," Spurnit said.

Pressing foreclaws and rear-arms against central cavity, folding up all four legs, Spurnit's weight shifted. The Sagopan child fell forward, tumbling end over end and picking up speed while rolling down the steep dune.

Upon reaching the bottom and unfolding all four legs, Spurnit brushed off the black sands and shouted: "Your turn!"

Qwix stared in wonder at the Sagopan child, unable to fathom the game. After a long pause, Qwix let loose a high-pitched whistle and seconds later, a sparkling flyer appeared over the other side of the dune. The Teiahman child stepped onto it and the magical device floated upward before gently descending to the bottom of the dune.

Qwix stepped off the flyer, mandibles grinding, and stood next to Spurnit.

"Efficient," Spurnit said, delighted. "But I think you missed the point."

"Here's what I don't understand," Gully said, setting down a microscanner on our worktable. "Two civilisations meet and one destroys the other. And yet there's not a scintilla of evidence of a war – or even a conflict. Where is the destruction? Where are the skeletal remains?"

I was having trouble concentrating since Fahlinjr's departure. The thought of waiting a year to tether made me anxious. With Ocura's population in decline, was it right to commit to wait so long to produce offspring?

"Kleev?" Gully said.

"Y-yes, an epidemic is making more and more sense. Maybe the northerners didn't have immunity to a southern disease."

"Normally, corpses would be consumed, but if they were diseased... "

"Mass graves," I responded. "There would be evidence of tens of thousands of graves."

"Unless they burned the bodies."

"Still, there'd be some evidence of death ceremonies, some account or depiction of the plague in their art, in the fragment of the song-tale we recovered."

"We haven't finished reconstructing all of it. The tale may yet end with a plague."

That morning I travelled to Blackscale City and stood again before Xemotaxadyl and the Explorata officer. "We've detected several preserved bone fragments in the substream sediment, near the debris wreckage of a northern vehicle. If we could study these Tieahman fossils, it might help us confirm – or rule out – whether the northerners fell prey to a disease. We need additional time, just a few more days, for the bots to extract the fragments."

In response, the Councilmember remained silent, the speaker staring away from me, as if I'd raised a topic unworthy of discussion.

Instead, the Explorata officer responded. "What does it matter what happened hundreds of thousands of years ago while our ancestors lurked in underground caves? I understand it's of intellectual interest, but we have to think now about the future, about our relationship with the alien species. Ten thousand bots will be swarming the cavern in the morning to extract the tactite. You'd best be gone."

*Story-Song #23B16* (continued):

[Recitative:] Over many sun-cycles, the Sagopans and the Teiahmans came to establish a new community. The Sagopans insisted, however, that the Teiahmans who, after all, had arrived uninvited and imposed their presence, assimilate into the community. The newcomers did not oppose the request. In fact, they relished the idea; the more time they spent with the Sagopans the more they found them fascinating. The Teiahmans spent much of their time learning about the history of the desert dwellers and their culture, their foods, their songs. Although the

Sagopans generally did not approve of the Teiahman culture, they were open to learning about the source of northern magic, which everyone eventually came to understand was not magic at all, but the manipulation of natural processes.

[Free-flowing melodies:] And on the night of the planetary syzygy, when the five planets aligned perfectly in the night sky, Spurnit invited Qwix and the other adolescents on the yearly pilgrimage to the Cliffs of Wonder. Once there, they sat on the edge, dangling their two front legs over the sides of the precipice. And together they sang the traditional triumphant arias of the Sagopan ancestors. Occasionally, Qwix and the other Teiahman juveniles would sing the brooding songs of the north, which Spurnit found poignant. Rich, deep songs full of a cold mourning, a mourning of something lost.

Qwix and the other Teiahmans bore the same four legs as any Sagopan but the vestigial legs that hung from their body cavity had vanished in the intervening years. Also, perhaps because of the desert sun, the newcomers had shed the fur on their arms and their scales had paled to a shade of gold that made them seem more Sagopan, more attractive. However, the Teiahman and Sagopan people were physically unable to tether. Some individuals had made the attempt – and suffered a horrible fate that was never spoken of. Still, Spurnit and Qwix had grown closer.

[Somber threnody:] "Do you miss the north?" Spurnit asked when they were alone in the cold night, basking in the warmth of the glow-orbs.

"The flooded lands became unlivable and we had no choice but to leave. I do occasionally miss the vapour in the air from my breath, the chill of our caverns. But if I hadn't left I would never have met you, my dear friend. My people are fortunate to have found yours."

"Fortunate? How? You're the ones who've brought all your 'magic' technology to us."

The Teiahman and Sagopan adolescents lay silent for a time, the question hanging in the air, before Qwix spoke.

"The flyers, the force fields, the tunnellers… They were all developed by our ancestors centuries ago. Before we came here, my people had become… idle." Qwix's mandibles had grown smaller and now resembled Spurnit's, but still flexed anxiously. "Although forced

217

upon us, the trip south has made our lives fuller. Given us a new home."

Qwix said nothing more. Instead, they joined together and sang a mournful song from the north. A song forbidden to be sung among the Sagopan people. For the Sagopans, although welcoming, had continued to insist that the Teiahmans make more of an effort to integrate, to be more... Sagopan. And the Teiahmans had done their best to comply.

Qwix interspersed southern melodies into the northern song and they harmonised, creating something new and rich.

"We're almost there," I shouted to Gully. We hung onto a line that lowered us down a narrow shaft. Araquils clinging to the sides of the wall scattered and fled into burrows. I tightened my back-scales at the sight of the vile male, female and xern vermin. One of them, evidently female from its large nostril, stared from a burrow.

"Having Tieahman eyes would be useful right about now," I said.

Fahlinjr would have laughed at the remark, but Gully just said, "That's why we brought infra-red eyewear."

I helped guide the bots as they navigated the riptide and drilled deep into the bottom of the river near the sunken Teiahman vessel where the bone fragments had been detected. If they could extract genetic material from the bone, it might well hold the answers to the mystery of the northerners' genocide.

"This is a mistake. The mineral-bots will be here any moment," Gully said. "If we're still here the cavern could come crashing down around us."

"Then best to focus. And move quickly."

We could see the bottom of the river through the images transmitted by the bots to our eyewear. The surrounding tactite interfered with the transmissions and required us to maintain a close proximity to the submerged bots. If we had more time I would have also retrieved the remnants of the sunken vessel itself.

A few minutes later, the bot emerged from the river, its pointed legs stabbing into the sides of the cavern wall to climb it. The bot had placed the prized bone fragments in a small, watertight, stasis box.

The bots above us pulled on the line and raised us higher until we reached the lip of the precipice. We raced back down the tunnel and into the cavern. At the far end of the chamber, the entire wall teemed with mining bots tearing the wall apart.

I held my breath, hoping the transtube still functioned, and exhaled when it began to ascend. As we reached the surface, the ground below us rumbled.

The next day I sat down in our lab to analyze the bone fragments. And after only a few moments examining it, the hot desert gust of disappointment swept through me. Despite the proximity of the sunken Teiahman vessel to the fossils, despite all of our efforts, we'd retrieved nothing more than an ordinary *Sagopan* torso bone.

Crestfallen, I wallowed in self-pity for some time before I learned that Gully had finished restoring the crystal recording of the story-song. I turned my attention back to the tale of Spurnit and Qwix.

*Story-Song #23B16* (continued):

[Recitative chants with interspersed free melodies:] Sun-cycles later, when on the edge of adulthood, Spurnit rode a flyer to meet Qwix at the Ouarian Oasis at the edge of Green Pond. The Sagopans had become accustomed to the all of the Teiahman technologies they once considered magic and now used them in every facet of their daily lives. In fact, Sagopan society had expanded past the desert to the mountainous regions that had previously served as a border. Using the Teiahman tunnelling technology, the Sagopans had become adept at accessing subsurface rivers and catacombs to navigate the continent.

When Spurnit arrived, neither Qwix nor any other Teiahman was present. Instead, a young Sagopan stood alone, staring out into the expanse of Green Pond.

Spurnit approached the youthful Sagopan, who said, "You're late. If we're going to dig for plant bulbs for sport, we might have more success earlier in the morning when the waters are further receded."

"Do I know you?" Spurnit asked.

A pause followed. "It's me. It's Qwix."

"Qwix?" They stood body cavity to body cavity and Spurnit stared ahead at what seemed like a perfect reflection. "You – you look exactly like me."

"Of course I do," Qwix said as if it was the most natural thing in the world.

"And your Teiahman siblings?"

"They, too, have become Sagopan. We fit in perfectly now."

[Somber cadences:] The first thought that came to Spurnit's mind was of the enchantment cast at the Mystical Wall when the Teiahmans had first arrived all those sun-cycles ago. The Sagopan elders had cast a spell to make the invaders disappear. And though the Sagopans had long ago abandoned the notion of magic, Spurnit couldn't help but think that somehow, some way, the enchantment had worked.

"Qwix," Spurnit said, trying to shake this thought of the malignant spell the Sagopans had cast. "Let's sing, shall we?"

"Certainly," Qwix said as they walked the shore.

And because sadness inexplicably filled the air, Spurnit said, "Let's sing a song of the north."

Qwix halted, mandibles flexing.

"What's wrong?" Spurnit asked.

After a long pause, Qwix said, "Strange, I seem to have forgotten the northern songs. Do you remember them?"

"No, not really," Spurnit said, straining to recall the brooding threnodies. "I only remember they were sad, beautiful."

"Shall we sing a glorious Sagopan aria, then?"

"No, that's okay," Spurnit said, no longer in the mood to sing.

Spurnit didn't quite understand the melancholy that had settled in the air. After all, it was good that Sagopans now had doppelgangers, good that the community had become purely Sagopan. In time, they'd all come to forget the name Teiahman.

And so the identical Sagopans silently walked side by side, leaving their indistinguishable footprints in the wet sand.

Over the next year, Gully and I and the rest of our team worked in a study room atop the Central Butte overlooking Utaru and listened to the recovered story-songs over and over. We studied visual recordings of the excavation site and analysed other remnants while I composed weekly report-songs to the Council, but we failed to achieve any significant insight on the mystery of the Teiahman extermination beyond the unusual tale of the story-song. Gully believed the fantastical story-song of Qwix and Spurnit spoke to deeper genetic truths that remained frustratingly just out of reach. I wasn't so sure. Perhaps the Explorata officer had a valid point about where our attention needed to be focused at this time: first contact with the aliens. We were undertaking a brand new future.

I thought of Fahlinjr every day, every hour. I'd delayed tethering for so long my body ached.

And then one day as if drawn by my thoughts, a bot entered the room and announced the Councilmember's summons.

When I entered the sublevel chamber, Xemotaxadyl and the Explorata officer stood waiting for me.

"Fahlinjr," I said, before either one could speak. "Is Fahlinjr back?"

Xemotaxadyl rumbled toward me and said, "Exposure to the aliens has had… unanticipated results. Both to Fahlinjr and to the tens of thousands of Wergens in the Explorata flotilla."

I expected Xemotaxadyl to say more, but only silence followed.

A bot guided me to an empty room where I waited until I heard steps behind me. Not the normal galumphing of rear legs clacking against the stone floor, but stilted, singular steps.

When I turned, an alien stood there.

"Kleev," she said. "It's me."

Her skin had the familiar triangular scales of a Wergen, a normal flat head crowned by a leafy *coronatis*, a familiar blue-green aura and black stormcloud eyes, but everything else about her was different. She had a large nostril that marked her as female, fewer appendages, and stood perilously perched atop her two remaining legs, waving two arms like a stunted infant.

"Fahlinjr? What – what did they do to you?" I tightened my back scales and gaped at her.

"No, not Fahlinjr. Not any more. With this new form, I've taken on a new name: Fahr."

"'Fahr?'" I didn't know what to say. I clenched my back-scales and gaped at her.

"The physical changes began after we first observed one of the aliens. They're so beautiful, Kleev. They're glorious. My body – the body of everyone aboard the seedship – reacted in this manner, transformed to match the beauty of the aliens."

"That's not all that's changed," I said.

She hesitated. "Oh, you mean this." She waved her hands over her robed torso and head.

"You're like an araquil," I said, shocked. The cave-dwelling vermin in the green- and black-sand deserts were partial beings, stunted, with unique gender markers. The females were efficient hunters with a keen sense of smell; the males smaller, affectionate child-rearers; and the xern, twice the size of females, were ferocious protectors known for their verbal trills. It took one of each to mate. Advanced life forms had long ago evolved beyond such gender markers.

"It's part of their beauty," Fahr said. "If only you could see them! Adopting a gender makes us more... like them, more beautiful."

She described the alien 'humans' — their genders, their delicate smooth skin and dazzling auras, their cleverness and blinding beauty. "I have to go back soon," she said. "I want to be near them again. We can help them. Come with me, Kleev. You can change as I have changed. And then we can tether as planned."

Her eyes were distracted. She couldn't stop thinking of her precious aliens — even when speaking of something as intimate as our tethering.

I imagined losing my natural Wergen form, becoming gendered, stunted, transformed into this... monstrosity. Even worse, would I become like her, focused on nothing but pleasing the aliens? I'd wanted so much to tether with Fahlinjr, but everything about this seemed... wrong.

I cleared my throat. "Fahlinjr..."

"Fahr."

"Fahr, I've run numerous genetic samples through MC. I'm compatible with one other, a member of our team. And I feel my place is here on Ocura. Do you understand?"

Fahr paused and stared at me. For an instant it seemed the spell had been broken, that she'd reestablished her connection with me. I expected her to ask me to reconsider, but instead she stared skyward — though she could see only the room's grey ceiling — and said, "You don't know what you'll be missing. The aliens are stunning, their beauty... indescribable." She laughed softly and spun on her two stump legs. "They're utterly charming. And now that we've updated the Council on our... changes, we've been cleared to return." She paused and placed her hands on my shoulders. "Incredible times lie ahead, Kleev."

Her touch still made my hearts flutter. "Of that I have no doubt," I said.

And then she turned and left without saying goodbye.

*Report-Song to the Council of the Grand Congress*
The pieces of the puzzle came together with Fahlinjr's reappearance as Fahr. The story-song was rooted in something real. And the answer, as our team suspected, lay in the superfluous strand of our triple helix.

[*Trill*]: History is biology is history is biology…

[*Free melodies:*] After months of analysing the genetic material in the bone fragments we'd recovered, Gully and I identified the gene that triggered the extinction of the Teiahmans. We initially called it the suicide gene though we soon came to recognise that designation as a misnomer. Sagopans, after all, might well have called it the revitalisation gene.

The Teiahmans hadn't been conquered by aggression or disease or interbreeding. They'd been conquered by an instinctive urge, a profound impulse to help the southerners. This urge activated dormant alleles in the third string of their triple helix, which we'd come to learn contains templates for hundreds of thousands of different phenotypic traits. This allowed the Teiahmans to take on the physical characteristics of the southerners down to the genetic level – in essence, to *become* Sagopans – reinvigorating them in the process. This bio-mechanism bore a striking resemblance to tethering, only on a macro-scale, with the absorption of one species into another. Teiahman society had been in decline and by turning into Sagopans, and merging their civilisations, the northerners had passed along their best traits and revitalised southern society, creating something better that flourished for millennia to come. Genetistorians around the globe and on the moon were now hard at work trying to better understand the impulse that triggered these morphic abilities.

And it explained why the fragments we recovered near the sunken Teiahman vessel appeared to be Sagopan bones.

[*Trills:*] Teiahman is Sagopan is Wergen is Teiahman is Sagopan is Wergen…

[*Dark aria:*] More troubling, this process, which benefits life on Ocura, has been activated by our contact with this alien species. This raises profound concerns about the inherent danger of interacting with these beings. A natural process has been triggered – and subverted – by the aliens. Our mere exposure to them presents an existential threat to our species.

[*Coda*:] With the sociobiological mechanism that allows species on Ocura to reinvigorate one another now hijacked by aliens, we are vulnerable, Great Council. Severely, utterly vulnerable. A quarantine must be imposed against all Wergen explorers who have interacted with the aliens. Those Wergens – and the aliens – must never be allowed to set foot in this system.

Gully and I flew over the burgeoning lunar city, lit purple and red, the first rays of sunlight peeking over the horizon. Above us, the forcefield generated a faint blue tint, which created the illusion of a fading aura. Gully – steady, reliable Gully – accompanied me as we surveyed the field's perimeter. The Council had authorised our proposed project to study the beginnings of Wergen life in the now-dry lunar seabeds. In this way we hoped to better understand the suicide gene, the origins of our morphic abilities and vulnerabilities.

"What are you thinking about?" Gully asked as we sailed above the city, the familiar question triggering a cascade of feelings. With my rear-arms I clutched the bunched-up tether connecting our skulls.

"Some view the Council's decision as extreme," I said. After Xemotaxodyl shared my report-songs with the Grand Congress, they'd accepted my recommendation and imposed the quarantine. The thousands of transformed explorers who'd ventured into the alien system – and Wergen colonists on nearby settlements – were now prohibited from ever coming back. They had no desire to return in any event. They wanted only to be near the humans. And any other Wergens venturing into deep space were prohibited from contacting these aliens.

"Those who oppose the decision don't understand the danger the aliens pose," Gully said.

I remained silent as our buzzer began its descent.

"What are you really thinking, Kleev?" Gully said again, this time more insistently. I didn't need to speak any words. I merely let down my guard and exposed my thoughts. Ever since we'd tethered, my mind had become crowded with Gully's thoughts, which mingled with mine until I didn't know where I began and Gully ended.

*Teiahman society was in a state of decline when they encountered the Sagopans. That's what triggered the suicide gene*, I thought.

Gully understood my concern. Wergen society had used fieldtech and wormhole engines for thousands of years, but what had been the last significant scientific breakthrough? What was the last great Wergen work of art? The last great Canticle? If our species were to die, what would we leave behind?

*Our civilisation is in decline.*

"We're still exploring, still expanding," Gully said, trying to comfort me, foreclaws outstretched towards the lunar horizon. *Yet the gene* was *triggered upon encountering the aliens*, came the ominous lingering afterthought. Now that we were tethered, Gully's thoughts were mine, just like my thoughts were Gully's.

*You're thinking of Fahlinjr, aren't you?* Gully said.

I couldn't deny it.

I concentrated and sealed off my mind. Gully shot me a disapproving glare. In time I wouldn't be able to do this any more. Eventually my mind would go blank and Gully's body would consume mine.

A warmness, a soft ache, filled my chest cavity when I thought of Fahlinjr. The humour. The enthusiasm. The kindness. Memories came flooding back – Fahlinjr teasing me, helping me. Would these memories survive my absorption into Gully? If not, with Fahlinjr gone, in the thrall of the aliens, everything we ever shared would be erased forever. A sad desperation overwhelmed me.

*Forget the past*, Gully thought. *Think of our merger, our offspring.*

I focused on this, as Gully directed, and I knew that, in time, the once-precious memories would dim, inevitably fading away to nothing.

# CHAPTER TEN
# The Exterminators of Langalana

## Langalana 2595 – 2600

I'd left Adrian stranded on Langalana where the settlers learned of the Love War only after it had ended. While Shimera and Phinny explored the continent of Argenta, Adrian resided on Inlandia where humans and Wergens worked shoulder to shoulder to tame a hostile world.

I only came to learn these tales of Langalana when the Wergen records maintained on Ocura became available to me.

### *Sunil*

My sister Tam and I floated on our backs in one of the swimming holes, squinting in the bright blue sun while the multi-tiered waterfalls created a soothing white noise. The warm saltwater collected into pink pools as it flowed downstream. The Wergens observed us from a raft floating three metres away.

"Shouldn't we be getting back, Sunil?" Tam said.

"Relax," I said. "No one will even know we're missing."

Tam had resisted the idea of ditching our VR lessons until I'd suggested swimming. With Mom and Dad and Tony at a Settlement Council meeting with Wergen leaders, we had the whole morning to play hooky.

"Sunil, do you like Tony?" Tam said.

"He seems nice enough." Mom had been seeing Tony on and off for about three months now and he'd been around more often than not lately. The way I saw it, if Dad had no problem with Tony, he was probably a good guy.

"Onyx! Hermillia!" I shouted to the Wergens. "Are you sure you don't want to get in?"

I splashed water at them, but their bodyfields flicked on, keeping them dry. They'd removed their robes and the white scales that covered their short, thick-bodied frames flickered in the sunlight. Each of them wore a red-leafed *coronatis*.

"We're fine," Onyx said. He didn't have any problem maintaining his balance on the raft.

Hermillia lay next to him on her stomach, hands beneath her chin, staring at us. "We can see you from here," she said.

"Are you sure you don't want to swim?" I said. "The water's warm."

"Leave them be, Sunil," my sister said. "You know they aren't great swimmers."

"Oh, come on! With their bodyfields they could walk the bottom of this swimming hole without any problem."

"Gee, *that* sounds like fun," Tam said, rolling her eyes.

She looked past me. "Hey, look!"

I couldn't see what she was pointing at, but she swam past me in the direction of the closest waterfall. I kicked my legs and followed behind her.

Swimming to the edge where purple-leafed plants swayed left and right, she climbed out of the pool, disappearing behind the tall vegetation. I followed, clambering over the rocks, pushing plants aside until I discovered a trail. The dirt path led to a shallow cave behind the falls.

I found Tam crouched, wide-eyed, staring at the curtain of pink waters cascading in front of her. "Is this amazing, or what?" she shouted over the roar of the falls. She pulled her wet hair back into a ponytail.

"Tam!" Hermillia shouted from the other side of the falls.

"Sunil!" Onyx called. "Where did you go?"

"It'll take them a while to find us," I said, plopping down next to her. "How did you know this was here?" I said.

"I didn't. I thought I saw something move in the brush," she said looking around. "But there's nothing here."

Blue sunlight streamed through the rose-coloured water, bathing the cave walls in a lilac glow.

"What do you say we christen this our official secret headquarters?" I announced.

Suddenly Onyx and Hermillia burst through the wall of cascading water and stepped into the cave. Although they'd leapt off the raft and through the waterfall, their bodyfields kept them dry. Their scaled, white skin took on a lilac pallor inside the cave.

"There goes the secret headquarters," Tam said, throwing her hands up.

"We don't like it when you hide," Onyx said.

When I was six years old I tried to teach Onyx hide-and-seek, but he hated losing sight of me even for a second. He was a kid himself – though not as young as me – but he didn't enjoy the game and refused to play again, even when I begged him. And it was unusual for a Wergen to refuse a human's request.

"Promise me you won't tell anyone about this place, okay?" I said to the Wergens. "We can come back here when we want to get away from the others."

"We won't tell. I promise," Onyx said, but I was sceptical. It was hard for the Wergens to resist spilling the beans on any secret, especially if a human asked them.

"Yeah, we can come here – if we aren't permanently grounded for skipping class, that is. Time to head back. Ready to go?" Tam asked, heading for the path.

She was about six metres ahead of me when I heard her piercing scream.

"Tam!" I ran, Onyx and Hermillia right behind me.

I found her curled on the ground. Attached to the side of her neck was a wriggling... snake-like creature. About ten inches long and blood-red, its protruding fangs had clamped down on her carotid artery. I tried to yank it off, but it wouldn't let go.

She moaned.

Onyx clapped his hands and a dozen bots came streaming through the vegetation and swarmed over Tam. A bot tried to inject the creature with a syringe, but the needle broke. Another bot released an electric shock, sending Tam into convulsions. The creature released its grip for a second. Before it could reattach itself, Hermillia pressed a button on her controller, trapping it in a containment field.

"Tam! Are you hurt?" Hermillia said, bending over her.

The bots continued probing Tam, monitoring her vitals. Within a matter of minutes, a Wergen contingent on landbuzzers arrived. They swooped down and lifted us out of the rainforest, speeding over the canopy of red trees in the direction of the colony.

"You're going to be okay," I said, holding on to her hand. "Everything's going to be okay."

Tam's eyelids fluttered and she shivered. The bots swarmed over her but her trembling had now turned into a full-blown seizure.

When her body finally stopped convulsing, she'd stopped breathing.

## Onyx

Sunil's attitude towards me changed after his sister's death. For many months, he became more distant and no longer confided in me.

One day, as I walked with him to the painting class taught by Tony Shetty, I asked, "Are we not we brothers any more, Sunil?" Sunil never introduced me as his Wergen friend to other humans, but as his brother.

He did not respond.

"What have I done?" I asked him repeatedly for days. "How can I make things right between us?"

He ignored my questions until one day he exploded in anger: "It's not what you did. It's what you didn't do." His eyes watered and his smooth brown skin flushed. "*I trusted you.* All of your tech… What is it good for if you couldn't even keep Tam safe?"

"Hermillia was Tam's shadow. Not me. And we did everything we could to save her. You must know that. Hermillia would have given her life for Tam."

"Then why didn't she?" He stormed off. "Leave me alone!"

There was a time – before development of the suppressor – that I would have been unable to comply with his request. At least not easily. But I acquiesced and gave him his space.

In time, he allowed me to shadow him again, but he remained distant for many months.

Growing up among humans, I learned long ago that if I stood too close to them, if I paid too much attention to them, they became resentful, sometimes even cruel. But if I feigned disinterest and kept my distance, they might accept – even welcome – my presence. As children, Sunil and I used to spend time on the shore of the Purple Sea, running, playing a marvelous game he called 'tag', in which I could let my guard down and chase humans around freely. They even permitted me to touch them briefly. Sunil would also chase me, but he would get angry when I let him catch me too easily.

Development of the suppressor helped me grow closer to my friends and to mend fences with my human brother. Wearing a whiffer allowed me to keep my distance and to modulate my feelings of love more easily. Once I started using the suppressor, Sunil confided in me more often. The walls he'd erected between us began to crumble.

We found a joint purpose that brought us together. Sunil and I committed ourselves to exterminating the creature that had killed Tam, a rare native organism called a grubber. At first her death was deemed a freak accident but then more grubber attacks followed with colonists being killed by the scores. This prompted the Settlement Council to summon specialists to help us with the infestation. Humans had a knack for extermination – delivering death to lower life forms with zeal, efficiency and creativity – a skill that far surpassed the abilities of my Wergen brethren.

First to arrive was Dr. Zooey Crest, a human scientist from the Argenta colony on Langalana's western continent. Named head of the extermination project, she proved particularly skilled in gengineering, manipulating the genetic makeup of native plants to make them edible and altering Earth crops to allow them to flourish in Langalanan soil. In addition to leading her team of gengineers, she also supervised the half-dozen exo-entomologists who arrived on an IS transport from the Sol System. (This pleased me and my brethren no end, for more humans meant more of an opportunity to experience their wit and their cleverness and their beauty).

For the next four sun-cycles until his eighteenth birthday Sunil volunteered to work closely with the new arrivals. This meant I, in turn, had the opportunity as Sunil's shadow to learn about the various methods of grubber extermination: baiting, trapping, pesticides – even proposals to gengineer a predator to eradicate them (a strategy deemed too dangerous to pursue).

Sunil studied extermination with a single-minded determination. He gained a particular expertise in toxins specially designed to kill the grubbers without affecting the multitude of natural plant life and the small, flying mammals that populated Langalana.

My focus – and Sunil's – changed yet again on a bright morning when the exit door of my hurth slid open and I stepped outside to find Sunil accompanied by another person, perhaps the most beautiful human being I'd ever seen.

"This is Lieutenant Adrian Guerrero, a new arrival on Langalana," Sunil said. "Dr. Crest asked me to give him a tour of the colony. He's joining the extermination effort."

I understood 'Lieutenant' to indicate a military rank. At two metres tall, he towered over me. His hair was closely cut to his scalp, and his eyes were as blue as sunshine. His aura radiated the brightest colours on the spectrum.

"There are more Wergens here than I expected," the Lieutenant said, gesturing to the rows of hurths.

"The Joint Venture Compact restricted the number of Wergens on this colony," Sunil said, "but the population limits have been relaxed with the development of the suppressor."

Sunil paused and glared at me.

I shook my head. I had been gaping, paralysed by Adrian's beauty, and had not realised I was not wearing my whiffer. I placed it over my breathing canal, inhaled deeply, and the intensity of my feelings subsided.

"Those devices," Adrian said, pointing at my whiffer, "are dangerous as hell."

"The initial kinks have been worked out, Lieutenant," I said.

"It makes it easier for the Wergens to work with us," Sunil added.

Adrian looked skeptical.

We walked the pathways that wound through the Wergen neighbourhood and into the grasslands, towards the glass towers at the centre of Inlandia.

"How long do you plan to stay on Langalana?" Sunil asked.

"Not long, if I can help it," Adrian said. "There's somewhere else I need to be, someone I need to find." There was a quiet desperation in his voice.

Sunil cleared his throat. "Dr. Crest said you led an expedition into Eremite territory..."

Eremites. Humans had actually made contact with the legendary beings. Beings made of light. When our fore-tetherers explored the cosmos they'd discovered the remnants of alien civilisations, but the Eremites themselves had vanished long ago. We assumed they had gone extinct.

When Adrian did not respond, Sunil continued. "EarthCouncil thinks your military expertise can help us with the grubber problem."

"Can I help?" I interjected. "I would be happy to assist any way I can."

He shot me a look. "What a surprise."

He squinted in the sunlight, gazing in the direction of the glass towers. "Well, EarthCouncil won't authorise my return to the Sol System until your bugs are eradicated." He turned back to Sunil. "So let's stomp some bugs."

Sunil smiled at this. "I can fill you in on the research performed by the gengineers, the pesticides being developed by the entomologists."

"I also need a full debriefing on all weapons available to us."

"Esperanza Quiles can fill you in on the number of laserguns and airpulsers in the colony."

"And I can provide a status report on available bots and fieldtech," I said.

"Good, good," he said, acknowledging my remark, which made my hearts race. "Let's move quickly."

Sunil smiled and hung on his every word. I wished I had an extra whiffer I could share with him.

### Sunil

The afternoon breeze whistled through the rustling grasslands. Onyx crouched in the red blades of grass beside me. All around us out of our line of vision, human-Wergen pairs closed the perimeter, tightening the circle.

"Field activated!" Hermillia shouted.

Onyx and I leapt up. We charged forward as one, pushing through the tall grasses alongside our teammates.

We converged on the containment field just inside the swaying grasslands. The trapped grubber – the same deep crimson as the grass – screeched; sharp thorns lined its exoskeleton. Scores of wriggling legs left a slimy trail in their wake and half-a-metre-long antennae squiggled in our direction. Fully extended, the creature stretched three metres in length.

"Unbelievable!" I said, my heart pounding. "I've never seen one this big!"

"There have been larger grubbers spotted on the western continent, but no need to worry, Sunil," Onyx said. "Our new fields are impenetrable." Typical of Onyx. Sensing my fear, he said whatever he thought would make me feel better.

"That's what you said about the forcefields of the Argenta colony, before the grubbers broke through," I said.

"Well… nothing is a certainty." He hugged his shoulders.

"I'm – I'm sorry," I said. "I know your people are doing the best they can."

Although most of these creatures were only a few metres long and could be disposed of by a single trained human or Wergen, one this size…

Pesticides initially worked to kill the creatures, but they soon developed a resistance. Clearing the grasslands and expanding the colony had only seemed to make the scummy things multiply.

"Clear the grass," came another shout, this from Adrian, who was leading this grubber-hunt.

Onyx planted the forcefield generator deep into the ground. The invisible field expanded with a whistling whoosh of air, flattening the grass. The other Wergens employed their own forcefields in the same manner, rapidly clearing the lands around us.

Within minutes, two dozen pairs of Wergen/human exterminators gathered in front of Adrian.

Adrian pointed to the grubber trapped inside the forcefield. "The field is a perfect sphere. Therefore, it can't tunnel into the ground; it can't scale up and over. And keep in mind, no matter its size, it still has the same vulnerability." He pointed at me.

"Its eyes," I offered.

"That's right," Adrian gestured at the row of bulbous eyes bisecting the grubber's triangular head. Removing a knife from his holster, he squeezed the handle, extending it into a spear. "Drop the field."

Hermillia and Arkania stared at Adrian in disbelief, but he refused to acknowledge them. Rumour had it Adrian hadn't encountered Wergens until he was in his late teens. Like most humans exposed to Wergens after childhood, he'd never quite adjusted to their presence.

Hermillia removed the spherical handheld controller from her suit pocket and pointed it at the grubber. The field dropped. The grubber charged at us, baring its fangs and Adrian thrust his spear into one of its six eyes. It screeched and collapsed to the ground.

"The creature's brain," Adrian said, wiping his spear on the grass, "lies two centimetres behind the eyes. Soft and vulnerable. With the right training, it's an easy kill."

As we prepared to leave the grasslands, Onyx pulled me aside. "Couldn't we simply have compressed the field? We could have crushed it without any risk to us."

"Its shell is strong. I'm not sure you could kill it that way," I said. "But you're missing the point. We're here to learn from Adrian, to hone our extermination skills. We may not always have fieldtech available to us."

I could see the wheels turning in his head, wondering why anyone would be so foolish as to walk through the grasslands without fieldtech.

"Best to be prepared for all eventualities. Okay?" I said, punching his shoulder.

He tapped the transparent whiffer that covered his breathing canal, releasing a dosage of the suppressor.

"We can learn a lot from Adrian."

Adrian had adjusted well in the months since his arrival on Langalana. Apparently he'd been transported here with Eremite technology, though he still refused to talk to me about it. He had a haunted look in his eyes, as if he'd suffered a terrible loss and would never fully recover from it. To think that he'd served in off-world battles between human and Wergen. Senior members of the Wergen Explorata had blamed the conflicts on an overuse of the suppressor. Some Wergens had apparently abused the inhalants, distorting their natural feelings of love for humanity. Fortunately, those times were behind us now. I couldn't imagine a Wergen ever trying to harm a human.

"Coordination," Adrian said to all of us. "Teamwork. Knowing what your fellow exterminators are doing before they even do."

Teamwork between humans and Wergens. It seemed redundant to put it in those terms. Onyx and I had been best friends – brothers – for as long as I could remember. We'd faced difficult times – our shared guilt over Tam's death, the loss of his mother before she could tether – and got through them together.

I refocused on the task at hand: travelling safely back to our campsite. Fortunately, we didn't expect to encounter any additional grubbers in this area of the grasslands, so close to Inlandia.

## *Onyx*

Sunil and I arrived at our campsite exhausted after exterminating a dozen small grubbers we had unexpectedly encountered on our trek eastward.

Our camp sat at the edge of the crystalline cliffs, overlooking the Purple Sea. At this distance from the grasslands, the danger of a grubber attack was remote. But being positioned on a cliff with no means of retreat made no tactical sense to me. When I asked Sunil why Adrian had rejected our offer to erect a protective field over the site, he had shrugged and said, "He must have his reasons."

In the distance, beyond the curving cliffs, the glass towers of Inlandia shone in the moonlight. The colony now stretched sixty kilometres across, built on the backs of human and Wergen settlers like my mother and Sunil's parents. If we had any hope of expanding further into the grasslands, the grubbers needed to be eradicated.

Our team of twelve humans and eleven Wergens had gathered together for only a few minutes before Hermillia, the boldest Wergen in our ranks, said to Adrian, "I would like to remind you that my people contributed the forcefield that contained the grubbers." She halted, awaiting a response.

Adrian said nothing.

"Yes, well, our people contributed Adrian's leadership skills," Antoinette said. She was one of the best human scouts, quick-witted and sensible. Sunil had indicated he wanted to get to know her better. "That makes us even, right?" She had a mischievous glint in her eye when she said this that Hermillia failed to recognise.

"But, but –"

Hermillia's flummoxed reaction made every human within earshot, including Sunil, burst out laughing. We had contributed our forcefields to the grubber-hunt and Hermillia now expected the humans to repay us in the usual manner they repaid Wergens. Hermillia anxiously paced the camp, hugging her shoulders, until Sunil intervened to bring an end to the joke.

"We're grateful, Hermillia," Sunil said, and her black eyes widened. "And we'd like to demonstrate this with our Expression of Appreciation."

With these words, Hermillia and I and my other Wergen compatriots congregated at one end of the campsite to face the human contingent.

Antoinette and her sister, Lizzie, brought out their blow-chords, and in a matter of minutes, the lilting harmonies of what they described as 'Martian folksongs' whistled in the evening breeze.

Sunil recited one of his poems, a ghazal about the ineffable nature of love and devotion. And then the humans all sang a dirge while we all watched in rapt attention. On other occasions Sunil expressed his appreciation by sharing his paintings or by performing a dramatic monologue. And we also loved to hear about their scientific hypotheses – everything from gengineering to wormholes – even though our scientific knowledge in these areas exceeded theirs. Sunil asked me once why we cared about their 'Stone-Age theories' and I had explained, "There is something... clever, ingenious, about the shortcuts you find for difficult problems. Even when you are wrong, there is a beauty in those efforts."

Sunil had thrown his arms in the air and said, "Argh!" in mock frustration. "You find our mistakes beautiful. Why am I not surprised?"

Antonio and Esperanza (both off-key singers) completed the Expression of Appreciation with a slow dance, what they called 'a seguidilla' with frenzied footwork, and when the final notes sounded and the final steps were taken, the performers all took a bow.

We had learned about applause – another ingenious human custom – and we clapped our hands enthusiastically.

### Sunil

I waited until Onyx had entered into the hibernation state that resembled human sleep before approaching Adrian. Wergens didn't share our sleep-cycle – in fact, they hibernated for a full week only twice a year – but they thought it made us more comfortable if they slept every evening like humans did, so they forced themselves to do so. Some scientists, like Dr. Crest, wondered whether the Wergens generally mimicked our behaviour to ingratiate themselves with us. Myself, I never thought about it in those terms. I considered Onyx an annoying kid brother, someone who looked up to me and wanted to do whatever I did. Half the time I resented him, but I loved him and wouldn't have had it any other way.

I stepped over the blanketed forms until I made it to the campfire, where Adrian sat alone, sipping from a flask. He'd kept to himself during the Expression of Appreciation. I still couldn't believe that he'd led an expedition to the far side of the Milky Way at Gliese 581-b, and had met the legendary Eremites.

I sat down across from him.

Adrian had delicate features, a button nose, thin lips, a cleft chin with several days of beard growth. He faced the moons and shifted his eyes in my direction without moving his head. "Nighttime on Langalana isn't anything like night on Earth," he said. He pointed to Axel, the largest and brightest of the three moons in the sky. "It's a wonder anyone can get to sleep with all this light."

I shrugged. "I came here when I was six years old. It's all I've ever known."

"You're lucky. This is a beautiful world."

We sat in silence for a few moments before I found the nerve to ask him about his history.

"Is it true? About your adventures in the Gliese system?"

"'Adventures'?" He smiled, one of the few times I'd ever seen him do so, but it was mixed with sadness. "If you call freefalling into hell an adventure, then sure, I had the adventure of a lifetime."

"Tell me about the Eremites. What are they like?"

"My memories have been mucked with, so I'm not sure whether they're even real, but I do remember that they're beautiful. So beautiful that it chokes me up to even think of them…" His voice quavered. He cleared his throat. "But you'll find out yourself soon enough. I understand EarthCouncil is in the process of negotiating joint projects with them. Soon we'll have exploration agreements in place with both the Wergens and the Eremites. Commitments to both species. I'm not sure that's wise."

I shrugged. "I don't see why not."

I wanted to ask more questions about the Eremites but he'd been so reticent to talk about them that after another long silence, I decided to change the subject. "Aren't we at a tactical disadvantage camping out here? If a grubber were to attack, we wouldn't be able to retreat."

"The time for retreat," he said, "is long past. If we expect to live on Langalana, we have to be prepared to fight for her. We can't keep counting on Wergen forcefields."

He had a point. Just as a new breed of grubbers had found a way to burrow past the forcefields that protected the Argenta colony on the western continent, it was only a matter of time before Inlandia faced a similar threat.

"Also, there may be an alternative to fighting," he said, "If Dr. Crest comes through with her gene-masker…"

Was it wrong that I wanted Dr. Crest to fail? That I wanted no alternative to exterminating the grubbers? "More than anything," I said, "I want to kill the grubbers. I want to wipe out every last one of them."

He stared at me for a long time. "Go to bed, Sunil."

But the last thing I wanted to do was to sleep, to dream of floating in the waterfall pools with Tam, to re-experience the same moment over and over again. Always with the same ending.

"We shouldn't count on any last-second miracles to eliminate the grubber threat," I said, as I stood to leave the campfire.

"No, we shouldn't," Adrian said.

## *Onyx*

Word of the last-second miracle spread throughout Inlandia a few days later.

Dr. Crest's gengineering team had perfected the gene-masker and all human colonists were required to be inoculated as soon as sufficient quantities of the compound became available.

At his parents' request, Sunil was called to the Central Inlandian Research Facility to meet with the other gengineers on Dr. Crest's team, and Adrian and I joined him.

Sunil said he had met Zooey Crest previously at his mother and father' home. It was apparent she had developed a deeper relationship with his parents than that of employer-employee – and I repeatedly asked Sunil to explain the situation to me. The esoteric interpersonal practices of humankind proved endlessly fascinating, but Sunil said he found my questions 'annoying as hell'. He explained that his parents, while married, had an 'open relationship', which was not uncommon among the colonists, and both had occasional trysts with different partners. Sometimes, if the relationships became more serious, his parents would introduce Sunil to their new partner. For example, Sunil said that over the years he had come to consider Tony Shetty a member of his family, a 'kindly uncle' who occasionally visited with his parents.

"Yet your parents are tethered – in the conceptual way that humans tether," I said.

"They're married but they have an arrangement. It's the way they've agreed to live their lives. No lies. No dishonesty."

I paused. "Tethered and yet untethered simultaneously. And they've found contentment in this inconsistency."

"You got it." Since he was tired of my questions, I suspected he would have responded this way no matter what I said.

Humans mated not solely for procreative purposes nor based on any genetic compatibility but purely for pleasure. They had no tethers that connected their craniums, no retraction that brought them ever closer. Instead, humans obsessed over imaginary social constructs: dating, open and closed relationships, marriage, divorce. I had heard these ideas for so long, but still found them fascinating and strange.

When we entered the lab, Sunil spotted his father on the far side of the room next to Dr. Crest. His father waved us over and introduced us to Dr. Crest, who stood about half-a-metre taller than Sunil's mother. A streak of grey cut through her cropped black hair.

"Sunil," she said shaking his hand. "It's so nice to see you again."

"And you remember Onyx?" Sunil said.

I extended my hand and she hesitated for a second before limply shaking it; I immediately took a whiff of the suppressor to mute my excitement. I could tell she felt as uncomfortable around my people as Adrian did. When I had previously met her she had addressed me curtly and only when necessary.

She turned her attention to Adrian. "And you are…?"

"Adrian Marquez."

"Of course," she said. "You've been leading the grubber-hunts. And I've also heard about your exploits with the Eremites, Lieutenant. Glad to finally meet you in person. Exciting news about the exploration treaty with the aliens."

"And I've heard your exciting news, doctor," Adrian said. "Congratulations."

"Thank you. The grubbers are a form of plant/insect hybrid we've never encountered before. The real breakthrough came when we came when finally understood their territorially driven tendencies."

"Yes," Sunil's father said. "Zooey brilliantly connected the dots between the rate of colony expansion and the increase in the number of grubbers."

"Our alien DNA is being targeted," she said. "As we spread, the grubbers multiply. But if we can mask our alien genes, disguise them so they appear Langalanan…"

"The grubbers lose interest," Sunil's father said.

"We used genetic material from manticola flowers to create a chemical mask," Dr. Crest said, "which has now been perfected." She held up a syringe, nodded at Adrian.

Adrian rolled up his sleeve, displaying his pink skin and bicep, and she administered the shot.

"Just like that?" Sunil said.

"Just like that," Dr. Crest said. "Follow me."

We walked with her past tables jammed with gene splicers to a rectangular depression in the wall. A half-a-metre-long grubber flitted around inside a containment field.

She removed a controller from her jacket pocket, pushed a button, and asked Adrian to stick his arm inside the permeable field. He obeyed without hesitation. The grubber continued circling around inside the field, ignoring his arm. "Masked individuals are invisible to the grubbers," she said.

As Adrian removed his arm, I stepped forward, and the grubber screeched and lunged forward against the field.

Dr. Crest had been avoiding eye contact with me but now addressed me directly. "The Wergens need to develop an equivalent mask for their genes if they're to survive on this world."

The fact she had addressed me directly immediately lifted my spirits.

"Yes, Pantillax's team will now be able to leverage your work," I said, "to complete an analogous genetic masker for my people."

She looked away from me, applying the syringe to Sunil's left arm as she spoke. "If your people weren't so damn secretive, we could've moved things along."

Sunil's father smiled uncomfortably.

"Our biology remains a private matter," I said. "Provisions of the Joint Venture Compact —"

She waved her hands in the air. "I know, I know. I don't need to hear the technicalities. Just expedite your work."

Dr. Crest turned away. She and Sunil's father then conferred with the dozen members of the team who were working on replicating the masker.

Sunil patted me on the back; I took a whiff of the suppressor. "Don't mind her," Sunil said. "She's an old-timer from Argenta, from the first wave of settlers."

"I understand," I said.

Before we developed the suppressor, the first generation of human colonisers felt so uncomfortable around us they negotiated limits on the number of Wergens allowed per colony. Our attraction to them only pushed them away. But the suppressor allowed us to mute our feelings somewhat; it made it easier for us to pretend not to love them as much as we did. Once we wore whiffers the next generation of human colonists called us brothers and sisters.

"The important thing," Sunil said, "is that we can finally turn the page and focus on the expansion of Inlandia now that the colony is safe."

### Sunil

The fall of Inlandia began six months later, long after the grubber-hunts had stopped and a few days after I'd begun a new position in city planning. It had taken the Wergens several tries but they finally developed their own version of the gene-masker. With this, our worries about the grubbers faded into the past and all our efforts were redirected to clearing the grasslands and further expanding the colony's borders. I'd spent so many years obsessing over the grubbers that I found it difficult to focus on my new duties. I hadn't dreamt about Tam in weeks.

The end of the threat to the colony also meant Adrian would be leaving Langalana. When I'd seen him a few days earlier he'd expressed frustration at missing the last interstellar vessel back to the Sol System. The next one wasn't scheduled to arrive for six months. Personally, I didn't mind having the extra time to get to know him better. He'd remained tight-lipped about his personal background, but if I was reading him correctly I thought he might be interested in getting to know me better, too. I was dating Antoinette at the time, but we didn't have an exclusive relationship and she'd been forthright about the fact she'd also been seeing Esperanza, one of our former teammates from the grubber-hunts.

Onyx and I surveyed the foundation where bots had broken ground for colony expansion. I probably should've told Onyx I needed my privacy that evening and left it at that, but I made the mistake of mentioning I was meeting Adrian at the town centre for drinks later that evening at Amethyst, one of the watering holes where colonists congregated after work. This led to a barrage of typically annoying Onyx questions. Some of them – about friendship, dating, and exclusive relationships – I'd answered a million times before. Others – about my sexual attraction to men and women – I'd addressed a few times before and refused to discuss again. And still others – about my specific sexual proclivities – I'd refused to answer at all.

"Why don't you go find yourself a cute Wergen to date and figure this stuff out on your own?" I'd said.

The absurdity of the remark stopped Onyx in his tracks. He stared at me dumbfounded, unsure how to respond.

"Relax," I said. "I'm kidding." Wergens, of course, didn't date or have sex or even find each other attractive, as far as I could tell. Instead, they tethered and fused with a genetically compatible mate. It bothered me to think about it, but one day Onyx's time would come. And whether he was the absorber or absorbee, he'd never be the same after tethering.

"I understand you were joking," Onyx said. "I only hesitated to marvel at your terrific humour."

"Get a life."

Our exchange was interrupted by a scream. When I stared down at the pit where the foundation had been laid, I spotted two grubbers tunnelling up through the ground. They both latched onto the legs of a Wergen worker.

A third grubber appeared. Then a fourth and a fifth.

I didn't have my weapons available.

A security guard opened fire, but the grubber that fell was quickly replaced by another.

Onyx removed his controller from his robe pocket and pointed it into the construction pit. A large spherical field encased all five grubbers. "I've got them!" he said.

The grubbers' antennae crackled and each of them pushed through the field slowly but steadily like a blade through molasses. The field collapsed.

Dozens of grubbers, several as large as a truck, burst upwards.

"Let's go!" Onyx said, pulling my arm. We raced away from the colony in the direction of the harbour, joining the masses of fleeing colonists.

We later learned that over a hundred humans and fifty Wergens were killed in the first hour alone. Panic spread throughout Inlandia once it became obvious the grubbers could see through our genetic masks, and that no forcefields could stop them. Until then, the grubbers had always limited their movement to land covered by vegetation. Wergen seedships had tried to assist in the evacuation by landing on the colony's grounds, but something about the vessels' vibrations caused them to be immediately swarmed by grubbers.

With the fields down, grubbers of varying sizes dug up through the foundation of the colony and into the glass towers where thousands of trapped colonists waited for the swarm to work its way up stairs and elevator shafts.

Wergen and human defenders fought valiantly side by side.

Inlandia fell in a single day.

Onyx and I boarded the *Endurance*, a passenger ship, along with thousands of displaced survivors fleeing the massive infestation.

My head was spinning. I tried – but failed – to process the pandemonium. Onyx kept repeating, "Everything's going to be okay," but his words blended into the chaos. I gazed across the deck of the ship and spotted Adrian hanging over the side of the ship as if about to throw up.

I ran to him. "Adrian!" I shouted.

"Look what's happened," he said in a voice barely above a whisper. "We fell asleep. We let down our guard. My God…"

In the distance, the skyline of glass towers seemed eerily pristine and unaffected. The *Endurance* sped forward over the Purple Sea.

"Sunil!"

I turned to find Dr. Crest among the survivors haunting the deck of the ship.

"Sunil, thank goodness you made it! Your mother and father are safe below deck."

"How could this have happened?" I asked her. "I thought we were invisible to them."

"The initial attacks honed in on Wergen workers." She looked past me and pointed at Onyx. "They were unable to mask themselves effectively. It triggered some kind of response in the grubbers, allowed them to see past all of our disguises. They're to blame for all of this!"

Others aboard the ship stared at the commotion.

"Pantillax replicated your approach to gene-masking," Onyx said. "But it must not have translated to Wergen physiology, at least not on a permanent basis."

"You're responsible!" she shouted. "You killed all those people!"

"Stop it! This isn't helping," I said.

I pulled Onyx away and took him below-deck away from the angry crowd that had started to gather. "Is she right?" he asked me. "Are my people responsible for all those humans dying?"

"Wergens died as well, Onyx." I said. "Whatever happened, it was an honest mistake."

I searched through the cabins until I found my parents. Mom wept and hugged me while Father stared past me, clearly in shock. So much of our lives had been devoted to settling Langalana, to creating a thriving colony. When Tam died, I swore I wouldn't let the grubbers win. And now...

"Sunil," Mother said. "Our best hope is to abandon not only Inlandia, but the northern continent."

"Yes, Wergen scouts have already explored the Isle of Splendours, part of the Equatorial Archipelago, and found it free of grubbers," Father said.

I cleared my throat, finding my resolve. "The grubbers may have lain claim to the northern and western continents – for now at least – but the islands of the Equatorial Archipelago can be ours." I squeezed my father's shoulder. "Everything will be all right. We can make a clean start and call Splendour our new home."

That night I dreamt of lavender pools and waterfalls that turned blood red, and of my sister's screams.

## Onyx

My fellow Wergens and our human partners fled the Isle of Splendour a year later, but not without a fight. Who could have predicted that the grubbers would prove to be such a formidable and relentless force? That they could see past the genetic masks? That they could penetrate forcefields strong enough to withstand the gravity of a gas giant? The grubbers had found a way to generate a bioelectric charge that allowed them to push though our defenses. And who could have thought they would swim across the vast Purple Sea in pursuit of us? Fortunately, we spotted the approaching swarm before it reached us, allowing us a few days for preparation and panic.

Sunil and I helped program the bots that constructed the eastern seawall. I was overseeing their progress when Sunil and Adrian pulled Dr. Crest aside. I observed from a short distance as they spoke to her. "I don't understand," Sunil said. "The grubbers are territorial creatures, indigenous to the northern and western continents. We've retreated, given up those territories. Why are they still following us?"

Dr. Crest still sparkled with the beauty that all humans had, but her hair had gone completely gray and she spoke with much less authority than when I first met her. "The team has a new theory, one born out by what the grubbers are now doing. We were wrong about the true nature of these creatures. Fundamentally wrong. They're not insects, not plants." She paused. "They're antibodies. *Planetary* antibodies looking to exterminate alien genes that have invaded its ecosystem. Langalana herself is treating us like an infection, a plague to be eradicated."

Adrian stared open-mouthed. "But that's cra –"

"It's the best hypothesis we have based on the evidence available," she said. "This world is not amenable to being settled."

"Your track record, doctor, doesn't instill me with confidence," Adrian said. He shook his head. "If we'd known this earlier we could've evacuated sooner. Made plans to leave this world. Now all we can do is hope to survive."

He stormed off, leaving me and Sunil alone with Dr. Crest.

I stared down at the seawall, keeping my back to Sunil and Dr. Crest. After a few seconds, she said, "Sunil, have you talked to your father?"

"Actually, I've spoken to Mom."

"I see. That's good." She opened her mouth as if to say something, but added nothing else. She turned and headed back toward the shelters in the town square where Sunil's father was staying.

A moment later, I approached Sunil. "What did Dr. Crest mean?"

"Nothing of consequence under the circumstances. Father and Mom have decided to end their marriage. He's decided to stay with Dr. Crest."

"I do not understand," I said. "I thought the three of them found some measure of contentment in their relationship, simultaneously tethered and untethered."

"They did for a time, as many others do. It's just… people change. Relationships can be difficult."

"I do not understand."

"Truthfully, I'm not sure I understand either. Something about Father's relationship with Dr. Crest crossed some invisible line Mom didn't approve of; I suppose being in a state of constant crisis can drive people closer together – or further apart – than perhaps they'd ever intended."

I wanted to ask Sunil more questions about his parents and Dr. Crest, but I could tell the subject made him uncomfortable and this was not the best time.

When the grubbers came to shore they struck with the force of a dark hurricane. A mammoth grubber the size of a Bendellian bluetonk crashed through the seawall. With its antennae generating a crackling electrostatic charge – visible even from a distance – the forcefields collapsed. Adrian, Sunil and I stared in shock from our vantage point on higher ground. The filth that followed – a vile wave of wriggling grubbers that stretched into forever – froze us in horror until Adrian stood up, cupped his hands against his mouth, and shouted, "Let's go!"

We hopped aboard our landbuzzers – about a thousand Wergens and humans – and charged into the battle. Within seconds we were immersed in chaos, blood, laserfire, airpulses, sizzling all around us.

And the wave of grubbers was met by a wave of bots that blanketed the shore, turning the warm white sands into an iron-gray slate. Adrian led the charge, diving into the grubber hordes, slashing his electric spear into eye sockets with one arm, firing his lasergun with the other.

Sunil buried his spear into the head of grubber after grubber, whirling around only to be faced with another. And I stood by his side, as always, firing my weapon, surrounded by bots I instructed to shock the advancing creatures. We stayed there until our arms ached and I thought we could no longer hold back the rising tide. At that point, I leapt in front of Sunil and erected a forcefield that halted the grubbers in their tracks to provide us a reprieve. But only seconds later, the grubber swarm had piled up against the field until it sizzled, crackled and collapsed.

I leapt backwards but a grubber the size of five humans had crept up behind me, its fanged mandibles no more than half a metre from my face.

Sunil threw himself in front of me.

"No!" I screamed.

The grubbers swallowed his upper torso whole, lifting him up, his legs kicking.

I fired at the grubber's carapace, its head and eyes out of my reach, but the laserfire deflected off of it.

Someone grabbed my arm and pulled me back.

"Onyx!" It was Adrian, accompanied by Hermillia. "Let's go!"

"No! Sunil! I –"

A bot shocked me, making me lose control over my body, though I remained conscious. Adrian threw my limp body over his shoulder. He scaled the hill and we were soon joined by Pantallax, Antoinette and several others exterminators. As I dangled over Adrian's shoulder, I looked down the hillside. My brethren, every last one of them, hung back, sacrificing themselves to save their human partners. As I had wanted to save Sunil. I should have. Why had I not died instead?

Adrian set me down, and Hermillia pulled me by my collar as I regained my footing until we had climbed to the hill's summit. The mammoth grubber had decimated the outpost. Buildings under construction had collapsed and a rubble field filled the valley.

"Sunil's parents?" I said. "Dr. Crest?"

Adrian shook his head.

We raced downhill, towards the bay on the other side of the island, an inlet to the Purple Sea, where we had docked the passenger ship. We traversed a ramp, scores of human survivors streaming aboard the vessel with only a few Wergens among them, including me and Hermillia.

At the sight of the first grubbers flowing over the hilltop, Adrian waved his arms over his head and shouted, "Go! Go! Go!" We lifted anchor, pushed rapidly away from shore by an expanding forcefield that surrounded the ship.

And as I hung over the side of the vessel thinking of my brother – *oh, Sunil, why did you do it?* – the lavender waves rocked the vessel from side to side. The humans still on shore panicked when they realised the ship had departed without them. Several of them mounted two-person landbuzzers that allowed them to fly to the safety of the ship's deck. But the large majority had no buzzers. Many of them used living Wergens as shields, crouching behind their torsos and firing into the swarm.

It continued in that manner until every last one of my people was dead and the grubber swarm overwhelmed the remaining humans.

### *Sunil*

I floated on my back in the water that streamed down from the multi-tiered waterfalls, squinting into the blue sun.

"Hey, look!" Tam said.

I flopped around in the water at the sound of her voice, turned to find her, but I only caught a glimpse of her in the splash. She was already exiting the pool, clambering over the rocks and into the purple vegetation.

"Wait!" I swam furiously to the side of the swimming hole and climbed out, chasing after her. "Wait!"

I pushed past the plants, found the dirt path and ran after her.

When I arrived at the den behind the waterfall, she was waiting for me, her hair already pulled back into a ponytail.

"Tam," I said, trying to catch my breath. "Tam, don't go back out there. There's a poisonous creature in the plants. It's not safe."

She sat on a large rock, staring at me calmly, and patted the space next to her for me to sit. I did, but there was less room than I remembered, maybe because I was an adult. "Tam," I said. "I'm sorry. I'm so sorry." My lips trembled, but I forced the words out. "We shouldn't be here. It's my fault. *My fault.* I convinced you to play hooky.

And then I couldn't save you." I'm not sure she could understand me through the sobs. "I was supposed to protect you…"

I buried my face in my hands and she patted my head for a long while as I wept. When I finally calmed down, she said, "Isn't this place amazing?"

I wiped my nose, looked around at the lilac-hued cavern, the lavender waters flowing directly ahead of us. "Our secret headquarters," I said.

She smiled at this.

"It's time to go," she said, standing up.

"No, wait! You can't go back onto that path."

"No, silly. Not that way. This way." She pointed behind us, into a cavern that extended into darkness.

I hesitated. "I'm afraid."

She rolled her eyes and held out her hand. "Come."

## Onyx

We sailed to a neighbouring island in the archipelago and climbed the snowy peak of Mount Scorn, the tallest mountain on Langalana.

Only about a hundred human survivors and a handful of Wergens had made it. We had lost the colony, so many of my people, but all I could think of was my brother.

Adrian and I sat at a lookout post, shivering, dressed in multiple layers of clothes. I clicked on my controller to no avail; it had been damaged. My ability to generate even a modest bodyfield had been compromised. Maybe it was for the best. If this was to be our last stand against Langalana, I wanted to face her head-on, with no barriers between us.

"From this location," I said to Adrian, "we will be able to see any approaching grubbers. I do not know why they have not pursued us yet."

"They're planetary antibodies. They'll follow eventually," Adrian said.

After a long pause, I said, "Sunil…

"I'm sorry," Adrian said.

"I failed him. Just as we failed his sister, Tam."

"You don't have a responsibility to sacrifice yourself for human beings. What we just saw... All of the people on the beach using Wergens as living – willing – body shields... I don't have the words."

"Sunil gave his life for me."

"Sunil is one person. Hundreds of others..." He shook his head, as if trying to rid himself of the memory of what he'd seen. "This whole relationship between humanity and the Wergens... I don't know. I just don't know."

"What do you mean?"

The wind whistled, making it difficult to hear him. "Your love and devotion... It seems to bring out the worst in us."

But my thoughts again turned to Sunil, and I could not disagree more.

"The reality," he said, "is that we have new agreements in place with the Eremites. I'm not sure this relationship is worth preserving."

"You are wrong," I said. "We have come so far. Learned so much from each other."

"You're naïve," he said. "Hermillia helped me send IS transmissions to EarthCouncil and to Wergen outposts. I've updated them on our status. We just need to hold on until the seedships arrive and hope that they don't instantly draw grubbers, as they did in Inlandia. They can transport us ten at a time to the moon base on Axel until the larger interstellar vessels arrive."

When the seedships arrived a few days later, we fled to Axel as Adrian predicted, where I was assigned to serve as attaché to Argenta's Wergen Ambassador, Shimera, who had survived an attack on that colony before its destruction. Adrian returned home on the next IS vessel to the Sol System, on a mission, he said, to find something – although I think he really meant some*one* – he had lost. To this day, I am not sure whether he found it, but I hope he did.

After several weeks stationed on the Axel lunar base, an Earth Emissary arrived to deliver a message to the Ambassador. After he left, I went to the meeting room to inquire what had transpired but I could not find Shimera. What I *did* find, carefully placed on a table, was an unopened envelope. I looked over my shoulder, ripped open the envelope and pulled out a yellow sheet containing human handwriting. I held it up to see it in the glow cast by Langalana, which hung in the sky forever out of reach. While I'd learned every spoken human language, I had not yet mastered all their written communications. All I could make out were rows of indecipherable squiggles.

# CHAPTER ELEVEN
## The Fading Echoes of Love's Song

### Ocura – Year 2620

The rocky world lay at the centre of the Goldilocks Zone, orbiting the giant red star Ulas in the inner spiral arm of the Milky Way. Even from this distance, signs of an advanced civilisation were evident: the atmosphere teemed with fluorocarbons, and faint traces of light reflected off forcefields surrounding its four moons.

Alex and Lily sat with me at the triangular Tactics Table while Rafi examined the incoming telemetry at his station. A holo of the orange and green-tinged planet floated over the table.

"The Wergens wouldn't need to live on a planet within the habitable zone of a star's orbit," Lily said. She spoke with an undercurrent of self-doubt, as if she didn't think she deserved to be in a position of authority. "With their fieldtech they could just as easily settle on a frozen asteroid in the periphery of this system."

An obvious point, I thought, though the three other persons on deck marvelled at the observation.

"Yes, but the Wergen *homeworld*," Alex said in his slow Martian drawl, "is unlikely to be any old outpost in the outskirts of the system." He looked remarkably young and healthy for a 90-year-old. Like most Charismatics, he'd benefited from expensive gene therapy to ward off old age. According to EarthCouncil, Alex had been selected to serve as Chairman of the corpship *Rapprochement, Inc.* – and Lily and I as Executive Directors – because of our 'familiarity with the Wergen mindset'. But I suspected there was more to it. EarthCouncil chose us, I believed, because we all had an axe to grind with the Wergens. When he was a child, Alex's family owned a Martian vineyard with Wergen servants he came to despise; Lily spent years in isolation surrounded only by Wergens who'd deceived her; I went to war against the Wergens and wound up sharing my mind with an Eremite hitchhiker.

*My companion.* I still felt an aching emptiness when I thought of her; I missed her voice in my head.

"Duncan?" Lily asked. "What do you think?"

I shrugged. "Why speculate? We'll know soon enough whether this is the homeworld."

"That's helpful, thanks."

The execs on deck stared at me with contempt for not showing more respect to Alex and Lily. Unlike the others, sharing my mind with an Eremite had rendered me immune to their Charismatic charms. EarthCouncil had offered me Charismatic status as well, but I turned them down flat. I didn't need more phony love. I'd had enough of that dealing with the Wergens.

"Rafi?" Alex said, nodding at Lily's brother.

He leapt to his feet, "Yes, sir?"

"How quickly can we deliver the anti-suppressor into the atmosphere?"

"Valentina's team in Delivery estimates they would only need a few minutes after we enter orbit. Then it would take the compound forty-eight hours to incubate before it becomes effective," Rafi said.

When Alex nodded his approval at the response, Rafi looked as if he might pump his fist in the air.

"How long will it take us to reach orbit?" Alex said.

"Two days on impulse. We can't risk stressing the wormhole engine any more."

Alex frowned and Rafi hung his head.

The Wergen tech we'd grown so dependent on had started to fail and we had no ability to repair it. We hoped the Wergens would lend a hand, but in our last encounter with them twenty years earlier, they'd perfected a suppressor drug to control their feelings of adoration towards humanity. The anti-suppressor we'd developed as an antidote restored the Wergens' feelings to their natural state. Our orders were clear. If the Wergens proved aggressive – or uncooperative – we were to engender that love again using all means at our disposal.

"Alex," Rafi said. "We have an incoming transmission."

"Go ahead," Alex said. "Patch it through."

The planet hovering over the command table disappeared, replaced by the image of a Wergen – only this Wergen had a jutting jawbone and half a dozen antennae dangling just above its compound eyes. Its sudden, twitching movements didn't resemble anything remotely Wergen.

"You shouldn't be here," the alien said in a gravelly voice.

"Why hello, old friends," Alex said with a big smile. "We've come a long way to visit our former partners. I'm the Chairman of this corpship, Alex Decinces. On my left is Lily Juarez and on my right Duncan McGuire, my two Executive Directors. You are...?"

"Antillia."

"Our warmest greetings, Antillia. We are –"

"– not welcome here. I've established no visual links to your ship," the Wergen said. "I cannot see you. And have no desire to hear you."

"We have crucial matters to discuss," Alex said, his Martian drawl becoming more pronounced. "Matters best addressed face to face. Can you provide us landing coordinates?"

A pause.

"Your kind is every bit as arrogant as I remember," Antillia said with a half-laugh, an insect-like click to her voice. "I'll consult the Grand Congress, but it's unlikely you'll be allowed to set foot on our world or its moons. You're far too dangerous."

"Dangerous?" Alex said. He smiled more broadly and stretched his arms out. "We're here to reconnect with old friends, that's all."

"Keep your distance from Ocura," Antillia said.

"How long will it take to hear back from the Grand Congress?"

The holo vanished, replaced by the spinning orange-and-green sphere.

Rafi left his station and approached us. "I know that Wergen," he said. "She looks different, but I remember her name. Decades ago, when I was stationed on the Pluto outpost prior to the war, she assisted our colony leader with research. She turned on us, joining the renegade splinter group that waged the all-out attack against Earth."

"Not the ideal representative to talk shop with," Alex said. "But we'll find a way to make it work."

I was on the edge of sleep, my recurring dream of falling just begun again, when the wall-monitor beeped. Alex's face lit up the panel. I sat up in bed, turned down the volume of my earbuds – the sound of a voice in my head relaxed me and helped me sleep – and Alex relayed the news we'd been waiting to hear. The Wergens had transmitted landing coordinates. He requested I put together a small landing party while Lily remained aboard *Rapprochement* to ready the anti-suppressor for possible use.

I trudged across the corridor to Lily's quarters and knocked. She opened the door, bleary-eyed. "What?"

"The Wergens have agreed to meet with us."

"Really?"

I sat on an ottoman at the foot of her bed while she put on a robe. "What's the matter?" I said. "This is good news, right?"

She frowned into the mirror and brushed her jet-black hair. It took her a long time to respond. "I don't trust them. I did once, foolishly, a long time ago, but never again."

"You think Alex is the trusting type?"

"No, but he can be overconfident."

"He suggested you stay aboard the ship and on alert, should it become necessary to give the order to deliver the anti-suppressor."

"Good, best to remain cautious."

"Alex and I are shuttling down to the surface for negotiations. I want to bring Rafi with us. He's been studying the planetary telemetry and seems to have a good handle on the environment."

"He'll be pleased."

"He's ambitious," I said.

"To put it mildly. He wants to be Charismatic, like his big sister."

"And you don't approve?"

"It's complicated." She sat down on the side of the bed and pulled the robe over her legs, still staring into the mirror.

She'd confided in me about the condition that had horribly disfigured her and sent her to live among Wergens. Before EarthCouncil cured her. And I'd shared my own story of the war, of the freefall. But when it came to the subject of her brother, Rafi, she tended to be more circumspect.

"You think I *want* to be Charismatic?" she said. "It's as if I'm back on that outpost being studied by Wergens. Every mid-level exec stares at me, puts me on a pedestal."

"You poor thing."

"No, I'm serious."

"Then why did you agree to take the love drug?"

"EarthCouncil wanted to maximise exec loyalty aboard the ship. For the good of the mission they demanded I take the neuromone. And I..."

"Found it hard to resist." Since all EarthCouncil reps were Charismatic, every person – unless they themselves were Charismatic – wanted to please them.

She bit her lower lip.

"I understand," I said. "They asked me to take the neuromone as well. If not for my immunity, I'd be Charismatic myself."

"It's a relief to talk to you, Duncan. You and Alex are the only persons aboard the ship who treat me as if I'm a normal human being. And Alex... Well, he has his own issues."

"Oh, yes. He's been Charismatic for years and likes the attention a little too much."

She smiled.

"Will you come with me to break the news to your brother?" I said.

"No, it's best you tell him yourself. Rafi wants to be like me, but he resents me. He admires me, but he's angry at me. As I said, it's complicated."

And this mission was complicated enough, I thought.


As I entered the recreation deck, I spotted Rafi and Valentina, head of Delivery, in the deep end of the pool. They'd been doing their mandatory laps, part of the physical and mental regimen demanded of the fifty ship execs aboard *Rapprochement*. Around them, mid- and low-level execs waited at the pool's edge for the swimming lanes to clear. An overhead holo of the noon sun projected light and warmth.

The execs took notice of me. Ordinarily they'd retreat in the presence of the three senior staff members – in fact, Alex and Lily *insisted* they keep a 'respectful' distance – but I presented an odd situation as the only non-Charismatic senior officer. Everyone knew I'd been appointed Executive Director because of my military experience and symbiotic relationship with an Eremite, so they had some measure of respect for me, but nothing like the deep admiration elicited by the neuromone. A few individuals stepped aside when I approached, but about half a dozen remained at the pool's edge.

I manoeuvred around them and crouched down, wiggling my fingers in the water. The pool reminded me of a time long ago, when I was a naïve student competing on the college diving team, when my biggest worry was my best friend finding out I was in love with him. So much had changed since then.

Rafi and Valentina swam over to meet me. I'd heard the two were involved romantically, though I couldn't tell from the way they interacted with one another. They seemed single-minded in their devotion to Alex and Lily.

"We're glad you stopped by," Valentina said. "Rafi and I were just talking about our Delivery team. There's a feeling all our hard work on anti-supp wasn't being... appreciated. It seems all Alex and Lily think about is the Wergens."

I laughed. "Our *mission objective* is to think about the Wergens, to reestablish relations with them."

"I understand. It's just that we don't want senior staff to lose sight of all our efforts, that's all. There's a whole ship of devoted execs willing to do whatever it takes to make this mission a success. Instead, there's only talk about the Wergens, about their tech, about what great partners they'll make. It's not good for corpship morale."

I was no stickler for corpship formalities, but it seemed presumptuous of her to raise this topic directly with me here. "A word in private," I said to Rafi.

He climbed the ladder out of the pool, grabbed a towel and followed me to the far side of the pool, where fewer people were present.

"Rafi, I wanted to give you the news in person. We've been impressed with your contributions to the mission. I've added you to Liaison. The skimmer to the Wergen world departs at 1300 hours. You're to join me and Alex in the shuttle bay."

"I – I hadn't realised the Wergens agreed to meet with us. This is great news. Yes, I'll be ready," he said. "Thank you, Duncan."

"You've earned it."

I turned to leave and as I reached the lift doors, he came rushing after me.

"One thing. I'm hoping... Would it be possible to put in a good word with EarthCouncil – when the time comes, if you think it appropriate, I mean. I'm on the wait list for Charisma."

Like most non-Charismatics, Rafi lived under the delusion we lived in a meritocracy where hard work – and not wealth or other connections – earned you Charisma. He did have his sister in his corner, but Lily wasn't happy with her own Charismatic status; she'd be unlikely to back his request.

"I'll consider it," I said.

Our skimmer glided through a cloudless indigo sky away from the sprawling cities and into the deserts that filled three quarters of this world.

I sat at the controls, Alex and Rafi on each side of me.

Rafi studied the datastream. "Metropolises extend kilometres below the surface on this world and its moons."

"We're approaching landing coordinates," I said.

Below us, the desolate terrain of swirling green sands created the illusion we were descending onto the lush grasslands of a savannah. I brought the skimmer down to a smooth landing and as we unfastened our safety restraints, Rafi studied the environmental data coming in on ship telemetry.

"The air is breathable," he said. "Temperatures and radiation levels tolerable. We don't need safesuits."

"No surprise," Alex said. "They're oxygen-breathers, after all, who lived side-by-side with us."

I didn't like the thought of leaving the ship without suits. Instead, we cooled the safesuits down to a comfortable temperature. Alex also suggested setting them on 'transparent' to reveal as much of our face and body as possible to the Wergens.

Alex ordered us to stay aboard the vessel while he descended the ramp that unfurled from the skimmer doors to the fine-grained sands. From the plexi, Rafi and I observed an endless ocean of sand surrounding our skimmer. Sporadic dunes broke up the flatness of the horizon, and the sweltering heat caused the vista to shimmer.

"You have a sharp mind," I said to Rafi. "Do you think we should be reestablishing our partnership with the Wergens?"

He seemed taken aback by the question. "It's not my place…"

"Tell me anyway."

He considered his response before speaking. "There are twenty billion people on Earth, Mars and the colonies dedicated to serving the Charismatics. Isn't that enough? Why do they also need these aliens?"

I'd expected him to address the ethics of bending the Wergens to our will. Instead, like Valentina, he sounded jealous at the attention we were giving them.

"Still," Rafi said. "If EarthCouncil believes this a prudent course of action, I defer to them."

"Of course you do."

After a long pause he looked at me, opened his mouth as if to say something else, then shut it.

"What is it?" I said.

"There's something I've been wanting to ask you, but I don't know if it's appropriate."

"Go ahead."

"What were they like?" Rafi said.

"Who?" I said, though I knew exactly whom he meant.

"The Eremites."

"It was just one Eremite, an ambassador," I said. I considered leaving it at that, but Rafi continued to stare at me and before I knew I added, "It was like having a warm, soothing current in my head. I was never alone. She – she knew my innermost thoughts, felt my feelings. Even unconscious feelings. At first it was a nightmare. I tried to fight her. But as time passed I dropped my guard and opened up. She shared herself with me, too, though I struggled to make heads or tails of her thoughts and memories – as she did with mine. Then I woke up one morning… and she was gone."

My face must have reflected my devastation because after a short pause Rafi said, "I'm sorry."

More importantly, when the Eremites abandoned us, they took their gifts with them: micro-crystals that generated unlimited energy, portals that provided instantaneous transport anywhere in the galaxy. They'd broken their promise to uplift us, leaving us only with the aging technology we'd received from the Wergens decades earlier, technology we couldn't replicate or repair.

"Rafi, if the Wergens choose not to partner with us… You have no reservations about enslaving them again?"

He stared at me.

"Yes, 'enslaving,'" I said, "Wergen biochemistry compels them to help us, to serve us. Similar to the neuromone that compels you to serve the Charismatics." I paused to see if he was putting two and two

259

together, if he could grasp the nature of his own enslavement. "This chemical manipulation of emotions... I suffered from it firsthand during the war. And it's wrong."

"But Alex and Lily deserve..."

My grunt turned into a laugh. "Look, I know you find Alex and your sister wise and infallible, but your emotions are being warped. Surely you know that."

"Of course I know. We were always close, Lily and I. It's unfair she now has this... advantage over me. It makes me angry I find her so *wise*, so persuasive. That's why I want to become Charismatic, like her. So we can be on equal footing, so we can be close again." He set down his scanner. "I'm the hardest working exec aboard this ship. If I keep performing well, I'm hoping I'll have a chance to become Charismatic myself."

He didn't recognise that his naïveté was also the product of the neuromone's effects. "How many people do you know who've worked their way up the ladder to Charismatic status?" I said.

"There are stories of some."

"Hmm." I leaned in close to him. "I'm trying to wrap my mind around the cognitive cartwheels you have to perform to view our EarthCouncil leaders as fair and kind and beneficent."

"They are elected by the people they serve."

"Unanimously! It's a charade," I said. "They divvy up the wealth and power among themselves. Then the enthralled population rubberstamps their decisions."

"Duncan, Rafi." Alex's voice came through the suit comm. "You can join me now."

I scooped up a handful of green sand and let the grains fall between my gloved fingers.

"Suit sensors indicate there are traces of manganese and boric acid in the grains, which could explain the colour," Rafi said.

"There's an entrance to an underground cavern not far from here," Alex said. "Strangely, the large cities on this planet are mostly abandoned. But there are massive life readings that stretch for kilometres beneath the surface of this desert."

With no Wergens to greet us, a thought nagged at me. "You did receive permission to land, didn't you?" I said to Alex.

"Actually," he said, "I didn't hear back from Antillia, but I did receive an invitation from another Wergen, who promised us safe passage to this site."

"But who –?"

Alex answered with a single raised eyebrow that communicated a clear message: *I'm Chairman, Duncan. Drop it.*

On his belt Alex had attached a canister of the anti-suppressor, which could disperse the gas in a fifteen-kilometre radius.

As we hiked under the orange sky, we came upon sparse plant life in what we initially thought to be a desolate landscape: flat, black, single-leafed growths that Rafi knelt to analyze. And in the distance crab-like creatures – nearly identical to bots – darted from one burrow to another.

After a few minutes we arrived at the entranceway to the subsurface, a tunnel made of a rubbery black material.

A shadow swept over the horizon.

"Look!" Rafi said.

A circular emerald-green Wergen vessel – darker than the desert sands – landed a hundred metres away.

Two figures emerged from the alien ship. They wore no clothes and bore the familiar chalky Wergen scales, but they moved on four limbs instead of two. Skittering across the sands like insects, they stopped five metres away. Their flat-topped elongated heads had dozens of wires – no, antennae – swaying along their brows above bulging black eyes. Spiked tails undulated a few metres off the ground. And a transparent whiffer masked the breathing canal at the centre of their faces.

"You shouldn't be here," said the first, who moved slower and had flaking scales.

"I am Antillia," said the other. She rose from her four-legged stance to perch on her hind legs. "And this is Korte."

"You're both… unlike any Wergen I've ever seen before," I said.

"We've formed a partnership with a species we encountered decades ago in the Cygni system, the Ch'kk-tk," Korte said. "Adjusting our shape makes us more… acceptable to them. Just as we altered ourselves for the Visians, generation ago, then for you humans."

I'd always wondered about the general similarity between the Wergens' humanoid shape and ours, their feelings and use of language. The odds seemed astronomical we'd encounter aliens so like us. It never occurred to me they could adjust their physiology – just to please us.

"One of your team members has trespassed into the great halls," Korte said, pointing down the ramp.

I turned around. Alex was gone.

Antillia and Korte raced into the sloping entrance followed by bots that emerged from their ship.

"Wait here," I shouted to Rafi. "If you don't hear from me in 30 minutes, inform Lily."

"Wait!"

I ignored him, descending the steep incline behind Antillia and Korte, who'd already disappeared into the darkness. Damn Alex's recklessness! He'd get us all killed. The ramp forked into different tunnels and, unsure of the direction in which they'd gone, I chose a random passageway.

The tunnel forked and I went right, emerging after a few minutes into a well-lit cavern.

There was no sign of Alex, Antillia or Korte, but at the centre of the chamber, an ancient Wergen sat on a pillowed high-backed chair. Turning, she gasped when she caught sight of me. She appeared more human than any Wergen I'd ever seen before. Except for her large eyes and scaled skin, she resembled an elderly human grandmother.

"I'm Duncan McGuire of the Earth vessel *Rapprochement*," I began. "We're here on a mission –"

"A mission of conquest," she said.

"You misunderstand. EarthCouncil has revisited its decision to break off relations between our peoples. We're here to propose a-a reconciliation."

"Yes, I communicated privately with your leader when I'd heard your ship had trespassed into our system and provided him these coordinates." She stood and bots holding elongated red staffs scurried to support her. Gripping two staffs, she took a laboured step in my direction.

"I am Shimera," the ancient Wergen said. "I was an ambassador to your people on the Langalanan colony of Argenta, where I grew up alongside humans."

*Langalana.* I'd breathed its salty air, walked through its red grasslands. I'd left my best friend, the love of my life there.

"Together, Wergens and humans worked shoulder to shoulder to build something special on Langalana." Shimera closed her eyes and inhaled deeply. "Those days are just far-off memories now... I've been working here in the great halls on what you humans call an 'art project', dedicated to our time together." She'd been staring at me out of the corner of her eyes but now turned to face me head-on. "You remind me of someone I knew a long time ago."

After an uncomfortable silence, I responded. "You don't look like the other Wergens."

"It's a... physiological response. I've yet to meet our new allies, the Ch'kk'tkk."

*Because you're still thinking about us*, I thought. *Even after all this time...*

"I don't believe the Grand Congress would have approved your request to meet with us, but I felt I owed it – to the memory of what we once shared – to listen."

"EarthCouncil believes that re-forming our alliance can be mutually beneficial," I said. "That we acted rashly in not giving the partnership a chance."

Shimera smiled and shook her head.

"This is something your people wanted," I pointed out. "Desperately. You wanted us to reconsider."

"Decades ago," she said. "It's funny our 'wants' are so important to you now. Tell me. What's changed?"

"EarthCouncil reassessed the situ–"

"The Eremites left you, didn't they."

I paused. Alex would have been able to spin an appropriate response to this question.

"Your hesitation speaks volumes."

"Yes, one day the Eremites vanished. Without any explanation. And I –" I stopped myself. I wanted to speak of how I'd felt personally betrayed, how I always wondered if I'd done something wrong, if she'd ever return.

"And this has caused your people... pain?"

I nodded.

"Good," she said.

"Is reestablishing relations something your Grand Congress might consider? EarthCouncil believes –"

"What do *you* believe, Duncan?"

She moved closer, her head reaching the middle of my sternum. Even with her unsteadiness, she carried herself in a dignified manner that demanded respect – and honesty.

EarthCouncil would have wanted me to answer her by saying a human-Wergen alliance served both our interests. But instead I said, "We've developed a drug. A drug based on our research on Wergen physiology. Individuals who take this neuromone – Charismatics, we call them – become irresistibly persuasive. Earth and most of the colonies, are now led by Charismatics who care about nothing but their own wealth and power. The majority of humanity is now happily oppressed. This… This is what Wergen-human relations produced."

"So you are now enslaved by your… love for these Charismatics." The irony wasn't lost on her.

Three Wergens and a wave of bots swarmed into the cavern and surrounded me.

"Lady Shimera, are you safe?" shouted an Explorata officer, identifiable from his blue *coronatis*. These Wergens bore the same insectoid shape as Antillia and Korte.

"I'm fine," she said, raising her hand and signalling for them to back away.

"The other human?"

"Sensorbots indicate he entered the Hall of the Grand Congress," Shimera said.

The bots shepherded me out of the chamber and we rounded a bend leading into another cavern. Alex emerged.

"There you are," he said as the bots surrounded him.

Before we were led off, I glanced into the immense cavern, constructed of the same black rubbery material as the ramp. A sea of white-skinned torsos extended as far as the eye could see, packed together in odd positions, all tethered by elongated cords that extended skull to skull to skull. I gasped. The figures had no limbs. They resembled unformed tadpoles sitting in a stadium-sized vat of ooze.

"The Grand Congress is beautiful," Korte said. "But not meant for your eyes."

I reversed course and slowly ascended the ramp back to the surface.

Back outside under the desert sun, Alex cleared his throat. "A pleasure to meet you in person, friends," he said, turning on the charm. "Can we go somewhere to sit and speak? We have much to discuss."

"You must leave immediately," Korte said. "You've defiled the hall of the Grand Congress."

"We've travelled enormous distances searching for this world," Alex said. "My people greatly regret ending our partnership before exploring other productive opportunities. We learned much from each other, friends. There's still more to learn."

The Wergens' tails undulated in the sand.

"The Grand Congress shall decide. But you must leave," Antillia said.

Alex bowed. "Inform your Congress we've ended our alliance with the Eremites. We're here, with open hearts, willing to negotiate and to start our relationship anew. Should your leaders reject our offer, we'll leave and you'll never hear from us again."

"Return to your vessel in orbit," Antillia said, "and we'll advise you of the Grand Congress's decision."

"Very well," Alex said. He bowed again.

That's when I saw the jiggling canister of anti-suppressor hanging around his belt. Open and empty. He'd dispersed the gas into the hall of the Grand Congress.

"That drug was intended for defensive purposes only," I said once we were back aboard the ship. "And only if the Wergens proved hostile – though, frankly, we're lucky we didn't get blasted to bits after landing on their home planet without permission."

"Shimera made arrangements for our safe passage – and there was no chance of that in any event. I know the Wergens well," Alex said. "I grew up on Mars with Wergen servants who *begged* for my attention, who worshipped me. They're weak-willed. The best approach – always – is to take a firm hand with them."

"By drugging their leaders?" I said.

"By *ending* the effect of their own suppressor drugs –"

"I've seen another side of the Wergens. They can be brutal, ruthless."

"But to what end?" Alex said. He leaned forward. *"To make you love them."*

"And what about the millions of lives lost on Earth?"

"For God's sake, that was during the war!" Alex said. "We're not battling the Wergens any more. We're giving them exactly what they've always dreamed of, an honest partnership that –"

"'Honest'?"

"Stop bickering," Lily said. "There's no point to it. I should tell you, Duncan, while you engaged with the Wergens in the desert, I gave the order to Valentina's team to release the remainder of the anti-suppressors into the atmosphere."

"*You what?*"

"Alex and I discussed it before you left. Preemptive action is the wisest course to take with the Wergens," she said. "The stakes are too high."

"Why wasn't I consulted? EarthCouncil assigned me to this corpship –"

"– for your piloting and tactical skills," Alex said.

"You can register whatever complaints you have with the Board when we return to Earth," Lily said. "Right now we need to plan for our response to the Wergens when they contact us. What do we want from them first? There's also this new alien species they've allied with to consider."

Alex nodded. "We'll need to find out their weaknesses from the Wergens."

I was about to storm off when Rafi appeared on the bridge. "We have an incoming message from the Wergens," he said.

The holo of Korte's face hovered over the table.

"You've responded more quickly than we expected, friends." Alex said. "Good news?"

"The Grand Congress noted you'd dispersed a chemical agent in the chamber. We've also detected that your ship released the same substance into the atmosphere. Fortunately, the compounds were inert – and ineffective. But your treachery reminded us of the complicated relationship we had with your people," Korte said. "Should your ship fail to leave orbit immediately, we will destroy it. If any other Earth vessel approaches this star system – or any of our colonies – we will destroy it. Never attempt to contact us again."

The image blinked off.

Alex whirled and pointed at Rafi. "You!" His eyes bulged. When Rafi stepped backwards, he charged at him and grabbed his shirt collar. "You were supposed to be supervising the Delivery team. The anti-suppressor was inert. Ineffective. You idiot!" He barked each word, tightening his grip on Rafi's collar. "I risked my life to release the compound in that chamber!"

"There's no time for this," I said. "We need to leave. The Wergens aren't bluffing."

"You're right," Lily said.

I accelerated the corpship. The lights dimmed and I felt the familiar tickle in my stomach that followed entrance into the wormhole generated by our engines. The hull trembled; lights flickered. Barely operating Wergen technology – now decades old – had been pushed to its limits to help us search this part of the galaxy for their homeworld. Now we were counting on it to take us home.

"Do you know what your ineptitude has cost us?" Alex said, nose to nose with Rafi.

I pulled Alex off of him. Rafi raced off the bridge and down the corridor as Alex shouted, "Get back here! Get back here, you fool!"

I descended two levels to the execs' quarters and banged on the door to Valentina's room, where I assumed Rafi had fled.

The door opened and slid shut behind me as I entered her quarters. As expected, Rafi was with her.

"What happened?" I asked.

"The anti-suppressor failed," Rafi said.

"But how is that possible?" The compound had been tested and retested.

"Were Lily and Alex upset?" Valentina said.

"To put it mildly," Rafi said. "I could be brought up on charges for incompetence."

"You aren't incompetent," Valentina said. "There's a theory I may be able to sell. The Wergens we encountered on the planet developed certain changes to their physiology. Those mutations may have rendered the chemical agent ineffective. It makes sense, right?"

"Well, yes." Rafi paused. "But what do you mean you may be able 'to sell' this theory?"

She turned away from us.

"Valentina?" Rafi said.

"I-I sabotaged the anti-suppressor," she said.

I froze. "I don't understand."

"Not just me. My entire team neutralised the chemical agent with water vapour, rendering it ineffective."

"But... why?" I said.

"Lily, Alex, all the Charismatics at EarthCouncil, all they cared about was the Wergens. They were obsessed with the aliens. You know that! They were ignoring us – and all our hard work. How much worse would it have gotten once the Wergens returned? We'd never get their attention again. But if the anti-suppressor failed... Well, that would solve the problem, wouldn't it?"

Rafi stared at her, dumbfounded. "Why didn't you tell me?"

"In case things went wrong, I didn't want you involved. I'm sorry."

A fist pounded on the door behind me.

When Valentina opened it, Alex stood there accompanied by two security guards. "Duncan, I see you found him," he said. "Rafi, you and Valentina have been relieved of duty. You'll be confined to quarters until we reach Earth, where there will be a formal investigation of this fiasco."

Hours later, I retreated to my quarters to think about the consequences of our failure. Without Wergen help, we'd be unable to repair the aging wormhole engines. In time, we'd have to rely on ancient propulsion systems to navigate through space, which meant confinement to our own solar system.

My wall-monitor beeped and it took me a moment to acknowledge the alien face staring back at me on the screen. Shimera.

"How did you...?"

"This is a targeted transmission for your eyes only, Duncan. I wanted you to know the Grand Congress had seriously considered re-partnering with humanity. I counselled against it. After thinking about the interactions between our people and the harm it's caused, and what you told me about the Charismatics, I've come to realise our relationship was more self-destructive, more toxic, than I ever imagined." She paused, fingering a fist-sized sphere in the palm of her hand. "If this is to be goodbye, forever, I want something positive to come from it... I have compiled here some of our stories."

"Stories?"

"We've kept careful track of our interactions with humanity. Most Wergens were fitted with recording lenses and asked to provide regular reports to the Explorata." She held up the sphere, pushed a button on it, and my wall-monitor flickered, the result of an incoming signal. "These transmissions tell some of the stories. Our stories. Chronicles of the human-Wergen partnership. I've spent years reviewing these accounts, these tales of love between friends, colleagues, lovers, family members. So many shades of human love... And I still don't fully understand it." Her eyes widened and she smiled at me, as if expecting me to solve the mystery for her. When I stayed silent, she continued, "Maybe your people will learn something from these stories, especially when you see them from the Wergen point of view. But there's something else... These transmissions are in a frequency that alter your theta brainwave ranges. Humans viewing these transmissions will be freed from the effects of the neuromone you call 'the love drug'. Consider this our final parting gift. Fare well, Duncan."

"Thank you, Shimera," I said, although the screen had already faded and she couldn't hear me any more.

A moment later the files uploaded onto the ship's computer system. I viewed the transmissions: my story, Shimera's, Lily's, so many others. I re-watched them, recording an introduction explaining the context of each story. When I finished, I asked the computer to play the transmissions on all wall monitors in every room aboard *Rapprochement*. And then, thinking of Rafi, of his belief in the fairness of an inherently corrupt system run by Charismatics, I arranged to beam the transmissions to Earth and all of the colonies in the Sol System.

"Ship, take us in closer to the inner planets," I said.

I sat in the seat Alex would have occupied, Lily's empty chair to my left.

"What's the situation?" I asked.

Rafi studied the data feeds. "Volatile, as you might expect. There have been revolutions on Mars and Earth, just as we saw on Titan and the colonies in the outer system. Given the small number of Charismatics in charge, it's no surprise the governments were all toppled so quickly."

"EarthCouncil?"

"Dismantled. It'll have to be reconstituted without Charismatics, which means new global elections."

The clear-headed execs aboard *Rapprochement* had expressed confidence in me because of my prior leadership experience and voted me interim corpship Chairman. My prior refusal to become Charismatic had been a factor in their decision.

"There's something I've been meaning to tell you," Rafi said. "On the planet, when you and Alex and the Wergens descended into the subsurface, when you ordered me to wait outside?" He lowered his head. "I violated your order and followed you. Only I entered a chamber adjacent to the one you entered. Inside, there was... Well, maybe it's best to show you."

He projected a holo he'd recorded with his safesuit: an image of a bright chamber filled with countless rows of towering stone statues. The figures were human. Women, men, children. The fifteen-metre sculptures stood in different positions and bore different expressions: happy, sad, angry, pensive. One particular statue stood at the fore, a lean young man with shoulder-length hair and a wide grin. Despite the vast differences between the statues, the sculptor had captured a shared intangible quality, the essence of their humanity.

The image extended deeper into the chamber. There seemed to be no end to the statues.

"Shimera told me she'd devoted herself to an art project..." I said. But this was no art project. These were monuments.

When I got up to leave the bridge, Rafi nodded at me. "With everything that's happened... I'll be searching for an old friend now," I said. "Someone who I can welcome back into my life again."

"Oh?" Rafi said.

He seemed curious and stood there for a few seconds but he didn't press for any more information, and I didn't offer any.

On the way to the recreation deck, I passed by the brig and got a glimpse of Alex in his cell, his arm in a sling. He lay asleep on his bunk.

Lily scowled at me from the cell next to his.

I went to bat for her, but the rest of the crew voted to keep her confined after learning she'd ordered release of the compound into the atmosphere. When the time comes, she'll be dismissed from the Board but likely suffer no other punishment. She was as much a victim as the rest of humanity, after all, a slave to the Charismatics' charms.

"This is not so bad as far as prisons go." She paused and her mask of bravado dissolved. "All I wanted was to make sure the Wergens would help us."

"Maybe it's time we got our hands dirty and helped ourselves."

Like most things I said, this made her roll her eyes and smile, but there was no question innovation had been on the decline with the rise of the Charismatics. The enthralled masses focused more on subservience than creativity. It might take time, but with the end of the neuromone, I had a feeling we'd be on the right track again.

I found Rafi and Valentina on the observation deck on the lowest level of the ship. Earth, a pearl sitting on black velvet, grew larger in the window. Rafi kissed her neck and she held his hand, the first time I'd ever seen any public display of affection between them.

Their feelings for each other ran deep apparently. They likely hadn't realised how deep, having been consumed by their attraction to the Charismatics. I would take Rafi aside later and he would say, "I loved her before, but in a lesser, muted way. Now it seems more profound, more *real*."

"EarthCouncil?" she asked.

I told her about the revolutions on Mars and Earth, the overthrow of the Charismatics.

"Is it wrong to admit," Valentina said, "that I'll miss them? A little bit? Life was easier with someone else calling the shots."

"Nothing wrong about admitting that it's scary being a grown-up," Rafi said. "But it's time to take care of ourselves."

She turned to face him. "You're so attractive, so wise. My knees are buckling."

"Glad to see you're thinking clearly now," he said.

She punched him in the ribs, and they kissed.

If you've viewed these eleven transmissions, you've been freed at last from the love drug's shackles. The artificial love that clawed its way into your heart and took root there has been dissolved at last.

Shimera did include an additional transmission, an addendum never viewed before by anyone, even her: a letter she said remained unread for years.

I include it for the sake of completeness.

# Addendum

February 15, 2588

Dear Shim:

I've wrestled with this letter, starting and stopping it so many times, I wasn't sure I'd ever finish it. Or ever send it. But after everything we shared, I feel I owe you an explanation. I need to tell you why I left Langalana, why I never returned.

I know my decision caused you pain, and the thought of hurting you... Well, all these years later and I'm still tormented by the thought of having done so. But I also know that the pain I made you feel was only temporary – *and necessary*. That it allowed you to shake off your feelings for me long ago and find peace of mind. The effect human physiology has on the Wergen mind has been proven to lessen with distance and the passage of time. And I wanted to free you of your fixation on me, Shim, to free you to live your life productively and to its fullest potential. I wanted you to be happy.

I imagine by now you may have forgotten many of the details of our childhood in Argenta. Do you even remember after all this time what it was like, exploring a vast new continent? Racing through the pathways in the grasslands. (Oh, those grasslands!) Meeting on the overhang above the Purple Sea where we shared our hopes and dreams and where you tutored me on your language? I have to confess, I didn't think I'd find much use for Wergenese, given the knack your people have for human languages. It just goes to show you what poor predictors we are of our own future.

After I left Langalana, I returned to Earth. I wanted time away from the joint colonies, away from Wergens who made me think of you. Lois and I resettled in a village outside of Dublin, in a small hamlet far away from the crowded cities where I found work teaching spoken and written Wergenese to linguists fascinated with the phonology and morphology of an alien language. (I've published several textbooks on the subject). The location where we lived reminded me of Argenta with its heavy vegetation and the scent of saltwater in the mornings. I'd wake just before sunrise every day to stand in our backyard overlooking the Irish Sea, to bask in the gentle breeze and think of days gone by. Still, it wasn't Langalana. I found the greenery mildly unsettling. I missed the crimson grasslands and the way the blades used to dance back and forth – as if in delight. I missed the glorious Purple Sea, the rose-coloured streams and indigo clouds. I missed the adventures of settling a new land, the discoveries, the dangers. Most of all, I missed you.

I've often wondered, were the colours really brighter and more vivid on Langalana? Or did it only seem that way because I was with you?

Lois and I divorced after two years together. After a year litigating child visitation rights, she moved to New Ethiopia and took my son with her. A few years later she relocated to Iapetus 2, a minor outpost on one of Saturn's moon. I understand she remarried and had another child before divorcing again. I know that these concepts – divorce, separation – are stressful to you so I won't linger on the details. But suffice it to say that I didn't get to be the father I hoped to be to my son. I still felt a paternal connection to him, I still loved him, but I wished we'd known each other better. Still, I've asked him to deliver this message to you – his work sometimes takes him to the Langalanan system – and when the time comes I believe he will endeavor to fulfill this last request.

I'm writing this letter to tell you that a day hasn't passed when I haven't thought about you, Shim. Of everything we shared. I know that your feelings for me were driven by a quirk of biochemistry, that by now I'm just a faded, distant memory to you. But my own feelings... If only I could have shaken them as easily.

I came to realise that I love you, Shim. I always have and I always will. And that my love for you is real, as real as sunshine and seawater, as real as the air I breathe. But after I'm dead and buried I can't help but wonder... What happens to that love? Will it vanish with me into oblivion or can it still exist, eternally, separate from the mind that conceived it? Can I preserve it by revealing it to you? (I hope you'll forgive my idiosyncratic musings, but I'm old, Shim, and I find that writing of my love for you makes me feel young again).

For all of the studies conducted on the chemistry of love, the biology of love, I believe it boils down to one truism: the heart goes where the heart goes, Shim. And I love you.

With eternal love and eternal regret,

*Phinny*

# About The Author

Mercurio D. Rivera lives in the Bronx in New York City and is a practicing attorney. He has a passion for weekend paddleball, *I Love Lucy* reruns, fine dining, travel and all sci-fi-related things. His short fiction has been nominated for the World Fantasy Award and has won the annual readers' award for *Asimov's* and *Interzone* magazines, respectively. His work has regularly appeared in venues such as *Analog, Lightspeed, i09, Nature, Black Static, Abyss and Apex, Space and Time* and numerous anthologies and "year's best" collections.

Stories set in his Wergen Universe have been podcast at *StarshipSofa, Transmissions From Beyond,* and *Kaleidocast* and taught in literature courses at the University of San Francisco, Columbia College (Chicago) and Instituto Pedagógico de Caracas (Venezuela). Tor.com called his short story collection *Across the Event Horizon* (NewCon Press) "weird and wonderful" with "dizzying switchbacks." His fiction has been published in China, Italy, Poland, Spain and the Czech Republic. You can find him online at mercuriorivera.com.

# Also from NewCon Press

## Burning Brightly edited by Ian Whates
Celebrating 50 years of Novacon, featuring a mix of original fiction and first time reprints of stories written by Guests of Honour for the annual convention booklets. Includes **Iain M. Banks, Peter F. Hamilton, Stephen Baxter, Justina Robson, Paul McAuley, Jaine Fenn, Adrian Tchaikovsky, Anne Nicholls, Geoff Ryman, Ian R. MacLeod, Juliet E. McKenna,** and more...

## Blackthorn Winter – Liz Williams
Something is coming for the Fallow sisters, for their friends and their lovers, and their mother Alys is no help as she's gone wandering again; though she did promise to return by Christmas, and December is already here... In this sequel to *Comet Weather*, four fey sisters are drawn from the familiar world of contemporary London and their Somerset home into darker realms where no one is who they seem and nothing is to be trusted...

## The Wipe – Nik Abnett
A story that develops in two timelines as we follow Dharma Tuke's search for her roots in a dystopian post-pandemic future where familial ties are taboo. Sometimes touching, sometimes harrowing, but always fascinating; a tale of determination and perseverance against the odds and, ultimately, a story about the importance of family, friendship, and love.

## Simon Morden – Bright Morning Star
A ground-breaking take on first contact from scientist and award-winning novelist Simon Morden. Sent to Earth to survey and report back, an alien probe arrives in the middle of a warzone. Witnessing both the best and worst of humanity, the AI probe faces situations that go far beyond its programming, and is forced to improvise, making decisions that reshape the future of a world.